# DRAGONFLY

# DRAGONFLY

## THE NINTH NOVEL IN THE SEAN O'BRIEN SERIES

### BY

### TOM LOWE

**K**

KINGSBRIDGE ENTERTAINMENT

# Also By Tom Lowe

A False Dawn

The 24th Letter

The Black Bullet

The Butterfly Forest

Blood of Cain

Black River

Cemetery Road

A Murder of Crows

Destiny

The Jefferson Prophecy

Wrath

The Confession

Library of Congress Cataloging in—Publication Data, Lowe, Tom, 1952

ISBN - 9781731224231

*Dragonfly* by Tom Lowe - First Edition, 2019

1. Dragonfly—Fiction. 2. CIA—Fiction. 3. FBI—Fiction. 4. Bahamas—Fiction. 5. Ponce Inlet, FL—Fiction. Title: *Dragonfly*

*Dragonfly* (A Sean O'Brien Novel) is distributed in ebook, paperback print, and audiobook editions. Audible Studios is the publisher of the audiobook.

Cover design by Damonza.

Interior by Ebook Launch

# ACKNOWLEDGMENTS

My thanks and deep appreciation for the people that helped put this novel together. To my wife, Keri, who works tirelessly as my "sounding board," first reader and superb editor. To Helen Ristuccia-Christensen and Darcy Yarosh for their extraordinary beta reading skills. To Carlton Lindsey, retired CIA officer. Thanks to Adrian, John and Dane and the talented team at Ebook Launch. To Alicia, Damon, and the graphic designers with Damonza. And finally, to you, the reader. Thank you for reading and being part of the journey. I hope you enjoy *Dragonfly*.

Life is neither good or evil, but only a place for good and evil to exist.

- Marcus Aurelius

For Sandra Brewer

# ONE

## Ponce Marina, Florida

New names painted on old sailboats are often a form of invisible ink made clear when the boat owner cuts the anchor to his or her doubts and fears. At that point, sailboats follow the wind with moveable graffiti tattooed on their tail feathers. Sean O'Brien thought about that as he watched the woman paint something across the transom of a sailboat. He didn't know what the finished word would be, but he was fascinated by the approach she was taking.

The sailboat was up on jack stands in the boatyard at Ponce Marina on the east coast of Florida, and the woman using the paintbrush appeared to be a perfectionist. She stood on a wooden ladder, the noon sun against her brown shoulders, slowly forming the second letter with the detail, skill, and flair of an Old World calligrapher. The first letter, *D*, was followed by a second letter, *R*, the black paint glistening against the bone-white boat transom in the hot Florida sun.

She wore cutoff jean shorts, a powder blue halter-top, and her dark hair in a ponytail. O'Brien guessed she was in her mid-thirties, pretty and a purist. The woman stepped down from the ladder, backing away and surveying the two painted letters. She stood for half a minute.

Motionless.

A soft breeze rattled the fronds of the royal palm trees next to the marina office, the sweet smell of jasmine in the tropical breeze. The diesels from a shrimp boat gurgled in the water as bronzed deckhands lifted lines and pushed off from one of the docks.

O'Brien found himself curious and amused at the same time by the woman's passionate attention to detail. It seemed as if she was envisioning the sailboat at anchor in a tranquil cove at the break of dawn, the boat's new name reflecting off the quiet surface of a remote bay. She wiped the sweat from her brow with the back of her left hand and climbed to the top of the ladder, beginning to paint the third letter.

Having just paid the rent slip for his boat, O'Brien stood in the shade of an awning outside the marina office, watching. From a distance, O'Brien tried to picture and guess the word. It was a used sailboat, probably forty feet in length, fresh bottom paint, a beam of sunlight coming through a tall palm and bouncing off the new stainless-steel prop.

Hundreds of boats—sail and power, were tethered across the marina, long piers from A dock to N dock. O'Brien's boat, *Jupiter,* was at the very end of L dock, slip L-41. Ponce Marina was less than a mile from Ponce Inlet and its access to the Atlantic Ocean. He watched a man in a Top Gun, 39-foot, racing boat docked at the marina fuel station, buying gas. The man was dressed in jeans, white T-shirt, deep tan, neatly trimmed black beard. He looked across the boatyard at the woman on the ladder, slightly bent forward.

O'Brien surveyed the marina, boats coming and going, gulls laughing in the warm Florida breeze, the scent of brackish water, creosote and charcoal grilled grouper in the air. O'Brien, mid-forties, dark hair, hazel blue eyes, six two, was 190 pounds. He sported five-days-worth of whiskers on his chiseled face, wearing faded shorts and a black T-shirt, his biceps stretching the sleeves.

Maxine, O'Brien's ten-pound dachshund, stood next to him and studied two pelicans as they stood on dock pilings, the birds eyeing a charter fishing boat entering the marina, the boat filled with tourists, fish and tales of the one that got away. O'Brien folded the rent receipt and put it in his wallet. Max barked once, trotting toward the pelicans, each bird larger than her. She paused on the dock and looked back at O'Brien, her brown eyes seemed to say, *I'm not waiting for you.*

O'Brien smiled. "Max, you'd fit in just one of those pelican pouches. You're lucky that they prefer redfish more than a reddish dachshund."

Max snorted, tilted her head, scampering toward the big birds. They looked down at her, large yellow eyes inquisitive as Max paced twice and then lost interest, sniffing a mullet head on the dock near a fish cleaning station. She quickly backed away. O'Brien chuckled. "Bet that's ripe. Even the pelicans won't touch it. Come on, kiddo, let's head down the dock to *Jupiter.* She needs a power washing." He motioned with his hands, Max appeared to nod as she scampered in front of him, prancing, toward L dock.

O'Brien glanced at the boat and the woman, she was painting the third letter, her brush strokes sure and fluid, the black paint seemed to form the letter **A.**

"Lovely, isn't she?" The man's question sounded amused.

O'Brien turned around as Dave Collins stepped from the Tiki Bar, an open-air, thatched-roof restaurant that sold food amid beer and rum drunks. Dave grinned, his creased face tanned, hair the color of cotton. He was in good shape for a man in his mid-sixties, wide shoulders and no sign of a beer gut in spite of his love for craft brews. He wore a blue-and-yellow tropical print shirt, partially unbuttoned.

"Yes, she is lovely," O'Brien said.

Dave gestured toward the woman painting the sailboat. "Her name's Katie Scott. She's the daughter of a good friend of mine. Katie and her husband, Andy, bought that Beneteau-42 a month ago in Jacksonville. They brought her down through the Intercoastal to Ponce Marina for bottom paint, new plumbing, a partial refit, and a rebirth, if you will."

"Rebirth?" O'Brien glanced at the woman, now putting the last touches on the third letter. "Somehow I assume you don't mean a new life for a used boat."

Dave nodded. He glanced down at Max. "Miss Max, Nick has been asking about you. He has a fresh catch in today. Some of your favorite, grilled snapper."

Max looked at Dave and scurried to him, her tail wagging. He leaned over to pet her and then straightened, cutting his eyes to the woman on the ladder and back to O'Brien. "Speaking of her husband, Andy. He's arriving now."

O'Brien watched a man park a silver Audi in the shade of three royal palms and walk over to the woman. He spoke with her, the woman smiling, and coming down from the ladder. Dave grunted and said, "They had a little girl who was killed in a car accident. Katie was severely injured. In a way, the crash may have saved her life."

"How so?" O'Brien watched the man hand his wife a bottle of water.

"After the X-rays, MRIs, poking and prodding, doctors found ovarian cancer in Katie. On top of the death of her child, it was as if a slow death sentence had been pronounced for Katie. She underwent heavy chemo, changed her diet and now a big change in lifestyle."

O'Brien watched Max stalk a brown lizard on one of the creosote-stained dock pilings, the lizard's coffee-colored humpback blending in well with dried barnacles. He said, "I take it that the sailboat will play a big role in a lifestyle change. Are they going to be live-a-boards?"

"Don't know. Maybe. I do know that they're planning an extended cruise through the islands. They met in college years ago. Had great careers, fast tracking. Andy rose in the ranks on Wall Street, a trader—private equity, hedge funds. Katie was a vice president at an advertising agency. And now, they've traded it all to be vagabonds for a while."

"Sounds to me like a better way to live. You said they came down the Intercoastal, most likely using the engine. Can they sail?"

"Let's go find out. I'll introduce you to them."

"Do they have a friend down here at the marina?"

"I think I'd qualify. I've known Katie since she was born."

"How long do you think the guys in the Top Gun-39 have known them?"

Dave looked in the direction that O'Brien motioned toward. He spotted two men, now standing behind the wheel of the orange and dark blue boat, a vessel designed for speed. The man standing wore wrap-around sunglasses. He held a phone to his ear, his gaze on the

4

woman and her husband. Dave nodded and said, "Maybe they simply enjoy watching a pretty woman walk up and down a ladder."

The man at the wheel in the Top Gun, cranked the engines, set the phone down and eased the stiletto-style boat away from the marina gas pumps. O'Brien watched him maneuver to the far side of the marina, turn left and merge into the Halifax River, going south in the direction of the Ponce Lighthouse and the inlet.

O'Brien eyed the couple standing next to the sailboat, the third letter on the transom finished. It was an **A**. He shifted his gaze to Dave and said, "Maybe that's all he was doing. Maybe not. One thing for certain is he paid for his fuel in cash. You don't see that happen much anymore. It takes a thick wad of bills to fill up that tank. Most people would use a card."

Dave chuckled. "Did you actually see him pay cash from that distance?"

"I saw the attendant count back money to him. Yeah, it was a cash buy. And unlike the transom of the sailboat your friends are painting, there's very little room on a stern-drive cigarette boat for a name to be painted. So, we have an unknown man in an unnamed boat paying attention to your friends."

"Let me introduce you to them. We'll find out if there is an acquaintance to the guys who just left." He stared at the sailboat, the woman beginning to paint the fourth letter. He looked over at O'Brien and asked, "Want to take a guess at the name Katie's painting on her boat?"

O'Brien watched her for a moment, part of the next letter now visible. He smiled and said, "Considering the room left on the transom, where she started, it looks like it'll be nine letters. She's painted the **D** ... **R** ... and what appears to be an **A**. I'd guess it might be *Dragonfly*. It's got nine letters and would fit well across the rest of the transom."

Dave folded his arms across his thick chest, grinned and said, "Well done, Sean. It is *Dragonfly*. When you meet Katie and Andy they'll tell you why they're christening their boat with that name. After the explanation, you may never look at a dragonfly the same way."

# TWO

Don Blackwell had waited thirty years for his tee-time. He stood at the first tee of the Westchester Country Club near Manassas, Virginia. Blackwell, mid-sixties, five-ten, thinning gray hair, thick wrists, slipped a glove on his left hand and teed up his ball. He looked like millions of other men in America. Nothing physically distinguishable. That's one of the attributes that made him an excellent former field agent for the CIA. The other things included a quick mind, amiable personality, and the ability to talk with anyone about anything, from opera to quantum physics.

He played golf with three other men, all about the same age. All retired from government jobs within the last three years. Today was the first day Blackwell enjoyed a game of golf as a full-fledged retiree, and he'd thought about this moment for three decades. He didn't wear a watch anymore. Didn't bring a phone on the golf cart. Didn't have to. The lack of a schedule, he felt, would lower stress and allow for better concentration. He knew his game would improve.

What he didn't know is that he'd be dead before the sixth hole.

• • •

Sean O'Brien walked next to Dave Collins as they approached the sailboat on jack stands, Max running ahead, the boatyard half filled with boats on dry land—more power than sail. Dave said, "We'd ask permission to come aboard, but that might be a challenge."

Katie Scott stood at the top of the ladder, paintbrush in her right hand. She flashed a wide smile and started down the ladder. She said, "Uncle Dave, you don't need our permission, but you'll need to walk up the ladder to get topside."

Dave grinned. "Think I'll wait until she's back in the water."

Katie's husband, Andy, came from around the bow area of the boat, holding a dirty towel and sandpaper. "Hey, Dave," he said. "We're getting there. Should be a few more days, and we'll have her back in water. You are invited to *Dragonfly's* christening before the inaugural sail as a newly named sailboat."

Katie stepped to the ground and Dave said, "Katie, Andy, I'd like for you to meet Sean O'Brien and his companion, Maxine, known around the marina as Miss Max."

Katie glanced at her right hand, black paint on it, and said, "It's a pleasure to meet you. I'd shake your hand and Max's paw, but I've managed to get more paint on my hands than on the boat."

"No problem," O'Brien said, extending his hand to Andy. "Good to meet you both."

"You too," Andy said. He smiled, blond whiskers on his face, his cheeks and forehead red from the sun.

Katie squatted down and said, "Hi, Max. She's so cute." Max scurried over to her, Katie reaching out her clean left hand and petting Max. "I always wanted a dachshund. If you ever need a dog-sitter, don't hesitate to ask us. Andy and I grew up with dogs." She stood, her green eyes catching the late morning sunlight, a sprinkling of freckles across her bare shoulders.

O'Brien smiled and said, "I just may take you up on that one day. Max enjoys sailing, too." He looked at the transom. "You're doing an expert job with the lettering. That's not easy."

"Thanks," she said, glancing over her shoulder for a moment, looking at the boat. "I did a lot of graphic work coming up through the ranks in advertising and some calligraphy years before that for fun. I guess the artistic part sticks with you."

Dave cleared his throat. "I was telling Sean that the name of your boat, *Dragonfly*, was a name with special significance for you both."

Andy nodded and said, "Katie chose the name, but you're right, it has a lot of meaning for both of us."

Katie said, "This is probably something best discussed over a glass of wine, but the short story is that the dragonfly is symbolic to a big change in our lives. Andy did very well on Wall Street. My career at the ad agency was at its pinnacle when our daughter was killed in a horrible car crash. After, I was diagnosed with stage three ovarian cancer. Andy and I decided to put the world, at least our corner of it, on hold for a while and make it a priority to find more meaning in our lives." She looked away from O'Brien and stared at the boats in the marina, a charter boat cranking its big diesels on C dock, a puff of white smoke drifting above the stern.

Katie cut her eyes from Dave to O'Brien. "The significance of the dragonfly has to do with the dragonfly's remarkable change. It lives most of its life underwater, living the last fraction of its time on earth flying above water. The dragonfly's iridescent body and wings capture the light of the moment. It's vision, at this point in its life, is second to none. Andy and I want to live in the moment, to capture life as it happens … because it is so damn short." She smiled and glanced down at Max, who was sniffing the base of a jack stand.

Dave nodded. "Well said, Katie. I do think this particular moment in time calls for that glass of wine you mentioned. Why don't you two join us for drinks and dinner? Our dock mate is Greek, a helluva fisherman and an even better chef. If we're lucky, maybe we can entice Nick into cooking up some of his catch. He got back from a seven-day run yesterday. His grilled red snapper is to die for."

Andy wiped his hands with the towel and said, "Sounds good, thanks. What time and where."

"Cocktails at six. Dinner whenever it's ready. My boat, *Gibraltar*, near the end of L dock."

"Thank you, Uncle Dave," Katie said.

Dave nodded, glanced at O'Brien. "I might as well be Katie's uncle. I watched her grow up from a snaggletooth kid to a beautiful, smart and talented woman. You're a lucky man, Andy."

"You're right," Andy said.

Dave looked up at the partially completed name on the boat. "It'll be spectacular when you finish. And this model sailboat, like the dragonfly, will fly across the water." He looked at O'Brien. "Katie's dad, Sol, worked with me at the CIA for more than twenty-five years. He stayed on longer than me. How's your dad enjoying his retirement?"

"Great. But I think he's driving Mom a little crazy. For a man who was away from home a lot, being there all the time now is quite a change for both of them."

O'Brien said, "I really like the metaphor you and Andy are using in choosing your boat's new name. What made you decide to go sail over power?"

Katie touched the dragonfly necklace lying against her chest. "That was easy for us. All our lives, we've been … it seems, in a hurry. We even got to the point where we ate our food fast, and it wasn't fast food." She smiled. "A sailboat was our only choice because we are no longer in a hurry to do anything. The wind will either guide us or push us, or it won't."

O'Brien nodded. "Do you have friends here at the marina with powerboats … like the sleek racing cigarette boats?"

Andy shook his head. "No, we haven't had much time to socialize. But we're going to make that change when we sail into new harbors."

Katie asked, "What made you think we might have friends with racing boats?"

"Nothing, really. I'd just noticed two men in a Top Gun cigarette boat, watching you two. Maybe they were just curious. Sort of like watching paint dry as you and Andy worked around the boat."

"What man?" Andy asked.

"He's gone. He was refueling at the marina pumps, and then he left. A boat like that can be in Miami or Jacksonville in a short time. They can run offshore at more than seventy-miles-per hour."

Andy looked to his far left, toward the marina fuel pumps. A trawler was pulling up for diesel, two gulls circling it. He said, "Those racing boats are not in our wheelhouse, excuse the pun. We're in the slow lane now."

• • •

Don Blackwell approached the fifth hole feeling good about his golf game. He was six over par after four holes, and thus far, he had the lowest score of the four. His friend, Robert, was close. But close doesn't count in golf. Sinking the ball in the hole does. He used a white rag to clean the face of his driver, stepped up to the fifth tee and looked out across the winding fairway. The hole was long, the longest of the course, a par five with two doglegs. It was surround by thick woods and a few swayback hills.

• • •

The killer was one of the most sought-after assassins for hire. He had a reputation as the best of the best. Never missing. This coming after more than two hundred documented kills across seventy countries in the last ten years. His skills were in high demand by people with the money to afford him. He had a leathery face, dark hair feathering from the edges of a black knit cap. Unshaven. His penetrating black eyes looked through the riflescope with a predator's sense of stalking. Like a lion standing motionless in the chest-high savannah grasses, watching for wind to part the grass and catch the movement of a gazelle.

The assassin had been following Don Blackwell for almost a week. Monitoring his movements. Looking for a place and time with a clear shot. A place of few people and a quick, convenient escape route. He found it at the Westchester Country Club. Bull Run Road was less than three hundred meters from the fifth hole. The hills surrounding the golf course offered great angles to shoot down onto the course from a long distance.

The killer had his CheyTac M200 rifle on a bipod, propped atop a flat boulder on the side of a hill. He had a clear point of view over the tops of the pines and poplar trees.

He sighted in on the man—Don Blackwell, as Blackwell chatted with his friends. The assassin was eager to take the job. The American ex-spy was probably talking about all the lies he'd spun, the governments he'd help topple, the puppet people he'd help put in place. *Didn't matter*, the killer told himself. *Nothing matters but staying out of harm's way, plenty of money, women, and a lifestyle that wealth can buy.* He sighted the crosshairs over Blackwell's chest and followed him as he walked from the golf cart to the tee box.

• • •

Blackwell used a new golf ball. He placed a red tee under it and pushed the tee into the soft earth until the ground touched his fingers. Then he lifted it up about a quarter inch, high enough above ground for the big driver club to clear and power the ball as far as possible. At age sixty-four, with the wind at his back, he could still manage a 225-yard drive on a good day. The breeze smelled of fresh-cut grass and a whiff of cigar smoke.

He stood parallel to the ball, sighted down the long fairway, turned back to his friends and said, "Keep your eye on the ball. I have a feeling this baby's gonna be so airborne it'll fly like a bullet."

"Let's see it," said one of the men. "Ten bucks says your ol' slice will return." He chuckled.

"Not a chance," said Blackwell. He stood, holding the club. A robin hopped to the far right of the fairway, chirping. Blackwell slowly pulled the club back and swung, the club squarely connecting with the ball. *Whack.*

There was another sound—the distant crack of a rifle. Before the golf ball reached its peak, Don Blackwell's head exploded. He fell dead on the fifth hole just after hitting his longest drive in thirty years.

# THREE

Sean O'Brien liked the clarity of thought during and after a good
run. He jogged along the surf near Lighthouse Point Park, close to
Ponce Inlet, Max romping behind him, her short legs alternating
between a run, trot, and an accelerated rabbit hop. The warm trade
winds from the east delivered the hint of enigmatic floral scents caught
in an airborne stream over the Atlantic. The trade winds across the
ocean were as mysterious as the currents beneath it. Both crisscrossed
the earth and left no tracks.

Max paused, sniffed a beached starfish and continued jogging.
O'Brien slowed down, allowing her to pass. Each time she did, Max
almost grinned, prancing through the shallow breakers, white flotsam
scattering like confetti around her head, barking at the snickering gulls.

O'Brien thought of the conversation he and Dave had with Katie
and Andy Scott. He liked their motivation for learning to sail, the
parallel analogy to the life of a dragonfly. He admired their grit and
boldness to make the leap from the bounds of corporate America into
the abyss of sailing into waters with no boundaries. What he didn't like
was the uneasy feeling he had when he observed the men in the racing
boat watching the couple. *Maybe it was nothing,* he thought. *Just a
couple of guys looking at an attractive woman climbing up and down a
ladder.*

O'Brien slowed as Max stopped to inspect a conch shell that rolled in with one of the breakers. The opening to the shell was soft pink, shimmering in the late afternoon sunlight. O'Brien picked up the shell and walked into the ocean up to his chest, gently releasing it. Max watched, barked twice and dared to run into a small breaker, retreating quickly as the wave lifted her up. O'Brien smiled. "I know you think you're a Labrador, but you do have other talents. Surfing isn't one of them, kiddo."

He walked out of the water and said, "Let's do another hundred yards and head back to the dock. We have a dinner party and Nick's cooking." They ran down the beach, Max's long ears flapping, O'Brien thinking about the challenge that Katie and Andy would have as first-time sailors heading for the islands at the beginning of hurricane season. And he thought about the dark cloud of suspicion he felt earlier today watching one of the men at the fuel pumps and then standing at the wheel of the Top Gun boat. He replayed Andy's comments, *"Those racing boats are not in our wheelhouse, excuse the pun. We're in the slow lane now."*

• • •

A half hour later, the sun was turning the horizon into wide streaks of crimson and burgundy to the west of Ponce Marina, the mangroves on the banks of the Halifax River becoming silhouettes. O'Brien picked Max up as they crossed South Atlantic Avenue and walked toward the marina.

They entered the parking lot, and he set her down as they approached the screened door to the Tiki Bar. The restaurant was a fish camp on stilts, or large pilings above the water. The isinglass windows were rolled up allowing the heavy aroma of fried fish, coleslaw and beer to drift across the marina. It was the kind of restaurant where no one batted an eye if a dog entered. O'Brien opened the screened door, and Max ran ahead. More than two-dozen sundrenched tourists sat at the long bar and around the circular dining tables, formerly large wooden spools that utility companies used for wire and cable. The spools were shellacked and turned on their sides—vertical, four chairs could fit at each table.

Max scampered up to the roughhewn bar, her eyes bright. She caught the attention of a weathered charter boat captain who sat on a barstool, a sweating bottle of Budweiser in front of him. "Hey, Max," he said, his pale blue eyes glassy, nose scarred from patches of cancer that had been removed from years in the sun. Max sat at the base of his barstool, cocking her head.

O'Brien asked, "How are you, Captain Leon? You make a run today?"

"Oh, hell yeah. Crack of dawn we took out a party of four guys from Buffalo, New York. We got into some mackerel and redfish. One caught a cobia. They were happy." He lifted a piece of cheese from a paper plate and tossed it to Max. She caught it in midair. "Wanna beer, Sean?"

"No thanks. I have to hit the shower. Max and I are a little gamey after a run on the beach."

The charter captain took a pull off his beer, grinned, and said, "I thought that smell was from oysters in the can out back." He made a coughing laugh.

"Maybe it's both. Come on Max."

O'Brien started for the back-exit door when the Tiki Bar owner, Florence Spencer, approached him. She was in her late fifties, smiling brown eyes, graying hair worn up. She said, "There's my favorite mystery man and his sidekick, Maxie. How you been, Sean? Haven't seen you in a while."

"We're doing well, Flo." He glanced around the restaurant. "Looks like business is good."

"It's improving. I hired a new cook. He knows seafood and burgers. He's qualified. I'd love to hire Nick Cronus. Even part-time. However, every time a pretty girl walked in, Nick would be out of the kitchen to become the host. Speaking of the ladies, someone was in here looking for you."

"Really? Who was it?"

She gestured to the bartender, Lee, stocky man with a Marine Corp bulldog tattoo on his right forearm. He came closer, and Flo said, "Lee, the girl in here lookin' for Sean … what was her name?"

"She didn't tell me her name, but she knew the name of your boat, *Jupiter*. She wanted to know if you were on your boat. Told her I didn't know. That was about three hours ago. She said she'd go look for herself … wanted to know where to find it. Told her it was at the end of L dock."

O'Brien said nothing for a moment. A solo singer in one corner of the restaurant sat on a stool, adjusting his guitar, his white fedora hat casting half of his tanned face in shadow. O'Brien glanced at the bartender's T-shirt, which depicted a curvaceous oyster in a bikini wearing sunglasses. The subtitle read: *Eat 'em raw at the Tiki Bar, Ponce Marina*. "Did the woman say whether she was going to my boat?"

"Didn't say. And I didn't ask." He grinned. "You know, what happens at Ponce Marina stays at the marina. She was a looker, though. Long, dark hair. Sort of exotic."

"No editorial comments needed." Flo said. "A friend of Sean's is a friend of ours. Just watch Nick around her." She chuckled.

O'Brien smiled. "No sweat. Thanks." He turned to leave, Max trotting ahead, the singer in the far corner now crooning a Jimmy Buffet song, *Son of a Son of a Sailor*. They walked out of the restaurant, started toward L dock, and then he stopped. "Max, let's see if Katie finished painting the name on her sailboat."

O'Brien gestured with his head, and Max followed him past the marina office, the manager, a wiry, middle aged man in a Marlins' baseball cap, was locking up for the day. O'Brien stopped and asked, "Hey, Wes, you have any cigarette boats listed for sale on your bulletin board?"

The manager removed his key from the deadbolt and said, "Not recently. You'll find more of those in the Miami area." He grinned. "You feelin' the need for speed, Sean?"

"You never know."

"If you want to put your Bayliner on the market, I can probably find a buyer."

"If I ever return to sailboats, I'll keep that in mind. See you around."

"Yep."

The manager headed for the parking lot, a wad of keys hanging from his belt, bouncing off his hip as he strolled away. O'Brien walked toward the boatyard. Among the three-dozen boats in the yard, Katie and Andy's sailboat stood out. They were gone, but their boat had a presence—even out of the water, the deep blue hull, fresh bottom paint, and a transom now wearing the new name: **Dragonfly**.

O'Brien stood there for a moment, admiring the perfect lettering, the breeze tossing an American flag attached to a short wooden pole secured to the cockpit. He watched the flag and thought about something Katie said. *'The wind will either guide or push us, or it won't.'*

The sound of a man whistling interrupted his thoughts. One of the marina employees, a black man with salt and pepper hair, walked up from the fuel station, heading toward the parking lot beyond the yard. O'Brien motioned for him and said, "Wes just locked up. Looks like he got out of here before you."

The man stopped and grinned. "I had to fix a breaker box on E dock."

"Happy to report all seems to be well on L dock. We have more than our share of pelicans, though."

The man glanced at Max and then up at O'Brien, smiling, and said, "That lil' dog ought to be able to run off the pelicans."

"She has her passive-aggressive moments."

"Sounds like my wife." He chuckled and started to walk away.

O'Brien said, "I saw you servicing the Top Gun cigarette boat earlier today. Are those big engines all gas or are they putting diesels in them now?"

"That one was gas, and it took a lot to top it off. And the dude paid in cash. Don't see much of that anymore." He paused, a slight sheen of perspiration over his dark, furrowed brow. He massaged a callous on one knuckle. "Matter of fact, I don't recall puttin' diesel fuel in one of 'em cigarette boats. Not that we see a lot here at the marina."

"Do you know if that one was for sale?"

"I doubt it. The fella seemed like one of those international playboy types that fly into Miami Beach, rent expensive toys, and fool around the waterways 'til they break something."

"Maybe he's back down in South Beach now."

"Could be. Or he could be heading out to the Bahamas. He asked me how far the closest island was to Florida. I told him if he headed east straight outta Lauderdale, he'd run into Bimini in about an hour in the boat he had."

"You think he'd try the Bimini run?"

He shrugged his shoulders. "Don't know. He wanted to know how long it'd take in a sailboat. I tol' him it depended on the boat, the wind, and the sailor. A racin' sailboat can do it a lot faster than a wide beam boat like 'em old Morgans." He paused and looked over to *Dragonfly*, pointing with his wide right hand, part of his index finger missing. "The dude asked me how long it'd take for a boat like that one … *Dragonfly,* to make it to the islands."

# FOUR

If a ten-pound dachshund could strut, it was Max. She strode down L dock like a conquering warrior in a parade looking for a hero's welcome. She and O'Brien walked past dozens of moored boats. Japanese lanterns hung from one houseboat, the orange and red lights swaying in the breeze, a Kenny Chesney song, *Pirate Flag*, coming from the salon. O'Brien heard a woman laughing, more of a giggle, as if she were being tickled. It was getting close to dinnertime, the smell of lighter fluid and smoldering charcoal coming from a trawler and a sailboat, white smoke drifting from the cockpits.

As he and Max approached the end of the dock, they got closer to a boat that had the lineage of an ancient mariner. *St. Michael* was a Mediterranean designed fishing boat—sweeping high bow, towering wheelhouse, able to plow through rolling waves at sea. The sound of Greek music was coming from the galley inside *St. Michael*.

"What's happening, Sean?" Nick Cronus stepped from his open salon onto the cockpit. His skin was as brown as a roasted coffee bean, faded swim shorts, tank top, wide shoulders, and muscles sculpted from years at sea. He sported a thick, walrus mustache and a mop of corkscrew, black hair combed by the ocean winds for so long that he'd have to steam out the locks to ever get them untangled.

Nick carried a white and blue cooler filled with cracked ice and fresh-filleted fish. He was a transplanted Greek fisherman, meaning he thought he was first cousin to a porpoise. As a young man, growing up on the island of Mykonos, Nick would dive for pearls and sponges. Today, he worked as a commercial fisherman.

"Come here, Hot Dog," Nick said, holding his big, calloused hands out for Max. She trotted to the edge of dock, tail wagging. He reached over the transom and lifted her into his Popeye forearms. "It's been almost a month since Uncle Nicky has danced with you." He spun around the cockpit, one arm extended horizontally, as if he had a dance partner to his right side, Max cradled in the other arm, his bare feet moving in rhythm to the music. After a couple of turns, he paused looked up at O'Brien, moustache lifting in a wide smile, and said, "Plato, probably my Greek ancestor, taught us that the first thing an educated man needs to learn is to dance."

"Are you sure Plato said that?"

"Absolutely. And it's got nothin' to do with philosophy. It has everything to do with a happy heart and a happy woman. In my case, it is the women. But one day, I will dance my way in to the heart of the right woman, and we'll have a big, fat Greek wedding. You, Sean O'Brien, will be my best man." Nick laughed and snorted at the same time, the sound like a kazoo mixed with the call of a wolf. He winked and set Max down.

"I'll be there," O'Brien said.

"I'm gonna take these fish to Dave's boat, fire up his grill, and create what surely will be another masterpiece. I hear we have company comin' to join us. Dave said they're a young couple—newbie sailors looking to head out to the islands."

"She's the daughter of an old friend of his."

"From Dave's time in the CIA?"

"That'd be a good bet." O'Brien looked to the opposite side of L dock. Dave's boat, *Gibraltar*, a forty-two-foot Grand Banks trawler, was tied to the cleats. The windows open, movement in the salon, light jazz coming from the stern. O'Brien glanced back at Max and then Nick. "Can Max hang with you? She got to play in the surf. I need a shower."

"Maxine would go with me anyway 'cause she knows Nicky's got the food. C'mon, Hot Dog. Let's make a Greek salad and get this fine fish over to Dave's boat."

"Thanks, Nick." O'Brien walked about fifty feet farther down the dock, to the end, where his boat, *Jupiter,* was moored at slip L-41. It was a Bayliner-38, and in good shape for a boat with thirteen years on the same diesel. He stepped over the stern railing and onto a short ladder leading down to the floor of the cockpit. He glanced around the boat, checking for any signs that it had been boarded since he was last here two weeks ago.

There was a sure sign.

A note.

And it was wedged in the frame of the sliding glass doors. He lifted the envelope. His name was written in a neat penmanship, the handwriting had a feminine stroke.

Not always a good sign.

# FIVE

O'Brien opened all the windows on *Jupiter*, allowing a steady easterly cross-breeze to move through most of the boat. He set the envelope down on his bar in the salon. The salon was roomy—leather couch, two canvas director's chairs, a slice of ancient bald cypress wood for a coffee table. The piece had been cut out of the trunk at the waterline decades earlier after the tree had stood in the Everglades for centuries. The table had serrated edges, shellacked and supported by four cypress wooden knees.

O'Brien stepped over to the three-stool bar and used a knife to open the envelope. He read it slowly. *Dear Sean, I hope this note finds you well. I was in the area and had the urge to stop by just to say hi and see how you're doing. It's been a while since you saved my life that day. I think about it often. I think about what we went through together, and how it proved Joe Billie was an innocent man. I saw Joe yesterday, and he'd asked about you. As I reflect back, I'm not sure if I ever even thanked you. If not, I'm very sorry. Maybe I could make it up to you over a glass of wine. I've included my number. Just a thought. If not, I understand. Take care and give my love to little Max.*

*Wynona Osceola*

O'Brien stared at her signature for a few seconds and set the letter down. He looked out the port window to the marina, a sixty-foot Hatteras easing out of its slip, deep-throated diesels warbling, the silver-haired captain in dark glasses. O'Brien walked to the large head near the master berth, turned on the shower, stripped down and stepped under the torrent of warm water. He closed his eyes, the water beating across his face and chest.

He'd often thought about Wynona Osceola—the keen intelligence and depth she possessed. Her wide smile. Her laugh. Her playful brown eyes. He thought about her former career as an FBI agent before stepping down after she shot and killed a man who was murdering his own daughter. Wynona had no regrets. She'd returned to her home, the Seminole Tribe to work as a detective on the reservation in South Florida.

O'Brien ended the shower, dried off, put on shorts and a fresh polo shirt. He picked up an unopened bottle of gin from his bar and looked at a framed photo of his wife Sherri. She was standing on the beach, turning around just as O'Brien had snapped the picture. He didn't know it then, but it would be the last time she spent on a beach, with the sand between her toes, and a golden sun setting soft against her tanned face. Ovarian cancer would claim her life in eight months. She'd leave him a wound that never healed completely and a little dachshund that always reminded him of Sherri.

He picked up the note and envelope left by Wynona, slid open a drawer, and dropped it inside, closing the drawer.

• • •

Katie and Andy Scott arrived at *Gibraltar,* she with a bottle of chardonnay in her hand and Andy carrying a second bottle, red with a black label. Katie wore a powder blue summer dress. Andy in shorts and a golf shirt, a Nike logo above the pocket. "Permission to come aboard," she said, standing on an auxiliary dock that ran the length of the trawler back to the large cockpit.

"Please, join us," Dave said with a grin, pouring an icy martini from the stainless-steel shaker. He walked over to the steps and reached his hand out to help steady Katie as she came down the three steps.

"Thanks," she said.

"Welcome aboard, sailors," Nick said, opening the cover to a standup barbeque grill. He used a paintbrush to slap a Greek barbeque sauce laced with crushed garlic over large prawns, the sauce and juices dripping into the mesquite wood and hot coals. Max trotted over to greet the guests.

"Hello, Max," Katie said, stopping to pet her. She stood, looked at the grill and Nick. "It smells divine."

Nick grinned. "That's 'cause it's inspired by the Greek god, Bacchus."

Dave sipped his martini and said, "I believe Bacchus is more associated with wine than food."

Nick closed the cover to the grill. "Wine and food are inseparable."

Andy stepped forward and said, "Speaking of wine. We bought a chard and a merlot. Didn't know what you were serving, so we wanted to cover the bases."

"Well covered," Dave said, taking the two wine bottles and stepping into the salon to set them on the bar.

O'Brien stepped from the salon to the cockpit, greeted Katie and Andy and then said, "I saw that you'd finished painting *Dragonfly* across the transom. You did an excellent job."

Katie smiled. "Thank you. I was painting by the numbers and trying to keep the paint between the lines."

O'Brien laughed and said, "You might fool Nick, but I've already found out you have an artistic history."

Dave's phone buzzed. He picked it up from the bar and looked at the caller ID. *R. Lewis.* It was from a former CIA colleague. Although a friend, Dave and Robert Lewis hadn't spoken in a few years. One of the last conversations was not too long after Dave retired.

He started to answer the call but didn't want to be on the phone while greeting Andy and Katie. Dave set the phone down, paused a moment, wondering if Lewis would leave a message. If so, Dave hoped it would be some good news. But his gut told him otherwise.

Dave watched Nick and Sean welcome Katie and Andy. He wiped his hands on a white bar towel and heard the *ping* of a voice-mail message as he stepped from the salon across the cockpit.

# SIX

"I'm Nick the Greek," he said, extending his hand.

Katie and Andy shook Nick's hand, she smiled and asked, "It's good to meet you Nick the Greek. Is 'the' your middle name?"

Nick turned to Dave and O'Brien. "I like her. Maybe the *the* oughta be my middle name 'cause my parents never gave me one. In Greece, a middle name is not needed. My surname is Cronus, it goes back to the time of the Spartans, or so we we're told."

Katie said, "You can always get your genealogy tested."

Nick grinned. "Hey, if I don't look Greek, the fishes don't have gills. Speaking of fishes, I hope you like seafood. I got some fresh-shucked oysters. Prawns on the grill. Then I'm gonna cook some red snapper using olive oil, Key Largo lime juice, a touch of garlic, ginger, lemon, and some secret Greek spices."

"Sounds delicious," Katie said.

Andy nodded. "Did you buy or catch the fish?"

Nick looked at him, disbelieving, dark eyes wide and playful. "I have never bought fish in my life. Not even a goldfish. What you eat tonight was swimmin' in the deep blue sea a few hours ago."

Dave said, "How about a drink before we serve the wine and food. Come, sit around the table."

Katie glanced at Dave's martini and asked, "Can you make a margarita?"

"My dear Katie. How long have you known me?"

"All of my life."

"Then perhaps you remember when you and your parents visited me during my first summer in Florida. We sipped margaritas at sunset … margaritas I made."

She smiled. "Yes, I do remember."

Dave glanced at Andy. "How about you, Andy? What can I fix for you?"

"A margarita sounds good, thanks."

They sat around a wooden table, a nautical blue tablecloth with the image of a compass in the center. They sipped cocktails and ate oysters in the half shell in a bed of cracked ice, the music of Miles Davis coming from speakers behind the bar. A Catalina-38 sailboat entered the marina, the sails down, the diesel barely audible as the man behind the wheel headed toward M dock.

Dave stirred his martini, ate a blue cheese olive and said, "I shared with Nick what you told Sean and I about the reason you renamed your sailboat, *Dragonfly,* but you haven't told us where you plan to sail. I know you're going to the islands, the Bahamas, but have you charted a route, picked out harbors, plotted sheltered coves in the event of bad weather?"

Andy sipped his margarita. "We're leaving out of Lauderdale, heading east. Bimini will be the first stop. After that …" He glanced over to his wife. "After that, we're going to follow the wind and our instincts."

Katie pulled a strand of hair behind her right ear and said, "We thought about sailing north after Bimini, into Grand Bahama, spend as long as we want there, and then head over to Great Abaco … stopping in the nooks and crannies, all the hidden harbors along the way. From there, as Andy said, we'll make it up as we go along the journey."

O'Brien sipped a Hendricks gin and tonic and said, "That sounds like a good start. How are your sailing skills?"

"Pretty good," Andy said. "I spent summers sailing from Province-town down to Nantucket. My uncle had a Tartan 26, and he taught me how to sail."

Katie smiled. "I know nothing about sailing, but I'm a quick learner."

O'Brien nodded. "You can quickly pick up navigation, anchoring, seamanship … but the art of balancing the wind and water is kind of like riding a galloping horse. Those who do it well make it look effortless, the rider and horse in sync, working together as one. When you and Andy are at the helm, learn not to fight the boat, but to ride with it, harnessing the wind, not so much to push you, but rather to pull you along, gliding, like you were part of an unseen train."

Andy leaned back in his deck chair. "You seem to have a heck of a grasp on the art and magic of good sailing. You told us earlier that the Bayliner across the dock is yours. So I gather that you've had some sailing experience."

"My wife, Sherri, and I had a Beneteau, the same length as yours. We spent a lot of time on the water."

"Where's the boat?" Andy asked.

"I sold it a few years ago."

Katie moistened her bottom lip. "May I ask where is your wife? And I don't mean to pry."

"Sherri died. Ovarian cancer."

"I'm so sorry."

"She'd given Max to me before she passed, so it's been just the two of us. I hope that you and Andy enjoy sailing as much as Sherri and I did."

Nick cleared his throat and reached for his beer. "Sailin' isn't hard. As long as you got fair weather, you'll figure it out. By the time storms show up, and they will, you'll pretty much have a handle on it." He stood and walked over to the grill, tending the fish and prawns, white smoke billowing up in his face.

Katie watched the owner of the Catalina tying the boat's ropes to the dock cleats. She said, "I like what you said, Sean, about gliding the boat and how it's not unlike riding in sync with a horse. The horse is alive, and so is the sea, with the currents, the swells, and life right under the keel. I'm looking forward to sailing with the wind, not against it. It'll be a nice change and experience. And it'll be so nice to watch sunsets from faraway harbors and experience starry nights from hidden coves and bays."

Nick finished grilling the fish and prawns, brought them to the table on a long serving dish and set it down, steam drifting from the food, the scent of butter, garlic and white wine in the mix. He grinned and said, "Bon appetit!"

After the first few bites of food, Katie sipped from a glass of chardonnay and said, "Nick, this is so good. Thank you."

Andy nodded. "It's the best seafood I've ever eaten, and I'm from the Boston area. Where'd you learn to cook like this?"

"I watched my grandfather when he'd come back with a catch. And at sea, on my boat, I cook every day with the freshest of fish, oysters, crabs, and shrimp. You learn."

They ate and talked sailing and navigation, Andy and Katie asking dozens of questions. Dave finished his second martini, excused himself to hit the head. As he walked by the bar, he stopped, picked up his phone and carried it with him. At the door to the larger of two heads near the master berth, he stopped and played the message.

The man who left the message sounded fatigued, his voice raspy. Robert Lewis said, "Dave, it's been too long old friend. I hope you're enjoying retirement, doing all those things we talked about after decades with the agency. I hate like hell giving you bad news … so I won't do it on a voice-mail. Call me back as soon as you get this."

Dave slipped his bifocals on and hit the button to return the call. "Hey, Dave," Lewis said answering on the second ring. "My apologies for the rather ambiguous message I left you."

"Robert, you're right, it has been too damn long. I hate to start a conversation off by you telling me some bad news. But, the message you left, I assume it's not some sort of a good news, bad news scenario. What do you have?"

"It's Don Blackwell … he's dead. Murdered."

"Murdered?" Dave reached for the doorframe, gripping it tight. "What happened?"

"Maybe murdered isn't the best term. He was assassinated. Don was playing golf at his favorite course with three other guys. Some from the agency. Others retired feds. They said that Don stepped to the fifth tee box, lined up his shot and a second after he hit the ball, someone shot him through the head."

"Why now?" Dave whispered. "After all those years with the agency … all the close calls, he's hit after retirement on a golf course."

Robert Lewis, thin, bags under his eyes, shorts and yellow polo shirt, stood on the front porch of his home in Scottsdale, Arizona, and looked at a single cloud in the bottomless blue sky. "Hit is the appropriate word. There is no doubt that a hit man had him in his sights. Our guys with him said the shot came from the direction of a knoll or small hill. The golf course is in a slight valley surrounded by hills. It's the Westchester Country Club outside of Manassas. FBI and the agency are combing the area. Nothing yet, of course. It was a single shot. Estimated distance at least three hundred yards."

Dave said nothing. He glanced back over his left shoulder, Katie and Andy laughing at something Nick was telling them. Sean had Max on his lap. Dave said, "It doesn't make sense. Had this happened five years ago, it'd be one thing … but now it doesn't unless …"

"Unless what, Dave?"

"Unless it was an old vendetta."

"An old score could have been settled before or in the first year after Don's retirement."

"Maybe not. Not if the assassin or the person who hired the assassin didn't have the means or money to settle the score … or that person, for some reason, was not in a position to do so. Robert, you and me, Don Blackwell, Simon Rivers, and Sol Lefko were the team working at Gitmo as some of the worst of the worst were being processed down there. We had to extract intel from dozens of enemy combatants. Maybe there's a connection."

"That doesn't seem plausible. Not after all this time. Regardless, Dave, the worst of the bad asses are still locked up and will be for the rest of their sorry lives."

"Don Blackwell was very close with Simon Rivers."

"Yes, I know. Their families spent a lot of time together. Too bad Simon's only son, Carter, died a couple of months ago."

Dave massaged the bridge of his nose. "I wasn't aware his son passed. How'd it happen?"

"Freak car accident. Went off a cliff on the Pacific Coast Highway north of Santa Barbara."

"I'm sorry to hear that. Don and his wife Marti knew Sol Lefko and his family well, too. Coincidentally, Sol's daughter, Katie and her husband, Andy, are having dinner with some friends of mine on my boat. I hate like hell walking back to the deck and telling her Don Blackwell was killed."

"She probably should know."

"Have you told her father?"

"No. You are the first in our group of five that I called. When we get off the phone, I'll call the others."

"Okay. This one really hurts. We had each other's back through some of the worst times in the worst places on earth. And all five of us survived. Bruised and battered, but we made it back alive. Watch yourself. Whoever killed Don may have us in his sights, too."

# SEVEN

D ave made another martini and rejoined the dinner party. Nick was giving Katie and Andy some sailing tips. O'Brien looked at Dave and knew something was not right. Dave sat back at the table, his eyes scanning the adjacent docks and boats. He said, "I want to propose a toast to our guests here tonight and their start on a new journey in life. Cheers!"

Nick reached for his beer. O'Brien lifted his gin and tonic. Andy and Katie lifted their glasses of wine. Dave said, "To Katie and Andy … to your courage to make a dramatic change in your lives. To your reasons for doing so. To safe passages, fair winds and memories you will share the rest of your lives. And to coming back here to Ponce Marina at the end of your journey to share your experiences with us around this fabled table. To the voyages of *Dragonfly!*"

"I'll drink to that," said Nick. The glasses and bottle all clicked in a toast, people sipping and O'Brien eyeing Dave, wondering what he was now concealing behind eyes filled with affection for Katie and Andy.

"When do you guys sail away?" O'Brien asked.

"In a few days," Katie said. "We can't wait to get our boat back in the water, now with its new bottom paint. And a new name splashed right across its lovely rump. I know the word is transom, but to me a boat as sexy as *Dragonfly* has a nice curvy backside there. Boat butt sounds better."

Nick lifted his beer. "Amen. I may never look at my boat, *St. Michael*, the same way ever again." They laughed and shared nautical talk, enjoying the food and drink.

An hour later, after Turkish coffee and Key Lime pie, Katie yawned and said, "This is one of the … no … it's probably the best seafood meal I've ever eaten. Thank you so much."

Dave said, "It was all Nick. I just provided the table and a few of the adult beverages.

O'Brien said, "I brought Max for the entertainment. I don't have to take a doggy bag back to my boat. It's on four short legs."

Nick drained the remains of his beer and said, "I like good food and good friends. You and Andy are now our good friends. Sean can't cook, but he's got other talents."

Katie turned her head toward O'Brien and asked, "What are those talents?"

Nick blurted, "My man, Sean … he's sort of a consultant. Dave always says Sean's the kind of guy you'd want with you in a foxhole. He'd find a way to get you out."

O'Brien shook his head. "I've been lucky, and I've lost about as many as I've won."

Nick leaned forward. "You won the big one for me." He looked at Katie and Andy. "Sean saved my life."

"What happened?" Andy asked.

"It was late. I was comin' out of the Tiki Bar when three bikers jumped me. One hit me hard with a sucker punch and then all three of 'em came at me with brass knuckles and bats. Sean, pulled up in his Jeep, saw what was going down, and he got a tire iron outta his Jeep. When the dust settled, he'd broken legs, knees, a few wrists and shoulders, lots of knocked out teeth. One guy was in the hospital a month. Today, I'm Sean's blood brother for life. I'd take a bullet for this guy." Nick's eyes moistened. He blinked twice and took a pull off his Corona.

O'Brien said, "The bikers were like a rabid pack of dogs on Nick, I knew he was about one baseball bat hit away from a coma or death. I just got lucky. Surprise attack."

Dave sipped his drink and said, "For a big fella, he's humble, too."

"What do you do for a living, Sean?" Andy asked.

Before he could answer, Nick said, "Sean's a birddog."

Katie smiled, her lips red from the ice in her after-dinner margarita. "Birddog, what does that mean?"

Nick said, "Sean finds stuff. Lost things … lost people. He even found a World War Two German U-boat on the bottom of the ocean. He used to be a detective down in Miami, and before that, Delta Force—"

"I'm retired, at least from all that," O'Brien interjected. "I didn't find the U-boat. I accidentally hooked my boat anchor on it. I'm a part-time, private investigator."

Katie sipped the margarita over the salty rim of the glass. "Finding a World War Two submarine sounds fascinating. What ever happened to it?"

"It's still out there, about sixty miles due east from the lighthouse. When you and Andy return from your Caribbean adventures, we can swap sea tales."

"Sounds like a plan," Katie said, catching herself in a yawn. "I'm sorry. I've been working ten-hour days on *Dragonfly*."

Andy nodded. "We should be getting back to the hotel. We're putting *Dragonfly* into the water day after tomorrow. A lot to wrap up before then. Can we help you with the dishes?"

Dave poured two-fingers worth of scotch over a single ice cube in a heavy glass and sipped. "Absolutely not. That's why I use durable paper plates. When you get my age, time seems to become costlier because there's less of it. Doing dishes is one of those things I eliminated, at least to some extent."

O'Brien watched Dave a moment, wondering if he was going to say something while Andy and Katie were on *Gibraltar*, or after they left. He scratched Max behind her ears and set her on deck.

Dave leaned back in his chair, stars now bright in the night sky, the sweep of a beam coming from Ponce Lighthouse cutting through the inky dark and grazing the surface of the Atlantic. Dave said, "Katie, your dad and I worked closely with a lot of bright and patriotic people at the CIA. We all did what we did because we believe deeply in the

U.S. Constitution." He paused, shifting his gaze from her face to the lighthouse. "Have you spoken with your mom or dad today?"

"No … why? Is something wrong, Uncle Dave? The last time I heard you talk like this was when you caught my friend Leslie and I taking shots from Dad's bottle of scotch at a party my parents were having. I was about seventeen at the time."

Dave chuckled. "I do remember that. I hope you learned your lesson." He exhaled. "Your father and I worked closely with three other men at the agency. In a way, I suppose, we had different skillsets that complemented each other. You know Don Blackwell and his wife, Marti."

"Yes, I met them a few times. Mr. Blackwell taught me, and my friend Rhonda, a card trick. Did something happen?"

"I just received a call from Robert Lewis, he's another one of our former contemporaries."

She shook her head. "I met him, too, a few years ago. Very nice man."

Dave nodded. "Yes, he is. Robert told me that Don was killed today. I'm sorry, but I thought you should know."

"Killed?" She looked at Andy, inhaled a deep breath through her nostrils. She cut her eyes back to Dave. "Was his death an accident?"

"No. He was shot while playing golf with friends."

"Shot? Oh my God … was it robbery?"

"The round was fired from a distance. They haven't found the person responsible. The killer took the shot from one of the hills overlooking the golf course. Robert Lewis is phoning your parents to let them know. Maybe you should give them a call sometime tomorrow to check in and see how they're doing."

Katie stared out into the harbor, boats gently bobbing in the rising tide and light breeze, a sailboat halyard clinking at the top of a mast. "I will. That's horrible. Do they have any idea why he was killed?"

"No, not yet."

Katie said nothing, her thoughts veiled. She bit her bottom lip. O'Brien detected an unconscious tremor of her shoulders, as if she fought back a chill on a warm Florida summer night. She looked at Dave and asked, "There's no reason for my father to be in any danger … right?"

"Correct, at least no direct reason that we know of at this time. If you talk to your dad before I do, tell him I'll touch base with him soon."

"I will." Katie and Andy said their goodbyes, Katie hugging Dave, Nick and O'Brien. She bent down and petted Max and then said, "Thank you, everyone, for welcoming Andy and I into your marina family. We so appreciate it. This may be *Dragonfly's* home port after our time in the islands."

"Let's plan on that," O'Brien said, walking with them to the steps leading up from the cockpit.

Andy shook their hands. "I appreciate the hospitality. Next time, we'll do it on *Dragonfly*."

Andy and Katie left, holding hands as they walked down L dock toward the Tiki Bar and the parking lot. Nick watched them for a moment and said, "She's a fine lookin' woman. Andy's a lucky dude. Let's hope he's a good sailor."

Dave smiled. "I just hope he's a good guy. He can learn to sail, it's hard to learn the other if it's not there. Right, Sean? You've dealt with enough evil in your careers to last many lifetimes."

O'Brien stepped back to the table, looked at Dave's phone on the table and then lifted his eyes to Dave. "We can talk about evil when you share with us what really happened today. No doubt evil played a part. What I want to know is this … what did your friend do to attract it … why after he'd retired? And are you in danger?"

Dave looked up in the sky beyond *Gibraltar's* transom, the three-quarter moon bright. He lowered his eyes and watched the lighthouse for a few seconds, the white beam moving across his wide, black pupils like a meteor, thoughts behind his eyes darker than the most remote part of the universe.

# EIGHT

Moonlight cast the shrimp boat, *Aphrodite*, in silhouette on the dark face of a flat ocean. Captain Santos Kalivaris turned off his lights, the boat drifting near the GPS coordinates that had been prearranged two weeks earlier. He stood behind the wheel, smoked a Camel down to the last half-inch, the tips of his fingers pale yellow, smoke haloing above his head in the boat's wheelhouse.

He was in his early forties, black hair and eyes, old scars on his hands and forearms. Hard muscle under a loose-fitting white T-shirt. Dirty jeans. Orange rubber boots. Near constant sun and salt water had parched his whiskered face like saddle leather. He wore a gold hoop earring in one ear. He raised a pair of binoculars to his eyes, scanning the dark sea. Nothing.

Kalivaris looked at his watch as a deckhand entered. At six-four, the man was larger than a bale of hay in the chest and gut. He wore a cut-off blue jean jacket. No shirt beneath it. Fur on his chest and upper arms. Forearms filled with ink. A wooden ship's wheel tattooed on one arm. The other arm inked with a human skull wearing an Indian eagle-feathered headdress, the skull's mouth was wide open in a sinister grin. The man went by the name of Bear. He said, "They're over a half-hour late."

Captain Kalivaris dropped the remains of his cigarette into an open Dr. Pepper can. "Tell me something I don't know."

Bear grinned. His black beard parted, round face crinkling at the corners of his bloodshot eyes. He smelled of reefer and beer. "What's got you pissed off? It's not like this is the first time we've done this."

"Right now, it's 'cause they're almost forty minutes late. I hate like hell sittin' a hundred-fifty miles out in the Atlantic waitin' for somebody to show up outta bum freakin' nowhere."

"How many are they off-loading tonight?"

"Two more."

"Arab types?"

"I got no idea."

"I wonder what happened to the last two we took ashore?"

"I don't know, and I don't want to know. Those son-a-bitches would cut your heart out and eat it with the blood drippin' from their long fingernails. You notice that? It's like they don't trim up their fingernails. Could be it's a culture thing."

Bear chuckled. "Maybe it's like ol' Samson in the Bible. Dude cuts his hair, and he loses his mojo. Could be the same for fingernails."

"Where's Johnny?"

"Last time I saw him he was sittin' near the nets on a plastic bait bucket playin' his harmonica."

"He'd better not be smokin' a bunch of weed. Not 'til we get this shit over with."

Bear looked out through the wheelhouse window, the glass speckled from dried ocean spray. "Capt'n, it's not like these dudes are gonna try to take your boat. They need us to smuggle their brothers into port in the dark of night. We turn 'em loose at the docks and they vanish. And we get paid well. We're sorta like a water taxi disguised as a shrimp boat. The Uber of the seas. That's better than the chicken of the seas."

Kalivaris shook another cigarette loose from the pack in his shirt pocket. He stuck the cigarette behind his right ear and opened a wooden cabinet to the left of the wheel. He lifted out a half empty bottle of Crown Royal, pouring a double shot into a glass with three melting ice cubes in the bottom of it.

Bear said, "I've run weed, coke … you name it. But I've never smuggled people. How'd these guys contact you anyway?"

Kalivaris sipped the whiskey, his face darkening for a second. He wiped his lips with the back of his scarred left hand. "I'd just come back from a nine-day run and didn't get enough shrimp to pay for the fuel. I was feelin' pretty bad, thinkin' I ought to go back to brick layin', bad knees and all. I headed for a little bar in Tarpon Springs called the Sand Flea. Sat by myself at the bar. My wife had filed for divorce two months before that. I was feelin' pretty shitty. Some guy sat down beside me. We got to talkin', and I told him about my time in the Marine Corp, how I thought the country had gone to hell since I came back. We talked about the screwed-up immigration policy the country has, illegals coming in and out like a damn merry-go-round. He said what the hell's a few more if these people would pay their fair share to be here. I looked at him sorta shitfaced, and he said there's big money in pickin' up select people at sea or on one of the out islands and taking them into some hole-in-the wall port anywhere in Texas, Louisiana, Mississippi and Florida. Well, the money kept my wife from taking off—she sure as hell likes spending the stuff."

"How'd this guy find you?"

"I got no damn idea. I've only seen him once. He appears to be American, got no accent. But he works for somebody he said I'd never see. And that's how it happened. Now I make more than I did shrimpin', and I don't have to deal with a perishable product like shrimp and ice. Just load and off load a few dudes and get paid for the trip. The way I look at it, since the country has such a screwed-up immigration policy, it don't make a hell of a lot of difference. I got a feelin' the guys we're takin' in aren't here to pick fruit and vegetables."

"We're takin' them in … what happens when they want to come out?"

"What do you mean, what happens? Not my damn problem."

"What if you get a call to take some of them out of the country, would you do it?

"Don't see why not."

"If it ever comes to it, I will most likely pass on that job." Bear grinned.

"Why?"

"Because they need us to get into port, to drop them off in the dead of night. If we're asked to ever take them back … back out here or to one of the islands in the Bahamas, it could be a different story."

"How's that?"

"Their job, whatever it is, it's probably done at that point. They don't need us anymore. And if we find out they did some really bad shit while they were in the states, we'd be the last people to see their faces, meaning we could eat a bullet."

Kalivaris sipped his whiskey, burping once. "I'll keep that in mind if I'm ever asked to do a return trip."

"Look … port side. Lights. We got a boat coming toward us. If it ain't the dudes we're expectin', that fast-runnin' boat could slam right into the side of *Aphrodite.*"

"I'll hit the lights when they're a little closer."

Bear stared at the approaching green, red and white lights. "At the rate their coming, I'd bet they'd be here in less than ten minutes."

Kalivaris reached back inside the same cabinet and picked up a Sig Sauer 9mm. "Go get Johnny ready. Hide your pieces somewhere on you. We got company comin', and you just never know how it'll all go down."

Bear said, "We're on it." He turned and left the wheelhouse.

Captain Kalivaris watched the boat coming in the distance, moving at a high rate of speed. He knocked back the rest of the whiskey and turned on *Aphrodite's* bow lights.

# NINE

D ave freshened his drink at the bar, turned back toward O'Brien and Nick and said, "If I'm correct, assuming it's some form of revenge, this kind of evil can lie dormant, and when it resurfaces, can be handed down with a vengeance just as intense as when it originated or worse." He sipped his scotch and stepped back to the table, the boat bumpers groaning as the high tide squeezed them between *Gibraltar* and the dock. "Maybe retribution is like a brand on the human psyche, scarred for life. What do you think?"

O'Brien considered Dave's question for a moment. "People can change, the DNA in them can't. I guess the answer to that question is somewhere between human chemistry, genetics, and the bruises of life experiences."

Dave swirled the scotch in his glass. "So, what you're saying is that it's a roll of the dice."

O'Brien fed Max a piece of fish. "When I worked homicide at Miami-Dade, an older detective used to say evil was like pornography, tough to define but you knew it when you saw it. Evil, to some extent, is the same. The trick is recognizing it before it's dangerous to you or someone you love. Sometimes there is a slow reveal. Storytelling unveils intention without defining the process of it. Evil reveals intent, to some degree, without defining the root cause."

Nick looked down at Max, her head tilted, listening, ears lifted as high as a dachshund ears can go. He said, "Sean, you're confusing Miss Max. When she sees a bad guy, she goes for the ankle. It's instinct for her."

O'Brien smiled and said, "She has a nose that can sniff out fear, maybe good and bad, too. Speaking of bad," he cut his eyes over to Dave. "You want to tell us what's really going on with the death of your friend and former colleague? What's the story?"

Dave exhaled, pursed his wet lips and said, "In my elder years, is it that obvious, my concern? Can you tell I'm, shall I say, that preoccupied at the moment?"

"Something's on your mind, and I can tell it's heavy."

Dave laced his fingers together and leaned back in his chair, Billie Holiday singing *God Bless the Child*, coming from the speakers. "I knew Don very well. Knew how much he believed in the people and soul of this country. He was an intellectual and a warrior at the same time when it came to defending attacks against America, Americans, and our friends. Don and I made enemies trying to preserve and protect the nation. I've always expected someone, or a relation to a person we had to compromise or extract information, might come out of the sewer and try to settle a score."

Nick pushed a lime wedge into his bottle of Corona and said, "You think some killer, some guy from your past, came out of the toilet and shot your friend?"

"I don't know. But that's what it appears to be. A killer, a long-range assassin, used one shot from a hilltop to kill Don. It wasn't for money. It wasn't because Don was threatening to blackmail someone. It was for something that happened in the past … during the time he was a CIA field agent."

O'Brien nodded. "Any idea what that might have been?"

"Could have been any number of things. He found ways to expose double agents, infiltrate coups, and help topple dictators. In three decades, as a covert officer, you see it all. You make a few friends and a lot of enemies. And, too often, the lines are blurred."

O'Brien said, "Maybe this hit doesn't go back three decades. Maybe it's connected to some of the last work Don did. I have a feeling, whatever it was, he did it with you."

A slight smile moved across Dave's lips. "If that's the case, it might have something to do with one of our last assignments."

"I'm not sure I wanna know," Nick said, picking up Max and setting her on his lap. "If you tell us, would you have to kill us?" He grinned, his moustache rising.

Dave chuckled. "Maybe. Depends on the circumstances. Some of the last work I did with Don was between Washington D.C., Iraq, and Guantanamo Bay in Cuba. We dealt with people who had such a deep hate for America, our Constitution, and our republic, that it was their sole purpose in life to try to change that … to bring America to its knees any way they could. The administration and the news media called them enemy combatants. We referred to them by names that matched their diabolical personalities and agendas. Many were similar to Nazi war criminals, proud of cutting off heads like it was a blood sport."

Nick took a long pull from the Corona on the table, his face hotter, a perspiration shine on his forehead. "I say a prayer before I cut the head off a fish. I do it 'cause, when I'm spearfishing, I look him in the eye when I catch him. It's respect."

"The men we interrogated had absolutely no respect for us or any part of the West."

"How'd your team interrogate them?" O'Brien asked.

"It would depend on who we were dealing with at the time, and the circumstances, specifically whether the information we were seeking could immediately save lives. We ran deep psychological profiles on each prisoner. The first effort was to simply speak to them calmly with no hostility. We made sure to treat them with dignity, to make them feel as comfortable as possible in a cell, to try to gain a mutual respect. We knew we'd never befriend them in the true meaning of the word, but we tried for weeks to gain leverage by understanding their goals and histories."

"Did it work?" asked Nick.

"Sometimes, usually with the younger, less hardened men. Not at all with the others. And then we turned to other means of interrogation … sleep and food deprivation, waterboarding, too. But we drew the line at smashing faces and breaking bones. That doesn't work well because they'll simply lie to you."

O'Brien nodded. "In addition to the man killed today, Don, who else worked with you on that detail?"

"Four other guys, which includes me—five of us altogether. All of us senior officers, and all now retired."

"I assume the rest are well and alive."

"Yes. As well as can be, considering our line of work."

"Then maybe this killing isn't connected to something you five did collectively. Maybe it's linked to something Don did on his own ... either professionally or in his private life." O'Brien paused, a shrimp boat entering the marina, the boat's rigging lit like a Christmas tree, a crewman smoking a cigarette on the stern. "Or it could be that Don Blackwell is the first."

Dave was silent for a moment, watching the shrimp boat pass and head for the largest section of the marina. "I thought about that as I was on the phone with Robert Lewis, and I continued to think about it after we disconnected. If it's related to our time at Gitmo, it could be linked to any of them, but one man in particular said something to the five of us that I still think about from time to time."

Nick crossed his beefy arms. "Who was it, and what'd he say?"

"His name was Abdul Aswad. He said, if it took the rest of his life, he'd hunt each of us down and butcher us like he slaughtered and silenced the lambs."

O'Brien asked, "Is Aswad still locked up at Gitmo?"

"No. He was one of seven prisoners swapped or traded for the release of one American soldier held by Al-Qaeda. After the exchange, Aswad was in Qatar, at least for a few weeks. We can confirm that, out of the seven released from Gitmo, five are back in the terrorism business. And one of them, the most extreme in my estimation, was Abdul Aswad."

O'Brien considered what Dave shared and said, "Maybe the killing is isolated and has no bearing on the rest of you. Like you said, you made a few friends and a lot of enemies. It wouldn't hurt to keep your guard up some, Dave. If the killer has some personal vendetta against your team of five field operatives, one of you could be the next target."

• • •

O'Brien was somewhere between a light sleep and consciousness when he heard it. Or maybe he thought he heard it. He stretched out on his bed in *Jupiter's* master berth, a Plexiglas hatch in the ceiling propped open a few inches, keeping the dew out but allowing a cool breeze to circulate through the cabin. *Jupiter* swayed a bit as the current changed during the ebb tide, the boat bumpers making a sporadic creak.

But that wasn't what he heard.

It was something else. Far off, in the distance, maybe heading to Ponce Inlet and the sea. It was not unlike the roar of lions after a kill, the deep-throated growls, as the carcass of a gazelle is ripped apart.

He opened his eyes, staring at the half moon through the hatch, Max at the foot of the bed. She rose like a prairie dog, part of the blanket draped over her head, eyes and nose showing in the moonlight. And then she uttered a growl from somewhere in the back of her throat.

O'Brien knew types of growls associated with her level of alarm. This one was low, an early warning, as if something just appeared somewhere on her dog sense radar. O'Brien said nothing, listening. He heard the outlying sound of powerful engines in the distance, near the inlet. It was the unmistakable sound of a cigarette boat's guttural motors opened wide. He looked at his digital clock on the nightstand. 3:17 a.m.

O'Brien quietly sat up in bed. He whispered, "Max … maybe it's time for a late-night neighborhood watch. Let's take a walk."

# TEN

O'Brien slipped on his jeans, boat shoes, and a dark shirt. He lifted his Glock from the nightstand and wedged it under his belt in the small of his back. He turned his sleeves up to the elbow, unlocked the sliding glass doors leading from the salon to the cockpit, and stepped out into the night. Max followed him.

The night air was cool, typical for Florida in coastal areas fanned by ocean trade winds. He picked Max up and stood in the shadows of the cockpit, listening. He could just hear the soft babble of water moving around the dock pilings as the tide receded, the cry of a feral cat on the next dock. Max lifted her ears. O'Brien whispered, "No barking. Just a cat."

O'Brien carried Max from *Jupiter* to L dock and set her down. The dock was covered in dew. "Stay with me. Don't run ahead." She looked up at him and waited for O'Brien to take the first step. He could smell brine and algae under the thick wooden planks. A mist drifted from the surface of the warm water, slow dancing like ghosts turning pirouettes across the marina.

They walked quietly toward Dave's trawler, *Gibraltar*, on the right, and Nick's boat, *St. Michael*, on the left. There was a soft light coming from *Gibraltar's* salon, the light from his TV, flickering, bluish. After everyone had left, Dave probably had fallen asleep watching a documentary.

O'Brien could hear Greek music, the soft pluck of a guitar, coming from somewhere inside *St. Michael*. Nick, no doubt, in an alcohol enhanced deep sleep. Max trotted to the side of the dock closest to *Gibraltar*. She sniffed, picking up a scent, turning her head back to O'Brien. He stepped over and knelt down next to her, looking at the area where she'd sniffed. He could make out tracks in the dew.

Large tracks. Left by a big man.

Under the soft light from one of three low wattage lights on curved lampposts, along the dock, O'Brien could tell the shoe size was at least a twelve, closer to a thirteen. He studied the pattern from the configuration left in the tracks. It looked like boot tread. Not the usual footwear on a Florida dock in the summer. He glanced up and looked as far as he could down the dock.

The tracks led away from *Gibraltar,* as if the man had strolled the length of the dock, sightseeing in the middle of the night. He'd stood near the bow of Dave's boat, turned and left, the tracks leading back toward the marina office, Tiki Bar, and the parking lot at least eighty yards away. O'Brien pulled out his phone, filled the frame with the boot print, and took a picture. He stood and whispered to Max, "Let's see if we can follow these tracks."

He led her quietly into the night, into the mist, past dark boats tied to dock cleats, past barbeque grills still hot from dying coals, beyond the deep-water slips, getting into an area where smaller boats were moored. He followed the tracks back to the entrance to L dock, to the locked gate.

O'Brien stopped and looked at the deadbolt that kept the aluminum swing gate locked at night. Someone could still enter if they wanted to chance climbing up the very narrow, serrated slats in the gate, not designed as steps. And there was no way boots the size of the ones that left the tracks on the dock could have squeezed into the narrow spaces between the metal crossbeams on the gate.

O'Brien used his key to unlock the entrance, slowly opening it just enough for he and Max to exit, the gate making a squeaking noise as it opened. The dock led to a cement sidewalk that looped around much of the marina. It was here that the tracks stopped, the dew not heavy enough on the concrete to make a visible imprint from the boots.

"Hold on, Max," O'Brien said, looking at a security camera on the exterior of the Tiki Bar, the camera's lens aimed at the perimeter of the building and the adjacent docks. The Tiki Bar had long since closed for the night. For the most part, it was dark inside the restaurant. O'Brien walked around the building, glancing at the marina water swirling around wooden beams the width of utility poles. He and Max moved through an alleyway between the marina office and the Tiki Bar. O'Brien touched the grip of his Glock, the holster would allow an easy exit of the pistol, if needed.

As he walked down fifty feet in the dark alley, Max following, he could smell sour beer and urine near one wall. He came to the parking lot. There were more than two-dozen cars and trucks parked in the lot. No sign of people. All the vehicles were the property of boat owners, or their guests. O'Brien looked up at one of the streetlights, the buzz of electricity in the humid air, a bat flying in and out of the darkness, snatching moths circling the light.

He looked down at Max. "Can you pick up the scent ... the same one you found on the dock in front of Dave's boat? Max tilted her head, snorted, and walked over to the loose sand at the base of a tall queen palm tree. She sniffed a track left in the sand. O'Brien squatted down and studied it for a moment. He could easily tell that it came from the same boots that left the tread prints on the dock.

He examined the right boot, and then the one in front, the left boot track. This one had a deeper impression near the toe area. He could see why. The man had dropped a cigarette and stepped on it, but it didn't extinguish the smoldering tip. A tiny waft of smoke came from the ash at the tip.

O'Brien pulled a clean, white handkerchief from his pocket, carefully lifted up the half-smoked cigarette, the butt still wet from saliva. He examined the unfiltered cigarette, a foreign brand, knocked the ash off the tip, and gently placed the butt in the center of the handkerchief, folding the material. He stood and listened. He could hear the soft roll of breakers on the beach, just over the sand dunes, the trade winds delivering scents from faraway lands. Places such as the Mediterranean Sea and Morocco—the country where the cigarette brand was manufactured.

He turned and walked back to L dock and *Jupiter.* "Come on, Max." She wagged her tail, walking parallel to O'Brien. He knew where the cigarette in his pocket came from … and there was a chance the man with the big boots came from the same country.

*What's he doing on L dock around the 3:00 a.m. hour?* O'Brien thought. *Why stop near Nick and Dave's boats? Could the trespasser somehow be connected to the killing of Dave's friend on the golf course?* O'Brien thought about that as he walked slowly down the dock. *Maybe it was nothing. Just a coincidence.*

*Maybe not.*

# Eleven

The 40-foot cigarette boat circled *Aphrodite* like a great white shark circles a seal swimming far beyond the breakers. Captain Santos Kalivaris climbed down from the wheelhouse. He was now wearing a long sleeve shirt, untucked, the Sig Sauer hidden under the shirttail. He walked up to his deckhands, Bear and a younger man, Johnny Hastings, dirty blond hair cascading from under a Ray's baseball cap, dried bird droppings on the bill. He had sleepy eyes, a blond goatee on his face. Softball-sized biceps stretched his black T-shirt, a .25 caliber Browning in his jeans pocket.

The cigarette boat made a third turn, getting closer each time, the odor of gasoline fumes in the night air. There were four men on board. Two of them, the men near the wheel and console, wore sidearms. They pulled the boat close to *Aphrodite*, the shrimp boat's lights casting a glow across the cigarette boat and its occupants. All four men had short, dark beards. Olive skin. All appeared to be in their mid-to-late-thirties. The pilot of the craft stood and shouted, "Lower your dinghy! I'll pull up next to it, and the men can get to your ladder."

"All right," shouted Kalivaris. He gave the signal, and Bear hit a switch to lower a nine-foot, hard rubber dinghy into the water. Johnny adjusted the ladder, moving it closer to the dinghy. Bear tossed the men in the boat a stern line for the dinghy, one of them in back catching it and tying it to a cleat on the cigarette boat.

The first man, wearing a backpack, carrying a long and narrow suitcase, stepped onto the dinghy, dropping to his knees in the choppy water. He crawled to the bow of the small boat, stood and reached for the ladder. In less than a minute, he'd boarded *Aphrodite*. The second man followed the same path, crawling with a backpack strapped to him, carrying a similar long and narrow suitcase, holding onto the sides of the jostling dinghy. He grabbed for the ladder, his right hand slipping on the wet wood, a small wave lipped across the side of the dinghy, soaking the man's pants.

Bear leaned over the side of the transom, offering a hand. The man grabbed it, and Bear lifted him to the rungs on the ladder. The man climbed up and over, landing on his feet, almost slipping on *Aphrodite's* deck.

Captain Kalivaris shouted above the rumble of the boat's powerful engines. "Are one of these fellas carrying payment in a backpack?"

The man sitting next to the pilot at the console shouted back and said, "Nazeeh has your money."

Kalivaris turned to the two men and asked, "Which one of y'all is Nazeeh. And I hope it ain't the guy who took on a wave in the dinghy."

"I am Nazeeh," said the man standing to the captain's right. He was the first man who climbed aboard the shrimp boat. His black eyes were deadpanned. His mouth was small, an air of contempt in his accent. "Do you wish to see it now."

"Absolutely," said Kalivaris. "It's the only way I do business. No offense, it's just business. And I want to do more than see it. I want to count it."

The man removed his backpack and unzipped it. Kalivaris clicked on his marine flashlight, peering into the open bag. He lifted it and sat it on top of a large ice chest. He placed the flashlight under one arm, reaching into the backpack and leafing through the money, all neatly bound in rubber bands, and all in one hundred bills. After half a minute, he zipped up the bag, turned to the men and said, "Ever'thing looks good. We appreciate your business."

"One more thing," said the man behind the wheel of the cigarette boat. "There is not enough time for you to go around Florida back into Tarpon Springs."

"That's my home port. That's what I know."

"You are a captain of a large shrimp boat. You should be in a position to dock anywhere. We have made arrangements for you to dock at a place known as Gangplank Marina in the Florida Keys, Marathon Key. The GPS coordinates are in Nazeeh's backpack. You will have time to dock there, refuel and drop off the men. Someone will be there to meet them between midnight and three in the morning on Thursday."

"Wait a damn minute! I don't know the area. It's dangerous just to pull up somewhere and drop people off like FedEx drops off packages. The border patrol can confiscate my boat and send my ass to prison, along with my crew."

"In our agreement, you never were given a choice of where in Florida we wanted the drop off to occur. We never return to the same place three times. No offense, Captain. It is just business." He grinned. "Be there Thursday, or we will come looking."

The driver of the cigarette boat revved up the big engines, while the other man untied the line to the dinghy, and they roared away, heading east toward the Bahamas. The boat cut a large rooster-tail wake, the waves curling up, moonlight pouring through the crests, creating a trail of whitecaps in the dark sea.

# TWELVE

Two days later, a giant forklift cradled the hopes and dreams of Katie and Andy Scott. It was called the "marina water buffalo." In the early morning sunlight, they stood in the boatyard and watched the operator lift *Dragonfly* from the jack stands and slowly proceed to the area where boats are lowered back into the harbor. Katie squeezed her husband's hand and said, "What do we do if they drop her?"

"Let's hope we don't have to find out. It's not unlike how they used to move the space shuttles to the launch pad."

The massive forklift, diesels roaring, black smoke belching from the exhaust pipes, crawled from the yard toward the entry point, a deep-water area where boats and yachts are hauled out and returned to the water. The operator was a hardened marine mechanic, silver hair and sunglasses, an unlit cigar stogie in the corner of his mouth, and a grease-stained, white T-shirt. Two other men stood around the entry point, using hand signals to help guide him closer.

"I want to close my eyes," Katie said. "Then you can tell me when it's safely in the water." Andy laughed, and Katie playfully punched him on the shoulder.

When the man at the furthest end of the entry dock raised his thumb, the operator slowly lowered the sailboat. Within two minutes, it was floating. The workers removed the large belt straps that had supported *Dragonfly*. The forklift driver shut off the engine and said,

"She's all yours now. Hank and Chuck will tie her off for you. What slip are you gonna keep her in, you know?"

"N dock," Katie said. "Slip N-17. But it's not for long. We're anxious to sail."

The man leaned forward in his seat, the sun on the back of his craggy neck, and one callused hand on the controls. He thoughtfully gazed at the sailboat a moment and said, "That's a mighty fine cruiser y'all have. Treat her right, and she'll take you to places you've never dreamed of going. You'll be doing and seeing things you never knew existed."

"That's the plan," Andy said. "Like Katie said, we're anxious to get in some blue water."

"I like the name you folks gave her … *Dragonfly*. Closest I've ever seen to a name like that was *Gypsy Moth*. It was a beautiful boat, a forty-eight-foot Vagabond. The owner was about my age when he got into sailing. He lost his wife to leukemia, cashed in his chips, and sailed the world by himself. Called it saltwater therapy."

Katie smiled, the breeze tossing her hair. "We can relate."

The man nodded, chewed the cigar a second, fired up the water buffalo and drove it slowly toward a remote section of the boatyard.

"Let's go, Katie. The guys tied off the boat. Now, it's waiting for us."

"Hold on." She touched her husband's arm. "Let's just look at her for a minute as *Dragonfly* is in the stable. Soon she will be released to the wind and sea, and we're lucky enough to go along for the wild ride. I can't wait."

Katie and Andy held hands and stared at their sailboat, gulls shrilling above the mast, the marina workers moving on, *Dragonfly* secured to the dock. Katie said, "I so want Dave to see *Dragonfly* in all her splendid glory on the water. But I don't think we should break a bottle of champagne across her bow. We don't want to run the risk of leaving a mark in the new paint. Let's board her and motor over to Dave's boat. I'm anxious for Sean and Nick to see her, too."

As they started toward the pier and *Dragonfly*, Katie's phone buzzed in her pocket. She looked at the caller ID and answered. "Hi, Dad. Are you okay?"

"Yes, I'm fine. I spoke with Dave Collins this morning, and he told me he shared with you that Don Blackwell was killed."

"Yes, it's beyond horrific. I'm so sorry for his family and you, Dad. Mr. Blackwell shot and killed while on a golf course. Does the CIA know who did it?"

"They have no solid leads yet. Tossing around a few theories."

Katie pulled a strand of hair behind her ears, the breeze across the marina a little stronger. "Dad, I know that you, Dave Collins, Don Blackwell and a few others worked closely together. Tell me straight, okay … are you in some kind of danger?"

Sol Lefko, Katie's father, was a lanky man, black frame glasses, salt and pepper hair neatly combed. Conservatively dressed in a pressed designer polo shirt and tan slacks, he walked down his long driveway to the mailbox at the end of his drive. "Now that I'm retired, I'm not worth anything to anyone, outside your mother—and you." He smiled. "If it were ten years ago, maybe. We did our jobs, and one of the unfortunate parts is I could never share any of that with you or your mom. To do so would have potentially jeopardized your safety."

"I understand … it just doesn't make sense for someone to kill Mr. Blackwell in his retirement years."

"How are you and Andy coming with your sailboat?"

"We just put the boat back in the water with an overhauled engine, new plumbing, generator and AC, new sails and most importantly … a new name, *Dragonfly*. I'm going to shoot some pics and video on my phone and send them to you and Mom. If you guys followed me on Instagram, you'll see lots of pics."

"It's better when you send them directly. Social media isn't my cup of tea."

Katie licked her dry lips. "I so wish Madison was here to see this."

Lefko stopped just before the mailbox, red rose bushes around the base, the scent of blooming roses in the North Carolina air. "She might not be there physically, but I believe her spirit is going to sail along with you and Andy."

"I hope so, Dad."

"It sounds like Dave Collins and his friends put out quite the culinary spread for you and Andy last night."

"I had planned to call you today to tell you all about it, but you beat me to the call. The food was so delicious. Dave's Greek friend, Nick Cronus, has an incredible touch when it comes to grilled seafood. We met Dave's other friend, Sean O'Brien, and his little dachshund, Max. What a cutie she is. Andy and I now are considering getting a dachshund to take with us—or maybe we'll find a dog along our journey."

"As long as you have lots of islands where you can stop so the pooch can run and do its business. What's your impression of Sean O'Brien?"

"You can train a dog to use a pee pad, Dad, which is not so bad if you have a small dog. O'Brien's sort of the strong, semi-silent type. But when he talks, people listen, and you can tell he's very intelligent. I wish I had a girlfriend to introduce to him. His wife died of cancer. Nick said Sean was a former detective, and quoting Nick, he said 'O'Brien finds stuff and people,' whatever that means. O'Brien's some sort of private investigator."

Lefko placed his hand on the mailbox, smiling. "We'll, the way Dave tells it is that O'Brien has a sort of sixth sense. Keenly observant, and his bullshit meter can spot deception just by the way someone moves. He's the kind of guy the agency always looked for but rarely found. When do you and Andy set sail?"

"In a few days. We'll be getting used to *Dragonfly*, take her down to Lauderdale, buy provisions and set sail from there. Bimini is our first stop. I hope you and Mom can fly to one of the islands and join us for some sailing."

"We'd like that. Let us know when you're ready to receive guests. Right now, it's important for you and Andy to have some alone time."

"Love you, Dad."

"Love you, too." He disconnected, slipped the phone in his back pocket and opened his mailbox. He glanced inside, the sun reflecting off of a brass casing. His heart jumped, pounding in his chest. He stared at a .30 caliber spent rifle cartridge. It was standing vertical, the bullet gone, but the cartridge spoke volumes. Whoever killed Don Blackwell left a deadly message.

# THIRTEEN

O'Brien awoke thinking about the mysterious boot prints. He wanted to look at the video from the surveillance camera, but he needed to talk with Dave first. He showered, dressed, fed Max and unfolded the white handkerchief he'd left on his coffee table. He dropped the half-smoked cigarette into a plastic Ziploc bag and sealed it, placing the bag in his refrigerator.

O'Brien lifted his phone off the bar. He pulled up the image of the boot print, studied it for a few seconds, and then he emailed it to himself. He picked up his laptop computer, sat on the couch in his salon and opened the email. He saved the image of the boot print. He had two software apps that did comparison analysis on tire prints and shoe or boot prints. He entered the image and hit search.

Max jumped up on the couch, sat beside him, looked up with adoring brown eyes and let out a slight whimper. O'Brien glanced at her. "I know you need to find a patch of grass. We'll take a walk in just a minute. He cut his eyes back to the screen. The word in white text read: Match. He clicked on the image, identical to the image he uploaded, and then read the description. Maelstrom Tac Force, manufactured in Sterling, Virginia.

O'Brien shut down his computer, stood and said, "Let's take a walk, Max." They started for the door when his phone rang. He looked at the screen, Wynona Osceola calling. He thought about the note she left and answered. "Hi, Wynona. I got your note. Sorry I missed you."

"No biggie. You didn't know I'd be in town. I didn't know either, for that matter. It was spontaneous. Spontaneity is a learned thing for me." She laughed, walking across a parking lot, stopping next to her parked car, her long black hair blowing in the breeze. Flawless light brown skin, prominent cheekbones, full lips and almond eyes as dark as her hair. She wore faded jeans and a white cotton blouse.

"I remember you trying to become a little more impulsive."

She smiled. "I was on my way from South Florida … I'm heading up to Jacksonville for a conference on forensic science. Passing through, I thought I'd take a chance to see if you were home. You're sort of at the halfway point."

O'Brien smiled. "*Jupiter's* more of a hobby than a home. I have an old cabin on the St. John's River that has a real roof on it. It's a tin roof, but it keeps the rain off. It's maybe a step down from the Seminole chickees."

She leaned against her car. "Tin roof. I bet it's cozy on a rainy night."

"Where are you now?"

"In a parking lot. I stopped at a store for some bottled water."

"How have you been, Wynona? I've thought about you often."

"I've been good … for the most part. I still have some dark dreams about what we went through to help Joe Billie. But they're not coming so much anymore. I spent a little alone time in the glades, got back to my Seminole roots, talked to some elders in the tribe and returned to my job as the only female detective on the rez."

"I'm glad things are getting better for you."

"Sean, on my way back from the conference, maybe I can stop by … we could have lunch."

"I'd like that."

"Good." She smiled. "In two days will you be at your cabin or the marina?"

"I'm not sure. But it doesn't matter. We'll meet. I may be here because I'm going to bid bon voyage to a couple going on a long sailing adventure in their new boat."

"Sounds like a trip for me. Is the boat named for one of the planets, like yours, *Jupiter*?"

"No, it's an older refurbished boat with a brand-new name. She's called *Dragonfly*."

"*Dragonfly* ... that's an interesting name. When I was a girl, it was right before the summer Green Corn Dance, Sam Otter—the elder medicine man you met, told me a story about the dragonfly."

"What'd he say?"

"The dragonfly has been part of Seminole culture for generations. Dragonflies may appear to be just large winged insects, but there is a spiritual component to understanding the place they share in the world, at least in our culture. There is something about them that no other creature on earth shares."

"What's that?"

"When I see you, I'll tell you ... even better, maybe I can show you."

# FOURTEEN

O'Brien thought about what Wynona had said as he walked Max on the far side of the marina. The Tiki Bar wasn't opened yet. No way to view the video from last night. He returned back to L dock. Max ran ahead, sniffing and glancing up at the squawking gulls. They walked past Nick's boat, *St. Michael*. No sign of life. Music off. No scent of Greek coffee.

O'Brien and Max moved down the smaller auxiliary dock that ran parallel to the width of the Dave's trawler. O'Brien could smell the fresh-brewed coffee. Dave sat at the round table on the cockpit under the shade from *Gibraltar's* awning, sipping coffee. He looked up and said, "Join me. I cooked extra sausage links in the event that you and Max would venture over here. However, it seems odd to offer sausage links to a wiener dog." He grinned and sipped his coffee.

O'Brien picked Max up and set her down in the cockpit. He stepped over to the table, pulled out a chair and sat. "Max has eaten, but I'm sure she wouldn't turn her nose up at a piece of your sausage."

"How about you, Sean? I can crack a couple more eggs. Hungry?" He used a knife to cut off a small piece of sausage on a paper plate, handing it to Max. She gently took it from his hand. Gone in one bite. He poured a cup of coffee from a pot and slid the cup toward O'Brien.

"I'm not hungry. I ate at the crack of dawn."

"Why up so early?"

"It was a restless night."

"Can you blame it on the oysters. When I was young, they made me restless, too." He grinned.

"No, I blame it on the guy who stood near the bow of your boat somewhere around 3:00 a.m. or so."

Dave started to sip his coffee, but stopped, his white eyebrows rising. "Perhaps you will elaborate?"

"Max heard something. I heard her utter a low growl. It's the kind of growl that's part of her intuitive radar, almost on a subconscious level. But it was enough to wake me. I was curious, so I took a walk a little after a quarter past three."

"What'd you see?"

"Tracks on the dock."

"Did someone walk in paint?"

"No, he walked in heavy dew."

"He? One person?"

"Only one guy was on the dock in front of *Gibraltar* at that time in the morning. And here's what he left." O'Brien pulled out his phone and brought up the image of the boot print on the screen. He slid it over to Dave and then sipped his coffee. "Looks to be a big fella. Probably a size thirteen."

Dave moved his bifocals to the tip of his nose and studied the image. "From the picture, it's hard to determine the size."

"I supposed I could have placed a quarter next to the print for scale comparison. Trust me, this guy's Sasquatch."

Dave examined it closer. "Interesting tread pattern. Doesn't look like a boat shoe to me?"

"It's not. It is a boot—a combat boot. I ran a computer scan on it. American made out of Sterling, Virginia. It's a Maelstrom Tac Four. Not your typical Docksiders. So, the question is this … who the hell is scoping out your boat in the early morning hours and why? And, is it related to the shooting death of your former colleague, Don Blackwell, on that golf course?"

Dave looked from O'Brien to the morning sunlight reflecting like gold coins across the marina water. Then his pale blue eyes shifted back to O'Brien. "Maybe. I thought about that last night after everyone left. I thought about it so much I almost started out my day mixing a Bloody Mary."

"What is it, Dave? Who is it?"

"I wish I knew. The trouble is, when you're a field officer with the CIA for close to thirty years, you don't win friends and influence adversaries by following a Dale Carnegie manual."

"No, but when you start to examine the adversaries—the people that you and Don Blackwell focused on together, you can narrow your list of suspects."

Dave nodded. "But that's still a rather broad list, considering the scope of what we did, to whom and where."

"You said one of the last assignments was at Gitmo. Maybe someone there or a prisoner who was once held there is now pulling the trigger or paying someone to do it for him."

"Those boot prints you found on the dock, since my boat and yours are at the very end of L dock, maybe it was simply someone taking a walk. The guy reached the end of the dock and then turned around and headed back."

"My boat is a little closer to the end. He didn't stop there. He didn't stop in front of Nick's boat. He stopped in front of *Gibraltar*. I don't know if he took a piss off the dock, watched the fog, or watched your boat. I do know that's where he stopped. I followed his tracks two ways—from where he began, at the entrance to the dock, to where he stopped in front of *Gibraltar*, and how he turned around and walked on the opposite side of the dock all the way back to the entrance. Dave, he was scouting the area and your boat."

"All right. I guess, in retirement, I have to get back into defense mode. Keep a sharp eye out for anyone and everyone. Maybe carry a sidearm. But look at what happened to Don. He could have had a Secret Service detail around him. Wouldn't have made a bit of difference." Dave stared out and across the marina. "There are two fairly high boat storage buildings and the fifteen-story condo at the edge of the marina." He shook his head. "I do have a nice pair of binoculars. I can have a look before I go for my morning walks. Maybe I'll spot a shooter before he spots me."

O'Brien said nothing, the sound of gulls shrieking, a charter boat horn blowing twice as it left the dock, the salty smell of the ocean in the eastward wind. He watched the tall mast sailboat round the main area of the marina, coming from the boatyard toward L dock. He looked over at Dave and said, "We have visitors, and they're arriving by boat. Looks like Katie and Andy got *Dragonfly* in the water, and they're heading our way."

Dave smiled, sat straighter in his deck chair. His phone vibrated on the table. He looked at the caller ID and said, "I need to take this, Sean. It's Katie's father, Sol. Maybe he has some more information on the killing of Don Blackwell."

# FIFTEEN

O'Brien watched *Dragonfly* approach, standing out in the crowded marina. It was still about a hundred yards away, the morning sun bouncing off her deep blue hull, Andy at the helm, Katie standing next to him, holding what appeared to be a large paper cup of coffee.

Dave sat back in his deck chair and said, "Good morning, again, Sol."

"Hey Dave, Katie tells me she and Andy had a great time with you and your friends. She said if she wasn't going on an extended sailing trip, she'd seriously consider opening a seafood restaurant if your pal, Nick, would agree to be the chef."

Dave looked over his bifocals to see Nick approaching, looking more disheveled than usual, no doubt more hung-over than usual. Dave said, "We had a great time. I'll pass the compliment on to Nick. Looks like he could use it this morning. Anything more on Don since we spoke earlier? The agency have any leads?"

"I've been on the phone with Deputy Director, Ben Graham. They have nothing thus far. None of the usual suspects have claimed responsibility for the shooting. No physical evidence beyond the round that went through Don's head."

"You mean they managed to find it on the golf course?"

"Considering the trajectory and the fact it happened on the tee, a large area with very close-cropped grass, yes. The techs removed the round less than ten feet from where Don fell."

"What was it?"

"A .30 caliber. Winchester 300 to be exact. And we think it may have come from the spent cartridge that I found in my mailbox."

Dave stood slowly, watching *Dragonfly* now about fifty yards away and motoring toward L dock. "What'd you say?"

"I found the casing when I went to my mailbox at the end of my drive. It was standing up, vertical. Someone wanted the maximum effect when I, or my wife, checked our mail."

"When are they going to run tests on the casing?"

"The agency was quick … they just picked it up. The techs are doing the ballistic tests today."

"Was there a note with it?"

"No, but the casing sure as hell spoke volumes. Whoever killed Don knows where I live. The message I'm receiving is I'm a target. Dave, who do you think may be behind this?"

"I'm not sure. I do know that I had a visit at my boat somewhere around 3:00 a.m. Whoever that was, couldn't have been the same person that placed the cartridge in your mailbox unless he could sprout wings and fly from there to Florida."

"What do you mean by visitor? Were you threatened?"

"No, at least not overtly like what you found in your mailbox. My close friend owns a boat across the dock from mine. He and his dog heard something around that time of the morning. He left his boat to investigate and found boot prints, combat boot prints, in heavy overnight dew, and the prints stopped at the edge of the dock next to where my trawler is tied. So, sleeping in my cabin, I was less than fifteen feet from whomever was scouting the area and my boat."

"The question is why and who? You, Don, Simon and I all worked on one assignment collectively. And that was processing the detainees at Gitmo. If it was one of those guys … which one, where is he now, and how can we stop him before he puts a bullet in our heads?"

"Let's get Simon on a conference call and brainstorm. Maybe it'll lead to a cause and effect—a source, and maybe we can stop it."

O'Brien signaled Dave, motioning to the approaching sailboat. *Dragonfly* was less than one hundred feet away, the diesels creating a V formation on the water behind the transom. Nick stepped over the side of *Gibraltar,* tank shirt, faded swim trunks, bare feet. He poured himself a cup of coffee. "Mornin'" he mumbled.

O'Brien smiled. Dave nodded and said, "Sol … Katie and Andy are literally a couple of minutes away from pulling up beside my boat. You ought to see their sailboat here in the morning light. It's a work of moving art on water. They've both done a great job, sanding and staining. They're bringing *Dragonfly* around to the dock where I have a boat slip. We're going to have coffee with them."

"I wish I could be there. This impending trip is so important to Katie after she and Andy lost little Madison. And then Katie became a cancer survivor. They desperately need some down time and away time."

"That's understandable. They told me the symbolism behind the name, *Dragonfly.*"

"Dave, I need you to do a big favor for me."

"Sure. What's that?"

"Don't mention a word to Katie about the rifle cartridge I found in my mailbox."

"Okay … but don't you think she might want to know?"

"I don't have to tell you that wanting to know and needing to know don't always run parallel courses. The last thing she needs to be worried about is her pop's safety. I managed to dodge bullets for twenty-seven years with the agency. I can manage it now."

"All right, Sol. But how many times in twenty-seven years did you find a rifle casing at the end of your driveway, inside your mailbox? Someone is playing a very deadly game. Let's talk later." They disconnected, and Dave told O'Brien what Sol Lefko said about the rifle casing. "He doesn't want Katie to know."

O'Brien nodded and looked at the framed picture of Dave's daughter on the coffee table just inside the salon. He thought about how she resembled Wynona Osceola and said, "Your daughter, Linda, looks like a friend of mine."

"Who's that?"

"Her name's Wynona Osceola."

"That rings a bell."

"I mentioned her to you when I told you what happened in Joe Billie's trial. Wynona is a detective with the Seminole Tribe. She's coming through the area and meeting me for lunch soon. I'd like to introduce her to you."

"I'd like that, too. I don't see Linda much since she and Todd live in London."

"Out of the four guys that did the prisoner debriefing at Gitmo, do all of them have children?"

Dave paused for a moment, his brow wrinkling. "Let me see. Don Blackwell and his wife, Marti, didn't have children. Katie is Sol and Barbara's only child. My daughter, Linda, of course. Robert Lewis once told me he had wanted kids but, after living in a nasty, covert world and also being home in small spurts of time, it altered his thinking about bringing a child into the world—so I don't think he and Caroline ever had any. Simon Rivers' son Carter is the only other one."

"You'd mentioned that Carter died in a car accident near Santa Barbara."

"Yes, so Carter was the only other one. Why do you ask?"

"Because you mentioned that one of the prisoners you interrogated said he'd remove your team and their seeds from earth." He looked at the photo of Dave's daughter and then cut his eyes over to the approaching sailboat, Katie waving, the wind in her hair. "I'm wondering two things. Was the freak accident that killed Carter really an accident … and how safe are your daughter, Linda, and Sol Lefko's daughter, Katie?"

# SIXTEEN

Nick held the coffee mug in one hand, looked through the rising steam and said, "Andy handles the boat well under motor. Let's hope he's as good with the wind in her sails."

Dave asked, "Want some breakfast? Looks like you could use real nourishment."

"Just coffee right now. After I left you guys, I dropped by the Tiki Bar to have one drink with Shelia, the newest server. She was off duty. You know, Flo's rules. We ordered ouzo. One shot led to another. Next thing I know was that Shelia's boyfriend came looking for her around closin' time. I offered to buy him a drink. Told him about the history of ouzo, how Greek monks first made the stuff." Nick grinned, his eyes slightly bloodshot. "Let's just say the fella had no sense of humor. They left, and I took a slow walk back to my boat where I slept like Rip Van Winkle."

O'Brien smiled and said, "Before you left the Tiki Bar to find your way back to *St. Michael*, did you happen to notice a tall man at the bar, maybe a guy wearing large combat boats?"

Nick looked as his bare feet, cut his eyes up to O'Brien. "Combat boots? I'm over dressed in flip-flops. How big?"

"Maybe size thirteen."

"Not his shoe size. How tall? Taller than you?"

"Probably."

Nick thought for a second. "Naw, same ol' late night bunch. Nobody stood out, but then I wasn't watchin' for tall dudes in combat boots. Why do you ask?"

Dave stood and said, "Because someone in big boots walked down the dock and stopped in front of my boat late last night. Sean snapped a picture of the prints in the dew."

O'Brien slid his phone across the table, the boot print image on the screen. Nick's dark eyebrows rose. He started to say something just as Andy and Katie came closer in *Dragonfly*. Andy used the bow thrusters to keep the big sailboat away from the pilings and other boats. "Ahoy!" Katie shouted. "We can smell the coffee from here."

Dave, O'Brien and Nick walked to the back of *Gibraltar's* transom, Nick stepping onto the swim platform. "Toss me a line!" he said. "We'll tie you off. No real currents where you are right now. Tide's slack anyhow. Hang a couple of bumpers off her starboard side, and we'll snuggle like teens on a first date." He grinned, his dark moustache lifting.

Max barked twice, tail wagging from the center of the cockpit. They tied and secured *Dragonfly*. Dave brought two large ceramic cups of coffee and handed them to Andy and Katie. They stayed aboard *Dragonfly* and took the drinks. Katie said, "How come coffee tastes so much better on the water?"

Dave said, "Because you don't have to go through a drive-up window to get it."

Andy grinned and said, "I do like pulling up to your trawler and ordering take out."

As they stood and chatted in the morning sunlight, O'Brien glanced at the adjacent buildings around the marina, the three-story boat storage buildings, the high-rise condo less than three hundred yards at the edge of the harbor. He saw no movement on the rooftops. He looked over at Dave and noticed he was doing the same thing while chatting with Andy and Katie. She turned to O'Brien and asked, "Now that you see *Dragonfly* in her element, what do you think?"

O'Brien smiled, he looked at her and then at the sailboat's helm and new paint job. "She's a beautiful cruiser. All the work that you and Andy put into her really shows up nicely in the harbor. But where she'll really get her sea legs is when you guys motor through Ponce Inlet and raise the sails as you enter the Atlantic. That's when and where a sailboat like this is in her element, a nice wind, skies blue as the ocean."

A smile moved across Katie's lips. "We can't wait." She finished her coffee, as did Andy, handing the cups back to Dave. Katie said, "We're going to be in slip N-17, almost your neighbors, for the next few days."

Andy said, "None of you has seen what we did with her interior. Can you guys come over for lunch, say one o'clock? We'd love to show you around *Dragonfly*."

Dave nodded. "Sounds fine to me."

Nick looked at his watch. "That'll give me plenty of time to get cleaned up and make a run for ice, too."

O'Brien said, "I look forward to it. Can Max come?"

Katie grinned. "Absolutely. We wouldn't mind if little Max decided to become a stowaway on *Dragonfly's* maiden voyage."

"Max is a good sailor. She likes to ride on the bowsprit." They laughed, untied the ropes and started the diesel to slowly motor around L and M docks over to N and their slip. They waved, grins on their faces.

O'Brien watched them leave, Andy standing tall at the wheel, his wife's hand on his back, the breeze blowing her ponytail, three brown pelicans soaring just above the top of their mast. He could see the reflection of the transom off the harbor surface. The name *Dragonfly* was fragmented in the ripples from the V caused by the wake, as if an arrowhead dissected the perfect lettering.

Dave watched O'Brien for a second and said, "They seem very happy, and you have a somewhat troubled look in your eye. What's on your mind?"

O'Brien turned from the swim platform, stepping back into the cockpit, coiling a rope in his large hands. "I can't put my finger on it. Just an uneasy feeling. Assuming they don't hit bad weather and the hurricane season is kind, they should have the trip of a lifetime through the islands."

"I'm glad. It's been a long time coming for them."

"I know they want to be alone but try to stay in touch with them without being intrusive. Since a .30 caliber rifle casing was left in her dad's mailbox, and because the grown son of one of the guys you worked with died recently in a freak car accident, I think checking in with Katie and Andy needs to happen. And, Dave, you might want to call your daughter, Linda, to let her know what's going on."

"I hate to admit it, but you have a strong point. Maybe it's nothing."

"Maybe we can stop it from becoming something … something tragic and preventable. Max, let's take a walk."

"Where are you heading?" Dave asked.

"To see if a surveillance camera caught the image of a man wearing combat boots and coming to and from our dock a little after 3:00 a.m."

# SEVENTEEN

O'Brien knew that the video from the Tiki Bar's surveillance cameras was archived on a continuous loop hard-drive in the back office. He walked in the backdoor, Max following him. Seven paddle fans whirled from the roughhewn Florida pine crossbeams in the ceiling. Two servers, both women, were taking chairs off the tabletops and positioning them around the tables before the first lunch customers arrived. One server raised the plastic isinglass, the morning breeze moving over the wooden floor, some areas still damp from last night's spilled beer.

The owner, Flo, sipped coffee behind the bar. She wore a black Tiki Bar T-shirt and jeans, setting the cup down to count one-dollar bills into her cash register till. Music played from the speakers around the restaurant and behind the bar, Flo piping in to sing along with the Keith Urban song *Coming Home.* O'Brien got Flo's attention and said, "Good morning, Florence."

"Hi, Sean. You know ... you're the only one who can call me Florence and get away with it. After my divorce, I simplified everything." Her phone buzzed. She looked at the screen and said, "It's my youngest daughter. Lives in Dallas. I need to take it." Flo smiled, closed the cash register, and disappeared through a door behind the far end of the bar. O'Brien watched Max work the room, trotting over to greet the servers, both girls bending down to pet her, the unmistakable rumble from Harleys pulling into the parking lot, a trace of dust blowing through the open windows.

Two bikers, both in cut-off jean jackets, fur, bellies and ink under the fur, came through the main entrance. Max trotted over to meet them, her tail wagging. One guy, sporting a red bandana on his head, stopped and looked down at Max. He grinned and said, "We got a new hostess."

"I can eat that much for breakfast," his pal said, walking across the room to take a seat in one corner.

Flo returned, setting her phone on the bar. O'Brien said, "We had an unknown visitor late last night on L dock. Around three something in the morning. Mind if I take a look at your security video, especially from the camera on the west side of the building?"

"No problem. Did this unknown visitor steal something?"

"I don't think so. We have a pretty good neighborhood watch."

"Sure, c'mon back. You can shuttle right through the video. It's all digitally time coded. You won't have a problem finding video from three o'clock in the morning."

He followed her to the back office and led him to a wooden desk, antique, painted black, old cigarettes burns in the scratched paint. Three hard drives were stacked vertically on the shelf above the desk, four TV monitors on the wall. One camera captured the front parking lot, one captured part of the marina near N dock, and the other two cameras covered the interior of the restaurant. She showed O'Brien how to retrieve the images and said, "I've got some work to do at my desk. If you find something and want a copy or a still shot, that's no problem."

"Thanks, Flo."

She turned to leave, stopping and said, "Did you connect with your mysterious visitor, the woman lookin' for you?"

"Yes, we connected."

Flo grinned. "Good. You're quiet about her. That's a good sign. But then you're quiet about everybody. Take your time in here, Sean." She left the room.

Max sat beside O'Brien's chair, watching a small oscillating fan blow air across the office. O'Brien sped through the digital time codes and paused at 00:3:02. Under the marina streetlamps, the light fell in cones. He could see the soft lights from some of the moored boats, like nightlights bobbing in the current. There was movement. A large cat strolled by the dock, pausing to look over its shoulder and then sauntering on its way. O'Brien recognized the cat as Ol' Joe, a stray that roams the docks and is never without food or a temporary home—especially hanging near *St. Michael* after its return from a fishing trip.

00:3:04. Someone walked by the camera.

He wore a baseball cap pulled low. Sweatshirt hoodie and jeans. All dark. Black or dark blue. O'Brien stopped the video and moved it back a few seconds, studying the man's footwear. Boots. Large combat boots. "Bingo," O'Brien whispered. He tried to get a clear look at the man's face. The bill of the baseball cap cast a dark shadow under the streetlamps.

He pressed a button and let the video play. The man approached the locked gate across L dock. He stopped, looked to his right and left, never behind him in the direction of the camera. When he used two hands to open the lock, O'Brien knew the man was picking the lock. In seconds, he pulled back the gate, stepping inside, closing it behind him. And then he was gone.

O'Brien sped up the video until he saw the man emerge from the darkness and come through the entrance again. He closed and locked the gate, started to walk away. There was brief flash. It appeared to be heat lightning over the ocean. The man looked up at the clouds, and the lightning popped again, this time like a flashbulb in his face.

It was a face that O'Brien recognized. The face of the passenger—one of the men in the Top Gun cigarette boat.

# EIGHTEEN

O'Brien thought about the unfiltered cigarette in his refrigerator—the DNA. He spent the next ten minutes looking at video from the interior of the Tiki Bar from an hour before closing. There were no images indicating the man in the baseball cap had spent time as a customer before he decided to pick the lock and stroll down L dock to the bow of *Gibraltar*.

The camera overlooking one section of the parking lot from the Tiki Bar and the marina office did capture him. He strode quickly through the lot, a phone in one hand held to his ear, and a cigarette in the other hand, the tiny red glow of the ash moving in a pendulum sweep as he walked. And then he stopped, pausing long enough to step through the sand at the base of a palm tree in the lot. O'Brien could see the intruder take a final drag from the cigarette before dropping it in the dirt and stepping on it as he exited.

The man walked through the lot, soon out of the camera frame, vanishing into the night. O'Brien shuttled the video through a twenty-minute window from the time the man disappeared. There was no sign of a vehicle leaving or one entering the lot to pick him up. "So maybe you left by water," O'Brien whispered. "What did you do in front of Dave's boat, take a picture? Who'd you call at 3:12 a.m., and are you returning?"

Max looked up at him, cocking her head.

• • •

O'Brien sat in *Gibraltar's* salon with Dave and debriefed him. He played the video clips he'd transferred from the hard drive to his phone and showed Dave the still frame of the man's face when lightning had illuminated it. O'Brien asked, "Do you recognize him?"

Dave's eyes narrowed slightly, looking through his bifocals. "No. But with the cap on his head, the guy's short beard, it's not that clear. He looks Middle Eastern … possibly a Saudi. I'll send the image and video to the CIA. They'll have NSA run it all though facial recognition software. The technology is so good today that the images don't have to come from a databank of known felons. They can get pictures off of any social media site. It gives a whole new meaning to Facebook."

"He's one of the guys I saw in the Top Gun boat watching Katie and Andy working on *Dragonfly*. And now we know he picked a locked gate to trespass on L dock, coming down to *Gibraltar* for something."

"Why at that time in the morning?"

"Maybe he snapped a picture. Maybe he came to see if you were home and for some reason, something scared him off. Or maybe he was surveying the area for a hit later."

Dave set the phone on the coffee table and looked up at O'Brien. "Do you think he came to kill me?"

"He could have had a pistol tucked away under the hoodie. Could have had a garrote or a knife. You tell me you've always been a light sleeper. Do you remember *Gibraltar* moving oddly at that time in the very early morning, as in someone attempting to slip aboard in the dead of night?"

Dave sat back on the couch, removed his bifocals, setting them on his chest. The glasses were attached to straps from a neck lanyard. "A trawler this size and weight doesn't move that much when someone steps aboard, if that's what you're thinking."

"I'm thinking that he could have walked down the dock just about any time in the day. He could have looked like a boat surveyor, mechanic, or even a yacht broker. But, yet, he takes the time to pick a lock and come all the way down the dock to your boat. I think he came here to do you harm … but something happened."

"Maybe you happened. What if he saw you and Max coming out of *Jupiter's* salon, turned and retreated? It's a possibility."

"Max never barked, only growled, and she did so at a low level in my cabin. I was very quiet stepping onto *Jupiter's* cockpit and then up to the dock. I looked down here toward your boat and Nick's boat. Saw nothing. When I walked up to *Gibraltar's* bow, I spotted the tracks on the dock. And it looks like he paced back and forth a couple of times right in front of *Gibraltar*."

"You said fog was building off the water and around the boats. Maybe he vanished into the fog, and the fact of the matter is that he wasn't that far away from you. You just couldn't see him."

"From the images on Flo's camera, he was gone at that point. His tracks may have vanished when the sun came up. But I have one saved on my phone along with the video and a still shot of his face. And I have one more thing."

Dave's white eyebrows rose. "What's that?"

"His DNA. You saw the video from the parking lot. Last night I found his boot prints on the sand next to one of the big palms in the parking lot. He'd tossed a cigarette down and stepped on it. The cigarette wasn't crushed. I lifted it out of the sand, sealed it in a Ziploc bag and set it inside in *Jupiter's* refrigerator."

Dave grinned. "What was your closure rate as a detective down in Miami?"

"Not high enough."

"Ever miss it?"

"Miss what?"

"The work."

"I don't miss the bureaucracy. I do miss hunting and taking down evil, especially in a homicide."

Dave crossed his arms, stared out the open salon doors to the expanse of marina and the boats moored. A Bertram 57 Sports Fishing yacht entered, one man in the wheelhouse, two more in the wide and open cockpit. Dave cleared his throat and said, "It looks like evil is descending on my group of retired CIA friends. You don't have to inject yourself, Sean. It's not your fight."

"Yes, it is. Those tracks in the dew next to your boat are, to me, a line drawn in the sand. You're my friend. I will do whatever I can to help you."

Dave nodded. "Thank you. Somehow, we have to find out who's behind Don's assassination. Who's the man in the video, and where can we find him?"

"What if he came here to deliver something to you last night?"

"You mean something such as a spent rifle cartridge?"

"No, something like a bomb. Let's check *Gibraltar* from bow to stern."

# NINETEEN

After a half hour of looking in all of the nooks and crannies inside and out on *Gibraltar*, Dave turned to O'Brien and said, "Times like this I wish little Max was a bomb-sniffing dog."

"She has other talents." O'Brien smiled and looked at Max asleep on the couch in Dave's salon. "She doesn't snore."

"Now that I know *Gibraltar* is bomb free, I'm ready for another cup of coffee. I'm sticking with caffeine, too. How about you?"

"Sounds good."

Dave stepped over to his bar, put a fresh pot of coffee on, glancing at the photo of his daughter. "I tried to reach Linda. Left a message on her phone to call me. As you know, there's a six-hour time difference between here and London."

"Now that you've sent the video into the CIA for possible facial recognition, what's next?"

"Shouldn't take too long."

"Maybe, in the interim, you and your former covert associates can brainstorm … there should be some data that will start to sway the compass needle. Had Katie's dad, Sol, not received that rifle casing, Don Blackwell's death could have been chalked up to a vendetta, maybe a jealous person in some love-gone-bad triangle, or someone with a hell of a personal grudge. But, after the discovery of the casing, and the guy stalking your boat around 3:00 a.m., this appears to be linked to something you, Sol and Don worked on together in the CIA."

"If it's tied to Gitmo, there are two more—Robert Lewis and Simon Rivers."

•  •  •

Simon Rivers never forgot old habits. These were habits that kept him alive working as a CIA field agent in some of the most hostile places on earth. Years ago, he developed the habit of alternating his transportation routes to and from work, the grocery store, or anywhere he went frequently. He was excellent at deception, experienced at keeping low profiles, which, for the most part, kept him off counterespionage radar.

Although he never forgot old habits, he found that they took more of what every retiree wants—time. Rather than make his daily jog through the twisting residential streets of his Seattle neighborhood, he chose to run laps around a community college track open to the public. The track was on the perimeter of a football field, making a large loop around it.

Rivers, mid-sixties, had the look of a retired football coach. Wide face, a scarred nose twice broken, thick neck and chest. He wore a Seahawks T-shirt, shorts, and running shoes. The emblem across the front of the shirt was that of the team's mascot, the profile of a steely-eyed seahawk, the single eye vivid blue.

Rivers wore a fitness tracker strapped to his left arm. He checked it before beginning a slow jog around the track. It would be the first of ten laps, increasing speed up through lap number eight, using the last two laps to slow down and cool off.

The track was in the open, an upscale condo building across the street, the college gym and athletic building near the field. Two sets of bleachers were on opposite sides of the field. Rivers got halfway around the first lap when he noticed someone sitting at the top of the bleachers on the east side, the sun just behind the person's shoulders. *Maybe a student*, he thought.

Rivers kicked up his pace, running a little faster, the first drop of sweat falling from his wide nose. He felt his heart step up into the familiar rhythm of an athlete, the solid pounding that would give him a resting heart rate of forty beats per minute. He looped around the far end of the track, the smell of fresh cut grass in the morning air, a robin hopping near the goalposts, a cool breeze from the northwest.

• • •

The assassin at the top of the bleachers watched his prey run around the opposite end of the track. He wore a black knit cap, tousled hair around the edges, unshaven. Dead eyes. The killer had scoped out the college's football field and surrounding buildings. Today: prey number two. Most of the surveillance cameras were on the opposite side, the front of the buildings. The closest outdoor camera was on the exterior of the gym, the lens pointed at the field, but too far away in the morning sun to capture someone in the bleachers. It was summer, very few classes, and very few people.

The rifle he carried under a workout towel was short, a Stealth Recon Scout, only thirty-three inches long. He waited for Simon Rivers to loop back and head in his direction. He kept the rifle under the towel, looked at his rental car beneath the stands, less than a sixty-second fast walk. He watched Rivers approach the turn, the sun in his eyes. The assassin lifted the rifle, propping the bipod on the bench in front of him. He quickly drew a bead on the runner, lowering the crosshairs from the prey's face to the center of his chest.

• • •

Simon Rivers felt the blood rushing through his veins. Felt the serge of energy he always got on the second turn around the track. He ran toward the bleachers, a mockingbird calling out from an elm tree near the fence, as if the bird was cheering him down the stretch. He saw movement in the stands. The person seemed to be watching him. *Maybe through binoculars.* The sun was in River's face, casting the person at the top of the bleachers in silhouette.

He slowed a notch, lifting his right hand above his eyebrows to shield the direct sun from his eyes. It looked like the man held a blanket. *Maybe homeless.* He could see the blanket was really a large towel, and the man had it draped around something.

*A gun.*
*A rifle.*

The scope and the barrel aimed directly at Rivers.

The first and only shot entered the blue eye of the seahawk on the T-shirt, the .308 round destroying the heart and exiting through the back. Rivers fell backwards under the impact of the bullet into the near center of his chest. As he lay dying, he looked up at the only cloud in the sky. It was the color of snow, moved slowly, shaped in a wide V form like a bird of prey. In the center of Rivers' T-shirt, the single blue eye of the seahawk now hollowed out and blood red.

# TWENTY

Wynona Osceola pulled her car into the Ponce Marina parking lot, removed the Beretta from the glove box where she had stored it during the conference, and put it back in her purse. She looked around the lot, two bikers standing under an awning at the front of the Tiki Bar, smoking. One man with a long black beard, pointed to something on his Harley near the motor. The other man, dressed in blue jeans with ripped knees and a jean shirt with cut off sleeves, nodded, grinned and took a pull from a can of Busch beer.

Wynona sat there for half a minute, her car engine ticking as it cooled. She glanced in the rearview mirror, then the side view mirrors. Although born and raised on the Seminole reservation in South Florida, she had a lineage that connected back to Ireland. Her oval face had flawless olive skin, hazel eyes. Her long hair was black with an occasional strand of reddish-copper seen only in the sunlight. As a teenager, she was encouraged to enter the Miss Florida pageant. But her heart was not to follow a beauty pageant runway—it was to journey toward a career in criminal justice, her major at Florida State University.

After working for seven years as an FBI agent, she eventually returned to the Seminole reservation as the first and only female detective. She thought about her phone call with Sean O'Brien when she asked him about his boat. *"Jupiter's more of a hobby than a home.*

*I have an old cabin on the St. John's River that has a real roof on it. It's a tin roof, but it keeps the rain off. It's maybe a step down from the Seminole chickees."*

*"Tin roof. It sounds cozy."*

*"How have you been, Wynona? I've thought about you often."*

Wynona placed both of her hands on the steering wheel. Her thoughts racing back to the time she and O'Brien tracked down South Florida mafia kingpin Dino Scarpa and his soldiers in a former banana-packing warehouse in Miami. During a horrific shootout, Wynona was hit with a single bullet. O'Brien had saved her life—kept her from bleeding out, and he saved her spirit by talking the shadow of death out of her disjointed and frightened thoughts. He'd held her hand and cradled her head in a hot parking lot, as she lay on her back between the broken wooden fruit pallets and said, *"You're going to rise up out of this dark rabbit hole and live, you hear me?"*

Wynona blinked her eyes, thoughts returning to the present. Out of habit, she glanced around the parking lot, got out of her car and locked it, and started for L dock towards Sean O'Brien's boat.

• • •

Nick Cronus sat in the cockpit of *St. Michael* on a hard-plastic chair, a hundred yards of monofilament fishing line near the base of the chair. The old line looked like a giant spider's web swirling around his bare feet, a sweating can of beer next to his right foot. He was replacing new line on three of his deep-sea rods and reels. Greek music came from speakers in the salon, a lamb shish kebob, skewered with tomatoes, peppers, onion and mushrooms sizzled on a small charcoal grill near him.

He glanced up as Wynona Osceola walked down the dock toward his boat. Nick grinned and said, "You look like you're lost. Or maybe you smelled my fantastic Greek shish kebob, and you couldn't resist." He stood, the fishing line halfway up his thick calf muscles.

Wynona smiled and said, "It does smell really good. I got a whiff from a good distance up the dock."

"And you followed it here." He grinned. "The lamb's been marinated in garlic, olive oil, lemon juice and two secret Greek herbs from the island of Mykonos. Join me!"

"I appreciate the offer for lunch, but I already have plans."

Nick studied her a moment, his eyes playful, moustache rising in a wide grin. "You look like you got some Greek blood in you. If I'm right, that means you followed the smoke to my campfire, just like in ancient Greece. And, if you don't eat my food, you'll think about it the rest of your life, wondering what you missed." He chuckled.

"Sorry, not a drop of Greek blood in me. But I do love Greek food. We have two excellent restaurants in Miami and South Beach."

Nick clapped his hands once. "I recognize you. At least I think I do. I think I saw you here on the dock before. If not, I have seen your face a hundred times in the picture on your dad's boat."

"My dad doesn't have a boat. But, if you include his canoe, I guess he had a boat." She beamed.

"Aren't you Dave Collins' daughter?"

Wynona shook her head. "No, sorry." She glanced further down the dock to *Jupiter*. "Thanks for the lunch invitation. Bye."

"Wait … umm … you're lookin' at *Jupiter*, my closest friend's boat."

"You know Sean O'Brien?"

"We're tight as brothers can get."

"Brothers?"

"It's a long story. Hey, I saw Sean take Max for her walk … she really takes him. Anyway, they ought to be back soon. Max doesn't mess around with her tiny bladder. In the meantime, lemme, introduce you to Dave. You gotta see the picture of his daughter." Nick lifted the shish kebob off the grill and sat it on a platter.

Wynona looked back down the long dock toward the entrance. "That's a thoughtful offer, but maybe I should just wait for Sean on his boat. I know where it is."

Nick kicked the fishing line from his feet, climbed out of the cockpit and up onto the dock. He extended his calloused hand. "I'm Nick Cronus."

She took it. "Wynona Osceola. I'm pleased to meet you."

Nick looked over her shoulder, toward *Gibraltar*. "C'mon, I see Dave. You won't miss Sean. I can easily spot him when he and little Max get close. She's usually barkin' at a pelican." He waved and got Dave's attention.

Dave came around *Gibraltar,* his bifocals hanging from the lanyard to his chest. He paused when he saw Wynona, looked at Nick and grinned.

Nick said, "Dave, this is Wynona Osceola. Wynona, meet Dave Collins. He's retired from a government job that sent him all over the world except for Greece. Wynona is Sean's friend, and now she's our friend, too. That's how it works at our marina."

"Oh," she said, "I didn't know that. Well, thank you."

Dave nodded. "Your name rings a bell. I've heard Sean mention you. You helped him when Joe Billie was accused of murder."

She smiled. "It was more of the other way around. He helped me. Regardless, Joe was cleared of the charges. And that's the important thing."

"Do you work on the Seminole reservation?"

"Yes. I'm a detective on the rez."

Nick's eyes opened wider. He cleared his throat and smiled. "So, my man, Sean, had your back."

"Yes, thank God."

Nick folded his arms and rocked on the balls of his feet for a second. He cut his eyes to Dave and said, "I told Wynona that she looks like your daughter, maybe a twin."

Dave smiled. "Indeed. You're probably about the same age. Her mother is Italian, from Rome. I met her when I lived there. But that was a long time ago. I assume you're here to visit Sean?"

"Yes, I'm early." She looked over her shoulder, glancing down the pier. She spotted O'Brien just entering the entrance to L dock, eighty yards away. What she didn't see was the man who was watching her. He did it from the window of a condo in the high-rise building across the marina.

• • •

The assassin held a pair of binoculars to his face as easily as he held a riflescope to his eye. After killing the last man on the running track, he was prepared for the third victim. There were folders on the table next to him. The one on top was marked D Collins. A black-and-white photograph of two people, an older man and younger woman, was paper-clipped to the outside of the folder. He lowered the binoculars and studied the picture. The woman in the photo looked like the woman who now stood on the dock next to Dave Collins.

# TWENTY-ONE

Max saw her first. O'Brien and Max were coming closer to *Gibraltar* when Wynona waved. O'Brien was looking at the center-cockpit of an approaching Hylas 46, the sails down, the diesel gently purring. He glanced at the top of the mast. The highest point was the lightning rod or dissipater as it's often called in marine stores. O'Brien watched it for a moment, before something caught his eye in the same trajectory, but further way.

In the distance, a man stood on the outside balcony of a condominium, holding binoculars to his eyes. O'Brien could tell the man was observing the marina. *Was he simply watching the movements of the boats? Was he watching the movements of people? Or both?*

O'Brien dropped to one knee and pretended to be tying a shoelace on his right foot. Max started to trot on, and he said, "Wait a second. Let's take it slow." He turned his head to the left, looking back up at the condo balcony across the marina. The man was gone. *Maybe it's nothing. Lots of people have binoculars around marinas. But how many people seemed to be peering in the direction of Dave's trawler?*

O'Brien stood and continued toward the end of the dock. He spotted Wynona Osceola chatting with Dave and Nick near *Gibraltar,* and he noticed her wide smile when she saw him coming her way. Max ran down the rest of the dock, toward Wynona, Dave and Nick, tail wagging, doing her doggy grin. Wynona crouched down and extended her arms. "Hi, Maxine! I've missed you." Max almost jumped into her arms.

Nick chuckled, looked over at Dave and winked. "Okay, Hot Dog, you never greet me like that, and I'm the one who slips you a starfish bone to chew on."

O'Brien approached, smiling. Wynona stood and stepped over to him, hugging O'Brien. She said, "It's so good to see you. I've had a few minutes to get to know your neighbors. Nick was kind enough to offer his lunch to me."

Nick folded his arms. "Of course, it's the Greek way. A pretty lady comes by my boat, and I feel an obligation to share my food and wine with her. It's something that Bacchus handed down to generations of us." He grinned.

O'Brien said, "Nick's the goodwill ambassador here at Ponce Marina." He looked at Wynona. "It's great to see you. Are you hungry?"

"After getting a whiff of Nick's cooking, I'm beyond hungry. Not close to starving but heading in that direction." She looked toward *Jupiter* for a second. "The last time I saw you and Max was after we returned from a way too short boat trip to the beach at Canaveral National Seashore. It was so beautiful there. That's the primitive Florida the tribal elders used to speak of when they talked about the way it was."

O'Brien held up the paper bag with two bottles of wine in it and said, "I need to drop this off on *Jupiter*. After that, we can walk down to the Tiki Bar for lunch."

Nick held his hands out, palms up and said, "Why go there when I can cater it for you. Take that wine over to Dave's boat, I'll throw some more kebobs on the grill and deliver. Now that's a helluva offer."

Dave said, "Happy to oblige. It's up to Sean and Wynona. If you two want to have Nick cater the event, he's certainly close and comes with quite the culinary pedigree."

O'Brien looked at Wynona and asked, "What would you like to do?"

"I have a suggestion. I think Nick has a fine offer. I'd be honored to accept. And maybe for dessert, Sean, we can head to the Tiki Bar for their legendary Key Lime pie. That's according to the blurb I saw written on a chalkboard under the special of the day—grouper sandwiches." She smiled.

"Good," Dave said. "Let's make our way to the cockpit for a glass of wine. I'd like to hear what the tribal elders had to say about Florida before we drained half of the glades and covered much of the coast in eyesores called condos."

• • •

They dined at the round table on *Gibraltar*, under the trawler's awning, the brackish scent of a rising tide in the east breeze. O'Brien sat with his back to the salon, a clear view of the marina and the high-rise condo. Wynona finished her last bite of grilled lamb and said, "Nick, this was fabulous. Thank you so much for going to the trouble to cook such a great lunch for us."

"No problem. It's what we do at the marina. Fish. Eat. Play. Not necessarily in that order. You'll have to try my swordfish kebobs one day. Fresh caught … those I can boast about," Nick said, as he kissed his fingers and flung his hand open in the air.

"Fish. Eat. Play. That sounds like a prescription for the soul, or maybe a title for a book about how to live life well."

Dave sipped a glass of chilled chardonnay and said, "The marina and boating life are highly recommended. I don't know if I'll live long enough to determine whether or not it adds to longevity, however, I can assure you it most certainly adds to the quality of life."

Wynona leaned back in her deck chair, the breeze gently stirring her hair. "Quality of life … that's one of the reasons I left the FBI … or maybe the Bureau left me. Or maybe it was mutual." She paused and looked from O'Brien to Dave. "Sean told me a little about your background. I suppose you had no illusions working for the CIA, right?"

A slight smile moved across Dave's mouth. "If I did, they didn't last too long. I'd like to think the world is in a tad better place in some respects because of a few things we tried to dust off and put back together again … hopefully in better form."

O'Brien looked toward the condo. The balcony on the ninth floor was vacant. He eyed Dave and said, "The problem is … or can be …

whether you're working as a detective in homicide, investigating cases with the FBI or CIA, you often are exposed to parts of the job that may not completely leave when the case gets shelved, closed or you retire."

"You mean for the cold cases that aren't closed?" Nick asked.

"Not always. A case is primarily dangerous work because of the nature of good and evil. Often it reveals itself into a kind of good, bad and ugly. The bad seems to have a longer shelf life than what you would think."

Nick laced his fingers together over his stomach. "Sounds like you're talkin' about PTSD."

O'Brien said nothing. Wynona leaned back in her deck chair, the reflection of sunlight from the harbor surface skipping across her face as a gentle wake rolled and flattened. She said, "What we did in the Bureau, and I imagine that what you did or witnessed with the CIA, can lead to a form of PTSD. My last assignment was near Dearborn, Michigan. My partner and I had been staking out a home. The patriarch was moving money to Iraq and other areas … we believe to suspected terrorist groups. He ran a bakery. We'd wired his house and shop. We wanted to make sure his connections weren't planning a 9/11-type hit on the homeland. We were watching men, and a woman, coming and going from the house and bakery who also had aroused our suspicion. We were in a van near the home when we heard, through the bugs we planted, horrific screaming from a girl. By the time my partner and I broke through the door, the man was stabbing his teenage daughter to death in a so-called honor killing. His wife was holding the girl's arms down on the floor."

"That's a damn sick father and mother," Nick said, reaching for his bottle of Corona. "He's not a father. He's a butcher, and the mother is just as bad. What did you and your partner do?"

Wynona said nothing for a moment. She glanced at Sean and then leveled her eyes at Nick. "I emptied my clip into his body. Eight rounds. The bureau called it beyond the use of excessive force. In retrospect, I suppose they were right. After they put me on administrative leave, they wanted to place me in a sort of witness protection program, which I refused. Because details of the incident were kept mostly internal, they thought it best to put me in a desk job, so I quit."

Dave nodded. "I assume that was because of a possible retaliation from the followers of this guy."

"Yes. It was very real. And it might still be after four years. My partner, Michael Levin, was shot and killed in his front yard walking his family dog." She folded her arms. "Maybe the bad guys stopped after they killed Michael. Maybe they stopped after that … in some sort of an eye for an eye mindset. Or maybe they just haven't found me yet."

Dave sliced into a grilled mushroom and said, "I remember reading about your partner's death. Did he shoot the guy killing his daughter?"

"No, just me. I guess the crazed and distraught mother had no idea who did what. She was covered in her daughter's blood, and her husband lay dead on the floor beside her daughter's body."

"The man you took out. What was his name?"

"Masood Aswad."

"Was he born in Baghdad?"

"Yes. How did you make that connection?"

"Because, in 2003, his brother Abdul was picked up as an enemy combatant. It's a small world."

"Too small when it comes to terror."

Dave nodded. "Abdul Aswad was complicit in the 9/11 attacks and at least a dozen other terrorist's attacks around the world. We interrogated him outside of Kuwait before his detention to Guantanamo Bay where the interrogation continued."

O'Brien cut his eyes from Dave to the condo in the distance. There was no movement and no sign of the man with the binoculars.

Wynona pursed her lips for a second, inhaling deeply before asking, "What happened to his brother, Abdul?"

"The president released him in a prisoner exchange deal." Dave's phone buzzed on the table near his glass of wine. He glanced down at the caller ID. It was incoming from Katie's father, Sol Lefko. Dave had a feeling that the call would not be good news. He looked at Nick, Wynona and O'Brien. "I need to take this. I'll walk out on the dock."

# TWENTY-TWO

D ave stood on the dock near *Gibraltar* and spoke with a man telling a horror story. Sol Lefko quietly closed his front door, walked out on the porch next to a large hanging basket of ferns and two wicker rocking chairs. He said, "No witnesses have come forward. The shooter used one round. He took the shot from the vicinity of the bleachers on one side of the football field. The round went through Simon's heart."

"Same caliber?"

"We don't know yet. We should right after the autopsy. However, if the shooter is staying true to his dark melody—as in leaving a .30 caliber casing in my mailbox, I'd bet it's the same."

"I thought this might be connected to the Russian, Andrei Sokolov. As a group, you, Robert, Simon, and me worked our share of collective assignments together. Sokolov was one we approached as a team because he was connected to that double agent Richard Thurston. Sokolov is one of the most vengeful men I've ever known. We don't know where he is today. Also, one of the last projects we did jointly, at least before most of us retired, was the Gitmo interrogations. We dealt with the worst of the worst, and I'd suggest the vilest of the bunch was Abdul Aswad."

"Remember, he was released in the exchange a few years ago."

"And, one of the last things he said to each of us was a threat. No, he called it a promise. He said he'd systematically kill each one of us at different intervals until the last of us was running with nowhere to hide, was the way he put it."

"He was and is … beyond incorrigible. For a devotee and major proponent of Sharia law, he was well read outside of the Quran and the terrorist's manuals he devoured. He earned a mechanical engineering degree from Oxford. Comes in handy when you're designing bombs."

"If it is Aswad, where the hell are his operations? Who'd he hire to do the hits? First it was Don … and now Simon. Let's get on the phone with the directors of both agencies, CIA and FBI. We need to give them everything we have and suspect."

Lefko watched a robin foraging for insects in his yard. He said, "I'll coordinate the call, and we'll have Robert Lewis on the line with us, too. If this is Aswad, we need to send him and his boys the same medicine. The agencies need to bring in or choose coordinated assets who can track down Aswad and whomever he's hired. And, they need to do this quickly."

Dave looked toward *Gibraltar*. He could see O'Brien talking with Wynona in the cockpit and Nick teaching Max a new trick. "I'm looking at a guy who could be one of the best assets we'd find. Name's Sean O'Brien—he's a former Delta Force member and then worked homicide Miami-Dade PD. He takes an occasional PI job and doesn't do it because he needs the money. We just had lunch with his friend, Wynona Osceola. She was an FBI agent for seven years. She left the bureau after they gave her a desk job. They put her in indefinite time out from the field because she allegedly used excessive force in the shooting death of a Dearborn, Michigan, man for stabbing his daughter in a Sharia law honor killing. Wynona and her partner were on a stakeout at the man's home when it was going down."

"I recall that one. Too bad she had to take the fall for taking a guy out for all the right reasons."

"The guy she took out was Masood Aswad. Masood was Abdul's brother. There are or were five siblings in the family. Before his death in Dearborn, Masood was the eldest son. So, what we have is a former FBI agent now working as a Seminole Tribe PD detective, and she's the woman who killed Abdul Aswad's brother. She's a close friend of Sean O'Brien's, a man who I'd put up there with the best of the best from the FBI and CIA in terms of finding people."

Sol sat down on his porch step. He watched a black ant dart across one step. "Sounds like a great guy to have on the back burner. Hopefully, we won't need him or his talents. This should be done in-house. Also, you might want to debrief the former FBI agent, Wynona, to see if what she has to say about Aswad's brother could have any insight into all this."

"All right. Before you get everyone on the conference call, let me float this by you."

"What do you have?"

"We're about to bid Katie and Andy a nice bon voyage. No water cannons over their bow, but we're going to give them a nice send-off as they start a new chapter in their lives."

"I appreciate that. Just do a favor for me … don't mention the death of Simon Rivers to Katie. She has enough on her plate. The name on their boat, *Dragonfly*, is an allegorical for their new passage in life."

"I know it's counter to checking out and going on a sailboat journey for a year or two, but they might not want to let their guard down."

"Why, Dave?"

"Because of something Abdul Aswad said about killing us and removing our seeds from earth. I keep thinking about Simon River's son, Carter."

"What about him?"

"What if the freak car accident was no accident? What if someone caused it to happen? Would Katie be safe? Could Aswad find them at sea? And, is my daughter in London any safer?"

"Let's get Robert on the line and the agency directors. Maybe we'll come closer to answering that question. Oh, there's something else."

"What?" Dave asked.

"Under the wiper blades on Simon's parked car near the track … police found a typed note that said: *and then there were three.* Dave, could that mean you, me and Robert Lewis?"

# TWENTY-THREE

O'Brien could tell that Dave had changed. Subtle, but Dave heard something on the phone for the last thirty minutes that shook a man trained to be shatterproof. As he took his seat again at the table, he glanced at the framed photograph of his daughter in *Gibraltar's* salon, and then he looked at Wynona and said, "May I ask your age? It's not something that I often, if ever, ask a woman. However, I'd bet that you're close to the age of my daughter, but I could be wrong."

Wynona smiled and said, "I don't mind at all. Not that I embrace age, but I remember what a tribal elder said to my mother when her father died. He said never resent old age because too many people don't have the honor of reaching it. I'm thirty-eight."

Nick grinned and said, "Okay, Dave, how old is your daughter?"

Dave's eyes opened a little wider, his playful self now returning. "Linda is thirty-nine. I was close."

"Yes, you were," Wynona said. "Where's your daughter?"

"She's in London with her husband, son, and daughter."

"Do you see them often?"

"Unfortunately, not often enough."

O'Brien said, "I like what the elder member of the tribe said about aging. Was that Sam Otter?"

"No, his name was Johnnie Tiger. He wasn't a Seminole medicine man like Sam Otter ... but more of a revered tribal philosopher.

Before his death, he didn't think the tribe should have moved in the direction of casino gambling. Johnnie used to say that people aren't caught or trapped in the web of life … but rather that we are part of it. He'd say we, the human race, are but one single thread within the web. He also said that everything in life, and death, is connected. And that whatever we do to the web—to the earth, we will do to each other."

Dave nodded. "It sounds like he was an astute observer of human existence."

"He was. And to this day, I miss speaking with him." She looked over to O'Brien. "You said your friends renamed their sailboat, *Dragonfly*, correct?"

"Yes. It may be a perfect name for their boat and circumstances."

"This is what Sam Otter said about dragonflies one summer after the tribe had its annual Green Corn Dance. Sam said, the dragonflies are free spirits embracing a life short lived. Dragonflies begin their life in water, as do humans in the womb. And even in flight, they stay connected to their life source—water. No creature on earth has better vision, and no creature on earth can navigate the winds of change like the dragonfly. He said, if a dragonfly comes into your life, maybe lands very near you, looks at you with those large eyes, just watch it for a moment, and be very still. Never harm or kill it. Sam told us the visit of a dragonfly often brings or signifies a change is coming into your life. He said, the key is not to fight change, but to embrace it." She took a deep breath and leaned back in her chair.

Dave said, "What a suitable name for a sailboat. I believe Katie and Andy came up with an excellent choice."

O'Brien nodded. "It would be good if you could share that story with them."

Wynona smiled. "I'd be happy to share it. Where's their boat? Do they moor *Dragonfly* here at the marina?"

Nick said, "It's one dock over—N dock. They leave for the islands tomorrow."

"I've been on a few powerboats but never a sailboat. It's on my bucket list."

O'Brien said, "It was on theirs, too, they just moved the sailboat bucket to the top of the list."

"I hope I can meet them before they set sail."

O'Brien nodded. "We can make that happen." He glanced toward the condo balcony. No one was there, but there was a movement behind half closed drapes—the silhouette of a man just on the other side of the glass.

Dave said, "I haven't seen a dragonfly lately, however, there is a change coming into my life, and it isn't good fortune."

Wynona leaned closer to the table. "Are you ill?"

"No, not any more than a guy my age trying to contend with upholstery that's a little frayed and plumbing that robs me of the thing we retirees long for … a good night's sleep." He lifted his drink, ice clinking the glass. "I'll share this with you, Wynona, because in an odd way, by happenstance, you're beyond the ninth circle of a revenge inferno. But for myself and four other members of a CIA team, we are apparently at ground zero."

"What do you mean?"

O'Brien shifted his eyes from Wynona to Dave and said, "I'm assuming the call you took was not good news."

"No, it wasn't. The second member of our team, Simon Rivers, was shot once through the heart as he jogged outside around a college football field. Our remaining team members, Robert, Sol, and me, will be speaking soon with deputy directors at both agencies—FBI and CIA." Dave told them the call was in the process of being coordinated then cut his eyes over to Wynona and added, "We believe Abdul Aswad is behind this. One of his brothers was Masood Aswad, the man you shot and killed. This, indeed, is a small and, all too often, deadly world."

# TWENTY-FOUR

Wynona said nothing. Her thoughts raced back to the horrific night when she heard the cries and pleas of a young girl's looming death coming through her earpiece as she and her partner sat in an FBI van on a quiet residential street in Dearborn. She pursed her lips, looked up at Dave and said, "We know where Masood Aswad is today. He's buried in the Islamic Cemetery outside of Detroit. Where is his brother, Abdul?"

Dave's chest expanded with a deep breath. "I wish we knew where to find him." Dave sipped his drink and added, "Maybe the positive side of this fact is that you've been left alone for the last few years. Perhaps, when they killed your partner, it was considered sufficient in their retribution code of an eye for an eye. Maybe, at this point, you don't need to be worried or unduly vigilant anymore. I don't know, though."

O'Brien looked over at Wynona. "That could be the scenario, but the situation has changed. Abdul is out of prison, in seclusion somewhere, calling the shots, literally. We know he has a vendetta, Dave, for you and your teammates. Maybe it won't reach to Wynona, but I think she needs to be very cautious for a while."

• • •

The killer on the ninth floor of the condo started to make a call but paused to sip from a chilled bottle of Perrier water. He was long-limbed, had bony wrists, hollow cheeks, dark skin, and empty eyes. He was dressed like most of the tourists—a Cocoa Beach T-shirt, shorts, and running shoes. He set the glass bottle on the table near the open curtains, a shaft of sunlight coming through the opening in the drapes and hitting the bottle, the glass glowing. His hand and arm movements were fluid, military precision.

The killer held the binoculars to his dark eyes, licked his thin, wet lips. He studied the people sitting at the table on the trawler. There was the man with the short, white beard—Collins. A man with darker skin ... maybe Middle Eastern. The woman, no doubt, is Collin's daughter. And then there was a man who just slipped on sunglasses. *Who was he? He seemed to be staring directly at the condo. Why?*

• • •

Dave picked up a TV remote, aimed it at the fifty-five inch wide-screen above the bar and said, "I was told these assassinations are getting a lot of press because the news media found out that two retired CIA field agents were each killed with a single bullet within four days of each other." He turned on the set.

A cable news television anchorman, dark hair, square jaw, looked into the studio camera and spoke to a national audience. "In the era of school shootings and terrorist attacks, rarely, if ever, do we hear about CIA agents hurt or killed. Mostly because the nature of covert work is so secretive that the CIA usually doesn't confirm or deny the loss of life with its agents in the field. However, not so much the case with retired agents. Four days ago, a former CIA operative, Don Blackwell, was killed by an assassin's bullet as he played a round of golf at Westchester Country Club near Manassas, Virginia. And now, there appears to be another retired CIA agent gunned down across the country. Sheila Barnes has more on the story."

The live image cut to a reporter in the field, her brown hair worn up, standing near yellow crime scene tape, the football field bleachers in the background. Along the perimeter, a dozen reporters and camera operators were shooting video and filing live reports. Police and investigators from the FBI continued to work the scene. The body was loaded into a coroner's van.

The reporter nodded and said, "That's right, Alan. The man gunned down here, in Seattle, this morning was Simon Rivers. He apparently was shot in the chest as he went about his morning jog around the track behind me. Police aren't saying if they have any witnesses. We do know that no one has been arrested. Rivers spent almost three decades working for the CIA. We don't know where he was stationed."

She glanced down at her notes and said, "Also, Don Blackwell, who you mentioned was killed on a golf course in Virginia, worked twenty-seven years with the CIA. The agency itself is not confirming any of this. However, the information was corroborated earlier today when the Chair of the Senate Intelligence Committee, Senator Lloyd Grayson, was asked about it after he came from a closed-door session with CIA Director, Doug Martin. He wouldn't comment further. The obvious questions right now are this: Did the same shooter kill both men? Why, after a few years retired from the CIA, were they killed? And, had Don Blackwell and Simon Rivers worked on covert projects together that would have led to their murders after leaving the CIA? Now back to you, Alan, in the studio."

Dave held up the remote and muted the sound. He shook his head. "It'll be just a matter of time before somebody in the media digs far enough to make the connection that all five of us were working together at Gitmo, but we worked a couple of other projects together as well."

O'Brien asked, "Can you share ... what other projects?"

"The conviction of Richard Thurston. He was one of those extremely rare CIA officers who breached, sold out to the Russians, and eventually got caught. He ranks right up there with Richard Hanssen and Robert Pollard. We know Thurston received at least sixteen million. We suspect much more. He's been locked up in a supermax prison for years and will be for the rest of his life."

Dave leaned back in his chair, his face filled with fatigue and grief. "Simon and Dan were like brothers to me. We had each other's backs in some very dangerous times and places. After retiring, we all lived in separate areas of the nation, but we stayed in touch. It was just this year that the five of us were going to get together here in Florida for a reunion and do some fishing and play a round or two of golf." He paused, his usual deep voice now soft, just above a whisper. "I'm going to miss them dearly … and I'm going to do whatever I can to find their killer or killers."

• • •

From the condo, the killer made a call. The man on the other line answered with a soft voice in Farsi. The hunter, speaking Farsi, said, "I could almost make it two birds with one shot. Dave Collins is on his boat with his daughter and two other men. They are sitting at a table on the deck."

"Can you identify the two other men?"

"No."

"Use a long lens on your camera. Take a photograph and send it to us electronically. We may need it as reference."

"I understand. After I take the picture, I will take their lives. Who do you want to die first, Collins or his daughter?"

"The daughter. Try for a head shot."

# TWENTY-FIVE

Dave was silent, watching a Viking-48 sports-fishing yacht maneuvering away from its mooring, two men in the cockpit smoking cigars, one man on the bridge, at the controls. Dave looked over at Wynona and asked, "Can you tell me anything more about Abdul Aswad's brother, Masood?"

"Not much more than what I've already shared. In all the hours of visual and audio surveillance that we conducted, I don't recall Masood mentioning anything specific about Abdul."

"How about any soldiers … guns for hire that he or Abdul may have used to carry out their terrorist plots?"

"Masood was pretty tight lipped when it came to specifics about that sort of thing. He did talk about a family home in the outskirts of Baghdad, not far from Abu Ghraib. It was there that Saddam Hussein held many dissidents as prisoners. And it was there where Masood Aswad's youngest brother, Mohammad Aswad, was held and allegedly beaten and abused by U.S. Army personnel; people who were later tried, sentenced to prison, and dishonorably discharged."

Nick folded his arms across his chest and said, "Yeah, but the crap that came outta that gave terrorists even more ammo for their Jihadist's holy war."

O'Brien glanced at the condo, balcony and window. Nothing. He lowered his eyes to Wynona and said, "Nick's right. When you give a fanatic even more reason to believe he has the right and duty to kill you because you don't follow his religious doctrine, you toss gas on a two-thousand-year-old fire. That web Sam Otter told you about when you were a little girl could become a spider's web. The black widow is hiding in a lair somewhere with strands of webbing that circle the globe, from Abu Ghraib to Gitmo and even to Dearborn, Michigan. For these people, there is no expiration date on revenge. Just keep your head up."

Wynona said, "I hope you're incorrect. Yes, I shot and killed a man who was butchering his daughter with a large knife. Yes, it is coincidental that he was the brother of a man the CIA spent a lot of time and effort interrogating for alleged terrorist activities. I think, though, that's where the similarities end between the two. We were surveilling Masood because he was suspected of supplying cash to terrorist groups, some of it coming through Miami … and not because he was a terrorist. His connections were shady, but beyond being a money man, which is bad enough, we couldn't link him to any actual terrorist activity. Your description of Abdul, however, is that he is a terrorist, perhaps even a leader or organizer."

"Wynona, just because Masood appeared to be on the sidelines, that doesn't make his connections, especially with a brother like Abdul Aswad, less dangerous," Dave said.

O'Brien glanced up at the balcony and window. The window was now open. He spotted the millisecond reflection of sunlight off something. The man was no longer holding binoculars. He was hiding a rifle with a scope attached to it.

O'Brien bolted, turning the table over just as a round smashed through it. "Down!" He yelled. "From the condo!" Another round hit the top edge of the table. "Crawl into the salon! Take cover!"

Max barked and ran with Nick. Wynona and Dave followed, crawling on hands and knees. O'Brien left the table vertical and crouched down, rolling on the deck into the salon. "Dave, where's your rifle?"

"I'll get it." Dave left and quickly returned with a Remington 700, scoped rifle. He handed it to O'Brien and asked, "Did you see the shooter?"

"I saw the lens flare from his riflescope behind an open window."

"Where?"

"Condo. Ninth floor. Top left corner."

Wynona stayed under cover and looked through the trawler's cockpit toward the condo. Nick stood behind the bar, his dark eyes darting from O'Brien to Wynona. She said, "I'm a pretty good shot. Do you have another rifle?"

Dave shook his head. "No. A shotgun and three pistols."

O'Brien said, "Everyone stay low. I'm going up to the bridge. Maybe I can spot him." He turned and climbed the inside steps to the topside fly-bridge. He crouched low, finding a covered area with a partial view of the condo. He looked at an American flag at the top of a mast on N dock. Looked at the direction and approximate speed of the wind. O'Brien rested the rifle on the edge of the captain's seat, quickly sighting toward the open window where the shooter was standing less than a minute earlier. He moved the crosshairs slowly, looking beyond the window into as much of the room as possible. He spotted a bottle of Perrier water on the table.

A shadow moved.

It was the shooter. He'd set the rifle down and was holding the binoculars to his eyes.

O'Brien sighted in the crosshairs back to the binoculars just as Max trotted out onto the transom, barking at a large brown pelican that alighted on one of the dock pilings. A jet ski zipped across the marina a hundred feet from *Gibraltar's* transom sending a wake across the water.

The man set the binoculars down, picking up the rifle and positioning the bipod stand on the table. He took aim.

O'Brien moved the crosshairs again. *Maybe the shooter was going to fire a dozen rounds into Gibraltar's salon, hoping for a kill or kills. Maybe he was aiming at Max.*

O'Brien had the man focused in the riflescope, the small dot at the center of the crosshairs just below his hairline. And then *Gibraltar* rose a few inches in the jet skis' wake. O'Brien held steady, waiting for the trawler to settle back. He didn't move. Finger just touching the trigger. When the wake fell, and the trawler lowered, the crosshairs lined up again on the man's head.

O'Brien fired.

Through the scope, he saw a spray of pink mist come from the man's head as he dropped from view. O'Brien paused a few seconds, waiting to see if anyone else was in the room. Nothing moved. He crouched in the wheelhouse, staring at the open window and then he quickly descended the steps.

Dave asked, "Do you think you hit him?"

"Yes. I think he's lying dead up on that condo floor."

Nick folded his arms, glanced at the two bullet holes in the table, looked where one round embedded in the teakwood floor of the salon. The second round entered a wall near a painting of a Florida sunrise off the coast of Vero Beach. Nick made the sign of the cross and said, "Holy shit! How'd you know to flip that table when you did?"

"I spotted the sun reflecting off the glass in the shooter's riflescope."

Wynona said, "He got off two shots quickly. Do you think he had two targets in mind?"

Dave said, "Definitely me. Maybe you as well."

"But they wouldn't have any idea that me, the former FBI agent that killed Abdul's brother five years ago, would be sitting on your boat."

Dave nodded. "I agree." He stepped over and picked up the framed picture of his daughter. "But they probably know what Linda looks like. You have a striking resemblance to her. And from a stakeout on a condo balcony, or through a riflescope, they probably couldn't tell the difference."

O'Brien said, "I don't think anyone in the marina saw me take the shot."

Nick said, "They definitely could hear it."

"But that doesn't visually connect me to it. And the trajectory is so far from where we are, no one will have any real idea where the shot originated."

"Sean, what are you saying?" Wynona asked.

"We have a couple of choices. We can call the Ponce Inlet Police and tell them what happened. I returned fire in self-defense. Regardless, my bet is that international espionage and a jihadist terrorist cartel is a little beyond their pay grade." He shifted his eyes to Dave. "Or you can call the CIA and get one of their eraser teams to pick up the body and clean the condo. My guess is the shooter was alone up there and the unit was leased under a fake corporate name."

Dave looked in the direction of the condo, a sailboat putting across the bay. He nodded and said, "They've murdered two of my close friends. They just tried to kill me … or all of us. If it's Aswad, or someone under his direction, he's declared a personal war. It can't be fought or won with the local police and prosecutor's office. Also, if the news media start flocking around the condo and marina, it'll create even more of the psychological horror that Aswad wants to generate. All leading up and ending with what he wants … all five members of my former team dead."

# TWENTY-SIX

Katie and Andy were enjoying their very first lunch together, just the two of them, on *Dragonfly* when they heard what sounded like a firecracker. They sat in the cockpit around a small foldout table and ate kale and romaine salads with shrimp cocktails on the side. The bread had been baked that morning at a local bakery. Their chardonnay was chilled from a refrigerator inside *Dragonfly's* galley, the shore power keeping all of the boat's electronics humming.

Katie smiled and said, "Sounds like someone is anxious to set off some holiday fireworks before the Fourth of July rolls around next week."

Andy looked toward the far end of N dock and said, "That was either fireworks or a gunshot."

"Sounded like a firecracker to me."

"Depending upon the gun and the caliber of the bullet, they can sound somewhat alike, especially from a distance. The horrible shooting in Vegas that killed all the people at the concert, survivors said they thought the noise was just one of the resorts setting off some fireworks."

Katie glanced down at her glass of wine and then looked up at her husband. "That's one of the reasons I'm anxious to set sail and leave some of the insanity behind us. Every time I hear the word *'another,'* in reference to another school shooting, I want to cry. Let's go explore islands of flowers, crystal clear waters, and skies so blue they're off the color spectrum. Maybe we'll find the land of the Smurfs." She raised her glass and said, "To us, Andy. To you and me taking a new fork in the road less traveled. To a journey we'll remember and talk about when we're sitting around the dinner table at an assisted living facility in old age."

They touched glasses in a toast.

• • •

O'Brien unlocked the sliding glass doors to *Jupiter*. Wynona stood next to him, Max at her feet. He looked over Wynona's shoulder, down L dock, as far as he could see. Nothing but boat owners going about their business, some washing hulls and decks, some making small repairs, others walking toward the Tiki Bar. He said, "I doubt if someone called the police because they think they heard a gunshot."

Wynona's eyes were uneasy. "There are a lot of loud sounds coming from a marina, noisy boat motors and whatnot. Right before you fired the single shot, I heard what sounded like a lot of motorcycles entering the Tiki Bar parking lot."

O'Brien pulled back the glass door, and they entered the salon, Max trotting ahead and jumping up on the couch. He closed the door, looking down the dock again. "The CIA will have ops people here in a couple of hours. We have to find out who tried to kill us from that condo unit and where his fearless leader is hiding."

"What if the perp in the condo *is* the fearless leader?"

"We're about to find out."

"Maybe I should go up there with you when the ops team arrives."

"I don't think that's a good idea."

"Why?"

O'Brien moved over to his bar and pulled a stool out for Wynona. "I don't know if those two shots were meant for Dave, or whether one was meant for him and the other one for you. Besides, you're a police officer—although you're out of your jurisdiction, it may be called into question why you didn't call the local police."

"The shooter could have been about to kill all of us ... you, me, Dave and Nick. But you turned that table over so fast it blocked his line of sight."

"Maybe the shooter wanted all of us dead. Sometimes, as you know, that happens when a killer is concerned about leaving witnesses alive who can ID him. But this guy was three hundred yards away, perched up in a high-rise condo like a hawk. Had he killed you and Dave, there is no way that Nick or I could have ID'd him. By the time someone got to the condo, the shooter would have been halfway to the airport. I don't like doing what I had to do, but there was no choice. He had us pinned down. Not much protection from rifle bullets on a boat molded out of fiberglass and plastic." O'Brien sat on a stool beside her. He smiled, his voice easy. "I almost lost you in a parking lot when Miami mob bullets started flying. I don't what to chance that again. If you don't mind, just hang back for the moment."

Her brown eyes softened. She took a deep breath through her nostrils and said, "I'm so appreciative of what you did. You saved my life. But you didn't save my life for me to make pies and do crossword puzzles. I was a federal agent for seven years. I can, Sean, take care of myself. I have been in and out of dangerous places, and I survived. It's the risk we take when we sign up for the job. You can relate, you were a homicide detective once."

"But I quit. I left it all behind."

"Why?"

"For a lot of reasons. The primary one was the line I had to walk or cross over to get into the criminal mind. It's not a place I wanted to be any longer."

"I can relate."

"I know you can."

"When Joe Billie was in trouble ... when he was accused of murder and going to trial for a crime he didn't commit, you were there for him. Not only there, but you took the responsibility of finding the real killers and proving Joe was innocent. You put your life on the line for him. Nick Cronus shared with me a story of how you pulled three bikers off him before they could beat Nick to death."

O'Brien said nothing.

Wynona crossed her legs, positioning her body more toward O'Brien, a gentle breezed puffing the white curtains on the port and starboard windows. She looked thoughtfully at O'Brien and said, "And now you are helping your old friend, Dave Collins. It's what you do, Sean, because there's something in your DNA that demands it. And I believe that human trait is getting scarcer every day. Did you ever stop to ask yourself why you walk towards trouble, and not away from it?"

"I don't seek it. Never have. For me, it's always been an obligation to lend a hand to people who really need it. Why? If I tell you it's simply the right thing to do, that sounds too simple. But it's not complicated."

"You're hardwired for it, and you're hyper-aware of everything around you. Many of the seven-billon people on the planet aren't either of those."

O'Brien said nothing. He glanced at Max and then the framed picture of Sherri on the end table. He looked at Wynona and said, "Each of us has been given the privilege to exist on our little blue-green planet for a while. I think there's a divine force at work in the universe as invisible as gravity but felt by good people when the human spirit is crushed or blown out like a candle flame. I've never thought of our existence as anything but coexistence with others. Maybe it's not unlike what the old medicine man, Sam Otter, told you about the web. It connects all of us in the good, bad and ugly of humanity. But through all of its marvelous complexities, there are spiders in the dark recesses of the web, people ready to inject you with poison and suck the life out of you, leaving a mummy wrapped in silk. I just hope to walk a solitary strand one day at a time. And, when possible, I try to help someone trapped in a setting of malice."

Wynona looked at him for a few seconds before reaching out to clasp his hand. "Okay, I'll stay here, un-mummified for the moment." She smiled. But, seriously, be careful, Sean. I don't know what you're going to find in the condo, but I do believe it's from the darkest burrows of the web."

# TWENTY-SEVEN

In the world of organized crime, they are often called "cleaners" or "fixers." In the covert world of the CIA, they are known as erasers. They are highly trained crime scene investigators who work as operatives or ops officers. Some of their talents and skillsets are used to make the crime scene look like a suicide, murder, or to make it completely go away. This includes everything from body removal to eliminating every speck of trace evidence.

Within one hour of Dave's call to the CIA, four ops officers, three men and one woman, were on a private jet from Langley, Virginia, to Daytona International Airport. When they landed, the team was met by a ground contact in a dark blue van. Their equipment was loaded, and they were at the condo parking lot fifty-three minutes later.

That's where they met Dave and O'Brien.

Four members of the team, a mid-thirties woman, and three early forties men, wore coveralls with the words *Klean Pro* on the back of the uniforms. One man wore a dark sports coat, a blue button-down shirt, and gray slacks. They greeted Dave and O'Brien, made introductions, Dave going over more details of what happened and why.

The man in the sports coat, Randall Drake, forty-five, short black hair and light brown eyes said, "This is the agency's top priority right now. The president is very upset. And, on a personal level for us," he motioned to the other men and woman, "we have a problem with crazies assassinating people like Don Blackwell, Simon Rivers and trying to hit you, Dave. Men and women who spent decades in the trenches so that our constitution could stand the test of time and terrorists."

Dave nodded. "Thank you ... let's get in there and see if we can ID whoever tried to take my head off. This is your show, so how do you want to conduct it before the clean-up crew gets to work?"

Drake said, "I will meet with management to obtain surveillance video, and to keep our faces off of it. Right now, we're assuming no one knows there's a dead guy in that condo unit. Or if they did, police would have been here by now."

O'Brien glanced around the parking lot and said, "I've been in this building once. A friend of mine was thinking about buying a unit. I know there's a service elevator that goes all the way up to the top floor and leads to an exit in the rear parking lot near the dumpsters. And there is no security camera near the exit. You can take the body out from there."

The CIA ops eyed O'Brien with a new grade of approval. Drake said, "Sounds good. I'll take our search warrant to management. God knows what we'll find."

Dave nodded. "I know what we'll find. What I don't know is the dead guy's ID; and if we determine that, can we trace him to Abdul Aswad or whomever else is behind this?"

They entered the condo building through the open, well lit, lobby. Mediterranean cream-colored tile, ceramic planters filled with tropical plants—red bromeliads, philodendrons, and elephant ears—gave it a welcoming appearance. No one was in the lobby. Seven wooden paddle fans, hanging from the ceiling, slowly turned. A Gershwin tune, *Summertime*, played softly through hidden speakers.

The cameras weren't hidden. There were two of them in the lobby. Drake glanced around, turned to Dave and said, "I have the paperwork ... and now it's time to go to work. I'll find management. Meet you on the ninth floor."

"Sounds good," Dave said.

They walked toward the elevators, hauling their large plastic containers with handles on the top. The containers, which looked like fishing tackle boxes, were filled with chemicals—compounds for cleaning and erasing human biological matter. They entered the elevator, one of the ops officers pressing the button to the ninth floor, the doors slowly closing.

# Twenty-Eight

The CIA ops picked the lock and entered the condo unit with guns drawn. They wouldn't need them. The man's body was lying on the marble floor less than five feet from the open window. The body was on its back, eyes open, lifeless stare at the ceiling. The metallic odor of sulfur, like in a jar of old pennies, lingered in the room. A small pool of blood trailed less than one foot from the head, a hole the size of a nickel above the right eye.

A yellow blowfly entered the open window and crawled across bluish lips. A sniper's rifle and a camera with a long lens were on the table next to the window. After the ops cleared the unit, O'Brien and Dave entered. They said nothing as the task force assessed the situation and began doing their work, snapping pictures and inspecting the entire premises. They put on rubber gloves, opening the cases they'd brought, removing chemicals, cleaning materials and brushes.

One of the ops officers inspected the rifle and the camera. He said, "It's a T-5000, made in Russia, one of the most deadly and accurate rifles in the world. The camera has an 800-millimeter telephoto lens. He picked up the camera and looked at the last few pictures taken. He cut his eyes up to O'Brien and said, "You're on here. And so is a woman sitting next to you guys." He motioned for Dave and O'Brien to look at the digital screen on the back of the camera. "Before he started firing live rounds from one of the best sniper rifles in the world, he took these pictures."

O'Brien and Dave looked at almost a dozen pictures of them having lunch. Wynona's face clearly recognizable. O'Brien with dark glasses staring right at the condo. The ops officer looked at O'Brien and asked, "Maybe this was the point when you noticed the guy. You could be staring right at the camera." He paused and looked out the window. "From one helluva distance, too. So that's Ponce Marina way out there, correct?"

"That's it," O'Brien said.

"How in the hell did you take that shot from the wheelhouse of a boat, on the water, and hit this killer almost dead center in his head?"

"Just a lucky shot."

Dave eyed O'Brien and cleared his throat and said, "Sean is a humble man."

The female ops officer, Kylie Stuart, slipped on rubber gloves and approached the body. Kylie's hair in a ponytail, her probing blue eyes reflecting the inquiry and demeanor of a medical examiner. She looked slowly from the man's face to his boots, looked all around the body, at the fingernails and said, "Long eyebrows, curved nose, dark green eyes, wide face, and over six feet tall. He could be Persian."

The other ops officers nodded and moved around the unit, looking for the spent round that had exited the back of the man's skull. One of the men, close to six feet tall, stood next to the body and stared out the window. He turned and inspected the walls and ceiling. He walked toward an open closet, paused and looked back at the window, proceeding to the closet.

"Do you see something?" asked Kylie.

"Maybe," said the man, examining the hanging clothes. He noticed something on a white shirt hanging in front of a half-dozen other shirts, slacks, a hoodie sweatshirt, and one sports coat. He could see a bullet hole in the collar. The officer parted the clothes and looked at the wall, the round's point-of-entry at eye level. He used his knuckles to tap to the left and right of the hole, the sound denser below the area where the bullet entered. He turned back to the others and said, "The round went through a shirt and into the wall. It hit a support stud. I'll patch over the hole."

Dave and O'Brien walked closer to the body, Dave staring at the dead man's face.

O'Brien asked, "Recognize him? Maybe from Gitmo?"

"No, I've never seen him before. Granted, facial recognition is more challenging with a bullet hole in the forehead, but I don't recognize what's left of him. Did this man kill Don Blackwell and Simon Rivers … or are there more assassins?"

Randall Drake entered the condo, paused a few feet inside, assessed the area as the others continued the inspection and clean up. They photographed the body and placed it in a long vinyl body bag. They began scrubbing the blood with chemicals they'd brought. There were brushes and a portable vacuum in another container.

Drake walked up to the open window near Dave and O'Brien. He looked at Dave and asked, "Have you seen him before now?"

"No. Kylie said he looks Persian. But that could mean anything. He could be a gun for hire, working in that capacity for Aswad and his group. Or he could be a disciple of the cause and volunteered to kill a few infidels. He may be the solitary assassin that killed Blackwell and Rivers."

O'Brien knelt beside the body and looked at the soles of the dead man's boots. He stood and pulled up the picture of the boot prints he'd taken on the dock, studied the image for less than ten seconds. "This guy was the one standing next to *Gibraltar* the other night. Boot tread patterns match. He's wearing Maelstrom Tac Four. I'll give the image to this team."

Dave glanced down at the boots, looked at O'Brien's phone screen and said, "I'm damn glad you thought to take that picture."

"He was, no doubt, looking at the trajectory … figuring out the shot or shots he'd take." O'Brien turned his head and stared at the body, looking at the face. "What I wonder is how many of these guys Aswad—if it's him behind this—has here, in America, on standby—ready to take up arms like their own brand of radical Islamic minute men to go hunt and gun down retired CIA field agents?"

Dave shook his head. "I don't know. What we do know is this guy is probably one of two assassins working with a directive to murder Don Blackwell, Simon Rivers, Sol Lefko, Robert Lewis, and me. They've taken out two of the five, and I was almost number three."

"They want more than you five," said an ops officer standing by a wicker table in the corner of the room. He glanced through two file folders on the table and said, "They want your daughter dead, too. Her picture and dossier are in this folder. Your picture and info are in the other folder here … and there's folders in that briefcase on Don Blackwell, Simon Rivers, Sol Lefko and Robert Lewis."

Dave asked, "Do you have another pair of plastic gloves?"

"Sure," said one officer, reaching in his forensics kit and picking up the gloves, handing them to Dave.

"Thanks." Dave slipped on the gloves, stepped to the table, opened both folders and looked through them. O'Brien approached and looked at the information. Dave said, "The bastards have addresses for Linda and me. Linda's was her former address here in the states. They've listed information about her shopping habits. Places she frequents … with her kids. And they did the same for me." He read the data. "They know I go to the post office on Fridays. And I sometimes attend St. Aquinas Cathedral on Sundays." He walked over to the open briefcase and went through each folder and added, "They did the same thing for the others, Sol, Robert, Don and Simon." He set the folders back in the briefcase and said, "They're thorough … attention to detail. These dossiers are almost as good as something the CIA would put together."

O'Brien considered the images and data as Dave walked back to the window and looked out, his thoughts hidden, the rolling breakers of the Atlantic to his far right, Ponce Marina in the distance, hundreds of sailboat masts poking the horizon. He looked at O'Brien and said, "I need to call my daughter, Linda, immediately."

O'Brien nodded. "Unfortunately, being in London doesn't make her any safer."

"Yes, there are plenty of hostiles for hire there, too."

"We now know that Linda is in danger. What does that mean for Sol Lefko's daughter, Katie? Although her file isn't in the pile, she's about to set sail in what could become very dangerous waters."

# TWENTY-NINE

Wynona Osceola walked Max near the Ponce Inlet Lighthouse and thought about her conversation with Sean. Max sniffed at the base of a royal palm tree next to the parking lot. The lighthouse, standing 175 feet in the air above Ponce Inlet, wore a coat of paint the shade of ripe tomatoes. The red contrasted against an endless blue sky, like an inverted sapphire bowl surrounding earth.

"Hold on, Max," Wynona said, holding the leash, before Max could trot into the parking lot. A dozen tourists with children in tow came out of the former caretaker's red brick cottage surrounded by a white picket fence. The cottage was the lighthouse's office and souvenir shop, which was filled with T-shirts and picture postcards. The adults held brochures and led the kids to the lighthouse to climb the steps to the top and peer out toward the inlet and the uninterrupted expanse of the Atlantic Ocean.

Wynona was glad that O'Brien wanted to offer her protection, but she wouldn't have become a federal agent and later a police detective if she felt the burning desire for protection. She wrestled with being grateful and flattered and being offended at the same time as if he might think she wasn't good at her job. But she was good. All she ever wanted was truth and justice for crime victims. She wanted to leave the world in a little better place. No fantasies, just the satisfaction of feeling useful. Sean's words were on her mind. *Maybe it's not unlike what the old medicine man told you about the web. It connects all of us in the good, bad and ugly of humanity.*

A car door slammed, getting Wynona's attention. She picked up Max and saw a man in the parking lot that triggered familiarity. His skin was the color of hers, olive. He was paunchy with a close-cropped black and white beard. He turned briefly to look at her. The man had a striking resemblance to Masood Aswad, the butcher—the father—who'd stabbed his only daughter numerous times before Wynona and her FBI partner could kick down the door.

Wynona's mind replayed the night she broke into a house of horror in a neighborhood where children played hide-and-seek after school. It was a middleclass community where families held backyard barbeques and saved for years to afford a trip to Disney for their kids. And it was a neighborhood where an *honor killing* took the life of a sixteen-year-old girl whose crime was she sat in her friend's car at the curb and listened to a new song he wanted her to hear. That was her unforgivable sin under Sharia law.

Max watched a tawny cat come out of the red brick caretaker's cottage. She uttered a growl in the back of her throat. "It's okay, Max," Wynona said. "It's just the lighthouse kitty." She watched the man walk toward the lighthouse. Wynona felt her pulse rise like the fur on a dog's back. Her phone buzzed in her pocket. She looked at the caller ID and answered. "Hi, Sean, I'm almost hesitant to ask what you found in the condo. Also, I just saw a man walking into the Ponce Inlet Lighthouse who reminded me of Masood Aswad. It may be that I'm starting to see his face everywhere as old memories have surfaced—or …"

"Well, don't approach him. I'll have Dave get someone from the team here to take a look. Can you meet me at the Tiki Bar in a half hour?"

"Yes, Max and I went for a long walk. We both felt the need to clear our heads. We're still at the lighthouse. I'll start back."

"Just in case Abdul or his men are near there, go quickly. It's not safe for you to be there alone."

• • •

Dave Collins stood in *Gibraltar's* salon and made a call to his daughter. He glanced at his watch. He hoped that Linda was not yet in bed. She answered on the fifth ring and said, "Hi, Dad. What do I owe the pleasure of a second call from my father in one week? And, sorry, I was going to return your call tonight before I went to bed." Linda Shafer stood in her country kitchen near Watford, England. Her dark hair hung just below her shoulders. She wore faded jeans and a white cotton shirt, the sleeves rolled up at the wrist. A small gold cross hung from a chain around her neck.

Dave asked, "How are the kids?"

"Jessica and Daniel are fine. They're in bed, and hopefully they're asleep. Todd's project this weekend is to fix the garbage disposal. And I'm doing bills. I know that sounds mundane, especially compared to what you used to do, but sometimes ordinary has its perks."

"I miss you and your ardent sense of humor, kiddo."

"Dad, I'm thirty-nine, but I'm still happy to be your kiddo." She smiled and pulled a strand of dark hair behind her right ear. "How are you?"

"I've been better."

"Are you sick?"

"No, at least by the traditional and physical definition, I don't believe I qualify. Although at my age, that's a moveable bar scale." Dave sat in a canvas chair in his salon, looked out at the marina water, the top portion of the lighthouse a mile beyond the tree line. He said, "Linda, you're correct, sometimes the ordinary has its perks. Most of what I did in my career with the CIA I could never tell you or your mother for a lot of reasons, chief among them was your safety."

"What's going on Dad? Your voice sounds different. Are you okay?"

"No, sweetheart, I'm not okay. I hope to be soon, but not right now. I often wondered if my past would ever resurrect itself and cross the road with my present and change my future, or the future of those I dearly love."

"Oh shit … Dad, are you in danger?"

"Yes. And, to some extent, so are you. That's why I'm calling." Dave spent the next few minutes giving her as many details as possible.

When he concluded, he said, "I'm so sorry this is happening. The CIA's office in London has been alerted. They will be keeping an eye on you and your family until we can get through this."

"You mean we'll have bodyguards in our driveway?"

"No, for the most part, you probably won't see them. If you do, it's because they wanted you to. Just keep very vigilant, Linda. Watch the kids, Todd, and yourself. Notice the obscure, anything out of place … any new people that come into your life. And call me, day or night."

"How about you, Dad. You're sixty-six years old. Who's going to watch after you?"

"Don't put me in a walker yet. I don't even use a cane." He managed a smile. "I love you."

"Love you, too, Dad. Be careful … bye."

After she disconnected, Dave held the phone a few inches away from his ear, his thoughts moving from the time he taught Linda how to ride a bike, swimming lessons, to her first date … and then so much of her life that he'd missed. He set his phone down and picked up her picture, his eyes dewy. He looked at it for a long moment, and then looked beyond the harbor to the condominium in the distance. Dave thought about the dead man on the floor, knowing he was one of many foot soldiers they'd send.

# THIRTY

O'Brien sat in a rear section of the Tiki Bar, his back to the wall, watching the parking lot and a portion of the marina. He sipped black coffee with Wynona, the edge of his chair touching the walls in the restaurant—walls built from marine driftwood and weathered planks pulled off old barns. There were knotholes and wormholes etched into the wood and into America's past. Max lay down under O'Brien's chair, her eyes half closed, resting. A dozen customers were in the restaurant, some sitting at the round tables, some at the bar, the scent of fried shrimp and hushpuppies in the air.

Wynona said, "Before you tell me what you discovered in the shooter's condo, I can report that Max and I had bonding time, and I'm impressed how fast she can walk considering that her legs are so short."

O'Brien said, "Max thinks she has the legs of a greyhound." He sipped his coffee and told her what they'd found in the condo. "The ops people were in and out in about three hours. All visible and invisible traces of the body are gone. They're looking at the surveillance video to see if the perp was coming and going with anyone else, or whether he was alone."

"We know he's not alone," Wynona said, stirring her coffee. "He may be a sociopathic loner, but he's not alone. We assume he was working for Abdul Aswad. I guess we'll know that for sure when we find Aswad and politely ask him."

"Randall Drake said the CIA and the FBI are running the deceased's prints and DNA samples through all the databases. They'll use the close-up pictures they took of his face to run through the facial recognition files as well. To do that, they'll use forensic software similar to Photoshop to make the wound in his forehead go away."

"How about his phone? What numbers were on it?"

"It's a burner. He was careful to delete calls. There was no laptop or computer in the room, just the rifle and the camera."

"You said my picture was in there, too."

"The shooter took the photos of us on the boat, and you're sitting next to Dave in the photos. You could easily pass for his daughter, Linda. I believe when the perp fired his rifle, he was aiming for you first, followed by Dave."

Wynona said nothing, raising her shoulders a moment, as if a cold chill crawled through the pores of her skin. She said, "Although I'm off duty, I carry my Beretta in my purse. I hope I don't need to use it ... or better yet, if someone wants to shoot at me, I'm at least in range to defend myself. How did you come to the conclusion that the first round was meant for me?"

"From the moment I turned the table over, the first round hit very close to where your head would have been if he'd had a clear shot. The second round was four feet to the left, in the general area where Dave was sitting before everyone dropped to the deck."

"You actually read the patterns of the rounds in the wooden table to figure trajectory, or the possible targets? Impressive ... that's something they don't teach at Quantico."

"I could have been dead wrong.

"And we could be dead ... at least Dave and I if you hadn't flipped that table so fast. I'm amazed that your reaction time was better than the shooter's time."

"I may have had a slight advantage."

Wynona tilted her head, puzzled and curious. "What do you mean ... slight advantage?"

"It pares down to a half-second. I'd been watching the guy on the balcony before he moved to the window for the shots. When I saw the sun reflect from the lens on the riflescope, I did what I could in a split second."

"But you didn't know it was an actual riflescope at that distance. It could have been a telescope or binoculars. How *did* you know?"

"I didn't. I figured a few spilled drinks and food on the deck would be a small price to pay if I'd been wrong."

"But you weren't. What you did can't be taught at Quantico. It's an instinctive thing … sort of a sixth sense. You have some kind of bizarre gift, Sean. I hope you never take it for granted."

Two bikers pulled into the oyster shell parking lot, their Harley's rumbling, the reverberation causing the surface of the coffee in O'Brien's cup to quiver. He said, "I just get lucky sometimes. Dave spoke with his daughter and her family. They're on alert in London. But, right now, Aswad or his spotters believe, perhaps, that Dave's daughter is here in the Ponce Inlet area … and that you're Linda."

"Maybe that's the way it should remain until we find them."

"What do you mean?"

"As you said, the first round was probably meant for me. Maybe they wanted to have my head explode next to where Dave sat. The shot would have given Dave two seconds to process that horror. Then, before he could wipe the blood and brain matter off his face, the second round hits him. I was going back to the rez, but now I believe I'm needed here more. I have some vacation time. I think I could put it to good use by helping you and Dave … and keeping his daughter alive."

O'Brien said nothing, thinking about what she was volunteering to do. And then he said, "You'd be putting yourself in grave danger to say here. The CIA is following Dave's daughter, Linda. She will have some sort of round-the-clock protection. The agency or the FBI probably has, or will have, people staking out Dave's trawler, trying to intercept trouble before it happens." He paused and leaned closer on the table. "That wouldn't be the case for you, Wynona. You're not his daughter. You're a woman, a friend of mine, who happens to look a lot like Linda. There would be no government protection for you. You'd be a decoy playing a deadly game, someone to draw the attention of people hell bent on killing Dave and the others. They've already assassinated two … if the son of one of Dave's colleagues was murdered, it'd be three. And it looks like he was."

"I understand the risks. And to some extent, I understand the mind of people who are devout followers of Sharia law. I've seen it first hand, and I did something about it."

"They killed your partner. Who knows if they were looking for you before you left the FBI? You told me you traveled a while before taking the job on the Seminole reservation. Maybe they simply couldn't find you. At this point, are they shooting at you because they think you're Dave's daughter … or is it because they know you shot and killed Abdul Aswad's brother?"

"It has to be because I look so much like Linda. They had no idea I'd stop in to see you on a return trip from Jacksonville and that your best friend was one of the ones who interrogated enemy combatants in Gitmo. That kind of coincidence is rare, Sean."

He sipped his coffee, eyes watching the entrance to the restaurant when the screen door opened, and two bikers entered, the men walking up to the bar. "It is rare, and for the most part, I have little faith in coincidental events when it comes to criminal activity. It's usually a direct result of a deliberate action. In this case, it appears to be different. Your episode with Masood Aswad was four years ago. Dave and his CIA colleagues interrogated Abdul Aswad and others in the two years after 9/11. Abdul was in a military prison at Gitmo when you killed his brother. He would not be released for another eight years. The fact that they were brothers is very interesting, but not remarkable. What is remarkable is that you happen to be here, in this marina, as Abdul tries to close in on Dave, and you—the woman who killed Abdul's brother, was sitting right next to Dave. So, it begs the question … was the first shot fired toward you the result of a deliberate action that resulted in Masood Aswad's death … or was it because you could be Linda's twin?"

"We don't know. We do know they're not done. Maybe there is a way I could play the role of Dave's daughter, take the danger off

Dave's real daughter, Linda, and help trap these sick and evil people before they can kill again."

He looked at her, focusing deep into her chestnut brown eyes. "I want to talk you out of it. But I know that's not what *you* want me to do. This will put a direct target on your back. You might as well draw a bull's eye."

"I'm hoping no one will draw a bead on me as a target until we can take the upper hand. You did it on Dave's boat, and you pulled it off in the parking lot of a deserted banana warehouse in Miami with members of the mob shooting everything that moved. I know you'll have my back, Sean. I'm just hoping we can find them before they find us."

He nodded and said, "I'll have your back. But, sometimes, in my case or anyone else's for that matter, the law of averages plays out, and you draw a bad hand. There are times when you can reshuffle the cards; other times, you're out of chips. Let's go find Dave. You need to tell him you're willing to impersonate his daughter in what probably will be the most frightening act of your life."

She shook her head. "No, that happened in a single-family home in Dearborn. In a strange way, maybe it's prepared me for what Dave and the others are facing now."

O'Brien caught a movement out of the corner of his eye. He looked to his far left to see Nick Cronus approaching. Nick walked by the customers sitting at the bar, smiling at a thirty-something brunette in cut-off jeans and a tight T-shirt. She returned the smile. He stopped and said something to her before walking across the restaurant toward O'Brien and Wynona.

O'Brien watched the smile drop on Nick's face, replaced by concern. He came up to the table and said, "Thought I might find you here."

Max stood, tail wagging. O'Brien said, "Join us."

Nick pulled up a wooden chair, using his wide hand to knock peanut shells off the seat. He glanced around the Tiki Bar and lowered his voice, his black eyes shifting from O'Brien to Wynona and back. "Y'all seen Dave?"

"Not since after we left the condo," O'Brien said. "He was going back to *Gibraltar* to call his daughter, but I did talk to him on the phone briefly afterwards. He was just about to get on the call Sol Lefko coordinated between the CIA and FBI. And, I headed here to meet Wynona."

"He told me some of what you guys and the special ops team had to deal with in there. I went to my boat to get money to pay for my slip, walked halfway down the dock and turned around to head back to Dave's boat. Thought I'd see if he wanted me to drop his dock rent check off to Hank in the marina office, but I couldn't find Dave. No sign of him on *Gibraltar*. Man, considering what the hell's happening, I'm damn worried."

# THIRTY-ONE

Dave sat under the shade of a gazebo near the marina boatyard and unsnapped the straps in the leather binocular's carrying case. At this point, it was not unlike a holster, and inside was a Smith & Wesson 9mm. He looked at it for a moment, slowly lifting his eyes up at the boats tethered in the marina. A forty-foot Sea Ray backed out of its slip.

Dave watched a sunburned man in shorts and a tank-top shirt fillet fish at a cleaning station, fish scales flying up from a large mackerel and landing like silver confetti around the man's bare feet. The station was an A-frame chickee with a rustic roof of thatched palm fronds brown as cured tobacco leaves, dried pelican poop splattered on the fronds. The man rinsed the fillets at a sink under the palm fronds, wiping the knife on a white towel.

Dave scanned the other sections of the marina, the boatyard, large storage warehouses, the office and Tiki Bar restaurant fifty yards away from where he sat. He watched a dark-haired man in shorts and a lightweight hoodie read a newspaper on a park bench overlooking the dockside. The man turned the page, glanced up at the waterfront and returned to the paper in his lap.

Dave placed a call to the CIA's deputy director and said, "You have a helluva team down here. They left that condo unit cleaner than it's probably ever been. Do you have anything yet?"

Deputy Director Ben Graham stood by the window in his corner office in Langley, Virginia. His wavy, silver hair looked like it would defy a comb. He wore black-rimmed glasses and a charcoal gray suit. He watched the sea of cars in the parking lot and said, "We do have an ID."

"That was fast."

"Dave, even since you retired, the new databases are staggering. Anyone who makes his or her face public on any social media platforms is now in our system or can be accessed into it. Not that we want ninety-nine percent of the pictures, it's just part of the brave new world."

"I can't imagine a hit man had his face on Facebook."

"He didn't. But a street camera in London captured his image three months ago. He was in East London, coming out the side door of a mosque. He was with an Imam that M15 is investigating for his alleged role in recruiting and radicalizing young, disenfranchised Muslim men. The shooter was Bakur Saba. Born in London to a seventeen-year-old, unwed mother … was raised by his grandmother. No apparent male figure in his life. His mother either disappeared for safety reasons or was the victim of a mercy killing. At eighteen Saba was sent to Saudi Arabia for a year where he was immersed in the kingdom's Wahhabism or strict Sharia fundamentalist Islam. He married there before traveling to Iran and picking up some of the finer points of terrorism, courtesy Isis. In a letter to his cousin, he said strict Sharia Islam is more than religious beliefs … it's a competing civilization, defiant to everything and everyone in the West. We have no record of him entering the country."

Dave stared above his bifocals, watching the Sea Ray ease out of the marina, a small puff of bluish smoke behind the transom at the waterline. "It sounds like a bio that I've read or heard hundreds of times through the years. Do we know how Saba wound up working for or with Abdul Aswad?"

"Not specifically. They traveled within the same circles of influence. Apparently shared many of the same beliefs. But Saba's not alone. We believe someone else killed Don and Simon. Logistics from where they were murdered to where you are in Ponce Inlet are too far apart for it to have been the same shooter. And the caliber of rounds used to kill Don and Simon doesn't match the T-5000 found in the condo unit. That unit was rented for one month to a dummy corporation called A&C Inc."

"Cash payment to the property management company?"

"No, it was a money order. Non-traceable purchaser." Graham walked back to his desk, looked at a framed picture of his wife and only son. It was at his college graduation five years ago, his son in cap and gown. Wide smiles. "Dave, your friend … O'Brien."

"What about him?"

"My ops officers tell me the shot he took, maybe only ten people in the world could have done it. Who the hell is Sean O'Brien? He's your friend, and that's good enough for us to take a good look at his background. Maybe we can recruit him."

Dave managed a smile. "I doubt it. He doesn't work within traditional boundaries, even the loose restrictions we used in the CIA. He's ex-military—Delta Force. Former homicide detective, too. I found out that he had the highest confession record in this division. He has an uncanny ability, a talent, for reading people and the environment around him. It goes beyond just being observant, Ben. In a way, I suppose, it's a sort of unique talent he was born with and learned how to fine-tune it."

Graham sat behind his desk. "Maybe between him and our guys down there, you'll be okay, giving us time to hunt down and eliminate Aswad before he can strike again. We need to cut the head off the snake."

"We dealt with a lot of snakes during my time with the agency. I hope it's the head from the right snake. With these people, it's never catch and release. They'll always try to come back to bite you. And the head is still deadly for a few minutes after it's cut off. A poisonous snake doesn't die quickly."

"Maybe this one will."

Dave glanced toward E dock at the man sitting on the park bench reading the newspaper. The man stood and walked down the dock twenty feet, looking at a Carver 52, still within a visual of Dave. "Ben, do you have eyes on Robert, Sol and me?"

"Yes. We have resources dispatched, using the FBI, too. Hopefully, none of you will need them after Saba was taken out. Maybe that'll send a chilling message up the chain of command."

Dave set the binocular case near his right hand on the bench, holding the phone in his left hand. "It'll disrupt them for a while. But they'll keep coming until we can decapitate the snake, but right now we don't know where the snake's hiding."

"But we will. It's just a matter of time. In the interim, as I told Robert and Sol earlier today, stay very observant. You all have survived a lot of tough situations in your careers, and this is another one. Unfortunately, it's happening when you guys should be letting your guards down, playing golf, and teaching the grandkids how to hook bream."

"The kids and grandkids are the ones I worry about the most. Would one of your sentries here in Florida be about thirty-five, black hair, a quarterback's lanky frame?"

"Even if I knew what he looks like, you know I can't ID him … and for his sake, depending on what's around the bend, you wouldn't want me to."

# THIRTY-TWO

The text came in just as O'Brien was standing from the table in the Tiki Bar. He read it silently, looked at Wynona and Nick and said, "Dave's coming. He said he was on the other side of the marina near the boat ramp."

"What's he doin' there?" asked Nick.

"Probably on his phone speaking with the CIA, FBI or both."

"Considering the fact that he's got two bullet holes to patch up in *Gibraltar*, he oughta hunker down low."

"He's liaising with the CIA, trying to stop the source."

Wynona said, "That flow has a long history, and I'm not convinced it's containable."

"What do you mean?" Nick asked.

"After I witnessed a man butchering his daughter, and after I watched his wife—the girl's mother, hold her down in what they called an honor killing, I've done a lot of soul searching and thinking about how a mother could help murder her own daughter. I thought I knew the mindset of fanaticism. I didn't. Some of America's greatest strengths are the layers of immigrants who've worked to make the nation what it grew to be. That means ethnicities and religions blending into a melting pot of flavors and colors that is red, white and blue. But when a group refuses to assimilate, refuses to accept others for who and what they are—Americans, then there will always be division. Sort of like a leaky pipe that is never fixed and one day floods."

Dave came into the Tiki Bar through the screen door facing the waterfront and walked over to the table. Nick grinned and said, "I looked all around this place. Couldn't find you anywhere. Your vintage Mercedes was parked under the only oak in the lot. So, I thought you were here. I checked with Katie and Andy on N dock. They hadn't seen you. You had me worried, and I'm the no worries guy."

Dave nodded and took a seat next to Wynona. He said, "Thanks for the concern, Nick, which I agree is contrary to your laid-back ways. Nonetheless, it's noted and appreciated." He looked at the coffee cups and said, "I could use a gin and tonic."

O'Brien said, "What's the latest with the CIA and FBI?"

Dave told them what Deputy Director Ben Graham had said, and added, "I believe I have company. He's sitting in the far corner. Shorts and a gray hoodie. Looks like he could have played college football. The hoodie is great for hiding his sidearm. Lousy for Florida weather, though."

O'Brien said, "It's a compromise. Let's hope you don't need his expertise."

"The agency has eyes on Robert Lewis and Katie's dad, Sol Lefko." Dave paused, looked over his bifocals and said, "Investigators found a note left under the wiper blades on Simon Rivers' car. Someone wrote these words … *and then there were three*. So, if the note writer is referring to Robert, Sol and me—that sums it up. Two are killed leaving three of the original players."

O'Brien said, "The words on the note sound like a nursery rhyme or something from an Agatha Christie novel. Interesting."

Wynona said, "The FBI needs to use that in its further profiling of this sick perp." She looked at Dave and asked, "Is the reason that Katie and Andy chose Ponce Marina as a place to haul out and work on their sailboat because you are here? Or was this simply a great spot to prepare for the upcoming voyage?"

"Both, I think. I mentioned it to Sol, and he had Katie call me. I championed the virtues of the place, expertise with reworking boats from structure, electronics—plumbing to wiring. And I told them that the marina is like one large neighborhood watch. I said it's safe and would be the perfect place for them to practice living aboard before heading to the island. Little did I know that her dad and the rest of our group would be in the crosshairs of a fanatic we'd interrogated at Gitmo years ago."

Nick leaned forward in his chair. "You really think Katie might be in danger?"

Dave blew out a long breath. "Maybe. Simon Rivers' son, Carter, died in a car accident. No witnesses. No other cars involved. It was a new Chevy, wireless technology. Did someone hack the computer-controlled operating system?" Dave shifted his eyes over to Wynona and said, "And then there was the two shots fired at us on *Gibraltar*. One, as Sean pointed out … closer to you than anyone at the table. The second was nearer to me. We know the shooter had Linda's dossier. I've almost called you Linda a half-dozen times because of your remarkable resemblance to her. I was the lead CIA officer during the Gitmo interrogations. I think most of Aswad's anger and vengeance is directed to me, that's why Linda is a target. But Katie could be as well."

Wynona asked, "Has her father spoken to her? Let her know to be cautious?"

"Up until we found Linda's file in the condo, we didn't know for sure about the possibility of our adult children becoming targets, too. And now, that's changed. I spoke with Sol and Robert in a conference call with the agency. Sol said he'd talk with her and Andy. Oh, by the way, one of the agents checked out the lighthouse and found no one resembling Abdul Aswad."

Nick nodded and said, "Once Katie and Andy get sailing, it's a big blue ocean out there. I've spent most of my life fishing it. I worked for seasons fishing the islands of the Caribbean, lots of time in Greece, and here in the states. If you want to vanish, a sailing trip is a damn good way to do it. You don't leave tracks on the ocean."

Dave leaned back, his body language slightly more relaxed. He said, "Katie and Andy leave in the morning. I'll feel better when they have a lot of blue water between the marina and *Dragonfly*.

Wynona smiled, glanced over Dave's shoulder to the man in the shorts and hoodie in the far side of the restaurant. She said, "Dave, I have some vacation time. Lots of it, to be exact. I haven't taken much time off in my job. I shared this with Sean and now I want to tell you. My presence here may lessen the danger to Linda in her London home. I want to help you get Aswad. I dealt with one of his brothers in Dearborn. And I can work with you to help take Aswad down wherever he is today."

Dave scratched his white beard and said, "Are you volunteering to stay here at the marina, impersonate my daughter with me, maybe draw out these guys to help take them down?"

"Yes, that's exactly what I'm saying."

"Wynona, that's a very noble cause. And I deeply appreciate your offer. However, in good conscience, I can't ask you to put your life on the line for fanatics who are hell bent on killing me. If something were to happen to you, I would never be able to accept the fact that I allowed you to sacrifice yourself."

Wynona leaned in, placed both hands on the table, palms down and looked straight at Dave. "And if Linda and her family are murdered, your world would stop cold. Let me help you. As a former federal agent, I've had a long history with fanatical jihadists. That doesn't mean I will ever fully understand what drives them to atrocious acts of violence against innocent people and teenage girls. But I do understand how to combat them. I've done it before, and if I have to … I will do it again."

O'Brien said, "Dave, I believe she's going to do it regardless of whether or not you give her permission. I think our next step is deciding how, working with the CIA and FBI, to flush out Abdul Aswad and to do it before someone else is killed."

# THIRTY-THREE

Katie and Andy weren't sure how to take the news. Katie had heard some of it earlier in the day from her father, but the information they were hearing now sounded more ominous. They sat at a table in *Dragonfly's* spacious salon with Dave, O'Brien, Wynona and Nick, the cherry wood polished, the interior smelling like rose oil and lavender incense on the eve of their first sail.

Dave shared some of his conversation with Katie and Andy that he'd had with the deputy director of the CIA. He concluded by saying, "This is really unprecedented. In this business, we always receive our share of personal threats. But rarely, if ever, do the bad guys follow through. And it's usually because they're in prison."

Max slept next to O'Brien on the long seat. He scratched her head.

Katie sipped from a glass of chardonnay, looked at her husband and then at Dave. She said, "The last thing I would have ever thought to pack on *Dragonfly* was a gun. We don't even own one."

"And you may never need one," Dave said. "What we're saying is to be cautious. Be watchful. Be yourselves only ... be damn careful."

Andy asked, "Do you really think these people are coming after Katie and me?"

"I don't know. It's better to have a gun and not need it than to need it and not have one."

"Where am I going to buy a gun on the night before our trip?"

"I'll give you one," Dave said. "I have a Smith & Wesson 500 magnum. You may never need it. But cruising through the islands, even if we didn't have the trouble we have, it's good to be armed."

"Why?" Katie asked. "Pirates of the Caribbean?" She laughed.

Nick grinned. "It's rare, but there are modern day pirates. You guys just stay in the general sailing area we laid out for you, and you should not have a problem. Also, when you're in a harbor or big cove with other sailors, you got people watchin' your backs."

O'Brien said, "Nick's right. Pirates, or pirate raids, are rare in the islands. Usually it has something to do with drug running. Very few sailors, couples and families, have much of any value for pirates to raid their boat."

Wynona nodded and said, "The FBI gets involved in piracy cases when it involves the kidnapping of American citizens or American boats in exchange for a ransom demand, most often, money."

Katie said, "Let's hope the only pirates we see are the ones when Andy and I watch the Pirates of the Caribbean movies while we are anchored in quiet coves imagining the exploits of Blackbeard and Captain Kidd." She looked at Andy, grinning.

Dave said, "Katie, you and Andy are out of here tomorrow. I know what you've been through to get to this point. And I know that part of you would like to treat this information lightheartedly with the pirate jokes and the other part is saying do not be afraid. Don't hold your hopes, dreams, and life hostage to some sick people you've never met or never had a reason to cross your path. We'll find and stop them. I promise you that. In the meantime, go have fun, get the wind in your sails, breathe deeply and laugh loudly—just don't throw caution to the wind. Okay?"

Katie exhaled, pursed her wet lips and said, "Okay. As a little girl, . even as a teenager, for that matter … when all the kids were talking about what their parents did, I never had a clue when it came to my father. Yes, I knew he was a ubiquitous government employee with the state department, but that was about all we knew. Sometimes Dad would be home, like regular dads, arriving at our house around dinnertime and spending time with Mom and me. Other times we wouldn't see him for a month or so. When he was home, he rarely watched TV. Always reading something, whether it was files from his job, a non-fiction book, or National Geographic magazines. His mind was preoccupied; he always seemed to be thinking about something he couldn't share. I used to resent the fact that he didn't just decompress from his job when he came home. But I didn't know why." She paused and looked at Dave. "Now I do. It's because the job never left him … even today, long after he retired."

Dave leaned back in his chair, looked at the navigation station on *Dragonfly* and shifted his eyes to Katie. "Please don't blame your dad or resent him for what he did. Sol was one of the best of the best. He was a patriot, still is, of course. But during his career with the CIA, he made an enormous difference. Katie, let's put it this way … the world is better off because your father made a positive difference in many areas."

She smiled. "That's nice to know. I wish I could have celebrated those small victories with him, but I know that was not possible then, and it's not now." A smile moved over her lips. "I want to toast … to the journey Andy and I are taking tomorrow and to our friends here on the night before departure who are filling us with good advice and alcohol."

Katie, Dave, Nick, O'Brien, Wynona and Andy clinked glasses and Dave said, "We're delighted to be here. Sean and Nick are better at dispensing sailing advice than I am. Nick, as he'll tell you, was born with gills. Sean sailed for years before getting a powerboat. As for me, I've always loved a trawler. I did the great loop from Michigan, where I bought *Gibraltar*, down the mighty Mississippi, through the Gulf coast and eventually settling here at Ponce Marina."

"How'd you choose this marina?" Andy asked.

"The beauty of the surroundings is unsurpassed. The ease of access to the ocean, and, of course, the Intercoastal right at our backdoor."

Katie looked at O'Brien and asked, "Why did you go from a sailboat to a powerboat?"

"The short answer is that I sailed with my wife, Sherri. After she passed away, sailing didn't have the same appeal as it once did. I was resigning from Miami-Dade PD and a friend told me about a boat for sale at a DEA auction. I was thinking about changing careers to charter boat fishing. I saw *Jupiter*, made an offer. She needed work. Still does. But I managed to get her from Lauderdale up to Ponce Inlet."

"Did you become a charter boat captain?" Andy asked.

Nick laughed and said, "He tried, but the only thing my man Sean caught was a German World War Two U-boat sixty-five miles out in the Atlantic. His fishin' skills never kicked into gear. Sean can find *things*—lost things like people, secrets, artifacts, paintings … subs, but he can't locate fish even with a sonar fish-finder."

They all laughed, and O'Brien said, "Nick was my teacher. What does that tell you?"

Katie said, "I want to hear more about the submarine. But before you tell the story, I need to get my phone. I left it in the cockpit." She stood and walked through the salon to the steps leading up to the cockpit. When she stepped outside, the night air was cool, charcoal smoke in the breeze. A horde of moths circled in and out of a cone of light from one of dock lamps attached to the top of a creosote-stained pole. She noticed the silhouette of a man standing just beyond the edge of light. He appeared to be watching *Dragonfly*. He stood there for a moment, amber and red lights from a departing shrimp boat moving in the distance behind him. Katie watched the man for a few seconds before he turned and walked away. She picked up her phone from the console near the helm. There was one text message, and it was from her father. It read: *Call me ASAP. Urgent.*

# THIRTY-FOUR

Katie gripped *Dragonfly's* wheel, her palm warm and moist, the metal cool in her grasp. She phoned her father, the call going to his voicemail. She waited for the beep and said, "Dad, I got your text. Are you and Mom okay? I'm on the boat with Andy. Dave Collins and three of his friends are here as well. Anyway, call me when you get this. Love you." She disconnected and went back inside the boat.

As Katie approached the salon, Andy asked, "Is everything all right?"

"I don't know. Dad left a text message for me. Said it was urgent. But when I called him, it went to his voice-mail." She looked at Dave and said, "Maybe you could check on Dad. Perhaps he's with some of his CIA buddies."

Dave nodded. "I'll make some calls."

She managed a determined smile. "Thanks. Something else … when I was near the helm, I saw a man not too far down N dock, and he was sort of standing there, looking toward *Dragonfly*, just out of the light from the lamppost. He wasn't on his phone, and if he was taking an evening walk, he seemed to do more dawdling than walking. Maybe he's just a sailor and was admiring *Dragonfly's* lines and paint job. I suppose I'm just being more suspicious after our conversations, but I'm doing what you all asked, becoming vigilant without turning paranoid. Somehow, sailboats and saltwater have to be the antidote for paranoia."

Andy poured a cabernet in his wine glass and said, "While you were gone, Wynona was sharing what a Seminole medicine man told her about the mystery of the dragonfly."

Katie said, "Oh, that sounds intriguing. I don't want you to have to repeat yourself, so do you have a condensed version you can tell me, too?"

"Of course. As a little girl, I was told that dragonflies are free spirits embracing a life short-lived. The symbolism with the dragonfly, for us, is to focus on the moment, because all life is short-lived. It's how you live it. The dragonfly, with its iridescent wings and body, looks different depending on the way light strikes it, giving the insect a new coat of colors, almost as if it just flew through a beautiful rainbow and became part of the rainbow for a moment."

Katie smiled, her eyes bright, animated. "I love that. It's so true. How long did you work for the FBI?"

"Almost eight years."

"I imagine the stress level is somewhat lower on the Seminole reservation."

"It's just a different type of stress, but crime and greed know no borders, boundaries, or ethnic preferences."

O'Brien said, "Katie, the guy you saw on the dock … did you get a good enough look to see any physical features. Height? Weight? Maybe the shape of his face?"

Nick cracked one large knuckle on his scarred right hand and asked, "Could you see if he was a black guy or white?"

"No, it's too dark, and he wasn't standing under the streetlamps or dock lamps as they're called here. I did notice that he wore some kind of sweatshirt, like a hoodie and shorts."

O'Brien looked across the table at Dave and said, "That sounds like the guy keeping an eye out for you, Dave, at least the guy on this shift. I assume there are more."

Katie leaned closer, her eyes wide, unblinking, candlelight dancing in her pupils. "What do you mean … the guy keeping an eye out for you? Shifts?"

"They're from the CIA or FBI. I'm really not sure whom the agency deployed. But they're here to try and prevent someone from doing what was done to Don Blackwell and Simon Rivers."

"Are they bodyguards?" Andy asked.

"In a way, yes," Dave said. "But they don't follow me around like the Secret Service is attached to the president. They try to keep a visual perspective on us. They're wired with radios, and they're armed. Hence the hoodie."

Katie hugged her upper arms and asked, "Are they protecting my dad … mom, too?"

Dave nodded. "Your parents are under their surveillance, as is Robert Lewis, and me. And that alone is a good reason for me to bid you and Andy a goodnight until you cast off tomorrow."

Katie said, "You think your presence here could be dangerous to us?"

"At this point, I don't want to risk spending too much time with anyone, really, until we can contain and extinguish the threat."

"And how close is the CIA to doing that?" Katie asked.

"I don't know. But I do know that you and Andy owe it to yourselves to go have a good time and live life. After all, you didn't name this boat *Dragonfly* to be tied to a dock, right?"

Katie shook her head, "Yes. Time to cut the umbilical cord to civilization, whatever that really means anymore."

Dave said, "Regardless, some old ghosts from our past—what your father and I did, shouldn't be allowed to haunt you guys."

Andy touched the tip of his nose, looked from his wine glass up to Dave and said, "That gun you offered us. What kind is it again?"

"It's a Smith & Wesson 500 magnum."

"We appreciate your offer and will accept. I'll return it to you when we get back to the states. You want me to follow you to your boat and pick it up?"

Dave glanced at his watch. "No, no need to do that tonight. I'll bring it to you before you two shove off tomorrow."

Katie asked, "Are you doing that because you don't want Andy to risk something … to be in harm's way following you to your boat, or are you bringing it tomorrow because you're tired and you want to go to bed?" She smiled.

"Both. I'm fatigued because it's been a long day and may be a longer night. And, even with sentries on watch tonight, there's no reason for Andy to walk out in the open around me and possibly jeopardize what you two are about to do together. Very few people ever will have the chance to do what you're going to do."

Dave stood, his back muscles tight. Nick, O'Brien, and Wynona stood as well. They said their goodbyes, a round of hugs, Andy offering Dave a bottle of cabernet that was just uncorked. Dave said, "Cork it and share it on your first night in Bimini. Sean will tell you the best harbor."

O'Brien said, "There are a half-dozen good ones. The Bimini Bay Marina is excellent. You can clear customs in very little time."

As they left the boat and walked down N dock, Nick decided to have a nightcap at the Tiki Bar. O'Brien, Wynona and Dave headed back to L dock and toward *Gibraltar,* Max leading the way. They walked through wide pockets of shadow between the lampposts, some of the lights flickering, the whirring hum of electricity in the warm night air.

The tide was coming in, causing boat bumpers to groan as the rubber compressed against the docks and pilings. The marina water was flat and dark, boat lights and starlight reflecting off the black surface in a silent harmony. O'Brien looked over his shoulder, spotted a man sitting on one of the half-dozen wooden benches along the dock.

As they walked up to *Gibraltar,* standing in the dark shadows, O'Brien said, "Your sentry is at the midway position on the dock … maybe you should buy him a drink at the end of his shift."

Dave chuckled. "I wish I could. When we get through this, I'll buy him and his team a few bottles of Macallan eighteen."

O'Brien nodded. "They'll have earned it. Speaking of scotch, you want to join us on *Jupiter* for last call."

Dave glanced toward the lighthouse, the beam punching through the darkness and sweeping the face of the Atlantic. He looked at the man sitting on the bench two hundred feet away and said, "Almost any other time, it would be a yes. But I've just lost two close friends. I need some time to think through a few things. And I need to call Katie's dad, Sol, to see if he's heard anything more. At this point, I'm almost afraid to ask him."

"I understand."

Wynona said, "We're here if you need us. And that includes just talking, too."

Dave exhaled a chest full of air. He said, "I've never lived my life in fear. It's not that I've been fearless, on the contrary. I've always been cautious. But, right now … I'm anxious. Maybe it's my age. I fear for my daughter and my grandchildren. And after tonight, I fear for Katie and Andy. I remember myself in my prime and wonder where that person is today."

"He's still here," O'Brien said. "And you have every right to be fearful because the game has changed. But you're still at the table, Dave. Let's find a way to make the odds more in our favor."

Dave looked at *Gibraltar*, watched Max sniff a dock piling. He half smiled and said, "Thanks, Sean. At this point, I couldn't have two better-qualified friends to lend their expertise. I'm deeply grateful to the both of you. And what you're doing, Wynona, is far beyond the call of duty."

She smiled. "Let me worry about that, okay?"

O'Brien hesitated and said, "If you hear, see, or think you hear or see something out of the ordinary, call us. We're thirty seconds away."

# THIRTY-FIVE

Two federal agents sipped coffee as they looked for a killer. The agents sat in a black Ford Explorer under the boughs of a large mesquite tree, which was adjacent to the driveway across the street from a retired CIA agent's Arizona home. The agents, both veterans of fighting domestic terrorism, were based in the FBI's Phoenix office. They wore dark polo shirts and jeans and packed 9mm pistols, two twelve-gauge shotguns on the rear seat. They'd bought four large cups of coffee from a convenience store, sipping the black coffee and speaking in low voices.

One agent, close-cropped, brown hair, three days without shaving, said, "We still don't know what these ex-CIA guys did to have such a vendetta come down on them. In the bureau, as you know, we deal with everything from mobsters, gangs, hate groups of all shades, but rarely, if ever, do we have scumbags try to hit our retired agents."

The second man, head shaved, square jaws ruddy, said, "One of the reasons is because we put a lot of the bastards in prison for a long time, and the other reason is we're damn good at covering all of our bases. But, CIA, they're good as hell at covering their tracks. So ... something doesn't add up. As far as these five former CIA officers, I'm not sure anyone in the bureau knows specifically what happened. We do know it wasn't long after 9/11 and the CIA was drilling down hard on these enemy combatants—assholes who bragged about killing thousands of innocents in the World Trade Center. Our patience was getting pretty damn thin. I don't care if we had to waterboard them or break a few knees and faces. It's small in comparison to the deaths and damages they chose to cause."

"And look at all the bombings, shootings, and vehicle terror incidents they've instigated and continue to do around the world." He paused and sipped his coffee. "But you gotta wonder what really happened—exactly whose dick did they step on? In a week, we have two retired CIA officers gunned down, and we're told there are three more with targets on their backs. Let's make sure our guy in that house across the street, gets a lot more time to play with his grandkids. He's earned it."

"Too damn bad retirement means looking over your shoulder and packing a piece when you drive to the grocery store." He scratched his forehead. "It's warm in here." They lowered the windows on the driver and passenger sides and heard the high-pitched staccato chirping from a nighthawk perched at the top of an Indian willow tree. They watched the rustic, sand colored Adobe-Pueblo style home, soft amber lights around a tall cactus and desert willows in rock gardens bordering the home. In the distance, they could hear the faint sounds of a semi-truck going through the gears.

The agent on the passenger side looked at his watch and said, "We know he came home more than two hours ago. His wife is supposed to be out of town visiting her elderly mother in hospice … so it's only Robert Lewis home alone and probably warming up leftover meatloaf in the microwave."

The other agent smiled and said, "I need to stretch my legs for a few seconds. You think Lewis would have a problem with me knocking on his door asking to use the bathroom? A few years ago, I could hold my coffee longer. He stretched and looked to his left just as the bullet hit him in the back of his head, a hole the size of a golf ball exploding above his left eye, blood splattering across the windshield. He collapsed.

The second agent's hand wrapped his pistol grip as a round entered his temple, blood spraying the headrest.

• • •

Robert Lewis sat in his living room and watched the local Phoenix news, catching the weather forecast. He sipped two fingers worth of straight bourbon in a heavy glass and gazed at a shapely brunette on TV. She wore a tight blouse, talked about the heat index, tomorrow's highs and lows, and the humidity forecast. In a way, the woman reminded him of an asset he'd recruited while in Russia. She was killed when her double-agent status was compromised when his identity was exposed—exposed by a breached CIA officer. After her death, Lewis managed to exit Moscow late at night. His eyes were dark as he remembered the events leading up to her murder. *Such a waste of human life and potential.*

Lewis got up from the leather couch, his knees sore. The large room was decorated in a Southwestern motif, a russet Navajo throw rug under the solid wooden coffee table. Pueblo pottery and sandstone vases in some of the corners. Above the fireplace mantle, an expensive oil painting of a sunset over the Arizona desert, the sun's crimson rays visible through the upright arms of a large Saguaro cactus.

He finished his drink, setting the glass in the sink. He glanced at the kitchen clock on the wall and turned, heading upstairs for bed.

*There was a noise.*

*Wind chimes.*

He was puzzled. Normally he couldn't hear the chimes unless the door to the outside was open. He flipped on the backyard floodlights and looked through the glass in the French doors. The elevated terrace was bordered by an extended rock garden with partially buried boulders surrounded by large and small cacti and blue agave plants. The breeze made the wind chimes jingle again and something moved inside. It was the short white curtains hanging over one of the kitchen windows. *A breeze.*

*The window was open.*

And he had not opened it.

Lewis saw a reflection behind him in one of the glass panes on the French door. Just as he turned, a man in a black ski mask said, "You are number three." He fired a single round from a Maxim 9 pistol with a built-in silencer. The noise sounded like someone dropping a book on the floor. The round hit Lewis in the center of his forehead.

He dropped to the sandstone tile, lying on his back, a pool of blood seeping into the grout. The shooter, wearing gloves, lifted a piece of paper from his pocket and dropped it on Lewis' chest as he exhaled a final breath.

The killer stepped over the body, exiting through the back door, the wind chimes now silent.

# THIRTY-SIX

Dave Collins called his friend Sol Lefko and said, "Katie's worried about you. We were on her boat when your text message came through to her phone. Sol, are you okay?"

Sol stood in the hallway of a hospital wing next to a patient's closed door. He glanced at the chart in the plastic holder by the door, his wife's name, *Brenda Lefko*, at the top of the chart. "It's Brenda … she had a heart attack. Doctors are telling me that I got her to the ER in time. They believe she'll recover."

Dave sat on the couch in *Gibraltar's* salon and shook his head. "I'm so sorry to hear that. I wish I were there. Is there anything I can do?"

"If you still believe in prayer, that would help."

"I can do that. Have you spoken to Katie?"

"Yes, she and Andy want to postpone their sailing trip so they can come up here. I told them that wouldn't be necessary because there is nothing they can do." He rubbed his right temple. "Dave, in a way, Brenda is a victim of this tsunami of revenge that's already taken Don and Simon. She wasn't shot, but her heart is suffering from the added stress. After the death of our granddaughter, Madison, something died in Brenda. Her eyes lost some of their brightness. When we went through Katie's fight with cancer, Brenda was there with sleeves rolled up and the stiff upper lip from her British roots. But the one-two punch knocked her into a corner. And, after the deaths of Simon and Don, and fearful for me, she somehow seemed more fragile than I've ever seen her in thirty-five years of marriage."

"Just be with her, Sol. Whisper in her ear. Let her know you're there, and you love her. Remind Brenda that she's a fighter. And she can get through this fight, too."

There was a pause for a few seconds. "Thanks for the reassurance. She is a fighter, and together we're going to fight this."

"Does Robert know what happened to Brenda? Have you spoken with him?"

"No, not yet. Would you mind giving him a call? I need to get back in the hospital room."

"Happy to. Hang in there." Dave disconnected and placed a called to Robert Lewis. After six rings, the call went to voicemail. "Robert … it's Dave. Give me a call when you get this. Sol's wife Brenda had a heart attack. She's in the hospital. He'll give you more information."

• • •

O'Brien sat in the captain's chair in *Jupiter's* fly-bridge, Wynona on the bench seat across from him, Max resting beside her. He said, "Thank you for volunteering—for being willing to stay around the marina to help Dave and his daughter, Linda."

"You're welcome. Wynona pulled her feet up onto the bench. She looked across the marina, the glitter of lights across the water as the boats swayed and dipped in the rising tide. "It's the least I can do. In an odd way, Sean, I'm connected to this. Maybe it's part of the web that Johnnie Tiger talked about—the dark portion. Abdul Aswad is hiding in some spider's lair while his followers go into the killing fields. I emptied my clip into his brother's chest. It effectively ended my career with the FBI. I'm not bitter about that. But what frightens me is the way I felt about what I did."

"What do you mean?"

"I know I could have stopped after the second round. I could tell he was mortally wounded. But I didn't. When I looked at his dead daughter on that kitchen floor, when I saw the twisted, hateful look on his wife's face, her burning eyes … I stepped forward and fired another round into him. Then I took another step and fired again … and again. The final pull of the trigger was the sound of the hammer striking metal. I was out of ammo. And maybe, at that point, I was out of my mind. I've never killed before or since. For weeks I had nightmares, could smell the blood and gun smoke in my nostrils even after long, hot showers."

O'Brien nodded. "You said what frightens you is the way you felt. How did you feel?"

"After I killed him, I was sick to my stomach. I vomited in the bushes in front of the home. I didn't think my hands would stop trembling for the first couple of hours. But as I was putting round after round into Masood Aswad, I felt so justified, so authentic and so primal in a weird sort of way. Never in my wildest imagination would I have ever wanted to be judge, jury and executioner. In a split second, I become all of that and more."

"What's the more?"

She was silent a moment. "I could do it again."

O'Brien said nothing.

Wynona hugged her upper arms. "I would never want to be in that position. But I know there would be no hesitance on my part. It's something I didn't know until I experienced it. Those seven seconds changed me for the rest of my days. In an odd way, it made me even more protective of life." She paused and looked at the lighthouse in the distance, the light winking through the tall palms and Australian pines. "But I felt no remorse for having just killed a man. I felt horrible for the death of his daughter, as if a little piece of millions of daughters and sons … soldiers and victims was inside her as the light faded from her eyes … a little piece of me in there, too." She tilted her head, rubbed Max's shoulder. "Sean, in the bureau, we studied and profiled what we'd call natural born killers. And then there were people who learned to kill, either by circumstance, war, or self-defense. Often, the precious beauty of life itself somehow gets destroyed in the process. I fear that could happen to me."

O'Brien leaned forward in the captain's chair. "An old man I once knew told me he stopped hunting the first time he killed a deer. He said this just after his eighteenth birthday. He and his father had built a deer stand in the lower limbs of a large oak in Michigan's Upper Peninsula. He was eager for his first kill, a coming of age or rite of passage between the generations. And that any trepidation he might feel about his first kill would be gone after he did it."

"Did he kill a deer?"

"Yes, but he wasn't prepared for what happened."

"What happened?" Wynona felt a slight chill in the night.

"After the hunt, the men would gather at the old general store with its potbelly wood stove, hooped cheese under a scratched plastic container, pickled eggs floating in vinegar and sweet onions in gallon jars. They'd talk about the ones that got away—whitetail the size of elk. They'd pour bourbon from a bottle wrapped in a brown paper bag, breaths hard and reeking of pickled eggs, cigars, and Jim Beam. The old man said they wanted him to tell the story of how he killed his first buck. But the problem was that the boy mistook a young buck for a doe. Shot her in the gut. He followed the blood for a hundred yards. Found the young deer crouched in the underbrush, her brown eyes wide, frightened, blood mixing with body fluids and excrement. Death ugly, painful and not happening fast enough. He said the deer looked at him with frightened, questioning, pleading eyes. He didn't know if the doe was pleading to die or live. But living was beyond the question, and he found it hard to aim the rifle at a deer less than ten feet from him. But he did it, his trigger finger shaking, eyes welling, warm tears rolling down his hot cheeks."

"At least he put the doe out of her suffering."

"After the shot, he said the forest became so quiet, as if God demanded a moment of silence for the fallen deer and for him, the teenager who was physically ill and repulsed by what he'd done. He told me he never forgot that moment—carried it with him when he was drafted into the Army and deployed to Vietnam. He told me that after he shot and killed his first soldier, a young man almost his age, after the adrenaline faded, the memories of the deer resurrected. He couldn't shake the finality of death and how all life forms have hardwired connectivity. It was, at that moment in time—the summer of 1964, he felt a piece of him had died in combat, too, because a fragment of him was left behind—inside the man he just killed.

Wynona, when you killed Masood Aswad, justified as it was, maybe deep inside you, the aberrance you had for killing another human surfaced because we're the same species. And that goes back to the web Johnnie Tiger shared with you when you were a teenage girl. I think that's why you're willing to do what you can to help Dave, even pretending to be his daughter."

She smiled. "So, I do have some redeemable qualities, right?"

"Right. Ideally, we are our brother's keeper … unless your brother is Cain."

"The people around this marina, certainly Dave, Nick, and even Flo at the Tiki Bar, are like your family. It's refreshing to see how protective you are of Dave."

O'Brien sat back in his chair, looked across the dock to *Gibraltar,* a soft light coming from her salon. "I wish I could do more. Dave's hurting. Losing friends not to death by natural causes, but rather death by deviant causes—murder born from vengeance."

"What can you do?"

"I got lucky with the first guy I took out. It may not happen again. Dave and the rest of the retired operatives in his group are working with the CIA and FBI. He said the agencies have a deep covert dragnet out for Abdul Aswad. They just haven't found him yet. I don't like playing a waiting game, playing defense. Offense is what I do when I have to. But in Dave's case, the enemy isn't yet defined, at least in a geographic scope for me to be effective."

"It's not like you can fly to the Middle East and attempt to track this guy down."

"Maybe he's not in the Middle East. That's where he was sent after Gitmo, but it doesn't mean that's where he is now. What if he was calling the shots right here in America?"

# THIRTY-SEVEN

A short blast from a shrimp boat horn rang across the marina. Stars like diamond dust blown into the night sky, the humid Florida air somehow heavier. Wynona looked toward the north section of the docks and asked, "Why would Abdul Aswad be in the states? How could he be here?"

O'Brien said, "Why … because this would be the last place on the planet we'd hunt for him. How? That's easy. These guys don't enter the country through airports. They never see customs inspections. They come in on small planes from the islands. They enter by boat, arriving into a backwater harbor town in the dead of night. It's not hard to do. Or they slip across the borders of Canada or Mexico."

Wynona watched the shrimp boat approach the docks. "I wonder if they could have entered the homeland right here in Ponce Inlet and this marina." She pointed to the north section of the docks. "How do we know whether the shrimp boat that just arrived at Ponce Marina doesn't have illegal and undocumented people aboard?"

O'Brien looked from the north part of the dock back to her and said, "We don't."

Wynona glanced down at her unzipped purse, the grip of the Beretta just visible. "It's getting late. I suppose I should be going."

"I thought you wanted to stay to help Dave."

"I do. That's why I want your recommendation for a hotel in the area. I'll book a room." She smiled.

"You're welcome to stay here. There's plenty of room on *Jupiter*. You can have the master cabin or the guest's berth."

"Oh, I get my choice?"

"Yes."

"I don't want to displace you, so I'll forgo the master cabin for whatever is available. My suitcase is in my car. I'll go get it."

"No, you won't, at least not alone. I'll go with you. And don't argue, if you're going to play the role of Dave's daughter, you know the risks."

She tried to hide her smile. "So, you'll lessen those risks, huh?"

"Yeah ... at least I'll help level the playing field."

"Remember, I have a Beretta in my purse. I know how to use it. I'll be fine."

"No doubt. But it's time for Max to have her walk. The three of us can go."

"You, Sean O'Brien, are a persistent man."

• • •

Wynona unpacked her suitcase in the guest cabin and walked back to the salon. Max jumped up on the couch and curled into a ball. O'Brien stood behind the small bar and said, "Would you like a drink, or maybe a glass of wine?"

"How about a whiskey?"

"Sure ... what kind, Irish, Scottish or Tennessee?"

She grinned and sat on one of the three barstools. "You know us Indians really can't hold our whiskey. We call it firewater. However, a complex red wine to help make life simple would be great."

O'Brien smiled and pulled the cork from a bottle of cabernet and half filled two glasses. He handed her one and said, "It's a cab."

She took the glass and said, "Did you ever drink a cab in the back of a cab?"

"Can't say I ever did. Have you?"

"Once, and once is enough. It was my first time in New York City. I'd just graduated from college. My best friend at the time,

Michelle and I spent a couple of days in New York before we headed out on our career paths. The irony is that, right out of the gate, she landed a job back in New York working for a public relations firm."

"Is she still there?"

Wynona sipped her wine, her eyes suddenly remote. "No, three kids and two husbands later, she's living in Albuquerque and works for the state department of transportation, writing news releases and bored out of her mind." She looked at a framed picture on a table next to the couch. It was a mid-length shot of a dark-haired woman in a sundress standing on the deck of a boat, wind in her hair, wide smile. "Is that a photo of your wife?"

"Yes, that's Sherri. We were on our sailboat, just leaving Cat Island for Castaway Cay. She loved to sail, and she was very good at the helm, a natural. Sherri was a woman who could read the sea and wind, and she could use both to navigate the boat without ever fighting either."

"She's beautiful. I can tell how much you loved her just by the way you look at her picture."

"I miss Sherri, and always will. Let's go topside. That way we can keep a better eye on Dave's boat."

They sat back in the fly-bridge, Max to the left of Wynona on the long bench seat, O'Brien to Wynona's right. They watched *Gibraltar,* O'Brien glancing up at the condo across the marina, the top left corner unit black. Beyond the condo, the lighthouse hurled a beam across the face of the dark sea. A half moon rose over the Atlantic, the warm breeze through the tidal flats carrying the perfume of blooming mangroves mixed with the musty scent of breeding crustaceans caught in a receding tide.

Wynona said, "It's beautiful and so tranquil up here at night, water almost everywhere you look. I can see why you love it."

"The sea has a way of tossing a cast net over me. Once you fall into the spell of the ocean, the chant of the breakers or the rush of water across the bow of a sailboat, it seduces you with the whisper of song that mixes in your blood like salt in the sea air. Both are inseparable. It stays with you."

Wynona took a deep breath through her nostrils as if she was recognizing the coastal scents of the night air for the first time. "Something that's stayed with me, Sean, and always will, was how you saved my life in the parking lot. Nick identifies with that and calls you his brother for saving his life. I don't feel like I'm your sister, though."

O'Brien watched her brown eyes soften, and he asked, "What do you feel like?"

She positioned her body toward him, her eyes searching his face. "I'm not sure. That night we made love … it stayed with me, too. I have no illusions, but I know in my heart it was different, not that I have a lot of one-night stands. Trust me, I don't. That time with you, though, was different. The physical part was nice, but it went, at least for me, far beyond that. I felt a connection with you I've never had with another man. I'm not talking about love … at least I don't think I am. What I'm trying to say is I felt a deep bond that still whispers to me like the sea does to you."

O'Brien said nothing, waiting for Wynona to finish expressing her thoughts.

She pulled a lock of her dark hair behind her right ear and said, "I don't know if it has to do with the fact that you save my life two days later. Maybe a near death experience combined with meaningful sex results in some kind of an out of body experience." She smiled. "Whatever it was … it still is, for me."

O'Brien touched her hand. She pursed her full lips, exhaled, and said, "I'm so sorry, Sean. I didn't mean to pop back in your world and expect us to … to pick up like long lost lovers. I simply missed you. I thought if we could spend a little more time together, maybe see what, if anything, develops. God, that sounds so damn selfish. So all about me, and I'm not like that."

"I know, and I'm glad you're here. I felt something, too."

"You did? And you're really glad I'm here?"

"Yes."

"You know I'm really not a stalker." She smiled wide.

"Our challenge, like it was when we were trying to keep Joe Billie from death row, is navigating the waters of people killing CIA retirees and attempting to kill you and Dave. That brings a different dynamic to reconnecting."

"I'm the first to understand. In lieu of taking walks on the beach, we're trying to find a crack in the armor of what I believe is absolute evil. I've experienced it firsthand, and now I feel it's just off the fringe."

"You and I are engaged in an aberrant form of combat—a type of war in which our enemy is invisible. When one of us catches a glimmer of it, like I did in that condo unit, we might have the opportunity to do something. It's the unseen foe, the archers just beyond the ridgeline, that worries me."

She nodded. "You said it worries you … but does it scare you. Are you frightened, Sean?"

He cut his eyes from Dave's boat to Wynona. "What frightens me is what can happen to people I care about … you and Dave. I think that alone is what makes me reduce fear to an emotion and, instead, become fearless. It's the only way I can survive when people carrying guns are coming for someone who I care about … or coming for me."

"It's a war. Maybe declared two thousand years ago. Someone once said all is fair in love and war. I don't agree. Neither is fair, no more than the fairness of life. I do believe that war, the closeness to death it brings, can instill a sense of desperation or personal mortality and the longing to find the opposite … life and love."

O'Brien started to respond when he noticed a silhouette on Dave's boat.

A shadow moving in the shadows.

# THIRTY-EIGHT

Max lifted her ears. She stood on the bench next to Wynona. O'Brien was already standing, watching from *Jupiter's* fly-bridge across the dock to *Gibraltar*. He said, "Someone may be on Dave's boat." He kicked off his boat shoes, picked up his Glock from the table next to the captain's chair. He looked at Wynona and said, "I'll be right back," turning and moving silently down the steps.

Wynona lifted the Beretta from her purse. "Shhh, Max," she whispered, leaving the fly-bridge.

O'Brien was already across the dock, a round chambered in his pistol. He walked quietly in his bare feet, a trace of dew on the dock. He heard something behind him, turning quickly, Glock aimed. He saw Wynona coming, nodded and used a hand signal to point to the cockpit of *Gibraltar*. All of the trawler lights were off—dark, the boat barely swaying in the changing tide.

O'Brien lowered his Glock as he came closer. He could see it was Dave, dressed in a black T-shirt and dark shorts, looking toward the night sky, stars ablaze. Wynona came up behind O'Brien and said, "It's a great night for stargazing."

Dave turned around and looked at them. Even in the dark shadows, O'Brien could see his old friend was distraught. He said, "I'm not sure I've ever seen *Gibraltar* with all of her lights off. And I can't remember the last time you weren't dressed in a tropical print shirt. What's going on?"

"Come aboard. It's nice to go dark once in a while and stare at the majesty of the heavens."

O'Brien and Wynona walked over the gangway to the cockpit. O'Brien could smell the scotch on Dave's breath. He looked at them, glanced at their pistols and said, "I don't recall requesting the cavalry."

O'Brien said, "Didn't have to. Neighborhood watch is effective in a tightknit community, such as a marina. Are you okay, Dave?"

"I'm not sure I ever could define *okay* in my life. It's one of those sheepish words used to describe the human condition when something is tolerable, not so much acceptable, but too often sufferable."

O'Brien said nothing, letting Dave find the words he needed. After a few seconds, he continued. "I wanted some fresh air, so I turned off every light on *Gibraltar*, changed into my ninja clothes, planted my 12-gauge shotgun next to the cockpit table, and trudged like a bear coming out of hibernation and looking to the north for a sign of spring, the Aurora Borealis. Alas, here in Florida, we have a spectacular view of the Milky Way and the constellations. But the Northern Lights, with their dance of pale green and white illuminations, are a ballet of mystery. When I was a lad, my mother told me the lights were the angels twirling across the heavens. The Ojibwe Tribe near Lake Superior said the lights represented their departed friends—a dance of the dead." He looked at Wynona and half smiled. "Perhaps the Seminole have something similar for their dearly departed. However, the family members of my murdered friends have no brightly colored lights to equate to dark and bloody slaughters." He paused and looked from Wynona to O'Brien. "They only have death and taunting notes left behind. I just got word that Robert Lewis was murdered in his Arizona home."

"I'm so sorry to hear that," said Wynona, her voice just above a whisper.

O'Brien slipped his Glock under his belt in the small of his back. "I'm sorry, Dave. I remember you telling me about Robert—his work ethic and his love of classical music."

Dave granted. "Mozart was his favorite, but he loved them all."

"What happened?" O'Brien asked.

"The killer broke into Robert's house, shot him in the head and then left a printed note on Robert's chest that read: *And now there are two.* Two FBI field agents were shot as well. They had been staking out Robert's house. Both agents were shot at close range. And it appears the shooter used a silencer. The neighbors said they heard nothing.

O'Brien was silent, his thoughts racing. "Dave, let's focus on these notes for a second, the one the killer left, *and then there are two.* Prior to that the note left under Simon Rivers wiper blades read: *and then there are three.* These sound like lines out of the Agatha Christi's mystery novel, *And Then There Were None.* Why would Aswad or his assassins leave that on the body?"

Dave thought for a second, *Gibraltar* slightly rocking. "I don't know. The premise of that book deals with ten people lured to an island and each killed. Loosely based off the nursery rhyme, *Ten Little Indians* … and then there were none."

Wynona smiled and said, "*Ten Little Indians …* I beg your pardon."

O'Brien said, "The novel, though, dealt with how the perfect murders could go unsolved had it not been for the ego of the killer wanting credit."

Dave nodded. "Indeed, the irony, if there is one in a story about ten unsolvable perfect murders, is the piteous human need for recognition, thus the confession. This contradicts the goal of the perfect murders, defeating the original purpose of the crimes."

Wynona glanced at Dave and asked, "But why would that note, as mocking and sardonic as it sounds, be left on the body of a former CIA officer shot in his home? Another thing—"

O'Brien held up his hand for silence just as one of the planks on the auxiliary dock creaked. A shadow moved. O'Brien lifted his Glock, motioned for Dave to step inside the salon. Wynona, Beretta in her right hand, ushered Dave into cover.

O'Brien hid behind the alcove of the salon door. Three seconds later, his Glock was pointed dead center at a man's chest. "Don't move!" O'Brien ordered. "Slowly, set your piece on the dock and back up."

The man looked like a typical boater, cut-off jean shorts, untucked shirt, running shoes. He had a wide chest. His haggard face was shiny from sweat. Pistol in his right hand. He said, "Okay. I'm FBI—Special Agent Keith Purvis. Who the hell are you?"

"No Q&A until the gun is down."

The man complied, setting the nine-millimeter on the dock. Dave walked out from the dark shadows and said, "He used the *okay* word. I rest my case. And, Sean you can rest the point-blank stance. The gentleman you just ordered to relinquish his sidearm is, indeed, a federal agent."

O'Brien didn't take his eyes off the man. He said, "Wynona … can you please pick up this agent's gun, and then we can continue with the Q&A?"

"Sure," she said, walking across the gangplank to the auxiliary dock, lifting up the gun and returning to *Gibraltar's* cockpit.

O'Brien lowered his Glock. "Dave, maybe this federal agent would like to join us. It's your boat."

Dave nodded. "Special Agent Purvis, please come aboard. Sean and Wynona are friends of mine."

The agent scratched his right jaw for a second and came aboard. He stared at O'Brien and said, "Was all this Barney Fife gun waving really necessary?"

O'Brien almost smiled. "Dave just had another close friend murdered today. Two federal agents, just like you, were watching his house. They were shot and killed. And had you made a wrong move, you would have joined them tonight. Yes, the Glock was necessary. Now, it's my turn. What the hell are you doing approaching Dave's boat this late?"

"I saw motion on it and came to check it out."

"Had I been an assassin, that motion would have been a round through Dave's head. Where were you conducting your watch?"

He gestured toward the stern. "Directly across from this trawler on M dock is a houseboat the Bureau rented. We have three agents alternating shifts."

O'Brien looked at the boats lined up and down M dock. Most were dark. A few had interior lights on, shadows moving on decks. He said, "That's a great perspective, the houseboat, the only problem is, if you see something suspicious, it could take you too long to get over here to stop it."

"Maybe. We also have two rifles with night-scopes. I spotted movement, didn't see your sidearm drawn, but thought I'd come check it out."

Wynona said, "Originally there were two guns drawn, Sean's and mine." She extended her had. "I'm Wynona Osceola. I used to work at the bureau."

He angled his head for a moment. "That name sounds familiar." His eyes widened. "You were the agent who took out Masood Aswad near Detroit." He looked at Wynona as if he wanted to study her. "For what it's worth, I think what you did was justified. It sent a strong message to Islamic fundamentalists hell bent on doing harm in our homeland. It's good to meet you." He shook her hand.

"Likewise," she said, handing the agent his pistol. They talked for a minute about the recent changes within the FBI.

O'Brien looked at the dark houseboat tied to M dock. He shoved his Glock under his belt and said, "Thanks for dropping by *Gibraltar*. If you'll excuse us, I need to talk with Dave."

Special Agent Purvis nodded, handed cards out and said, "My cell number and the numbers to the two other agents are on the back of the cards." He looked at Dave. "Call us if anything or anyone looks suspicious." He turned and left.

O'Brien cut his eyes over to Dave and said, "We need to talk."

# THIRTY-NINE

O'Brien pulled the drapes over *Gibraltar's* salon windows. He peered out a crack in the curtains on the starboard side, watching the federal agent walk down L dock through the funnels of light cast by the pier lamps. Wynona sat in one of the canvas deck chairs, Dave on the couch. O'Brien turned from the window and said, "I think you need to blend into some form of witness protection program, whatever the CIA has to hide, relocate, or transform its retired officers into something that's not a moveable target."

Dave leaned back on the couch. "It's not safe anywhere. But it's safer here with a security detail, and limited access to the dock for the general public, especially after dark. Where the hell would I go anyway?"

"My cabin on the river. You've been there. It's secluded. Sits on three acres. The nearest neighbor is a mile away. You have the Ocala National Forest directly across the river. Much of the forest in the area is swampy, full of snakes and gators. Nobody's coming through that way. Stay there for a while until this thing ends."

"When will that happen? These people have armies of punch-drunk haters of all things West. The work my colleagues and I performed is simply fuel on the fire of their pompous doctrine of destruction. They've assassinated three former CIA officers in less than a week. Attempted to kill me. But they didn't plan on you being here,

Sean. We know the killer took photographs of us dining on my boat. They may already have your ID, probably Wynonna's as well. Nick may not be safe either. But immediately, it's me they want. I'm sure it's all over the news." Dave picked up a TV remote control off the table and turned on the set over the bar. He scanned through the cable news channels, stopping as a story unfolded.

The graphic to the left of the TV news anchorwoman read: *Third CIA Victim?* Dave turned up the sound and the news anchor said, "Three people are dead in an affluent neighborhood of Scottsdale, Arizona. Two are known FBI agents, and one is a suspected retired agent of the CIA. Brad Holden is live on the scene. Brad, what do you know so far?"

The live shot cut to a somber-faced reporter wearing a polo shirt and khaki slacks, standing in a neighborhood of upscale, adobe-type homes, dozens of flashing red-and-white lights from police vehicles in the background. The coroner's vans also were visible beyond the reporter. He said, "Detectives have notified next of kin and have released the names of the victims. This is the exclusive neighborhood of Paradise Estates near Camelback. Two FBI agents were found shot to death in their parked car. We're told they were on a stakeout, watching the residence of Robert Lewis. Lewis was found shot to death in his home by officers responding to a call from a neighbor who, returning from a walk, noticed the two deceased men in a car across the street from Lewis' home. The FBI agents have been identified as John Cohen and Matthew Spencer. Lewis, according to investigators, had retired from the CIA five years ago. He joins the list as number three of retired CIA employees recently killed—one shot to death on a golf course and the other shot as he went for his morning run around an outdoor track at a community college. These deaths happened in different parts of the country. That is essentially all the information we have at this moment. The CIA hasn't released a statement and is not offering information. Did these three men work together before retiring? If so, what did they do and, literally, where in the world did they work? None of that is known … or released at this time."

The image cut to a split screen of the reporter and anchorwoman. She asked, "Brad, do police have witnesses or suspects?"

"Not at this time on either account. One of the detectives told me that preliminary reports indicate that no one saw, or at least no one has come forth to say they saw anything suspicious before or after the deaths of the three men. Police believe the FBI agents were killed first and, from that point, the killer or killers entered Robert Lewis' home and shot him. Ballistic reports are ordered to determine if the same gun killed all three men. And to answer your questions about suspects, local and federal investigators are keeping tight-lipped about that for fear of compromising the investigation. However, the question remains … is this third death of a retired CIA employee the end … or are there others targeted and why?"

Dave muted the sound and said, "It's good to see that investigators didn't tell the news media, at least thus far, about the note found on Robert that read … *and now there are two.* The CIA has stopped and started foreign revolutions. We've helped bring down brutal dictators responsible for the deaths of hundreds and sometimes thousands of innocent people. And now, here in the homeland, a rogue enemy combatant is slaughtering retired CIA officers and taking out active FBI agents. This has to end now."

Wynona said, "Dave, I think Sean makes a strong point. A secluded cabin in a remote part of Florida might be better than here at the marina."

Dave nodded. "Yes, however, I'd imagine that you'd be quick to concur there is no safe place on earth with today's tracking devices. Regardless, I've never been one to be held hostage by another man's delusions. It is one of the things I've fought against all my adult life. Sean, I sincerely appreciate your offer. I'll think about it and let you know. I do consider it to be a viable option. I also know how deep our covert teams are penetrating Aswad's world. It's just a short time before he's shot like Gaddafi was—hiding in a sewer pipe somewhere in the Middle East."

"What if he's not in the Middle East?" O'Brien asked. "What if he's right here in the States or somewhere close enough to easily direct these killers?"

Dave almost smiled. "I doubt that's the case."

"When and where was Aswad last seen?"

"Two years ago. Iran, near Al-Fallujah."

"He could be anywhere today. The guy I took out ... what were the results from tracking the electronic forensics on his phone? Where'd he send the picture he snapped of us on *Gibraltar*?"

Dave reached under a stack of National Geographic magazines on his coffee table and lifted up a lined yellow legal pad of paper. O'Brien could see extensive notes on the first sheet. Dave put on his bifocals and read silently for a moment. He looked up over his glasses and said, "Not much data, of course, from the burner phone we found in the condo. The photo was encrypted and sent through dummy proxy servers. No real IP address. Very hard to trace."

O'Brien said nothing. He sat in a chair next to Wynona and asked, "Where is the phone?"

"CIA gave it to NSA. Why?"

"If we can't trace it through the Internet, we might try something else."

"What?" Wynona asked. "When someone buys a burner, they're anonymous. Telcom carriers don't ask for an ID. The buyer buys the phone and the airtime. That's it."

O'Brien said, "But there may be a record from the store where the phone was bought."

Dave said, "Not if he paid with cash."

O'Brien glanced at L dock, shifting his eyes to the houseboat and then back at Dave. "Sometimes people remember cash transactions because they're becoming rare. Regardless, maybe when the phone was bought, the clerk scanned the UPC code."

Dave smiled. "I like the way your mind works, Sean. If we can't track the bastards through the 'net, let's go terrestrial. Even when you're not on your phone, all cell phones 'talk,' if you will, to cell towers. Sort of like ships passing in the night. And in addition to a UPC code, phones, even burners, have an IMEI or ESN number code. That may have been scanned, too, at the point of purchase."

Wynona said, "Maybe the company that shipped the burners has a record of the phones they sold to each particular store, perhaps matching the IMEI numbers."

Dave looked at his notes. "Let's hope NSA is running all of that through its super computers, looking for matches."

O'Brien said, "Sometimes NSA and CIA, for that matter, the FBI, get so focused on international parameters—tracing through the Internet and via satellite, that burner phones, because of their use-and-toss technology, fall through the cyber cracks. Wouldn't hurt to call them in the morning. Maybe they found something already."

# FORTY

It was near 1:00 a.m. when O'Brien and Wynona returned to *Jupiter*, Max greeting them both like they'd been gone for days. O'Brien said, "We're back, kiddo. I'll take you for a quick walk."

Wynona folded her arms across her breasts. "While you two go for a stroll, do you mind if I use the larger shower?"

"It's all yours. Towels are in the closet to the left of the head. Extra bars of soap, too."

She smiled. "Thanks, but I packed my own. Not that I haven't ever used a man's soap. I have."

"I didn't know there was much of a difference."

"Trust me, there is." She grinned, turned and went to her cabin.

O'Brien waited a moment, picked up his Glock, slid it under his belt, shirt untucked. "Let's go, Max. Wynona calls it a stroll. That'll work, right?"

Max tilted her head, sniffed, and trotted toward the sliding glass doors leading to the cockpit. She walked alongside O'Brien, past *Gibraltar*, the trawler cast in dark shadows. They moved quietly past Nick's boat, *St. Michael*, the sound of Greek music just audible, coming from inside the darkened salon. They walked down the long dock, moths circling beneath the lamps in chutes of light, the brackish scent of algae and bare barnacles in an ebbing tide, the swirling gurgle of fast water moving against the pilings.

O'Brien looked over to M dock, toward the houseboat in silhouette. He wondered if one of the federal agents was watching him through a night-scope. He thought of Katie and Andy Scott in *Dragonfly*, the sailboat secured to N dock on the eve of their last day in the States for a long time. *They'll probably be safer in the islands. Let Dragonfly stretch her wings in the seas of anonymity.*

O'Brien unlocked the entrance to L dock, Max scampering by his boat shoes. He relocked it, and they walked near the Tiki Bar restaurant toward the marina parking lot. There were less than a dozen cars in the lot, most belonging to employees. He could hear conversation coming from the kitchen and bar area. Three motorcycles were parked under a building awning. "Come on, Max." He walked her to a large grassy lot, the sound of ocean breakers just behind the dark road and sand dunes filled with sea oats swaying in the night breeze.

O'Brien watched Max and thought about the talks with Dave. '*The premise of that book deals with ten people lured to an island and each killed. Loosely based off the nursery rhyme,* Ten Little Indians … *and then there were none.'* O'Brien looked up at the moonlight breaking through the saw-toothed fronds on a tall royal palm, his mind replaying conversations, '*The irony, if there is one in a story about ten unsolvable perfect murders, is the piteous human need for recognition, thus the confession. This contradicts the goal of the perfect murders, defeating the original purpose of the crimes.'*

The wind died, and he could hear the breakers rolling beyond the sand dunes, the night sky throbbing with starlight. He thought about the CIA eraser team that removed the body from the condo, and the file folders that they found in the room. How Dave's eyes narrowed as he read them, reading a profile of his own daughter. '*These dossiers are almost as good as something the CIA would put together.* O'Brien replayed Dave's comments about Richard Thurston, '*He's been locked up in a supermax prison for years and will be for the rest of his life.'*

"Max, let's head back. Maybe solving this will boil down to tracking the egos of the evil.

• • •

Wynona was sitting in a corner of the couch, in dark pajamas, reading a book under soft light from a lamp when O'Brien slid open the glass door, Max trotting inside *Jupiter's* salon, her eyes bright. Wynona looked up and said, "Welcome back. I assume all is quiet on the western front of Ponce Marina."

"As far as I can tell." O'Brien set his Glock on the bar. He sat in a canvas director's chair opposite the couch. "One of the reasons I enjoy long walks on the beach with Max is that it often helps me put complicated things in a little better perspective."

"Being by the water can do that."

"We assume that Abdul Aswad is behind these killings. Often, when a sociopath leading a terrorists group blows something up or murders people, the group is quick to take credit. That hasn't happened with the murders of three former CIA officers. What investigators have found are the notes … and now there are three or two. Ostensibly, reflecting the verbiage used in the Christie novel, *And Then There Were None.*"

Wynona set her book down. "Okay, you have my full attention."

"When a person or group enjoys taking credit for hurting or killing someone, the all-consuming narcissist's desire is for recognition … the ego rises out of the cesspool and exposes its Achilles heel."

"Sean, what are you suggesting?"

"We have to find that exposed heel now. We know that Richard Thurston certainly had or has the motive to retaliate against some of his former CIA colleagues, the ones who set the trap and caught him, resulting in a prison sentence for life. Dave said Thurston is known to have taken more than sixteen million dollars from the Russians, and it's believed that figure is on the lesser side. Before going to prison, what if he put together a plan to have his former coworkers assassinated, one by one, after he was locked up."

"Why wait so long?"

"Maybe it was because Dave and the others were scattered around the world as active CIA officers. Once they all retired, moved back to the States, led relatively sedentary lives, they became easier targets. If Thurston had millions stashed away, he could have cut a deal with someone, offering a few million to start the killing spree. He could have withheld instructions to claim the remaining balance until the last man was dead … *and then there were none."*

Wynona leaned forward on the couch. "Do you think the FBI, CIA and NSA are chasing ghosts in trying to capture Abdul Aswad when all along the mastermind is sitting inside a federal supermax prison?"

"It's possible. It's more than possible because Thurston, as a double agent—a mole, was one of the best of the best. Smarter and more diabolical than spies, such as Richard Hanssen or Aldrich Ames, two other former CIA officers convicted of passing secrets to the Russians. Dave said it was so difficult to catch Thurston because he didn't leave tracks in the traditional sense."

"Thurston would have intimate knowledge of how the CIA works, thus potentially keeping a smokescreen around his plans all the way through today … if it is him behind this. The question is how would the FBI and the CIA prove it?"

"By setting a trap."

# FORTY-ONE

The last time O'Brien glanced at the digital display on his bedside clock it read: 2:17. He stood next to the bed in the master berth, looking out the starboard porthole to Dave's boat. All seemed quiet and motionless. *Maybe the feds were doing their job.* He stretched out on the bed, his mind still thinking about scenarios that might catch a killer whether he is hiding in a mosque somewhere in Iran or sitting in a six-by-nine cell inside a federal penitentiary.

Fatigue built behind his eyes and soon sleep silenced his conscious mind and allowed the subconscious to rise in a kaleidoscope of disjointed images. One moment he was looking through a sniper's scope in the hills of Afghanistan juxtaposing immediately through the riflescope on *Gibraltar's* wheelhouse. The image cut to the frightened face of a teenaged girl he found walking at midnight on a remote back road deep inside the Ocala National Forest. When O'Brien slowed his Jeep to speak with her, the headlights captured the panicked look in the girl's eyes, wide—distrusting, like the iconic National Geographic image of the Afghan Girl as a teenager photographed in a refugee camp, her large green eyes staring straight into the camera.

There was nothing but blackness. The only sound was his heavy breathing and the crunch of his combat boots against the rocky terrain one hundred kilometers north of Kandahar. Then there was a sliver of

TOM LOWE

color. Crimson in the eastern horizon, the sound of Blackhawk helicopters coming—black dots against a cherry sky.

Something touched his leg.

O'Brien barely opened his eyes; moonlight coming through the clear skylight above his bed on *Jupiter.* He knew his Glock was three feet away. Three feet. Less than two seconds, and he'd be pointing it at someone.

"Sean," Wynona said, her voice silky in the buttery light. "Are you awake?"

"Part of me, yes."

"Which part?" She smiled.

O'Brien pulled a second pillow beneath his head. Wynona stood at the side of the bed, her pajama top unbuttoned, soft moonlight against her breasts. He looked in her eyes and asked, "You having trouble sleeping?"

"Yes … I am."

"And why's that?"

"Because I keep thinking about you."

O'Brien said nothing.

She came closer, reached out and touched the top of his hand, her fingers softly stroking his skin. "Actually, I've been thinking about you since last year when you stayed in my home for that one night. I've been wondering if it was really something magical … something that I wanted to find again. So, I thought, lying alone in my room, the only way to find out was to come in here." She glanced up at the moonlight coming through the skylight. And then she lowered her brown eyes to his face. "I don't know if you wondered the same thing. I hope so, but if you want me to leave, I understand. I'll turn back around and crawl in my bed. You don't have to share yours with me." She used her right hand to touch his bare chest, tracing two fingers across his chest muscles to his hard stomach.

O'Brien looked into her eyes—eyes soft, trusting and unguarded at the same time. He said, "Stay."

She nodded, a smile at the corner of her full mouth. "Max is on the couch. It's just you and me."

He reached for her hand, kissing the inside of her wrist. After a moment, she slipped out of her pajamas, getting into the bed and straddling O'Brien, bending down to kiss him, her dark hair falling around his face. Their kisses were gentle—testing, building. O'Brien could smell the sweet, soapy fragrance of flowers on her skin. He reached for her shoulders, directing Wynona onto her back, her hair cascading over the pillows and reflecting the light as if moonlight was rippling over the surface of black water.

O'Brien used one hand to cradle Wynona's face, kissing her tenderly, the kisses growing more passionate. He was in no hurry, using his thumb to push a strand of hair from her right cheek. She responded to his every move with desire, her heart beating faster. O'Brien took his time, taking her into his arms. He pushed up on his hands, kissed her breasts and gently entered her. She inhaled a deep breath through her nostrils, her eyes searching his face. Wynona met him with the unbridled passion of a woman who'd watched her lover sail away from the harbor and vanish into the horizon, lost between the sea, sky, and time. And now he had returned ... to her. The receptors in her eyes, her pores, her very being—longed for reassurance that the first time, months ago, was real for all the right reasons. A few late nights, alone in her bed, she'd awaken thinking about him. And now they were together again.

O'Brien pushed up from kissing her, looked Wynona in her eyes, shifting his body, entering deeper as he made love to her, quickly bringing Wynona to a powerful climax and repeating it again.

When it was over, Wynona lay next to him, a white sheet partially over them. She looked up through the skylight, stratus clouds moving in front of the moon. She heard the boat's rubber bumpers creak as the tide and current pushed *Jupiter* gently against the dock. For the first time in a long time, she felt a sense of peace. Here on a boat moored to a harbor filled with interesting people. And here with maybe the most interesting and enigmatic man she'd ever met. She felt she knew Sean well, and yet knew very little about him. He has an old soul ... and at times, she felt, a very troubled soul. It was something she told herself she would not try to fix. Because a voice inside her said it wouldn't be reciprocated.

But what she didn't know was why. Maybe in time, she would.

Maybe.

# FORTY-TWO

Katie Scott thought she might snag a fingernail when she untied one of *Dragonfly's* mooring lines. But she didn't care. She didn't care if she ever had a manicure or pedicure again. Even, at that moment, as the sun climbed over Ponce Marina, fingernail polish felt too heavy. From now on, it will be less clutter, less stress. More fun. At least that was the resolution that she and Andy raised their glasses to last night before making love for the last time, for a long time, in the United States.

And now it was almost time to cast off. Nick Cronus was going over some last-minute logistics and sailing instructions with Andy in *Dragonfly's* cockpit. Dave and O'Brien standing to one side, sipping coffee and talking quietly. Katie glanced over to Wynona and said, "Would you like more coffee?"

"Yes, thanks. Didn't get a lot of sleep last night."

"I can see why. What you're doing for Dave is so generous. You do have quite a resemblance to his daughter, Linda. I haven't seen her in a few years, but the likeness is almost eerie, like she's your twin."

"I hope to meet her after this is over, and we can all enjoy events, such as your bon voyage casting off without looking over our shoulders."

Katie crossed her arms, looking across the marina, the call of a boat horn in the distance. "I'm worried about my dad. He could never talk about his work to my mom or me. And now, that he's retired, I can tell he wants to discuss it, or some of it, but he's fearful. He was always so protective of us. One time I heard him tell Mom that people can't get something from you if it's not there. He was talking about one of the reasons he could never share his work. Dad was always concerned about how the adversaries would try to extract information from Mom and I when our family was overseas. Of course, nothing like that ever came close to happening … until now."

Wynona smiled and said, "You and Andy put all of this behind you, okay? Just enjoy your journey and remember that no matter how far you travel, the horizon will still be in front of you."

Katie smiled, refilled Wynona's cup from a large thermos bottle and said, "It was a rather sleepless night for us as well. We were like kids the night before Christmas morning, thinking about this magnificent forty-two-foot gift we were lucky enough to acquire and what it'll do for our lives."

Wynona took the cup, steam rising in the morning air. "It takes courage to do what you and Andy are doing. Certainly, nerve and skill to sail around the vast Caribbean but, it takes courage to sell your home, buy a boat, say goodbye to a lifestyle you've known for years … and to embrace change. Most people are the exact opposite. Change is often feared because it takes a commitment and it takes people out of their comfort zone." She sipped her coffee.

Katie said, "When we do return, I'd like to get to know you better. I think we could be darn good friends. You like shopping for antiques?"

"Love it."

"Me too. In a couple of years, let's do it."

"I'll hold you to it." Wynona lifted her coffee mug.

Katie did the same, the mugs clinking.

Andy stepped out of the cockpit and said, "All right. It's time. Nick has been kind enough to give me a final crash course in sailing, making sure to point out his favorite bars on the map."

Nick grinned, his mustache rising. "I had to narrow 'em down to the top dozen. And that took some deep thought, 'cause I tried to space 'em out from Bimini south through Grenada. That's a long stretch, y'all."

Dave said, "Indeed. Make sure you include Pete's Pub in Little Harbor, Great Abaco."

Andy smiled. "That's one of them that Nick listed." He looked at O'Brien and asked, "How about you, Sean. They tell me you've spent a lot of sailing time in the islands. Any harbor bars that are a must to stop for a drink?"

O'Brien glanced over Andy's shoulder to the condo in the distance. Within the immediate area, he could see a federal agent pretending to fish from an open space on N dock. He said, "It's hard to beat the Tiki Bar right here in our marina. So what I'd look for is an off-the-beaten-path experience in the out islands of the Bahamas. There are more than 700 of them. Mile after mile of white sand beaches, quiet coves, and places where time doesn't seem to move, at least not too fast."

Katie smiled. "God, take me to those places. Is there a quiet cove or a remote out island that you'd recommend?"

"There are many. A few stand out. West of Cat Cay you'll find a string of very remote islands. One in particular is called Spoonbill Cay. It's a small island. Last time I was there it still was not inhabited by anyone. It's probably fifty acres in size. And on the south side is one of the most beautiful, protected coves I've ever seen. You wouldn't be able to count the shades of blue in the water. The only bars are sand bars. If you're in the area, it's a great place to spend some time."

Andy nodded. "We'll try to make it a destination. That's what I love about this. We don't have to file a flight plan with anyone. Just explore the islands like pirates did 400 years ago. Thank you all for your encouraging words and your trip advice."

Dave lifted a brown paper bag at his feet and removed a pistol, a Smith & Wesson 500 magnum. He said, "Here's a little insurance policy, not that you and Katie will ever need it. I've included a box of ammo. There are no rounds in the gun but check it. Do you know how to use it?"

Andy held the pistol, turning it over and inspecting it. "Yes, I do. This is a powerful weapon. I heard people have hunted bear with these."

Dave nodded. "It has tremendous knock-down power."

Andy set it on a cockpit seat and said, "I'll store it below deck. Thank you very much. That was thoughtful."

"You're welcome."

Katie stared at the large pistol and said nothing.

Wynona looked at Katie and said, "You guys remember the significance of what and why you renamed your boat. A dragonfly landing next to you is a sign that change is coming into your life. That's happening as you depart today. Embrace it."

Both Andy and Katie smiled and said in harmony, "We will." Then Andy looked toward the marina exit and the wide Halifax River leading to Ponce Inlet. He said, "Well, it's that time. The time we've been looking forward to for months … maybe all our lives. We want a picture with you guys before we leave." They all posed, and Andy snapped a photo.

Everyone hugged and said farewell. O'Brien, Wynona, Nick and Dave stood on N dock. Andy said, "Can you untie and toss us the lines on your end?"

"Already doin' it," Nick said, squatting down, his knees cracking as he untied one of the bowlines, tossing it to Andy. O'Brien did the same and within a minute, *Dragonfly* was puttering out of her slip, the Yanmar diesel rolling the water, gulls chortling overhead.

Dave said, "Your umbilical cord is now cut. Go find new horizons."

"Thank you!" shouted Katie over the engine, as *Dragonfly* pulled right, heading toward the Halifax River, and a short jaunt to Ponce Inlet and the Atlantic Ocean. Within a few minutes, only the sailboat's tall mast could be seen as Andy navigated through the sea of boats moored in the marina.

Dave exhaled a deep breath and said, "Let's wish them fair winds and a great time the next couple of years. They'll come back changed, and that will be good." He glanced over at the FBI agent fishing, turned to O'Brien and said, "I'll call her Dad, Sol, and let him know they got off without hitting another boat in the marina, and that's a good sign of things to come."

Nick grinned, "Andy's got some good sea legs. He sailed as a teenager off Nantucket, and he's remembered a lot his dad taught him."

O'Brien watched *Dragonfly's* mast disappear behind the mangroves and tidal flats. He said, "After you call her dad, let's talk. I think this thing is even larger than Abdul Aswad."

# FORTY-THREE

They approached a corner table in the Tiki Bar. O'Brien sat with his back to the wall, facing the entrance and exit doors. Dave, Wynona, and Nick took seats around the small circular table. Less than a dozen customers sipped coffee and ate breakfast. The restaurant carried the smell of bacon, hash brown potatoes and onions. O'Brien watched the FBI agent take a seat across the restaurant.

Flo walked to the table with menus in her arms. She smiled and said, "Good morning, Joe's making cheese omelets with stone crab meat. Here's some menus, not that y'all need 'em." She looked at Wynona and said, "Now you might need a menu 'cause I've only met you once."

"Thank you," Wynona said. "But I'll have whatever Joe's making."

Flo grinned and said, "I like you. Abby will come take everybody's orders in just a minute." She looked over at O'Brien and said, "Not only is she pretty, Sean, but she's got class."

O'Brien smiled. "I agree."

"Did that video ever help you?"

"Yes, it did. It's helped us keep a closer eye out for the guy."

"Good. If I see him in here, I'll let you know." She turned and walked back to the bar, speaking with one of the servers.

After the first round of coffee arrived, Wynona said, "I snapped a picture of Katie and Andy when you guys tossed them the bow and stern lines. The smiles on their faces were some of the biggest, most candid, I've ever seen. Take a look." She pulled up the photo on her phone screen and passed it around the table.

Nick chuckled and said, "They're like forty-year-old kids. I'm lovin' it."

"I'd like to send that to Katie's parents, Sol and Brenda. Brenda is sick. This might help her," Dave said.

"I'll email it to you," Wynona said.

"Thanks."

O'Brien looked at the image. "That's a keepsake, and the transom with *Dragonfly* shows up well." He handed the phone back to Wynona. "Dave, tell me more about Richard Thurston, the CIA agent who breached."

Dave's white eyebrows arched, forehead furrowed. "May I ask why the interest?"

"Curious."

"I think you're more inquisitive, however, there's not much more to say than what I shared with you earlier. He was for the most part, always one step ahead of us. And, of course, that's because he was playing both sides, and we weren't suspicious of him yet. That changed."

"What eventually brought him down?"

"Greed. For years he was careful to pretend to live a lifestyle within the bounds of a CIA officer's salary. But toward the last year, he let his guard down somewhat. Took expensive trips. Had a mistress, and that was one of his downfalls because his wife was quick to share some of how Thurston spent money he took from the Russians, although she never knew the source or how much."

Wynona asked, "What made him breach? Was he in debt and needed the money?"

"He once said, after his conviction, because it was so damn easy. And money begets money. There was never enough of it. That propelled him to seek assignments within the CIA that would give him access to extremely sensitive intelligence information that the Russians would be eager to offer large sums of money to receive. Because Thurston has such an extraordinary photographic memory, he could assimilate, store and spew the data almost all from memory. And, on top of that, he was one of the world's best at deception. After half a dozen polygraph exams, each with a different examiner, he beat them all."

Nick set his coffee cup down and said, "I used to play cards—poker, with a guy who, for a price, would teach people how to beat the lie detector. He told me later, right before someone broke his collarbone on both sides, that his '*how to beat a lie detector*' lesson was just another bluff. He said people could never prove he was runnin' a scam because ninety-eight percent of them forgot everything he'd said when they were strapped up to the machine and the questions started coming."

Dave grunted. "Richard Thurston was the two percent who could beat it, and he never took a lesson."

Wynona said, "That's very rare. I remember the case. The FBI used that one and others in our training at Quantico. But Thurston's conviction stands out because he got away with it for so long, receiving millions from the Russians while leaving CIA officers out in the cold to be exposed and compromised."

Dave glanced down at the back of his big hands. "We know ten were executed because of the exposure. And our national security was greatly impacted, as if a cancer had spread through the system."

"Was the money traced?" asked O'Brien. "Did he spend it all?"

"No. He was excellent at dealing with offshore accounts. Laundering it from the Caymans to Canada and elsewhere."

O'Brien nodded. "So, a lot of it could still be out there."

Dave leaned back in his chair, glanced over his shoulder, taking in a visual of the patrons behind him, including the agent across the restaurant, and asked, "Sean, are you suggesting what I think you are? You believe Thurston is behind the killings?"

"Maybe."

"Preposterous. He's in a federal supermax prison for the rest of his life. You don't get much more isolated than that."

"Money, like water, has a way of getting through the cracks, the bars, and under locked doors." O'Brien sipped his black coffee and said, "Your three former colleagues, Richard Lewis, Simon Rivers, and Don Blackwell … let's toss in Katie's dad, Sol, for good measure—did each one of you have a hand in helping put Thurston behind bars?"

Dave said nothing for a few seconds, a waitress walking by with a tall Bloody Mary for a woman sitting alone at a table overlooking the water. Dave cleared his throat. "It was Sol and I who testified at the trial. However, all five of us worked to uncover evidence and trap Thurston. That was after Gitmo."

"Here's the question I've been thinking about, especially thinking about the notes the killer left on the bodies, the *And Then There Were None* reference. Did Thurston cross paths with any of the detainees at Gitmo?"

Dave pushed back in his chair, ran his tongue on the inside of his left cheek, watched a Viking-42 cruiser idle by the docks. "Unfortunately, the answer to that question is yes." He took a deep breath and added, "I need to lose some of this coffee in the restroom. When I return, I'd like to know … what made you think of that possibility?"

# FORTY-FOUR

Dave came from the restroom and didn't make eye contact with the federal agent sitting at a table against the wall. When Dave returned to the table, he said, "To elaborate on your question about Richard Thurston, he did work within a small prison facility we called Strawberry Field, near Guantanamo."

"Why was it near Gitmo and not in it?" O'Brien asked.

"Because it wasn't set up just to hold prisoners. Its sole purpose was to turn prisoners."

Nick leaned forward, grinned, and asked, "Turn 'em into what? Nice guys?"

Wynona said, "I don't think it had anything to do with changing personalities, maybe changing allegiances, I'd bet."

Dave almost smiled. "And you'd be correct. It was set up to turn detainees into, for lack of a better term, killing machines for us. There were promises of safety for the detainees and their families. And there were assurances of money. All they had to do was kill Al-Qaeda terrorists or join us to carry out those kinds of missions. Thurston worked for a few months at a black site in the Ukraine, one of the CIA's clandestine holding facilities. It wasn't much more elaborate than a traditional safe house."

O'Brien leaned forward in his chair, lowered his voice, and asked, "Did Richard Thurston know of or have access to Abdul Aswad?"

Dave's eyes opened a little more. "Sean, are you now suggesting that, somehow, Richard Thurston, from the insides of a supermax prison, connected and is collaborating with terrorist Abdul Aswad to murder my former associates and myself?"

"That's exactly what I'm suggesting."

Dave shook his head in disbelief. "It's not possible."

"Dave, almost anything is possible with enough money and motivation. Both Thurston and Aswad certainly have motive for the murders. Thurston may have a few million lying around to help fund Aswad. Let's put it this way, if Thurston sold out to the Russians, a move that had gotten ten CIA officers killed, why wouldn't he do it again? Switch players. Switch sides. Doesn't matter to him. As he sits inside that supermax cage for life, he has a lot of time to think, to plot, to seethe with anger."

Wynona said, "It's plausible. Thurston knows the inner workings of the CIA like the back of his hand. And he knows you and the other officers. He may not be in a position to direct or orchestrate the logistics or the murders, but he might have a hand in some of it. All it takes is paying off a guard to get a message outside and to bring one inside."

Nick crossed his Popeye-like forearms and said, "This is some serious espionage stuff. I'm feeling the urge for a Blood Mary, a double, with skewered shrimp, Greek olives, feta cheese and a scallion to stir it."

Dave said, "I need a little time to examine this. Not because I disagree with you—it's an interesting theory—just seems highly unlikely. I would like to do some research and see if Thurston did process or try to turn Aswad or others in that group. And, I need to rack my brain for what could be plausible touch points or connectivity to support this idea. It's been a long time, and my memory isn't what it used to be. Also, I wasn't working with Thurston as much as Sol Lefko was back then."

O'Brien glanced around the restaurant, scanning past the federal agent, who was eating breakfast while watching Dave's table. O'Brien said, "It was you and Lefko who testified at Thurston's trial. And you two are still alive."

Dave splayed his hands on the table. He scratched a small cut on the back of his right hand next to a dime-sized age spot. He looked up at O'Brien and asked, "What made you think of Richard Thurston? What made you associate or try to connect him with Abdul Aswad?"

"The notes left on the bodies. The files in the shooter's condo. As a detective, I often had to unravel a crime in reverse. It was, for me, the only way to do it. The crime had already happened. Time, people and events associated with it had moved forward. I needed to push all that backwards to see where the first domino fell and why." O'Brien stared through the large open isinglass window, a Leopard-40 catamaran leaving the marina. "When I looked at the files in the shooter's condo unit, the ones with your dossier and that of Linda's, it didn't look like something a ragtag terrorist group would have put together. It had all the professional touches, measurements, and data found in something that the FBI or CIA would have produced."

Dave shook his head. "The probabilities of Thurston producing those or having it done on the outside are slim to none."

"Someone did it, and it has the characteristics of CIA or FBI. Was it a hired gun working for Abdul Aswad? We don't know that. You'd mentioned that one of the things that attracted Thurston to the CIA was the fact that he always was fascinated by the perfect crimes, ostensibly how to solve them. But, later in his career, he became fascinated with how to perform them. And that, Dave, is the plot and theme behind Agatha Christie's novel, *And Then There Were None*. Who else would have those notes left on the bodies, the bodies of people who worked to convict Thurston and put him in a cage until he's wearing a diaper and doesn't know his name?"

Dave said, "That's a lot to fathom, a lot to consider."

"Can you speak with your CIA and FBI contacts and see if they can sniff out any communications Thurston may have had with someone on the inside to get to the outside?"

Wynona said, "And that usually begins with someone like a prison guard, medical clinician, assistant warden or warden or anyone in the penal chain of command."

Dave finished his coffee, pushing the heavy mug aside. "I will speak with the deputy directors of the CIA and FBI to let them know what you guys are thinking. Although I don't believe there is a snowball's chance in hell that Richard Thurston can be remotely involved. However, Sean, your insights into the criminal mind have left me amazed more than once. Maybe you'll do it again. If Thurston is, by some incredible stretch, involved with Aswad, this will go down as the worst CIA breach in the history of America."

O'Brien nodded and said, "When you speak with your agency pals, even if they can't find any evidence or indication that Thurston is behind this, or somehow involved, maybe then you get permission for me to visit him in prison."

"Sean, Richard Thurston is a master at deception. He's beaten every polygraph exam ever given to him. We had physical proof he took Russian payoffs and laundered the money in offshore accounts under the name of Burgh LTD. He denied it and sailed through the polygraph. You'll get nothing."

"That's a possibility. But a polygraph test leaves out one main component of deception, and that's the visual aspect. The machine can test blood pressure and breathing, but it doesn't have eyes. There's something I'll be looking for when I have Thurston sitting in front of me."

• • •

When Dave was alone on *Gibraltar,* he replayed the past in his mind over and over again—scenarios, conversations, possible link opportunities—anything that could support a connection between Richard Thurston and Abdul Aswad as O'Brien implied.

Later that afternoon, he picked up his phone and made a call to the CIA Deputy Director Ben Graham. He said, "Ben, I know this is going to sound odd, but hear me out."

"What is it, Dave?"

"Although we suspect Aswad is killing or calling the hits on our retired officers, I have a strong suspicion that he may be taking his cue from Richard Thurston."

"Thurston? Are you serious? Thurston won't ever see the sun shine for the rest of his sorry ass life. He's a shell of a man, pale. Lost a lot of weight and living like a crazed hermit in the bowels of the most secure penitentiary in America."

"Granted, but just listen why, okay?" Dave told him the reasons that he thought Thurston could be a suspect, and concluded by adding, "Let's look at possible accomplices. Guards, medical personnel, front office corrections workers, even the damn warden. Take a look at bank accounts and personal spending. Someone with an expensive car or new boat. Extensive home remodeling. Pricey vacation. Anything that would set them apart from the salary they'd normally earn."

Deputy Director Graham was quiet. He stood next to his car in his driveway. "Okay, but this will take some time, though."

"We don't have time. Please put all your resources, including FBI and even NSA, on this. My life, my daughter's life, and Sol Lefko and his family's lives are at stake. We know where Thurston is, there's no tracking him down. The tracking will be looking for and tracing any possible communications he may have had with anyone on the inside or outside, including his family and attorney."

Graham pinched the bridge of his nose, looked at a weeping willow in his yard, the long green limbs animated in the wind. "Okay, Dave. We have nothing to lose. What made you suspect Thurston?"

"I didn't. Remember my friend that I mentioned to you?"

"The O'Brien fella? Him?

"Yeah, him. Are you attending Robert's funeral?"

"Of course. I know that you and Sol Lefko will be there in addition to, at least, one senator and two members of congress. We'll have ample protection."

"Let's hope. There's nothing worse than a massacre in a graveyard."

# FORTY-FIVE

Dave Collins couldn't remember the last time he attended a funeral. During thirty years with the CIA, funerals were something he did in extreme moderation, if at all. Part of the job criteria could result in funerals, on both sides. But, too much visual evidence of those kind of results—it could slow down split-second decision-making, causing deadly consequences.

The funeral for Robert Lewis was taking place in the near center of Paradise Cemetery on the outskirts of Scottsdale, Arizona. From the large, tent-like awning where Dave sat with eighty-five other people, he could see the Camelback Mountain range in the distance against a hard-blue sky. No wind. Desert Willow and Chilean Mesquite trees stood motionless on grounds filled with monuments to the dead. Some people in attendance used hand-fans to circulate the hot, dry air. Others sat passively in the wooden fold-up chairs and observed the somber funeral services for Robert Lewis.

Around the perimeter of the cemetery, in the parking lot, and monitoring cameras from a satellite, were federal agents. In addition to Dave Collins and Sol Lefko attending the funeral, more than two-dozen CIA officers, some retired, others still active, were there. Also, a U.S. Senator and two members of congress were in attendance. Robert's wife, Caroline, sat in the front row next to her sister and brother-in-law.

The minister, a tall, gangly man with shaggy eyebrows, stood near the open grave, the casket secured above it, and concluded the funeral by saying, "Not only did Robert give to his country, he gave to his community. He worked tirelessly to raise money for organizations, such as Make-A-Wish, Wounded Warrior, and the Salvation Army, among others. Robert was soft-spoken. A good listener, and when he did speak, others listened. Every day of his life he displayed the best of who he was. Robert was a plainspoken man who managed to do extraordinary things. Sometimes it was because they fell into his lap, but more often it was because he wasn't afraid to move toward an obstacle or conflict. Robert Lewis will be sorely missed. And now he's in God's hands. Let us close in prayer ..."

Dave thought about his time working with Robert, how he was quick with a joke, but deadly serious when it came time to protect America's interests. *'Freedom comes with a price tag,'* he used to say, sipping a gin and tonic. *'But those costs far outweigh the alternatives found behind the cold eyes of tyrannical and autocratic demigods.'*

"We'll miss you, Bob," Dave whispered under a chorus of "Amen," from the mourners as the minister ended. Dave waited for many of the well-wishers to offer their condolences to Caroline Lewis. And then he made his way to the gravesite where the funeral director and his staff were making preparations to lower the coffin.

Caroline stood in silence for a few seconds next to her husband's coffin. She reached out and placed her left hand on the bronze surface. She wore her gray hair up, black dress, face filled with fatigue and stress, but still with the high cheekbones and clear skin that must have turned heads when she was a young woman. She set a sunflower on top of the coffin, made the sign of the cross and turned around to leave, her sister and brother-in-law waiting for her. She looked up, smiled wide and said, "Dave Collins ... it's good to see you. Thank you for coming."

"I am so sorry for what happened, Caroline." He gave her a hug, her hands felt hot and small on his back. He said, "I wish I had words. Bob made a positive difference in the world. I know he couldn't share with you much of what he was doing, but please know he did it well and it mattered to him and the nation."

"Thank you, Dave. It's good to hear that. The shame is, for so much of our marriage, it was ships passing in the dark. Not that it was bad … just different. But I got used to it, and we made the very best of the time we had together. I think the anticipation of seeing Robert again made me long for him even more. It was a precious honeymoon for thirty years. And now, in our retirement, the golden years … when we were really enjoying our time together, he's killed." She paused, looked toward Camelback Mountain as if searching for something. "They killed him in our home. The place that was our little sanctuary after living all over the world." She inhaled through her nose, eyes red, and asked, "Do you know who did this?"

"We have suspects, yes. And we're moving quickly to contain them."

"Contain … that sounds like something you do to keep a virus from spreading. But to really stop a virus, you must kill it. Go kill it Dave before these evil people take another life. Don Blackwell, Simon Rivers and now my Robert. Are you in danger, too?"

"Yes, I've been threatened."

"By whom?"

"Specifically, I don't know. It came in the form of two rounds from a sniper's rifle."

She looked at him, her eyes probing, something in her throat making a slight clacking sound as she spoke. "Is this coming from someone or something that all of you worked on with the CIA?"

"Most probably. Caroline, we worked on a number of things together during three decades. The CIA and FBI are drilling down to some of the most recent before we all retired."

She looked beyond Dave to the two-dozen or so people still mingling and speaking in subdued voices. "Sol Lefko is here. He was on some of the projects, wasn't he?"

"Yes."

"Is Sol in danger, too?"

"Yes. Here's something I hope I can articulate. Robert, Sol, me, Don, Simon, and many more CIA officers were and are in danger all over the world. Unfortunately, it's the nature of the job—the parameters dealing with tyranny and basic evil, as simple as that might sound. I wish to God we could have found and stopped these killers before they got to Robert. We will stop them. I promise you that."

"It's too late for my husband. Someone's already killed three highly trained CIA officers. I know that my Robert was being very cautious, and they got to him in our home. The CIA and the FBI combined haven't stopped them. God forbid that you and Sol could be next. Who's going to stop them? Who can stop them?" Her eyes welled. "I'm sorry, Dave. I'm just so tired." She squeezed Dave's hand, managed a short smile, turned to join her family, and together they walked toward the parking lot.

Men in dark glasses and earpieces watching her every move.

# FORTY-SIX

O'Brien was searching for a hidden connection. He sat on the leather couch inside *Jupiter*, Max stretched out next to him, her eyes closed. His computer was on his lap, looking for anything he could find about two people: Richard Thurston and Abdul Aswad. There was plenty of information about Thurston's federal espionage trial, conviction, and subsequent sentencing. Excluding information related to the charges about what he did within the CIA, no other facts concerning his career were available. He read the prosecutor's summation to the jury. Read interviews with two members of the jury after the verdict was delivered.

When it came to Abdul Aswad, almost nothing. Born near Baghdad in 1976. Educated at schools in England. Recruited by a radical imam, known as Wadi Botros, and trained for years in different terrorist camps scattered from Syria, Yemen, Libya, and Iran. O'Brien looked at the time Aswad was held in the Guantanamo Bay Detention Center, comparing it with the time Thurston was assigned there.

Wynona came out of the master head, her hair wet from a shower, dressed in a white terrycloth bathrobe. She asked, "How are you coming?"

O'Brien looked up, over the laptop. "Slowly. Not a lot online when it comes to classified CIA data. If it's there, chances are the agency put it there, and you never know for what purpose."

She nodded. "The FBI was good at that, too. Social media can be leveraged in many ways to influence, to change the perception of certain groups. Just look at Facebook and how that platform was used by Russia in the various elections. Not only here, but all over Europe and anywhere the Russian president wants to hawk influence. And, according to media reports, even Facebook employees were discussing how to control access or manipulate information. Not to mention the fact that those platforms, designed to share pictures of you and your friends or family, become dossiers where your ID can be hacked and stolen. People have no idea how vulnerable they can become once the genie is out of the bottle."

O'Brien said nothing. He looked through the sliding glass doors, watching a Viking-42 rumble through the marina.

"Sean, are you okay? You're staring off in the distance like you missed the boat. But the fact is, you're sitting on a boat." She laughed and sat down on the couch opposite him. Max opened her brown eyes for a brief second before yawning wide and continuing her nap.

"Yeah, I'm okay. Dave doesn't care for the word, okay. Says it's often used as its own opposite. Some people use the word okay when they're not fine. Just the opposite, they're hurting or upset. But that's Dave's analysis."

She smiled. "I'll make a mental note not to ask you if you're okay."

"You mentioned the genie being out of the bottle ... bottle being the operative word."

"What about it?"

"In the novel, *And Then There Were None*, the killer was a judge who'd seen a miscarriage of justice, criminals getting off due to talents of high-priced lawyers or some technicality. So, he takes it upon himself to invite ten non-convicted criminals to an island and systematically murders each one ... one at a time with no traceable, physical evidence."

"What's the bottle have to do with it?"

"The Achilles heel for the judge was his need to receive credit for the perfect murders. He wrote down his confession and put the note in a bottle, sealed it, and tossed it into the sea. He assumed, as we are led to believe in the story, that the ocean current would carry it around the world. Maybe after his death someone would find the bottle, open it, read the confession, contact Scotland Yard, and the mystery of the ten murders would be solved."

Wynona shifted her body on the couch. "But that defeats the purpose of seeking credit if the person doesn't live to experience it. It's like an actor playing to an empty house."

"However, if the judge or anyone facing death, maybe due to sickness, there often is the psychological need to seek his or her own brand of immorality before death. To hear the last round of applause before the lights fade to black and the curtain closes."

"But, of course, in the novel, it didn't end that way."

"Of course. The bottle was caught in the net of a fishing trawler and the bottle was uncorked, note read, and Scotland Yard had their man."

"What's the parallel with Thurston or Aswad for that matter?"

"Well, both are sociopaths, devoid of culpability or guilt. If Thurston believes he's pulled off the perfect crime, five murders, maybe more if we factor in the son of Simon Rivers killed in a freak car accident, maybe Thurston would confess as well."

"He'd have nothing to lose, considering the fact he's wasting away in prison." Wynona watched O'Brien close his eyes for a moment. "What are you thinking, Sean?"

"How to trap Thurston and Aswad—how to stop both in their tracks. We know that Abdul Aswad was held in Gitmo for more than three years. Part of that time, according to Dave, he was placed in the area known as Strawberry Field. The section where CIA officers and consultants worked hard to turn some of the radical jihadists into, as Dave suggested, killing machines, working for us against Al Qaeda. Richard Thurston had access and could have come to know Aswad very well."

"No doubt," Wynona said. "He spends all that time trying to reprogram a man's brain … he has to become extremely in tune with his subject. But, all of that went south in the prisoner exchange."

"And so, what we have is Richard Thurston using every skill he's learned to turn Abdul Aswad into a Frankenstein monster—part radical jihadist, part psychological survivor given the opportunity to live. If nothing else, maybe they established some sort of mutual respect and a bizarre bond. Later, Aswad vanishes in the Middle East. And Thurston is tried, convicted and sentenced for handing over data to the Russians. And now there is the movement of the perfect storm in terms of Thurston and Aswad conspiring to get what each one wants … revenge."

Wynona petted Max and said, "So, as Thurston's relationship with Abdul Aswad, is cemented for months in a detention facility neat Gitmo, all Thurston has to do is get word and money to Aswad to kill people they both hate, the other members of the CIA team."

"Bingo. During his trial, which lasted a month, Thurston took the stand, in his own defense, which is surprising. In cross-questioning with the prosecutor, Thurston alleged that he was set up, a scapegoat in dirty politics that went all the way to a former U.S. president. He told such a compelling story, that the jury was almost hung, this came in spite of overwhelming physical evidence against him."

Wynona wrapped her arms around her knees. "What does that tell you?"

"That he's a very clever sociopath who easily connects with a jury and almost convinces some members that he was a pansy in a government witch hunt. After he was convicted, and after sentencing, he looked over his shoulder at Dave sitting in the courtroom and said, "Enjoy your retirement. I'll have a lot of time to read now. Maybe a few good mysteries. I'll drop you a line one of these days."

Wynona said, "And now those lines that he or someone is writing seem to be a mocking reference from a classic murder mystery novel."

"Yes, unless we're completely wrong, as Dave believes about Richard Thurston. Let's hope the CIA and FBI can find out quickly, because now the targets are down to Sol Lefko and Dave. If the adult children are targeted, that could be Katie and Andy, because he's with her. And you, as long as they believe you're Dave's daughter. Just keep inside, lay low while Dave is out of town."

"I don't like waiting for someone to target Dave again, or me. We need to come up with a plan of attack before they do. We have one guy sitting in a supermax prison and the other probably in a base of operations in Iran. Both thousands of miles apart. How do we attack that?"

"By using a ploy to make them come to us."

# FORTY-SEVEN

Dave spotted Sol Lefko coming his way, extended his hand and said, "Sol, I wish we were seeing each other again under different circumstances."

Sol glanced at the coffin, workers turning a crank to lower it into the grave. He said, "Me, too, Dave. It's horrible. Never in all the decades we worked for the agency would I ever have thought we'd be burying our co-workers in our retirement years because they were murdered."

"How's Brenda?"

"Better, thanks. She's really tired and doesn't like her restricted food and daily pill regimen, but doctors say she'll be fine. We're fortunate."

"That's good news. Don's family and Simon's family both chose cremation and private services. I almost wish Caroline had made the decision for a private service for Robert. Being here reinforces the extreme vengeance and threats we're facing. We're the last two in our group. I want to make sure I'm not at your funeral or you're not at mine, unless I eat bad oysters and die of food poisoning." He smiled.

"Amen. Hey, thanks so much for sending that picture of Katie and Andy leaving the docks. That image says it all. We're going to enlarge it, frame it, and hang it in the foyer of our home."

"Katie and Andy are good people, as we used to say in the business. They'll do fine hopping around the islands. They chose a very good sailboat. She'll take care of them. The name *Dragonfly*, it fits them, the boat, and their journey well."

"They spent a lot of time trying to come up with a name."

"After they've been in the islands awhile, maybe you and Brenda can fly down and spend some time with them. It'll do the whole family good." Dave paused, glanced around the cemetery, staring at a statue of a winged angel next to an old grave. The angel's face looking up toward the sky, weather and time stained the stone face with dark streaks resembling traces of tears from her eyes. Dave said, "The note on Robert's body, the one on Simon's body, all appear to be making reference to an Agatha Christie mystery novel: *And Then There were None.*"

Sol shook his head. "Yes, it's odd, but we have no clue why. Both the CIA and FBI are looking at every conceivable angle on this thing. It's probably just a final nail in the coffin; excuse the bad pun, when the hit man made the kills. I got a spent round in my mailbox, not a note."

"That's because you weren't dead. Think about it, Sol … why the hell would Abdul Aswad leave those notes on the bodies? I doubt he's ever read a mystery novel. Regardless, you know as well as I do that when these groups claim responsibility for kills, it's all over their social media pages. And it usually includes some long-winded diatribe about the satanic West and how another group of infidels were killed. They boast. They don't leave cryptic notes."

"What are you saying?"

"Remember what we went through trapping, trying, and convicting Richard Thurston?"

Sol's hazel eyes opened wider, eyebrows arching. "Come on, Dave. You can't be suggesting that Thurston is involved in this, too. For all practical purposes, he's almost buried in concrete and steel inside a prison. Last I heard, he only gets one hour a day out of the cell to walk around the yard, alone."

"But the notes have the ring, the earmark, if you will, from something he'd say or do. And he has one helluva motive to do it. He shares that vengeance with Aswad, for god sakes, it was you and Thurston who spent the most time trying to turn Aswad. What if, after all these years, Richard Thurston, who is a disgraced CIA officer ... is in partnership with an Al Qaeda terrorist and his gang to murder former CIA officers?"

Lefko watched Lewis' coffin slowly being lowered into the grave. "It sounds farfetched, but I know Thurston as much as you can know a sociopath—I've watched him work. Considering some of the threats he shouted after his guilty verdict, I could see it happening. How though, since he's deep inside a federal prison, I just don't know."

"Remember how, before he was a suspect, he'd talk about the ease of committing the perfect crimes ... the perfect murders if they were well planned and carried out?"

"Yeah, he was always analyzing cases, looking for weak links, things that may have caused a different outcome, both for the prosecution and defense. I recall him saying that he wanted to teach criminology classes at a university when he retired. He certainly studied it, read a lot."

"And he read mystery novels. Agatha Christie's, *And Then There Were None*, is a classic. The whole premise dealt with how to commit the perfect crime and remain anonymous. The epilogue, if you will, was the delivery of justice by getting caught because the killer's vanity swelled as large as his ego. Let's walk over and speak with Deputy Director Graham before he flies back to Washington. Sure, we may be wrong, but with three of our group dead, we need to chase every lead. If we don't, odds are you'll be attending my funeral, or I'll deliver the eulogy at yours. Either way, both of us lose."

# FORTY-EIGHT

Katie Scott was mesmerized. She had never been in this situation in her life. She stood near the bow of *Dragonfly* and looked at the blue-green sea across a horizon in a 360-degree circle of ocean. She removed her sunglasses, the wind coming off the face of the Atlantic Ocean teasing her hair. She wore no makeup, just a bikini and a wide smile.

She'd said goodbye to the States a few hours ago, when they last sighted land. And now, before they moved into the region of the Bahamas, it was water, everywhere. She watched a pod of dolphins break the surface in the distance. "Yes! Oh my God!" she shouted looking back at Andy in the cockpit.

Katie turned and walked to where Andy stood, one hand on the wheel, the other on a cold bottle of Corona. She said, "This is such an incredible experience. It's as if *Dragonfly* had a mind of her own, seeking new lands, and we're just going along for the ride."

Andy sipped his beer and said, "She's one of the best and fastest sailing boats I've ever piloted. *Dragonfly* was built for the wind and sea."

"I love the simplicity of our new life. I came with no make-up, not even lipstick. Most of my clothes are shorts, T-shirts and sundresses. And the best of the best is we don't have an alarm clock beside our bed."

Andy lifted his bottle in a symbolic toast. "After twenty years of doing it, we finally began to realize priorities."

"If Madison hadn't passed … if I didn't get cancer … would we have returned to the suburbs, long haul, forty-five years earning money to plow into things that now seem so damn inconsequential?"

"Probably, although like millions of other people, we talked about living and working our lives differently from just adding to the GDP."

Katie smiled, the breeze tossing her hair. "I really like what Dave's friend Sean had to say about cutting ties. He said we all share most of the same fears. Death. Being alone. He said why fear the inevitable? Better yet, why not embrace the time you have? Because while we're here, that's really all we have. And when we have each other, it's shared time and experience. It just depends on how you choose to use it … or abuse it." She fingered a strand of hair behind one ear. "When do you think we'll see land and have the chance to shout land ho?"

Andy looked at his digital gauges built into the console, glanced at his watch and said, "If the winds stay as they are … I'd estimate about three hours."

She stepped down into the cockpit with her husband and removed her bikini top. "Does *Dragonfly* have auto-pilot?" she asked.

Andy grinned. "Yes, always. Especially during these times."

Katie kissed him and said, "There will be a lot more of these times now. We're finally all alone on the deep blue sea." She pointed to the starboard side. "Look … did you see the dolphins? There has to be a dozen of them less than fifty feet away." The pod broke water, jumping across the surface, keeping up with *Dragonfly*, smiles out of the corners of their faces.

Andy said, "Those are the bottlenose. They can swim more than thirty miles-per-hour, meaning they're making a concerted effort to slow down and hang with us."

They watched the dolphins for a few minutes, the mammals submerging, swimming under *Dragonfly*, and becoming airborne along the port side of the boat before vanishing in the turquoise sea. "They seem so happy. Like they're out here playing and letting us join them for a few minutes before moving on to other things."

Something caught Katie's eye.

She stared to the northeast for a second. "Andy, I can see a boat in the distance."

He turned and looked over his left shoulder. "Yeah, I see it. Just spotted the reflection of the sun off the boat's window. Can't tell how large it is from here. Probably coming from somewhere in Florida."

Katie slipped her bikini top back on and said, "Just as I was feeling we had the whole Atlantic Ocean to ourselves, we're not alone."

"That's not surprising considering the boat traffic from South Florida to Bimini and the other out islands in the Bahamas. We're about forty miles north of some major shipping lanes, too."

She said nothing, watching the boat in the distance. She pushed her sunglasses on top of her head, the wind whipping her hair. "They must have a pretty fast boat. It's getting closer."

# FORTY-NINE

CIA Director Doug Martin and Deputy Director Ben Graham listened intently in a corner of the cemetery under the shade of a ficus laurel tree as Dave Collins and Sol Lefko spoke, Dave leading the discussion. He concluded by saying, "What you literally see in front of you, Sol and me … are the remaining survivors. Aswad, most likely, led in some capacity by Richard Thurston, is gunning for us. And he's killing us one at a time. That's why I believe the investigation into Thurston is justified."

Director Martin looked from Dave to Lefko and asked, "You worked with Thurston and Aswad the most. Do you think Thurston, from a pen in a supermax prison, could be working with Aswad?"

"It's a possibility," Lefko said. Thurston is cold-blooded and very diabolical. I don't have to tell you that his actions sent at least ten officers to horrible deaths, compromised many more along with the human assets they recruited, and now he appears to be directing his sworn vengeance on us … the guys who worked to convict him."

Dave added, "We all joined the CIA wanting to do the right thing—to serve justice. To Thurston, I believe, it was just a game. I think the game meant more to him than money—the cash just a by-product of the game, not the motivator. Revenge would be part of the game. If that's the case, we could be his first round of targets … vengeance could extend to the agency."

Deputy Director Graham said, "And that could be a lot more people within the agency." A diesel engine growled, and cemetery workers began digging another grave fifty yards away from where Robert Lewis's coffin was lowered. "Doug, as we talked about on the way out here, Dave and I have been discussing this possibility. We're partnering with the FBI to exam bank accounts of all employees working at supermax in Florence, Colorado, with a special emphasis on all guards, all shifts, working anywhere near Thurston."

Director Martin folded his arms over his black suit coat, a shaft of speckled sunlight breaking through the ficus limbs and dusting his shoulder. He said, "In supermax, inmates like Thurston have very limited contact with more than a handful of guards or other inmates. They're kept in their cells twenty-three hours a day, food on a tray is slid in through a drop box in the bars on the cell. How could Thurston communicate with anyone under those circumstances?"

Dave said, "In a handful of guards, all it takes is one."

The director said nothing. Deputy Director Graham said, "I've spoken with Warden Jefferies. He said no one has been allowed to visit Thurston since he was incarcerated. He has one adult son. His wife filed for and got a divorce when he was convicted of espionage and treason. She apparently took an awful verbal beating by the public for no fault of her own."

Dave batted a gnat out of his face and said, "Doug, if Thurston is backing Aswad, and if they succeed in their killing spree, you will attend more funerals for retired and murdered CIA officers. That alone will send a message down to those recruits considering joining the agency, the message suggesting that it won't make any difference if you're in or out … your safety will always be sidelined."

Director Martin loosened his dark blue tie and said, "We are doing and will do everything humanly possible to eliminate Abdul Aswad and his gang. We have drones and special tactile commando units on alert and standby in every corner of the planet."

Dave started to say something when Deputy Director Graham held up his hand. He looked at an incoming call on his phone. He said, "Give me a few minutes. I need to take this. They wouldn't be calling me during a funeral if it weren't somehow related to the funeral."

• • •

When O'Brien returned to *Jupiter* from walking Max, Wynona was dressed in blue jeans and a white cotton blouse. She wore a necklace, the gold cross shining against her olive skin. She sat at the bar, laptop open, taking notes on a legal pad. Wynona looked at O'Brien and Max, smiled and said, "How was your walk?"

"Great, Max has her routine. I'm thankful there were only two pelicans perched along the dock or it would have taken longer."

"When I walked her, we chatted about girl stuff … you know. I asked her what eyeliner she used—appears to be permanent black eyeliner under those precious big eyes."

O'Brien smiled. "And how did she respond?"

"She said you ordered it online for her." Wynona laughed.

O'Brien grinned and said, "Aha—that wouldn't make it permanent!" He reached behind the bar and lifted a bottle of water, sipping. "I stopped by Nick's boat on the way back. He's invited us for lunch. Whatever it is … it'll be good."

Wynona laughed at his eyeliner catch and then said, "I can smell something delicious dripping on charcoal already." She looked at the laptop screen. "Richard Thurston has my curiosity meter pegging the dial. I understand, or think I understand, the domineering motivation behind people like Abdul Aswad and his sicker brother Masood, but someone such as Thurston, sworn American patriot from the get-go, throws it all out the proverbial window. What for? Cars? Fancy vacations? Drugs? Prostitutes? All or none of the above?"

O'Brien set Max on the couch and said, "What do you mean, none of the above?"

"In the FBI's behavioral analysis unit, we studied how some of life's more traumatic incidents, not just one, but a *blend* of things, can lead to personality disorders that often can't be screened until something comes along and digs down into that composite or human psyche and hits a deadly nerve."

"Are you suggesting that Thurston's selling out his CIA colleagues, and if he's behind the murders of retired CIA officers, is because something or someone found a way to penetrate all that emotional minutia."

"Minutia is more of the trivial stuff rather than the scars I'm talking about."

"You mean the tree rings that mark the years or leave lasting impressions."

She smiled. "That's a good way to put it in perspective. In one of the mental competency exams Thurston went through before his trial, according to the reports from the forensic psychologist, he mentioned an incident that happened when he was five years old. If he's to be believed, he said his father threatened to give him up for foster adoption while keeping his brother who was two years older at the time."

O'Brien nodded. "Sort of a Cain and Abel correlation. Does that report say what happened to his brother?"

"No, but years later, his father allegedly died from a fall off a ladder as he was removing leaves from his gutter. There were no witnesses. Just a man with a broken neck at the base of a ladder, and decaying leaves covering his face."

O'Brien said nothing. He looked through the blinds on the starboard side of *Jupiter*, white smoke corkscrewing up from a grill on Nick's boat, *St. Michael*. He turned to Wynona and said, "Why would the leaves fall on his face?"

"Maybe gravity has something to do with it." She flashed a wide smile. "What do you mean?"

"Assuming he lost his balance and fell … the odds are that, if he'd been removing decaying, wet leaves, they'd be on the ground—most likely wouldn't be covering his face. By the time he toppled and fell, if it was an accident, he's probably not using a trowel or his bare hands to clear the gutter at that moment. He's holding onto both sides of the ladder, or the top rungs. Maybe one or two leaves might have fallen on his face. But to be covered, indicates to me he either was pushed off the roof or the ladder was knocked out from under him."

"How'd you come up with that?"

"Often a killer, especially one that has an intimate knowledge of his or her victim, covers the face of the corpse. It's a strange, psychological phenomenon, but it happens. They can kill a wife, lover, brother, sister or mother … but they can't stand to look the dead person in those unblinking, dead eyes. So, they cover the face. With leaves all over the father's face … maybe Thurston was the source of an accident that was really a murder."

Wynona glanced at her computer screen and let out a low whistle. "If you're right, that may have been Richard Thurston's first murder."

"Just a guess. Doesn't prove a thing. See if you can find a current address for Thurston's mother?"

"Sure … why?"

"Maybe we can pay her a visit."

# FIFTY

K atie looked up from her rum punch at a marina waterfront table, *Dragonfly* tied to the docks, her eyes scanning the entrance to the harbor. The open-air restaurant had more than two-dozen diners sitting at tables topped with colorful umbrellas. The soft breeze carried the smell of spilled rum and fried conch. Katie smiled at Andy and said, "I must confess to a lot of first times on this journey already. Never in my life have I eaten conch. But in this salad, it has such a clean, almost sweet taste. I try not to think about the fact it is meat from a sea slug or a large mollusk that lives in a shell." She took a bite of salad.

"I've had it in chowder, but never in my salad. It's good. The server said it was delivered this morning."

"It doesn't get any fresher. Since we brought two fishing rods and stowed them on *Dragonfly*, I'm looking forward to you teaching me how to fish."

"You never tried?"

"As a little girl, my grandpa put a cane pole in my hand, baited the hook, and I pulled a bream out of his pond. As it flip-flopped around my bare feet, I remember looking down and feeling so very sorry for the poor little thing. I was afraid to touch it to try to get it off the hook. So, I gently lifted it up and set the fish in the water, hook, line and sinker, much to Grandpa's chagrin."

"If you catch a wahoo, don't do the same thing. They're delicious. And I don't mind baiting your hook for you."

She laughed and sipped her rum punch. "Is that how you caught me … baited a hook?"

"Absolutely, but as I recall, it was the other way around. I'll blame it on that little black dress you wore the night of that fundraising dinner."

Katie reached out to touch her husband's hand. After a moment, she looked toward the harbor and the sea beyond the docks and retainer walls.

Andy squeezed Katie's hand and said, "I've seen that look in your eyes before. You're worried."

"No, I'm not."

"Okay, you're concerned about something. Some of the brightness in those beautiful eyes is a little duller considering where we are and what we're doing. So, a penny for your thoughts."

"Not sure they're worth that, only because good thoughts have real emotional value. Bad thoughts, not so much." She sipped the rum punch and recalled her first conversation with Sean O'Brien. *'What made you think to ask if we had friends with racing boats?'*

*'I'd noticed a man in a Top Gun cigarette boat, watching you two. Maybe he was just curious.* Katie looked from *Dragonfly* to her husband's face, the sunlight off the clear water dancing across the red umbrella above them. She said, "That boat we saw about half way into our crossing …"

"What about it?"

"After we sailed through the Gulfstream, the waves were a little choppy. I used our binoculars to watch that racing boat in the distance. It flew through the stream, creating a lot of frothy waves from its bow. I could see two men in it. Not well, but I could see them. And I saw one, the passenger looking at us through binoculars."

Andy smiled, "Babe, that's why sailors and boaters carry binoculars and telescopes, to help keep our distance in shipping lanes, keep from running into each other or aground on sandbars. Those visual aids are in addition to the radar."

"I understand the rationale of all that. But the boat looked like the one that Sean O'Brien described when he was asking us if we had friends around the marina that owned racing boats. He said it was red and white. That boat, about twenty miles back, was red and white."

"There are a lot of red and white cigarette type racing boats making the run from Lauderdale to Bimini. It's only fifty miles, and those boats can easily top sixty miles per hour."

"After they saw me using the binoculars, they seemed to fade back some, then turned and went southwest. Why didn't they just pass us? We were going the most direct route to Bimini. Why head southwest and go around us?"

"I can't answer that. I can, I think, answer why your anxiety is up. You're worrying about your dad. Why don't you give him a call and check in with him or your mom?"

Katie was silent, the sounds of steel drum reggae music in the background. The breeze came across the purple and pink bougainvillea flowers spilling from a terrace near the seawall. "You're right. There are a lot of red and white boats out here. It's probably nothing but a coincidence. But if, for some bizarre reason, going way back to when my father worked for the CIA, if we're being followed … why?"

"I can't answer that any more than you can. But I can choose not to go there."

"Then answer this … that gun Dave gave you … exactly where on *Dragonfly* did you store it?"

# FIFTY-ONE

N ick Cronus removed the last thick slab of grouper from the grill
in the cockpit of *St. Michael* and entered the salon, Max
following, her tail flapping. O'Brien and Wynona were sitting at a
table near the galley. It was made from rustic cedar, the legs sanded
and polished with coats of shellac. Nick said, "I wish we could eat
outside and enjoy the nice breeze, but I understand it's not smart to do
that. Even with the FBI camped out in the houseboat and patrolling all
around, you can't be too careful."

O'Brien said, "We can minimize the risks, but why take unnecessary chances?"

"When does Dave get back from the funeral?"

"Tomorrow."

Nick shook his head, a shine of perspiration on his brown face,
moustache with a trace of white foam—dried beer, just about his lip.
"I've never seen Dave this way. He's not the type to get depressed, or
even be fearful of much. But this stuff—his friends gettin' killed, us
gettin' shot at on his boat … it's like a war that has no damn
boundaries. Somebody is gonna have to find these towel heads or go
inside that prison and pull the dude's head through the bars 'til he
talks."

Nick served large, thumb-sized, grilled prawns with grouper and a
Greek salad. He said, "McDonalds thinks it has the special sauce.

Well, lemme tell you the real story … the Greeks invented it. When you're feeding the gods, do you expect anything less?" He grinned and shrugged his shoulders, lifting his hands, palms up.

Wynona laughed and said, "It smells so good. This is way beyond what I define as lunch. This would be a great meal at a fine dining restaurant. How'd you cook everything?"

Nick winked at O'Brien and said, "First I have to swear you to secrecy."

"Okay. I swear to absolute secrecy."

"Good. The prawns were marinated in lemon juice, olive oil, a dash of salt, pepper, a lil' bit of garlic, tomato sauce and some merlot. The grouper was marinated in olive oil, basil, tomato, black pepper, a touch of tarragon and thyme. I put it all in foil on the grill so the spices meet the juices and let the food sex begin. Then I add in sweet onions cooked in olive oil and chives. I top the fish with feta cheese."

"You didn't have to swear me to secrecy. I'd never remember all that."

O'Brien smiled and said, "I often think that Nick simply uses what he has on *St. Michael* to cook. But one thing that stays the same is the freshness of the seafood."

"Bon appetite!" Nick said lifting a bottle of Sam Adams, condensation dripping from the bottom.

After the first bite, Wynona said, "This is delicious. And I was raised with parents and certainly grandparents who cooked fresh fish on an outdoor grill. That's the way it was for a long time on the rez. It was the old Florida of my childhood. Clear water in the 'glades and thousands of waterfowl rising up at sunrise … so many birds the sky would darken as they took flight. But those days are long gone in today's Florida."

Nick looked at her, nodded and took a bite from a grilled pawn, chewing thoughtfully, he said, "Yeah, I can see the changes in the ocean, too. Less fish. A lot of it has to do with the crap that flows in and out of Florida's biggest lake, Okeechobee."

Wynona said, "The Seminoles camped and fished from Okeechobee for generations. No longer. Sometimes you can't breathe the toxic air around the lake."

"And that's a sad testament to politicians and their evil offspring—pollution," O'Brien said. "In Florida, for far too long, there is a dangerous symbiosis between the two. The people in water management, connected by the hip to their political bosses, who are funded by big sugar and agricultural money, play a shell game. And Florida's heart and soul are being assaulted. They've allowed the sugar industry and farming to dump fertilizer and pesticides into waterways that feed the lake. The phosphorus in the water breeds massive toxic chemicals, green algae blooms. And all that water flows south into the Everglades and tributaries to the Gulf and Atlantic. Along the way, there are fish kills and beach closings."

Wynona folded her arms across her breasts and said, "Sean, you met Sam Otter. He's the eldest of the living elders in the tribe. He always said the ground we walk on represents the ashes of our forefathers and mothers. He said there is a power from the earth ... its soil. Life springs from it and death falls back to it. That's one of the reasons you always see him walking barefoot, to feel the power of the earth under his feet. And he sits on the ground, not in a chair."

O'Brien said, "I remember that."

"He was close with Johnnie Tiger before Johnnie's death. And the philosophy of the elders really comes down to the underlying principles of taking care of the planet that gives you life ... as in sustains it. You go into it when you die. So, in between life and death, why can't we be better shepherds of mother earth? What more signs do we need than the largest lake outside of the Great Lakes in America turning the color of green Jell-O?"

O'Brien's phone buzzed on the table. He looked at the caller ID and said, "It's Dave. Although he's coming from a funeral, let's hope he has some good news."

# FIFTY-TWO

"I'm not going to ask if you're okay," O'Brien said, the phone against his ear. "I know that word is no longer in your vocabulary."

"Not after events of late, it isn't." Dave was driving a rental car, the sun streaking through the passenger windshield partially smeared with insect blotches. "It's tough to bury someone you knew and worked with for so many years. On a more positive note, NSA and the FBI came up with some intel."

"Dave, can I put you on speaker? I'm with Wynona and Nick inside *St. Michael*."

"That's fine." Dave waited a moment and said. "After the funeral, speaking with various directors and deputy directors of the alphabet agencies, they got a hit on the point of purchase of the burner phone they found in the shooter's condo."

"That's good. Where?" O'Brien asked.

"Across the state from us. Specifically, Tarpon Springs. NSA, along with the FBI, pulled footage from the cameras inside the electronics store where the phone was bought. The video matches the shooter's ID. Agents were dispatched to Tarpon Springs. They're questioning store clerks, ride-share drivers, people at local airports and marinas. The shooter wasn't alone. We have video of another man.

From the description of the guy you gave me in the Top Gun speedboat, I'd say it's a match."

"Can you send the video to my phone?"

"I can arrange that."

"Another request … can you find an address for Richard Thurston's mother?"

"Sure, why?"

"She might have something to say. Do you know if anyone plans on questioning her?"

"Not that I've heard. She was interrogated as we investigated Thurston. So was his wife at the time … she divorced him after the trial. The ex has been dead a while now."

"How about Thurston's other family members?"

"Father is dead. Thurston's mother, if she's still alive, lives in Miami Beach. He has one son. Has or had a brother."

"Can you get me addresses for Thurston's son and mother?"

"Sean, I'm not sure it's worth the scratch and sniff efforts. Not a lot in any of those two places." Dave slowed the car and stopped at a traffic light. He watched a man, mid-twenties, cross the road with a little girl, holding her hand. Her hair was raven black. Dave thought of his daughter, Linda. "Wynona, how are you?"

"Can I say okay?" She grinned. "I'm fine, Dave. Chef Nick is taking care of me."

O'Brien looked toward the galley where Wynona was drying silverware and said, "Nick made us one of his light bite lunches." He smiled, his eyes scanning the docks and looking over to the houseboat, one of the FBI agents standing on the bow, sipping from a white Styrofoam cup.

Wynona walked closer to the phone on the table, Nick standing between the table and bar. She looked at the phone and said, "I hope things went as well as they could at a funeral."

"They did. It's one of the sadder days of my career. Although I'm not gainfully employed, and haven't been for a few years, the death of Robert took me back to the days we worked and survived together."

"I understand."

The light turned green and Dave drove on, slowly through the streets of Scottsdale. He looked in the distance, craggy mountains painted in the colors of rust. Uneven peaks, valleys—the rugged and rocky serrated spines of long sleeping leviathans, motionless after the tectonic plates shimmied and shook, molding and pushing them across the desert's dance floor thirty million years earlier. "Wynona, I really appreciate what you're doing for me and for Linda. However, after watching the coffin of one of my best friends lowered into a grave, it would be unconscionable for me to see you hurt or worse. Please, just walk away. Don't put your life on the line any longer, okay?"

"Dave, first … okay's not a word you pull out of your card deck. Second, you would not be the reason. The reason is simple … evil. It's palpable with these people. I don't know Richard Thurston like you do. I don't know any more than the case files Sean and I've read in depth. But I suspect he's cut of the same cloth as the man I saw slaughtering his daughter. So, you aren't the reason … *they* are. Yes, I'm doing this to help you and Linda. But, on another level, a psychological one that I don't even fully understand, I'm doing it for myself. I dealt with Masood Aswad … maybe I'm supposed to meet his evil twin."

Nick arched his eyebrows, folding his arms, a slight smile working in the corner of his mouth. He glanced over at O'Brien who was expressionless, standing at the weathered bar, waiting for Wynona and Dave to end the conversation. O'Brien could picture Dave's face after what she just told him. She wasn't going anywhere. And he knew it. She was too principled. Too committed to retreat. She was Seminole—a tribe that was never conquered. It was in her blood.

Dave said, "All right. I can see why Sean respects you as much as he does."

She looked up at O'Brien, her eyes soft. She moistened her lips and inhaled a deep breath, Max letting out a yelp as the cat came closer.

Dave cleared his throat and added, "I had planned to be back tomorrow, but I may be back in a day or two. I will let you know. Then we can all meet to discuss our next steps. We have to work parallel with the FBI and CIA on this. Maybe we can do some legwork and let them work the offense. They have the manpower and firepower."

"I agree. But when it comes to firepower … I spent years with the bureau, and I don't know anyone who could have taken the shot that Sean did under the circumstances and remove a hostile. I'd suspect you could say the same thing during the entire thirty years you were with the CIA."

Dave smiled, an eagle flying just above Camelback Mountain. "I hope, when this is over, we'll get to spend more time with you."

"Me, too."

"I need a last word with Sean. Is he still there?"

"Yes."

O'Brien picked up the phone and took it off speaker. Dave asked, "Why Tarpon Springs? Florida has cities with strong international arrivals, cities such as Miami, Orlando, and Tampa. Every day, hundreds of people from all over the world, including the Middle East, fly into those cities. We know emissaries, spies and newly recruited jihadists can slip through the checkpoints using counterfeit passports, IDs, along with their deceptive reasons for visiting."

"Tarpon Springs is a quaint fishing and tourists' town. It's filled with fishing boats. Maybe the feds should ask around the docks. Has anyone heard from Katie and Andy? They should have hit Bimini by now?"

"As I was leaving the cemetery, Sol said he received a call from Katie. She and Andy docked *Dragonfly* in Bimini. They'll spend the night there, and in the morning, they'll set sail for other remote islands. Right now, Katie's probably in the best and safest place ever until this thing is history."

# FIFTY-THREE

Twenty minutes later, O'Brien downloaded a video of the man he'd killed. He stood next to the small bar inside *St. Michael*, Wynona helping Nick clear the rest of the table, Max staring out the salon window and uttering a low growl as a large, tawny cat sauntered down L dock. O'Brien watched the surveillance video play on his phone screen. It was in black and white, the moving images slightly grainy, but there was no mistaking the man who'd fired upon Dave's boat. Tall. Big boned. A hawk nose. Short beard. He was a foot taller than the balding male store clerk.

Standing next to the man was another man. Shorter. Narrow face. And even in the video, his eyebrows looked like they were painted on above his eyes. Dark. Thick. Almost cartoonish. He glanced up at the security camera and quickly looked down. It was enough time for O'Brien to recognize him. He was the man behind the wheel in the cigarette boat. O'Brien watched the men finish the purchase of four burner phones, pay cash and walk out the door.

"Did Dave upload the video?" Wynona asked, wiping her hands with a white dishtowel.

"Take a look."

Wynona and Nick stood next to O'Brien as he replayed the video. He waited for the exact second the small man looked up at the camera and then stopped the video, the man's dark eyes looking squarely at the camera. O'Brien said, "That guy, the smaller one, he's the man that was behind the wheel of that Top Gun boat the first day I met Katie and Andy."

Nick folded his arms and said, "Dude looks like he could cut your heart out with a dull butter knife."

Wynona said, "Dave told you NSA retrieved the footage from an electronics store near Tarpon Springs. How'd those guys get there, and then how'd they find an expensive Top Gun speedboat to gas up here at Ponce Marina? Did they buy it? Did someone give it to them, and if so … where is the guy looking at the camera, and where's the boat?"

"All good questions," O'Brien said, setting his phone down on the wooden bar. "Right now, we don't have the answers. We do know that the big guy in the video was the designated shooter. He's wherever the CIA stores or obliterates bodies of enemy combatants. And we know they were in the Tarpon Springs area before they got here, according to the time stamp on the video … that was, most likely, more than two weeks before they showed up here. What I wonder is … are there more of them? Where are they? Who's bringing them in the country, and how are they doing it?"

"On the west coast of Florida," Wynona said, "from the panhandle down to Naples, and then the ten thousand islands, there are probably a few hundred ways to slip into the backwater country. They could get dropped off by boat and then picked up by someone in a car with darkened windows all around."

O'Brien looked at a text message. "Dave sent me the address of Richard Thurston's mother. Her name is Patricia Thurston. She lives in unit 1617 at 3349 Atlantic Way, Miami Beach. It's probably a condo, and with that address, it's on the ocean. I wonder how long she's been there, and how she bought a beachfront condo? Was it with her own money or was it a gift from her son?"

"I don't know if she will tell us, but it can't hurt to ask her," Wynona said.

Nick shook his head. "I'd like to ask her what the hell happened to her son for him to turn out with ice water in his blood."

Wynona looked over to O'Brien and said, "Sean, I can go question her. Maybe catch her in a receptive mood. Maybe not. I'd like to stop by my house. It's not too far from the Miami area, as you know. I need to water my plants. As much as I would love to, I don't have a cat or dog—I'm rarely home. Just a few plants that have been my silent roommates for years."

Nick said, "That's the best kind."

O'Brien laughed and said, "Ol' Joe is as fat as can be as much as he hangs around you and your boat waiting for gourmet fish scraps. He's one well fed cat." Then to Wynona, he said, "Both of us should go. Maybe we can tag team in a softball kind of way with an older person. Nick, could you keep an eye out for Max?"

Nick looked over at Max who was staring at the big cat that sat on L dock behind *St. Michael*'s transom. "Of course. I watch Hot Dog … she watches Ol' Joe the scarface cat. No sweat. You gonna tell the FBI agents you're taking off?"

"Yes. I'll see if they want to follow us or stay here and wait for Dave's return in the morning."

• • •

O'Brien didn't have to request permission to board the houseboat on M dock. As soon as he approached the transom area, one of the port doors opened, and a stocky, angular-faced man stepped out. Dark skin. Sunglasses. Blue jean shorts and an untucked, long sleeve denim shirt, sleeves rolled up to his elbows.

O'Brien said, "Greetings. I just spoke with Dave. He's still in Scottsdale. He said he'd let me know if he was returning tomorrow or the next day."

The agent nodded. "Thanks for the info. You're O'Brien, aren't you? Dave Collins' close friend?"

"That's me." He smiled.

"We heard about your marksmanship. You learn that during a tour of duty?"

"I learned it trying to survive in Afghanistan."

"I'm Marines. You?"

"Delta Force."

The agent removed his dark glasses, dropping them in his shirt pocket. "I heard the Afghans are some of the fiercest warriors on the planet."

"I'd agree."

There was a long pause. "I'm Special Agent Daniel Hernandez. We've been in touch with the team in Scottsdale. Lots of VIPs and higher ups all in one location in the cemetery. We pretty much surrounded it from ground and satellite surveillance. So far, so good."

"Maybe things will stay that way until you guys hunt down these people."

"That's the hope and plan. Sometimes there is a real quiet before a storm. I assume Wynona Osceola is still inside the fishing boat, right?"

"Yes, she is. She wants to head to her house near the Seminole reservation in South Florida to pick up a few items. Back tonight. You guys interested in following?"

"Are you going to be with her at all times?"

"Pretty much, yes."

"Let me check." He walked back inside the houseboat.

O'Brien heard mumbled conversation from inside the boat, the cough and sputter of a sailboat diesel starting up, and the toot of a sightseeing boat's horn leaving the marina.

Special Agent Hernandez opened the houseboat door, the knot of his 9mm barely visible under his shirt. He walked to the port side, glanced across the docks toward Nick's boat and said, "I'll escort you two to your vehicle. We'll tag along for the first thirty miles or so. If all seems quiet, considering her background and yours, too, and the fact that you're both carrying, you can take it from there. Just check in with us every couple of hours, okay? Here's my card."

"All right. Thanks." O'Brien took the card and turned to leave.

Special Agent Hernandez said, "Be careful. We know the radicals are after Dave and his daughter. Granted that Wynona bears a resemblance, but that doesn't mean they're not hunting elsewhere." He paused and looked across the marina and said, "Here's something to chew on … Wynona Osceola is held in high esteem among a lot of members in the bureau. I can't say I wouldn't have done the same thing she did if I'd broken down the door and found some crazed jihadist cutting his daughter's throat. She flat took out Masood Aswad. If his crazy brother is behind these assassinations, and if he finds out her real ID, I'd bet a year's salary he'd want her a helluva lot more than Dave Collins' daughter."

O'Brien said nothing. As he turned to leave, he said, "We'll be in the parking lot in twenty minutes." He walked down M dock to the main waterfront area, looked back over his shoulder at N dock and the slip that was a short time home for *Dragonfly*. He thought about Katie and Andy and what Dave had just said, *'In the morning they'll set sail for other islands. Right now, Katie's probably in the best and safest place ever until this thing is history.'*

He walked past the Tiki Bar, the smell of fried shrimp and hush-puppies coming from a large open window, people laughing, and the Huey Lewis song *Cruisin'* drifting from the speakers. O'Brien moved further toward L dock, looking at an eighty-foot charter boat returning from a half-day fishing outing. The boat, part of a commercial fleet, was loaded with pink-faced tourists, and the fish they managed to catch bottom fishing the reefs, the customers packed in like refugees.

As he walked down L dock, he heard the baritone rumble from deep-throated Detroit diesels. He turned and watched a shrimp boat chugging out of the marina, heading to the open harbor and the sea. The man behind the wheel wore a dirty baseball cap and white tank top. Two tanned deckhands moved about the big boat, adjusting nets and ropes. One wore a sweat-stained red bandana tied behind his head. Wild black beard. No shirt. Ink over his arms and the center of his chest. He lifted a large toolbox, biceps like rippled steel, a cigarette hanging from one corner of his mouth. He looked up at O'Brien, quickly turned his head and walked to the starboard side of the boat.

As a detective, O'Brien had seen the look many times. People not wanting to make unnecessary eye contact with strangers. It came like second nature to career criminals and people on the run. O'Brien stopped on the dock near a fish cleaning station under a thatched roof of fried palm fronds. He watched the shrimp boat move into the Halifax River, turning left toward Ponce Inlet and the sea.

*It could be gone two or three weeks at sea. Maybe a month.* O'Brien thought about the distance these shrimp boats could travel.

*Would the captain and crew return here to the homeport? Or would they come back someplace else?*

*Someplace like Tarpon Springs.*

# FIFTY-FOUR

Katie Scott had never seen a sunrise that appeared to expand the entire length of the horizon. But this morning, all the atmospheric elements were working in harmony, and the sunrise over the Atlantic Ocean seemed to stretch to the ends of earth. Before she and Andy untied *Dragonfly* from the slip on Bimini, she wanted to have a few minutes of quiet, watching the sun bloom over the sea. It was as if a yolk had broken and was oozing along the threshold where the heavens and ocean met, drops of gold dribbling into the dark blue sea, creating streaks of tangerine orange flowing into infinity.

She stood on *Dragonfly's* bow, a cup of steaming black coffee in one hand and a piece of toast in the other. Katie wore white shorts and a new light pink T-shirt she bought that read: *Bimini Bliss.* The shirt portrayed the silhouette of a woman in a hammock holding a margarita glass, the hammock stretched between two palm trees, the sun setting in the background.

She sipped her coffee and looked below the boat, schools of blue and yellow fish darting about in the gin clear water, the white sandy bottom easily visible. She pinched off a small piece of toast and dropped it. The portion drifted less than a foot under the water before a half-dozen small fish surrounded it for breakfast, the fish tearing into the toast with fervor. In five seconds, it was gone.

"It's a wonderful morning in the neighborhood," said Andy, coming from below deck, his hair disheveled, whiskers on his slightly sunburned face. He wore shorts and a new T-shirt with a wide-eyed SCUBA diver riding a large shark, the caption read: *Ride the Bimini Bulls.*

Katie smiled and said, "It is a wonderful morning in the neighborhood. Look at that sunrise. The colors change by the second. And take a deep breath. Even the air feels so much cleaner. Maybe it's all from the blooming flowers on Bimini. I can't wait to see the other islands. There are only seven hundred."

"Should keep us busy."

"You think?"

"Yeah, I do." He walked toward the bow and kissed his wife, the morning sun dancing in her eyes.

"Love you, Captain Andy."

"Love you, First Mate Katie."

Andy sipped his coffee and watched the sunrise. Two black boys, early teens, running an old Boston Whaler skiff, came around the far end of the docks. Bluish-white smoke billowed from the small outboard motor, the kids riding out a quarter mile to dive for fresh conch they would sell to the restaurants. Andy said, "There's a lot to be said for living this lifestyle."

Katie watched the minor wake trail from the little boat and said, "The key word is living. I bet it's hard to find clocks, especially alarm clocks, in the Bahamas."

"Maybe someone put the last ones in a big burlap sack, tied it and tossed it overboard to give the fish a reef to swim around." He chuckled. "I'm going below to plot out the sail up to Grand Bahama. From there, we'll make it up as we go along."

"Sounds good."

Andy went below deck, and Katie tossed the remaining small piece of her toast to the fish. She looked up at the marina and docks, spotting a moored red and white cigarette boat. She took a deep breath. *It's nothing,* she thought. *Just one of many boats. Nothing special.* She stared at it a moment. It looked at least forty feet in length. No one was in the cockpit, just the boat tied to the dock cleats, bobbing and dipping in the rising tide with the veiled innocence of a sleeping dragon.

• • •

O'Brien and Wynona pulled off Collins Avenue in South Beach and drove up to the gated and guarded entrance to the Harbor Reef Towers, two massive forty story condos of smoked glass and steel overlooking the Atlantic Ocean. The security station at the front entrance, made from hand-cut Italian beige sandstone, was meant to look as non-intrusive as possible and still deliver the message: *members only.*

O'Brien stopped at the gate and lowered the window in his black Jeep. He could see shadow movement beyond the glass window in the front section of the small building, two men, one with a clipboard. O'Brien looked at Wynona and said, "Let's hope Dave or one of his CIA pals got through to security before the shift change."

"We'll soon find out."

The door to the check post opened and a slender, middle-aged man in a white, short-sleeve shirt and black necktie, came over to the Jeep. He said, "Good evening, Sir. May I help you?"

"Yes, my name's O'Brien. You should have notification of security clearance."

The guard studied O'Brien's face and nodded slightly. "May I see your ID?"

"Of course." O'Brien already had his driver's license out and ready. He handed it to the guard. The man looked at the picture on the license and then cut his eyes up at O'Brien. He returned the license, glanced across the seat at Wynona.

"Wait here, please. I'll be right back."

When he reentered the guardhouse, Wynona said, "He'd be a good poker player. He acted like he didn't receive a clearance for us. Maybe something happened, and Dave didn't get it done."

"He got it done. The guard isn't that good with his poker bluff. He recognized my name."

"How do you know?"

"Because of the look of recognition in his eyes the same time he nodded his head. It was subtle, but there. And I only gave him my last name. He didn't ask for the first before he looked at my ID."

The guard returned and said, "Everything is in order, Mr. O'Brien. I see you and the lady are guests of Mr. Randolph Powers. His home is in the penthouse. Top floor. Have a good day, folks."

After the guard walked away, Wynona smiled and said, "Mr. Randolph Powers. That has a nice wealthy ring to it. How'd Dave and his contacts find that name so fast?"

"I'm not sure I want to know. Randolph Powers may be a personal friend, or he might be someone who's a funder for the current party in the White House and owes someone in the CIA or FBI a favor. I don't care as long as we can move through here at will. Cameras, no doubt, will be in most, if not all, of the common areas, as well as the front and rear access points."

"After all of this, let's hope Richard Thurston's mother is home."

They parked in the lot for guests to the far side of the Harbor Reef Tower number one. The grounds were awash with manicured landscaping, deep tropical greens, tall flowering plants, bird of paradise, augustums, giant pink and white lilies, philodendrons and soaring royal palms. They walked to the front entrance in the late afternoon sun, the cascading splash of water in a three-tier marble fountain directly in front of the tower.

As they approached the doors, Wynona said, "I doubt if you'd find a condo in this entire building under a cool million. She's on the sixteenth floor. I'd imagine the higher the view over South Beach and the Atlantic, the higher the prices."

"There are eight large penthouses at the top. And I'd wager that all of the owners are here only periodically at best, moving with the seasons, whims, and the money."

Wynona laughed. "Maybe it's my Seminole-Irish blood, but there is no way I would ever live in such confinement."

They entered the lobby area, bone white marble on the floors, rich woods with inlaid mirrors, more tropical plants and three elevators. One was private—direct access to the penthouses only. The others lead to a dozen different floors each. O'Brien and Wynona rode one elevator to the sixteenth floor, got out and walked down a long plush carpeted hallway with alcoves, softly-lighted paintings and black-and-white framed photography on the walls depicting the history of Miami Beach. They stopped at condo number 1617.

Wynona looked over at O'Brien and said, "This is strange."

"What do you mean?"

"All my professional career, in the bureau, as a detective on the rez, even working with you on the Joe Billie case, we'd enter a property either with a search warrant or the intent to find evidence of wrongdoing so the state could successfully prosecute."

"That's not the case this time."

"No, it's not. Richard Thurston is in prison for life. We're not looking for evidence to add time on a life sentence ... we're looking for evidence to save lives. And, if it does lead us to a supermax prison, will the elderly mother hold some answers?"

"Let's find out."

O'Brien pressed the doorbell, the chimes ringing like church bells on a Sunday morning in the distance. Within half a minute, someone was standing on the other side of the door.

# FIFTY-FIVE

O'Brien looked up and down the hallway for security cameras. He couldn't see any, at least not obvious cameras. Who knew if there was a lens in the fire alarm above their heads? He waited a few more seconds and rang the doorbell again. He could just see a slight movement on the opposite end of the peephole near the center of the door.

A voice with a Hispanic accent asked, "Who's there?"

Wynona said, "We're here to speak with Mrs. Thurston. Department of Justice. It's about her son, Richard."

The door cracked open and a slim, dark skinned woman wearing a nurse's uniform stood behind a brass chain lock.

O'Brien looked at Wynona. She took the cue and said, "Hi, I'm Wynona and this is Sean. We understand that Mrs. Thurston is home. As I mentioned, it's about her son, Richard."

"Why didn't security at the gate call us?"

"Mrs. Thurston is one of three people were seeing in the building. Perhaps he didn't get around to calling everyone."

The woman angled her head for a second. She had a round face, compassionate but guarded dark eyes. Black hair twisted loosely in a bun and pinned at the nape of her neck. "Mrs. Thurston is ill. She's in hospice care. I'm not sure if she's up to having visitors."

"That's why we're here," O'Brien said, smiling. "Her son, as you may know, is incarcerated and can't make it here himself. We're the emissaries between the federal prison and Mrs. Thurston. We just need to deliver a message to her. We won't be long."

"I don't know. I'll need to—"

"Who is it, Isolda?"

The voice sounded frail, sharp pitched, elderly. "Who's at the door?"

Wynona spoke up. "My name's Wynona, and my associate is Sean. We're here to speak with you about your son, Richard. It's Department of Justice business."

There was silence, only the whish of cold air through the vents. From somewhere in the room, the elderly voice asked, "Did he pass away … is he ill?"

"Can we come in so we don't have to raise our voices for you to hear us beyond the door?" Wynona asked.

"Hold on a minute." The nurse closed the door and was gone less than thirty-seconds before the sliding sound of brass on brass as she removed the chain on the lock. The door opened wide and the nurse said, "Follow me. She's not far, just inside the living room."

O'Brien walked behind Wynona as they entered the room. It was filled with leafy ferns in the corners, bromeliads, and white orchids near the windows. The cool air smelled of flowers and bleach. A vast collection of hardcover books lined a floor to ceiling Old World bookcase. A tall grandfather clock stood like a sentry in one corner. A television was on the wall, the sound muted, *Jeopardy* on the screen. Out the large picture window on the far side of the great room was a view of the Atlantic.

In the center of the room was an old woman, Patricia Thurston, in a hospice bed. She had long gray hair combed over one shoulder. Her face was pasty. Cheeks hollow. Eyes sunken and lined in dark rings. To O'Brien, she looked like a small bird left in a nest by itself, blankets draped around her withered frame. A rocking chair sat near the bed, the TV remote control on the chair. In addition to bleach, the room had a slight odor of urine and vomit.

The hospice nurse interlocked her fingers, holding her hands near her midsection and said, "Mrs. Thurston, I'll be in the kitchen if you need me."

"Thank you, Isolda." After the nurse left, the old woman looked up at O'Brien, her left blue eye clouded from cataracts. She said, "You remind me of my William. He was tall and wide shouldered. He passed away years ago. I forgot your name. What is it?"

"Sean O'Brien."

She touched her hair with her left hand. A thin gold band on her ring finger, hand bowed from arthritis, her skin the texture of parchment, a web of blue veins just beneath the translucent skin. "My William, on his mother's side, was all Irish." She looked at Wynona and said, "I remember your name because one of my favorite singers is Wynona Judd."

"I've always liked her singing, too."

The old woman nodded and stared at the wall of books lined on the large bookcase. Wynona said, "You have a marvelous collection of books. Have you read many of them?"

"I've read all of them."

"That's impressive."

"I didn't have the opportunity, or resources, for a university education. So, these books, and many more, were how I educated myself. World history, philosophy, economics, sciences … it's all there. And some good fiction, too. The classics from writers, such as Mark Twain, Faulkner, Hemingway, Jane Austen …." She tried to smile, her face weak. "Like me, my son Roger loved all kinds of books, too."

"Where is Roger?" O'Brien asked.

"Up north—Vermont, he likes the cold. He's a retired advertising executive. Unfortunately, he and Richard never got along—so very different. They haven't spoken since Roger went off to college."

O'Brien took a few steps to the bookcase, scanning the dusty book spines and their titles. His eye caught a book by C.S Lewis, *Mere Christianity*. On the adjacent shelf were some of the Agatha Christie books: *The Mousetrap, Murder on the Orient Express, Endless Night, And Then There Were None*. He said, "I see you've read Agatha Christie."

"Oh, my goodness, yes, of course. She's the best when it comes to murder mysteries. Hercule Poirot, he doesn't miss a thing."

O'Brien looked back at the books. "I see part of your collection includes *The Mousetrap, Murder of the Orient Express, Endless Night, And Then There Were None.* Which is your favorite."

"That's difficult. I love them all. But if I had to choose … I would pick *Endless Night.*"

"Why is that?" Wynona asked.

"It seems like a novel Agatha wrote when she grew tired of Poirot and Miss Marple. *Endless Night* was more of a novel about the forces of good and evil, especially evil. I thought about it for days after I finished it." After a few seconds, she said, "Richard liked *And Then There Were None* the best."

"Why is that?" O'Brien asked.

She thought a moment, staring at the bookcase, and said, "He told me that he liked the way justice was delivered to people who got away with crimes."

"Justice?" asked Wynona. "Those people were invited to the island and methodically murdered, one after the other."

She tilted her head toward Wynona and said, "Perhaps it was extreme justice that didn't fit all the crimes, but Richard loved the way the murderer played each person and kept anonymous until he wanted to reveal that he was the one who committed the crimes." She shifted her eyes to O'Brien. "Years before he read the book, I read the nursery rhyme to Richard. It was one of his favorites. He wanted me to read it over and over. Is my Richard ill? I haven't heard from him in a while."

Wynona said, "He seems to be doing as well as can be expected. He has time to exercise, read and write letters. He misses you, Mrs. Thurston."

"I'm trying to remember the last time he wrote me a letter. I know he writes to his son, my grandson, Jason."

"Where does Jason live?" O'Brien asked.

She thought for a moment. "Atlanta, but he was here just a few days ago," she paused, "said he was meeting up with some friends for a couple days of water sports. I expect he will be back soon because he left his laptop computer." She looked at a coffee table near a long beige couch, a laptop in the center of the table. O'Brien spotted a thumb-drive inserted in one side of the computer, a large black Bible on the same coffee table.

"When did he leave?" Wynona asked.

"Let me think … three … no, two days ago I believe." Her throat made a small clacking sound, breathing slightly labored. "He was here because he wants to be in my good graces, not that he deserves it. He knows my time is near. I've accepted that. Made my peace with the Lord. My grandson is the only grandchild I have. Richard is alive, but I'll never see him again … not in this life. And Roger has a bad heart and can't travel anymore."

"I understand, "O'Brien said.

She nodded and glanced over at family photos on one wall. "Richard bought this place for me to move into after I sold my house. From the time we married, William and I lived in the same small house for thirty years … until his untimely death. Upon my death, I would like to return this to Richard—he would like it here. But that doesn't seem likely unless…" She looked at O'Brien and Wynona. "Unless you are here to tell me they found evidence that my son was a scapegoat for the wrongdoing of others on the CIA. Is that why you are here?"

# Fifty-Six

O'Brien looked from the bookcase to the coffee table and decided to take a gamble. He walked closer to the hospice bed, removed the TV remote from the rocking chair, and sat down. He looked at Patricia Thurston's face—deep furrows, her brow creased, but yet hope coming through the fog of cataracts in eyes that still carried a subtle radiance. "Mrs. Thurston … you said earlier that you'd made your peace with the Lord, correct?"

"Yes. Not because I have cancer, long before that. Everybody dies. Death doesn't frighten me. What scares me is when I watch the TV news and see what's going in our world. The horrible way some people treat each other. My father used to shake his head and say the greatest rule in the universe only has eleven little words with large meaning, but it's the one rule most broken."

Wynona asked, "Would that be the Golden Rule?"

"Yes. Do unto others as you would have them do unto you." She looked from Wynona to O'Brien. "It seems so hard for so many people to truly follow that."

O'Brien nodded and said, "What do you think happened to Richard? He violated the Golden Rule and that resulted in the deaths of at least ten CIA employees."

"None of that was Richard's fault. He was a victim, too."

"No ma'am, sadly, he was not a victim within the CIA, he was a victim of his own greed and power. He chose to sell American classified secrets to the Russians and he was paid well for his services. That's how he could afford to buy and deed this condo to you."

"It's not true." She looked up at Wynona, searching for some affirmation she was right.

Wynona said, "I'm so sorry, Mrs. Thurston, but it is true."

The grandfather clocked chimed seven times. And then the room was quiet. The hospice nurse opened the door to the kitchen and asked, "Do you need anything, Mrs. Thurston."

The old woman shook her head, a strand of white hair breaking across her face. 'No thank you, Isolda." The nurse nodded and disappeared back in the kitchen.

O'Brien said, "Ma'am, the last thing that Wynona and I want to do is to deliver bad news to you, but I have to believe in your heart of hearts that you know, or suspect Richard did those things he was found guilty of doing. There is a mountain of hard evidence, proof—video and audio of Richard selling secrets and taking money. Some was cash. Some in electronic deposits to offshore accounts he opened under the name Burgh LLC."

Patricia Thurston coughed and looked up at O'Brien, cleared her throat, her face filled with repressed thoughts. After a moment, she lowered her voice to above a whisper and said, "I pray for his soul every night before I go to sleep. He was always such a good boy, bright and spirited. My husband, who spent a career in the military, used to push Richard really hard when he was a little boy. Too hard, I felt, and I would say so. William disagreed. Of the two boys, Roger was more studious, and I could say, pliant or less challenging in William's eyes. Richard was curious, creative, and inventive, something William never really understood. It seems that Richard was always trying to exceed his father's expectations. And that was truly impossible. When our family dog, Tucker, died, somebody in the neighborhood poisoned him. William blamed Richard because Richard left the back door open, and Tucker ran out. Richard was only eleven years old at the time. Just a freckle-faced boy who loved astronomy and animals." She paused collecting her thoughts like picking overlooked clothes from the back of the closet, her eyes moist.

"Take your time," Mrs. Thurston, Wynona said.

"Tucker died at our front door, trying to come back home and whining in such pain. My husband made Richard lift up Tucker's body from the front porch. He had to dig the grave in the rain and bury Tucker in our backyard. He fought back tears because he didn't want his father to see him cry, or maybe his tears were lost in the rain. And I think that day, right before sunset when Richard tossed the last shovel of dirt on Tucker's grave, something inside him changed. I could see it in his eyes as he stared at our backyard floodlights for a few seconds. Later that summer, after his father had mowed our lawn and berated Roger for some small thing—I think for not putting the rake on the right peg in the garage, Richard saw one of those small furry moles that burrow underground. It was trying to walk across the hot pavement on our driveway. Richard went up to it and stomped the poor thing to death. He kept stomping until there was nothing left. I screamed for him to stop. Somehow, the sweetness that was part of his freckles was gone. And it never came back. Years later, he raised his son, Jason, much of the same way." She leaned her head on the pillow. "I'm tired."

O'Brien reached over and held one of her small hands. He said, "None of this is your fault. You were, no doubt, a good mother. You did the best you could under the circumstances. Many people, unfortunately, grow up in abusive homes. That doesn't justify or give them the right to harm others. I think you followed your father's advice the best you could. I think you followed the meaning of the Golden Rule to the best of your ability."

She said nothing, a slight nod. The old woman's eyes seemed to signify she understood that she was somehow part of a grander plan, and on death's door, she was allowed to peer through the keyhole. Her face now more content. And in less than twenty seconds, she was asleep, sunken chest moving slightly up and down under the blue pajama top. O'Brien patted her hand and stood. He walked over to the laptop on the coffee table and quickly removed the thumb drive. And then he opened the door to the kitchen, the hospice nurse sitting at the table sipping a hot tea and reading a home decorating magazine. O'Brien said, "She's asleep. We can see ourselves out the door. Thank you."

"She doesn't get many visitors. It was good to hear her talking. She's a very smart lady."

O'Brien smiled and closed the kitchen door. In two minutes, he and Wynona were in the lobby. She stopped walking and said, "You never mentioned to her ... you never told her about the recent murders of the retired CIA officers, those who helped send Thurston to prison for his crimes."

"No, I didn't."

"Why?"

"What would that have accomplished? She's very old ... dying. Her bookcase was filled with books about Christianity. There was a large Bible on the coffee table. She wears a cross on a necklace. Patricia Thurston, I think, knows her son is most likely guilty. But she never gave herself permission to believe it. Every mother wants to believe her son grows up to be a good person ... a good man. Sometimes that doesn't happen. And I think she knows it."

Wynona smiled. "One day I'd like to compliment your mother because you did become a good man."

He smiled. "Define good. My mother died a couple of years ago."

"I'm sorry. I can imagine she was a remarkable woman."

He looked at the security camera across the lobby, a man using a squeegee cleaning the large glass windows. O'Brien said, "We didn't come here to tell Patricia Thurston what she doesn't already know in her heart. We came here to get information we can use and to corroborate evidence we suspect."

"You mean the reference to Agatha Christie ... *And Then There Were None*?"

"Yes. Patricia read the nursery rhyme to her son, Richard, when he was a boy. Obviously, the novel fascinated him. Later on, he became absorbed with pulling off the crimes ... perfect murders."

"Sean ... what if, somehow, that was part of his plan when he breached ... to unveil deep cover CIA officers he didn't like, or thought might be better than him, exposing them to the wolves, Russian assassins. Did he really think he was the smartest person in the room? And now that he's been convicted and is stagnating in prison, we believe he's striking out from behind concrete and steel bars. It's been said that he or she who has the last laugh, has the best laugh."

"He hasn't had that laugh yet. If we're lucky, he won't get it." O'Brien opened his right hand, the thumb drive in his palm. "I think, somehow, Thurston is getting messages out to Abdul Aswad. Maybe it's coming through simple letters written between a father and son, and then shared with one of the world's most ruthless terrorists—in some kind of code. My laptop is in the back of my Jeep. Let's open this thumb drive and see what's on it."

# FIFTY-SEVEN

O'Brien and Wynona sat at a back table in Starbucks and read letters brought up on the laptop computer screen, the air smelling of ground coffee beans. O'Brien minimized one letter and clicked on a file. A small light blinked on the thumb drive and in seconds there were two file folders on the screen. They were labeled: 1) *Invoices;* 2) *Letters.* Wynona glanced over at O'Brien and said, "Seems to be generic letters between Richard Thurston and his son, Jason. Chatty stuff, primarily from Richard. Not so much with Jason—just a few sentences. Let's see what else is behind curtain number two."

"All right." He clicked on the *Letters* file. There were five more documents—Word files. He browsed through them, some handwritten and scanned in, and the others composed on a computer. O'Brien said, "It looks like all of the handwritten letters are from Richard Thurston to Jason. And the text letters, composed with a keyboard, appear to have been sent from Jason to his father, Richard. O'Brien skimmed the letter, reading quickly. He said, "As far as the handwritten letters go, I'm sure the CIA can authenticate his handwriting."

"What does he say in this one?"

O'Brien zoomed in closer, the neatly printed words on the page. He read from the screen. "*Dear Jason: I hope this letter finds you well. You don't know how much your letters mean to me. I know they're not often, but I look forward to and cherish each one I'm fortunate enough to receive from you. Thank you for continuing to believe in my innocence. The sad thing is that what happened to me could happen to any American. There is no protection under the Constitution against political corruption and collusion that moves between covert and open sources to end a person's career when it comes to the threat of whistleblowing. Even the infamous CIA has standards of engagement that should be humane, and the agency must be held accountable for its action, and conversely, lack of action, enabling an evil cancer to foster and grow.*" O'Brien paused, glanced over to Wynona.

She said, "Talk about the pot calling the kettle black. Now I can see how Patricia Thurston was snowed. Her son is quite the con man, pointing fingers, refusing to accept responsibility even after the evidence and conviction."

"Let's see what else he had to say." O'Brien found his place in the letter and read. "*My hope is that one day the truth shall be known, and the truth shall literally set me free. In the meantime, please continue your journey in life. Visit your grandmother often. Don't give up your dreams. I encourage you to travel. It will broaden your horizons and scope. That was a good perk in my job, when the job was good. One of my favorite places was Italy. The Italians know the art of good living. If you get to Venice, have a drink in Harry's bar and toast me. Spain was another favorite, especially Barcelona. Have lunch at Vivanda on the square. And don't forsake the Middle East just because of some of the things you may hear in the news. I think Iran may be the birthplace of humanity, maybe even the Garden of Eden. If you get to Lebanon, have coffee in Café de Penelope in Beirut. The consumption of coffee began in the Middle East in the year 1,000, centuries before the rest of the world caught the buzz. If you make it to Café De Penelope, ask for the Arabian Special, the Sir Lawrence. The French were the first to export the bean outside of Europe, planting seeds and growing coffee in Hispaniola in the late 1600s. If you make it there, visit the caves of El Pomier, the Tito Indians—the first indigenous people to greet Christopher Columbus, left behind hundreds of cave paintings in the NW part of the island, dating back 2077 years ago. After that, have a toast of Clement Rum at Captain Cooks. They may still have a few bottles from 1952. It's superb, and it was distilled in the year of my birth. Follow your journey. Write to me when you can. I want to hear more about your adventures. Love, Dad."*

Wynona pushed back a bit from the table. She looked around the coffee shop at the dozen or so customers, most on phones or hunched over laptops with caffeinated drinks next to them. She said, "Richard Thurston sounds like a guy trying to encourage his only child to find his own way into the world. If we didn't know how really cold blooded he is, reading these letters you'd think he was a troop leader for the Boy Scouts."

"Maybe," O'Brien said, scanning through more letters. "Let's see what other correspondence is in here." He quickly read parts of three other letters. And then he read letters that Jason Thurston had written. O'Brien said, "Out of the batch of letters, two thirds were written by Richard to his son. At first glance, Jason's letters seem more businesslike. He writes that payments have been made to all utility companies on behalf of his grandmother. Her medication and doctors' trips have been paid. The question is … paid by whom, Richard or Jason Thurston?"

"Maybe Patricia had a trust fund from money left to her from the death of her husband. Jason could just be paying her bills out of whatever money she has in an account that's allocated for those types of expenditures."

"Maybe. But Patricia and her husband lived in the same small home for thirty years. How did she afford a pricey South Beach condo?"

O'Brien clicked on the *Invoice* file. It appeared to be a standard excel spreadsheet. He studied the entries, Wynona examining the numbers, too. She said, "Wow … wonder what Jason Thurston does for a living. Whatever it is, there appears to be a substantial flow of cash." She pointed to one column of numbers. "He begins with a seventeen-million-dollar entry. The first withdrawal was for two-point-five mil. It only lists the source of the deduction as two letters or someone's initials … b-a-b?"

"Wish I knew. There are three other debits at a little more than a mil each. There are no bank accounts or deposit routing numbers.

So where is the money coming from, and where is it going to? And who is … or what is b-a-b?"

"The bureau needs to pick up Jason Thurston for questioning immediately. Maybe you should give Dave a call to let him know what we found. He'll want to see this odd kind of a P&L sheet and the letters from Richard and Jason Thurston."

O'Brien said, "I think junior is the point person, the go between connecting Richard Thurston and Abdul Aswad … and I think there are codes in these letters, especially the last one we read. I'll email it all to Dave, let him, NSA, CIA and the FBI try to figure it out. I'd like to get permission from someone with the feds to allow me to meet face-to-face with Richard Thurston."

"Maybe Dave can get that arranged. What would you ask Thurston?"

"Not a lot. Not in terms of questions. I would say a few things and see how he reacts. Now that we've spoken with his mother, I know what to say."

# FIFTY-EIGHT

Captain Santos Kalivaris navigated *Aphrodite* toward Marathon Key with no moon in the night sky, one hand on the wheel and the other on the 9mm Sig Sauer under his belt. He looked down from the wheelhouse to his crew on deck. One man, Bear, stood in silhouette on the port side of *Aphrodite* smoking a cigarette.

Johnny was near the bow, watching the marina in the distance through night scope binoculars. He looked at the moored boats lying flat under the light of half a dozen dock lamps on utility poles scattered across the small marina. He searched for movement. People. There was no sign of life. Johnny lowered the binoculars and eyed Kalivaris, giving him a thumps-up.

The two stowaway passengers were in the crew cabin. The second man to board, Saleh Toma, watched through a starboard window, dried saltwater spray on the exterior. He surveyed the marina, looked at his watch and then back at the docks. He turned to his companion and in Farsi said, "We're about thirty minutes behind schedule. Let us hope they are waiting for us."

The other man nodded and responded in Farsi. "If not, we might have to kill these men, take their boat and make other arrangements."

"Shahid has the captain's phone number. I will see if he attempted to contact the captain." He quietly opened the door, slipped outside, stood in the dark shadows for a moment before climbing up the steps to the wheelhouse. He opened the door and said, "Captain, have you received a call or a text from our contacts?"

Kalivaris stood next to the captain's seat. He looked at Toma and said, "No. Not a fuckin' peep, pal."

Toma came closer. He took a deep breath, releasing it through his nostrils, his jawline popping as he gnashed his teeth. "Why do you Americans always have to use foul language?"

Kalivaris took a cigarette from his left ear, lit it with a silver Zippo, the smell of lighter fluid instantly in the wheelhouse. He wedged the cigarette in one corner of his mouth and looked at Toma through the drifting smoke. "Why do we use foul language? I can't speak for anyone else. You gotta remember there are 350 million of us here in the homeland. I'm swearing because I damn well feel like it. What I don't feel like is having my boat, my livelihood, confiscated by ICE, Border Patrol, the FBI or God knows what agency is down here in the Keys. This is probably the smugglin' capital of the whole country, and your compadres insisted we drop y'all off in some fuckin' marina I've never been to and frankly don't want to ever visit again. I could be less than a hundred yards away from having *Aphrodite* boarded and a dozen guns drawn on my men and me. I'd be handcuffed and carted off to some federal prison where I'd spend the next twenty years of my life. So, to more precisely answer your question, I'm swearing, this time, because I'm fuckin' pissed! You got a problem with that? If not, then get the hell outta my space and let me concentrate on bringing my boat through a layer of fog and into this lovely place, okay?"

Toma stared at him through hard eyes, said nothing, turned and left. Kalivaris lifted the Sig from his belt, placing the gun on the console. He used two hands on the wheel, the marina less than thirty yards away, a light fog building and creating halos of moisture around the dock lamps.

• • •

In a remote section of the marina parking lot, two men sat inside a black Lincoln Navigator, the engine off, windows down, crickets chirping. Both men had pistols on the seats beside them. The driver, scruffy short beard, narrow face, swatted at a mosquito and said, "I see them. They're not using many running lights on their boat. That could be a good and bad thing."

The other man, dark complexion, face stubble, ferret eyes that never stopped moving, nodded his head in agreement. "Fewer lights will draw less attention unless the captain is in violation of some absurd American nautical law."

"It's late at night. The marina owner has been paid well. No one appears to be awake and moving around the docks. This will only take one minute. As soon as they are off the boat, we get them and leave. Simple. We shall be in Miami in a few hours. From there we will await our next orders."

• • •

Captain Kalivaris approached the docks as quiet as he could with two large diesels rumbling, each engine capable of 850 horsepower. Bear and Johnny were in the wheelhouse, readying to secure *Aphrodite* to a dock for a few minutes, long enough to offload the two men aboard. They looked through the wheelhouse windows, a mist drifting up from the warm water on a humid night in the Florida Keys.

Kalivaris said, "I see a spot large enough for me to dock *Aphrodite* next to one of the longest piers."

Bear scratched a scab on his tattooed forearm and said, "You got better eyes than me. How the hell can you see through that stuff?"

"I've been doin' this for so long I can just about see through fog." He looked over at Johnny and said, "I'm gonna ease her up to the closest dock. I saw a sailboat and a trawler on either side about fifty feet down. Johnny, you get ready to jump off. Bear, you toss him a spring line. We sure as hell don't need to tie her up like we're gonna be spending a few nights at the bars in Marathon. We just need to hold her tight to the dock long enough for these ol' boys to get the hell off my boat."

Johnny nodded. "On it, Captain. Maybe we can make this real quick. I got an uneasy feelin' in my stomach about this place. It's foggy and too damn quiet for my tastes. We can't get the hell outta here fast enough."

# FIFTY-NINE

Before O'Brien and Wynona left the coffee shop, he'd sent Dave the correspondence between Richard Thurston and Jason, asking Dave to channel it to the CIA and FBI for evaluation. On their way to the parking lot, opening the doors to the Jeep, O'Brien looked at his watch and called Dave. When he answered, O'Brien filled him in on the conversation he and Wynona had with Patricia Thurston. "We believe that Jason Thurston is the conduit between his father and Abdul Aswad. Wynona and I think Richard is calling the shots through that innocuous looking mail he's sending Jason."

Dave sat at a table in his hotel room, his computer open and said, "Maybe. I've been reviewing the letters. I don't see much, if anything, that can be construed or used to orchestrate the kind of coordinated effort it would take to find, stalk, and kill former CIA officers."

"For a man with his skills and background, knowing you and your team, it doesn't take a lot to find men who are no longer undercover and living overt lives." O'Brien sat in the driver's seat of the Jeep, glanced at Wynona on the passenger side and said, "Patricia Thurston said she expects her grandson, Jason, will be back any day to pick up his laptop, which he left in her condo. Maybe agents in the FBI's Miami bureau can pull him in for questioning … do some fishing without tipping him off. They can take a look at the letters. Wynona said one of the agents in particular, assuming he's still assigned there, is extremely good at interrogation." O'Brien looked at Wynona again and asked, "What is the agent's name?"

"He's Special Agent Mario Hernandez. Last I heard he was still there."

O'Brien nodded. "Dave, could you hear her?"

"Yes. Mario Hernandez. I'll speak with the deputy director at the CIA to see how they want to handle it. I'm sure they'll agree with the FBI questioning the son at this point. The CIA want the bigger fish, so they won't question the kid yet—surveillance maybe, but not a face-to-face."

O'Brien said, "Jason, who lives in Atlanta, could come and go at any time. I hope the CIA can get the FBI to step it up then. I could use anything they might garner from questioning Jason."

"Why you, Sean? What do you mean?"

"Because I want to talk with Jason's father ... Richard Thurston. Can you pull strings to get me into the supermax prison in Colorado and a meeting with Thurston?"

"Something like that usually takes a little while to go through prison protocol, and there's no guarantee that Thurston will agree to meet with you. Even if he does, he might not say a word. He's like that. He simply doesn't care what you or anyone else thinks."

"I don't buy it. He very much cares what others think ... especially now, and I'm betting he specifically cares about what *you* think and feel. You were the lead investigator in the team that caught and convicted him. That's one of the reasons he's doing this. He wants you to think about him—to despise him for accomplishing what he's doing from prison. He, like the executioner in the novel, *And Then There Were None*, wants credit, wants the fame to become infamous."

"You said one of the reasons. What's the other?"

"Revenge. He wants to take you guys completely out because of the slow death sentence you helped yoke him to. Thurston's mother, Patricia, said the nursery rhyme that the novel loosely is based upon was one Richard asked to hear over and over as a kid. And when he became an adult, the novel was a silent passenger in his psychotic wheelhouse. When the CIA did personality profiles way back in the day, I wonder if the shrinks caught the fact that little Richard

Thurston grew up in an abusive, passive-aggressive home. His mother spoon-fed him while his career military father pushed him to near boot camp levels as a child. The kid was never allowed to be a kid. And now look at the monster that arose from that assault."

"I'll make the calls to see if we can get you a meeting with Thurston."

"Let's do it as soon as possible." O'Brien rubbed his temples. "A lot's a stake, beginning with your life and that of your daughter. Wynona can only pretend to be Linda for so long, and then they may go looking for her."

Dave pushed back in his chair. "I deeply appreciate what she's doing. And with her background in criminal justice, I'm glad she's with you, Sean. Normally, you just go it alone. I think she brings a lot of value."

O'Brien looked over at Wynona and said, "I agree. She does. Something else ... what's the status of the CIA or FBI's investigation around Tarpon Springs? Those burner phones were bought there. Either the perps were passing through, or they were entering the country from somewhere over there. There are a lot of commercial fishing boats that work the area."

"The FBI knocked on some doors. As I understand it, they looked at all transportation hubs: rail, bus, and boats. They worked with city police, inquiring at marinas, the sponge docks. Came away empty."

O'Brien said nothing. He started his Jeep..

"Where are you and Wynona now?" Dave asked.

"Leaving Miami. Heading back to Ponce Marina."

"Sol Lefko and I spent some time with Robert's wife, Caroline. There wasn't much we could really do or say, though. It was as if she'd expected this all her married life, but certainly not in his retirement ... shocked and heartbroken. She had the thousand-yard stare of a warrior trapped in battle fatigue. She was a woman who thought she'd get a knock on the door one day and a somber faced federal official would deliver the tragic news to her that her husband was deceased. She would never know exactly how he died, where, or who may have killed him. She finally had let her guard down before recently ramping it back up with the latest murders. Another tragedy within this desolation is that Robert's death may have been caused by Richard Thurston, a man who ate Thanksgiving dinner in that same kitchen in the early part of his career and whom they had, at one time, considered a close friend."

"I need to look Thurston in the eye and speak to him. If we find Abdul Aswad … I believe that information will come from Thurston."

"Sean, you don't know this guy. You can't break him."

"I don't need to. I just need to find a rusty spot in his armor. And I may know where to look."

# SIXTY

Russell Douglas smelled the diesel fumes first. His eyes were closed, drifting in and out of sleep. He awoke on a small cot under the canvas eave of his 38-Chris Craft, *Vixen,* a boat that was more than twenty years old. He enjoyed sleeping outside on warm summer nights in the Keys, something he did often at sea.

Russell lay there—listening. His long ashen beard was on top of the discolored sheet that covered his lean body. He slept in boxer shorts. The scent of diesel fumes through the fog reminded him of his years at sea on crab boats from the Bering Straits through the Florida Keys. Sometimes he missed the work—days and nights at sea, the camaraderie of loners who often became brothers, sailors who soldiered rough weather and places. But he didn't miss the odor of crabs. *My days of eatin' bottom feeders are behind me*, he thought.

He retired to an old boat of his own after working for dozens of captains through his twenty-seven-year career. When he retired, Russell rented an apartment after years of going to sea, following the fishing seasons like a cowboy chases the rodeo circuit. After two months on land, he felt seasick.

Tonight, he stared across the marina at one of the lamps on a fifteen-foot creosote-stained piling. He watched the fog swirl through the light. There was no breeze, the mist making its way on unique vapor trails under the light. In the year and a half he'd lived aboard his boat at the marina, he became accustomed to the sound of the diesels on most of the boats moored here. Each had a unique voice, a different rumble or pitch, similar to how a Harley sounds unlike other motorcycles.

He listened to the resonance of the diesels. *Got to be caterpillars.* He looked at his watch in the dim light. 2:59 a.m. *Who the hell is comin' in at this time in the morning. Somebody delivering somethin' that they don't want nobody to see.*

He sat up, his mouth tasting like flat beer and copper pennies. He reached under his cot and picked up a red towel, unwrapping it and lifting out a .38 Ruger.

• • •

Captain Kalivaris looked at *Aphrodite's* depth finder. Looked at the tide charts. He motioned to Bear and said, "It's shallow. Most of the Keys are too shallow for me. I'd be surprised if they have any large sailboats tied up here. Come low tide, the big ones could have a hard time gettin' outta the marina into the channel. We're on a high tide, and I'm still concerned."

Bear said, "Last thing we want is to hit ground in this whole-in-the wall place."

Johnny stared at the digital numbers on the screens and said, "No shit. I'm goin' down there now. Bear, I'll need you to toss me a couple of lines." Johnny turned and left the wheelhouse.

Bear rubbed the stubble on his face, the sound like sandpaper on drywall. He glanced over at Kalivaris and said, "That's why these dudes picked this marina. There's nothin' but a few crabbers and day sailors down here. How the hell did the outsiders find it? That's what I'd like to know." Bear watched the approach for a few more seconds and left.

Kalivaris worked the controls, slowing *Aphrodite* to a crawl. The mist lifted enough for him to better see the docks now that the shrimp boat was less than fifty feet from the closest pier. He used the thrusters to position *Aphrodite* closer, the bow almost alongside the dock.

Johnny waited until the boat was two feet from the mooring before jumping off. Bear tossed him a line and Johnny found a cleat, quickly securing the rope. Bear threw a second line and Johnny tied it to one of the pilings. He looked toward the wheelhouse and gave Kalivaris the thumbs up. Johnny glanced back over his shoulders at the marina community. He could see lights in a few boats. The majority were dark, bobbing silhouettes under the dock lamps, a whiff of gasoline and rotting seaweed in the clammy night air.

Bear opened the door to the crew's cabin, looked at the men and said, "We're here, fellas. Time to hit the road."

The men said nothing, each getting his bag and walking past Bear to the port side of the boat where Johnny stood lighting a cigarette, pacing. He watched the men approach, both speaking in low tones. Johnny had no idea what language they spoke. He looked up at the first man and said, "Lemme take your suitcase."

The man nodded and handed him the long and narrow case. The other man did the same. Johnny said, "What the hell y'all got in here?" He grinned. "That's okay. I really don't want to know."

The two men stepped over the port side and dropped three feet to the wooden dock, both quickly picking up his bag.

Johnny took a step backwards, cut his eyes up at Kalivaris and shook his head. Bear stood next to the gunwale, his right hand inches from the pistol under his shirt. Something caught his attention behind Johnny. He lifted his Beretta .32 out of his belt.

From the curtain of fog, two other men appeared. Johnny raised his left hand in a feigned greeting, taking the cigarette from his mouth. He made an awkward grin and said, "I guess you fellas are the designated drivers."

The first man stared at Johnny for a moment, unblinking. In a thick Arabic accent, he said, "You are late."

# SIXTY-ONE

It was close to midnight when O'Brien and Wynona pulled into the gravel parking lot at Ponce Marina. He parked the Jeep near four tall royal palms and shut off the engine, the cooling motor ticking in the humid night. He counted eleven cars in the lot near the Tiki Bar. In O'Brien's rearview mirror, he watched two bikers get on Harleys and ride away. A small raccoon came from behind a dented metal trashcan, waddling toward mangroves on the far side of the boatyard, a chicken bone in the animal's mouth.

Wynona looked over at him and said, "Last year, before we were actually tracking Dino Scarpa, I noticed how you always scope out places. Always watchful for cars, people. Makes sense right now, of course. But it's as if you can't let your guard down."

"It comes with the territory. Part of the scars. And, I'm sure you'd do the same." He smiled. "Let's go find Max. If Nick's asleep, we'll let her sleepover on his boat. Between *St. Michael* and *Gibraltar*, Max has extended living quarters."

"She's endearing. And so are your friends. The people here at the marina seem like a big family. Flo at the Tiki Bar. Nick and Dave in particular. They know you always have their backs."

"It's mutual. But right now, I have to do more because there's a target on Dave's back, and I don't know where the next shot is coming from, and it might not be from a gun."

She looked beyond the parking lot to the dark fringe of sand dunes and sea oats. "I understand how much you want to help Dave—to protect him from these assassins. Unfortunately, they know more about him than we know about them, at least in terms of where they're located."

"I know where one is located. I'm hoping he can lead me to the others."

"Maybe you'll get in, and possibly you'll get something from him. How will you approach Thurston?"

O'Brien scanned the parking lot, the sound of a reggae song coming from speakers inside the Tiki Bar. He said, "Let's go find Max, and I'll tell you."

• • •

Johnny Hastings could feel the grip of the gun close to his spine under his belt. He knew the two men coming within twenty feet of him were carrying, but their guns were not visible. He assumed the two passengers had packed any number of weapons in their bags. *Maybe it won't come to that … not tonight.* He thought of his pregnant wife, Renee. Johnny grinned, a poker bluff, and said, "I'd say thirty minutes behind schedule is pretty damn good considering the fact that we had to come from way the hell out in the Atlantic. Captain Kalivaris got your men here before a lot of other captains would have, I can guaran-damn-tee you that, pal."

The man with beady, nervous eyes, looked up at the wheelhouse. He gestured with his right hand, signaling for the captain to come down.

• • •

Russell Douglas heard voices. Muffled. Sitting on his cot, he could feel *Vixen's* rubber bumpers grinding as the high tide pushed her nearer to a piling topped in seagull droppings. Russell's boat was close enough to make out that at least one of the men spoke with an accent. And it was an accent that Russell had heard before, working the shipping channels one summer on a freighter out of the Great Lakes.

Two of the crew had been from the Persian Gulf area … great seaman, but their accents were thick as ice in Lake Superior during April.

Russell stood, slipping on a pair of dirty jeans and a Western rancher shirt. He wedged the Ruger under his belt, tightened it a notch and swatted at a mosquito. He listened, angling his head toward the muffled conversations.

After a moment, as if he was waiting for a faraway signal in the dark, Russell stepped off *Vixen* and disappeared in the mist.

• • •

As O'Brien and Wynona walked down L dock, he stopped and stood in the shadows, looking at the houseboat the FBI agents were using to stakeout Dave's boat and the general area. It appeared dark.

Wynona said, "They could be watching us right now."

"I hope so. Or they could have called it a night because Dave's out of town."

She shook her head. "I don't think so, at least not under these circumstances. If Thurston and or Abdul Aswad know Dave's attending a funeral, maybe they'd send someone in here to place a bomb onboard *Gibraltar*. Then, when Dave came home, it could be rigged to detonate in many ways. From him stepping on the boat, opening one of *Gibraltar's* doors, or even remotely." She glanced at the twinkling lights of the condo in the distance. "Even from there. Although I doubt they'd go to the same place twice."

O'Brien said nothing, staring at the houseboat and then looking down L dock to *Gibraltar* directly across from Nick's boat, *St. Michael*. "There are eleven cars in the marina lot. Two of them, the black Ford Explorer and the dark gray Chevy Tahoe, are the agents' SUVs. There's a third, a Ford Escape, but it was not in the lot."

"I didn't know that you knew what they drove. Maybe one of the special agents is asleep while the other is in the wheelhouse behind an infrared scope keeping an eye on Dave's boat."

"Let's hope the agent isn't asleep at the wheel." O'Brien smiled. "You're probably right about the condo in terms of using the same place twice."

They walked further, approaching *St. Michael.* The salon doors were open, Greek music drifting out the doors, a galley light on inside.

O'Brien pursed his lips and made a short, two-beat, whistle. Within seconds, Max popped her head out one corner of the open door and trotted out onto the cockpit. She spotted Wynona and O'Brien, Max's tail moving like a hand-held broom.

Nick lumbered out of the salon, drink in one hand, swim shorts, bare-chested. "Hot Dog," he said to Max, looking up at O'Brien and Wynona standing on the dock. "I shoulda known it was you, Sean. Maxine would be barkin' her head off if it were Ol' Joe the cat. Come aboard. Let's have a drink. I just pulled the cork on a new bottle of ouzo. I wanna hear about Dave."

O'Brien said, "Dave's expected back tomorrow. He stayed over to help the family."

Nick looked toward one of the cones of light from a dock lamp. "He never should have gone. If they'll kill a man on a golf course, they'll shoot him dead in a cemetery or somewhere else in Scottsdale. Not a lot of trees out there to block a sniper."

Wynona said, "There were dozens of government agents and police present. I think he was probably more secure there than the marina."

Nick sipped his drink. "Yeah, stubborn old coot. He wants to stand his ground. What's the latest? FBI or CIA any closer to finding these freaks?"

Wynona said, "The FBI should be questioning Jason Thurston soon. He's Richard Thurston's son. They'll want to see if he's the link between his father and Abdul Aswad."

"How the hell would that happen?"

"Maybe in the letters written between father and son … some kind of code. We don't know, but it's worth pursuing."

Nick sipped from a jelly glass, the white ouzo catching the subdued light from a pier lamp.

O'Brien reached over the cockpit and lifted up Max, setting her on the dock. He asked, "That music coming from your salon, are the musicians from Greece?"

"No, most of the guys are from Tampa. I caught 'em playing in a little club over at Tarpon Springs. I bought their music."

"How well do you know Tarpon Springs?"

"Good. I get there a couple of times a year. It's Florida's Greektown."

"I'm going over there. You care to join me?"

"Sure, but with all this shit goin' on with Dave, this might not be the best time."

"It could be the best time."

"Why is that?"

"Because that's where the FBI found video of two guys buying burner phones. One was the killer that fired down at Dave's boat from the condo. The other guy, I think, was the one behind the wheel of that Top Gun boat I spotted the day I met Katie and Andy."

Nick said nothing. He walked over to one of the canvas deck chairs near the small stainless-steel grill and sat.

Wynona said, "The FBI questioned merchants, marina and boat owners in Tarpon Springs, looking for a possible portal of entry, but they found nothing."

Nick cleared his throat, leaning forward in the deck chair, a gold cross hanging from a chain around his neck, the cross barely moving like a polished brass clock pendulum. He looked up at O'Brien and said, "If the FBI couldn't find anything, what the hell can we do?"

"Dig deeper. Go to places they didn't. A lot of the commercial fishermen speak Greek when they're among their peers. Maybe you'll overhear something."

"They're some tough hombres over there. Sponge divin' is brutal work. They're a salty bunch, and most of those dudes won't give us the timc of day."

"Then we won't ask them that. We'll ask them something we don't know."

# SIXTY-TWO

Captain Kalivaris shut off the diesels, wedged his Sig under his belt beneath his shirt and climbed down from the wheelhouse. He walked over to the port side and said, "I don't have time for small talk. My men and I need to get the hell outta here. We delivered these fellas to you, so y'all can go on about whatever business it is that you do."

The man with the ferret eyes took a step forward. He said, "You, Captain, are part of our business." He grinned. "What we do ... we could not do it without you."

The other man with the steel wool beard said, "That is why I have been asked to tell you we request your services again."

Kalivaris looked at him suspiciously. "When? What did you have in mind?"

"Soon. Within a week or so. This time we will need you to take some of our men back out to sea to meet one of our boats in the Bahamas."

Bear looked over at Kalivaris, blew out a breath and said nothing.

Something moved on the edge of the fog and darkness down the dock.

Bear saw it out of the corner of his eye. He could see a man standing behind a boat davit, the small crane holding a Boston Whaler suspended three feet above high tide. But he couldn't see if the man had a gun or if he was a wearing a security uniform. Bear lowered his big hand to the grip on his pistol, gestured with his head to Kalivaris. Both men could now see the man standing there.

The guy with the edgy eyes looked back in the direction. He motioned to his partners and in Farsi said, "I saw someone down the dock."

Johnny looked up at Captain Kalivaris and Bear, flipping the remains of his cigarette into the marina water and said, "Oh shit."

Russell Douglas knew he'd been spotted. He couldn't see any guns on the men. Rather than try to run, he decided to play ignorant. He walked toward them. When he was about twenty feet away, he smiled and said, "Y'all need any help tying her down? I spent better part of thirty years on shrimp boats and hundred-twenty-foot crabbing boats outta Alaska. I'm a light sleeper. Comes with the package when you're pushin' seventy. Heard your diesels. Cats, right?"

Kalivaris said, "Yep. You got a good ear. We appreciate your offer. We got it covered, partner. Sorry we woke you, bud."

"No problem. Y'all have a good night." He nodded and turned to leave.

Ferret eyes said, "If you could hear the engines, I would think that you could hear us. Listen carefully right now. There is a gun pointed at your back. Do not take another step."

Russell froze. He lifted his hands and slowly turned around. "I didn't hear nothin' on account of the engines. Whatever the hell y'all are doin' out here is your business. Not mine. So, if you'd excuse me, I'd like to go back to bed."

One of the men spoke in Arabic and said, "Do not use a gun. Too loud. A blade will do fine." Both of the men who'd been passengers on *Aphrodite* nodded and approached Russell. One said, "Come with us."

Russell stood his ground for a few seconds. He said, "Okay … I haven't heard or seen a damn thing so there's nothin' I could tell anybody." He walked with the men back to the end of the dock where the others waited.

Captain Kalivaris folded his arms across his chest and said, "He's just a tired old man. Y'all got no right to hassle him. Ever'body has what they want. Let's call it a night."

The man with the anxious eyes pulled a long, serrated knife from under his shirt. "Maybe we cut the old man's tongue out."

Russell reached under his Western shirt and found the grip on his Ruger. Within seconds, the men attached him like wolves. Ferret eyes shoved his knife to the hilt just above Russell's navel, and pulled hard up to his sternum. The killer's eyes, black as coal, burning with hate of his victim and ecstasy of a kill. He withdrew the knife, grinned and used one foot to kick Russell off the dock into the dark water below.

Johnny said, "You're fuckin' crazy! This ain't part of the deal!"

The men ignored him, guns out. They looked up at Kalivaris and the man with the woolly beard said, "Our deal is with Captain Kalivaris. We'll call you in a week … to ten days. Be ready to do what we tell you to do. If not, each one of you will become food for the crabs."

All four men backed away, heading down the dock, one walking backwards, pointing his pistol toward the shrimp boat. Within five seconds, the fog swallowed them.

Johnny scrambled aboard the boat, breathless. Bear helped pull him over the gunwale and said, "We didn't sign up for murder."

Kalivaris said, "Shut up! None of us did."

Johnny stood on weak legs, his lips cracked and bleeding. He said, "I told you I had an uneasy feelin' about this place. That poor old man. Shit!"

Bear said, "They're expectin' us to haul their asses back to the islands. Capt'n, it's like the mafia. Once you get in, it's hard to get out alive."

Kalivaris said, "Cut the lines. We got to get outta here. Cut the line. Use a knife. Now!"

● ● ●

Russell Douglas clutched a barnacle covered piling under the docks. His fingers bled from the sharp edges. The outgoing tide threatened to pull him from the post. He could feel blood flowing from his deep knife wound. "Got to hang on," he mumbled. He watched as the shrimp boat backed away from the marina. Russell didn't have to see if the boat would turn around for him to read the name on the transom. It was on both sides of the high-pitched bow. He mumbled, "*Aphrodite.*"

# SIXTY-THREE

O'Brien and Wynona sat in the dark. They were inside *Jupiter's* fly-bridge sitting on the bench seat, Max asleep to one side. There was no moon visible, the night sky shimmering with starlight. Wynona touched his hand and said, "The trip with Nick to Tarpon Springs might yield something, or it could be a huge time suck."

O'Brien looked at the boat lights across the marina. "That's always a risk in a criminal investigation. The good thing is that if nothing appears illicit, you rule it out and move on to the next fallen domino."

"Are you leaving tomorrow?"

"Yes, as soon as possible. Dave's back tomorrow. Although I have faith in the FBI's stakeout here, would you keep an eye on him?"

"Of course. After all, I'm his daughter, so it makes sense that I can pop over to visit Pop from time to time." She looked down at Max. "You want me to keep an eye out for the sleeping princess, too." Max partially lifted her right ear, one eyelid barely opening.

O'Brien smiled. "Nick will be with me, so he can't take her down to the Tiki Bar at happy hour. He says Max is an ice breaker with the tourists, women, who are visiting the area."

"Really, is it a seasonal thing, or does Nick find a steady flow of ladies visiting the area?"

"I wouldn't know."

She smiled and shook her head. "You know, I really believe you. Women don't find guys like you at a bar."

"Oh, where do they find guys like me?"

"They don't. I say this only because I never met a man like you before in my life. And for me, I didn't *find* you, but I did get to know you during a murder investigation. That's not a typical gathering place for ninety-nine-point-nine percent of the world's population."

"Really?"

"Really. I wouldn't recommend it over a traditional dinner. But, at least for me, the threat of danger, watching you work … watching your absolute dedication to righting a wrong for Joe Billie, I found myself attracted to your … commitment. To whatever it is in your heart that propels you to take such risks for others. You're a noble knight, Sean O'Brien … your moral code and chivalry are things that I thought expired for most men in the seventh century."

O'Brien smiled. "Sometimes I wonder what it would have been like to live in those times. I'd like to think the human race has become a little more civil since the seventh century. But I have no delusions. What about you, Lady Wynona?"

"If I were a lady back then—being Seminole and Irish, I probably would have been in trouble constantly," Wynona said laughing, "and given the nickname Lady Rebel." Wynona looked at the horizon, the sweep of the lighthouse over the dark sea, the stars seemingly from one tip of the horizon to the edge of the earth. "It's ethereal out here, in the dark, in your boat's fly-bridge. Although we're surrounded by a sea of boats, it feels like it's just the two of us."

"At this moment, it is just the two of us."

"I have no delusions either, that's why, when you kiss me, it'll put the *real* in ethereal." She smiled.

O'Brien leaned over and kissed her softly. When they finished, he said, "I hope that felt real."

"Real good," she said with a sensuous smile. "Maybe it has something to do with the gentle rocking of the boat, the gorgeous heavens above us, and the vastness of the sea beyond the breakers."

"For me, it's all of that and the beautiful woman sitting next to me."

"Thank you," she said softly. A moving light caught her eye. "Look, Sean, a meteor in the sky over the ocean." She pointed. The meteor shot through the eastern sky in a fiery burst before fading to black. Wynona said, "Sam Otter used to tell us that shooting stars are a sign of good fortune, especially if you saw one the night of the Green Corn Dance. I hope Dave and Sol Lefko saw it."

"Maybe they did. I wish Dave would spend a few days at my river cabin."

"I know you do. Dave gives the impression that, since he spent a career chasing or being chased by cutthroats, he's not going to allow them to intimidate him into moving. And I think he feels there are few places that he could escape them for long. So, he's resigned to fight from his Alamo." She paused. "Sorry about the analogy, but three ex-CIA officers have been assassinated in the last two weeks. The killers can come over the fort walls because we don't know where they're coming from to stop them."

"That will change. We just have to keep Dave, his daughter, and Sol Lefko safe until …" O'Brien stared toward N dock.

"Until what, Sean?"

"As you know, we found dossiers in the shooter's condo. They included Dave, his daughter, Linda, and the other four ex-CIA officers, including Sol Lefko. However, there wasn't a folder on Sol's daughter, Katie."

"Maybe it's because there are other assassins and someone else who could have Katie's dossier."

"But with Katie Scott right here—right in this marina and not far from Dave's boat … why wasn't there a dossier on her?"

"Maybe the perps weren't aware she and Andy were staying here, prepping for their launch."

"Could be … or Thurston, if he's driving it, may have other plans for Katie. They could be targeting her when she's in the islands."

"Why? If they want her dead, why not try to do it stateside? It's quicker, probably a lot easier than trying to hunt a sailboat among hundreds, if not thousands, scattered all over the Bahamas and the Caribbean islands."

"It could be because Thurston enjoys the cat and mouse game of hunting and systematic elimination. We know that one of two men in that Top Gun boat is dead. Where's the other guy, and where is the boat?"

Wynona rubbed Max's chest and said, "You told Katie and Andy about the boat that day they were working on *Dragonfly* in the boatyard. You said you gave her a brief description of it and the men on it. Seems to me like Katie and Andy might be watchful for a boat like that. If one comes inside their comfort zone, they can radio call for help. Or use a satellite phone. They do have Dave's pistol if someone comes too close, and Andy says he knows how to use it."

"If I don't see Dave tomorrow, maybe you can ask him to get in touch with Sol Lefko, just give him the heads up and maybe he can check on Katie. There are some good Internet connections on most of the larger Islands in the Bahamas."

"You started to say something else about Richard Thurston before we talked about Katie Scott. Jason Thurston has no apparent reason to flee. The FBI's Miami bureau will question him, probably tomorrow. Maybe he'll know a lot more than can be theorized in a few letters. I'd like to give the Bureau a few additional questions to ask."

"I can help you with that, too."

"If you get a meeting with Richard Thurston, how will you approach the questioning?"

"That will depend on his demeanor ... what he says or doesn't say. The way he looks at me. The posture of his body. The movement and blink of his eyes. The way he uses his hands to make a point. How often he speaks in past tense when it should be in present tense. For a sociopath, even one as well trained as Thurston, his ability to pretend to be normal is often only as good as the information he has offered to him about what you expect."

Wynona hugged her upper arms in the cooling night air. "In the Bureau, we were extensively trained to investigate, interrogate, and eventually help prosecute sociopaths and the violent psychopaths. But, evil as they were, and although many shared the same psychological traits, there was always something that would happen that wasn't covered in training or something you learned from dealing with the previous criminal mind. I think you're going to find that with Richard Thurston."

"No doubt, but to get what we need ... a link to finding where Abdul Aswad is today, I have to go back into Thurston's past ... all the way back to the time his mother read and reread the nursery rhyme, *Ten Little Indians*, to him. For most kids, the nursery rhyme was used to teach counting, although the story was told from ten to one, the process of elimination. And for most kids, the counting—or subtraction, is what they'd get out of it. But, for a sociopath in the making, it was a nursery rhyme with a dark core—a core of killing and genocide. I think that's where it began for Thurston. And, as dark as it is ... I'll have to travel there to find what we need to save lives."

# Sixty-Four

Russell Douglas thought, if he could move fifty feet closer to shore, he might not die ... at least not tonight. He clung to a piling under the dock, the receding tide pulling hard at his shirt and jeans, his boat shoes washed away. He looked up under the dock. Boards, two-by-six sections of timber, ran between the pilings, almost like sturdy latticework designed to co-support the boardwalk directly above the pilings. "Gotta get a hold of one," he whispered in the steamy night air.

He used what little strength he had left to hoist himself up, reaching for the nearest section of lumber. He grabbed it with his right hand, held tight for a second, and then used his left hand—placing it in front of his right. From there, Russell labored to move through the rushing water, hand-over-hand, from the end of the docks toward the midway point, one hundred feet. At age seventy, years of pulling fishing nets and crab traps had given him a grip stronger than most men half his age.

Russell moved further down the pier, his stomach on fire as the salt water moved in and out of his gaping wound. He held on, right hand moving in front of the left and then the left moving in front of his right—slowly, the timbers wet, hard to grasp. Blood from the barnacle cuts in his palms ran down his wrists, dripping onto his forehead. "Just a little more," he said, grunting. "Gotta hang on ...

gotta get help." He pulled harder. Getting weaker from the loss of blood. Bile moving up his throat.

Something touched his feet.

Sand. He'd pulled himself far enough under the docks for his feet to touch the bottom. He still used his hands for another yard and finally let go. He stood, water rushing around his chest. He plodded on through the current, crabs scurrying from under his feet as he took steps. And then he was in three feet of water. He braced himself on a piling and moved toward the shore less than twenty feet away. He fell, his head going under the water for a second. He emerged, finding adrenaline from somewhere in his body.

Russell walked out of the water and up onto the docks. He felt in his back pocket. He phone was there. He pulled it out and saw the screen filled with water. He tried to walk up the docks to a boat where he knew the owner well. He came to a Helmsman-37 trawler. The lights were off, the boat completely dark. Russell knew his friend, Craig Moore, was home. Russell eased onto the transom and cockpit, clutching the cavernous wound in his stomach with his left hand.

He almost slipped in the dew-laden cockpit as he stumbled to the door to the salon. He pounded on the window with the palm of his bloody right hand. Within a few seconds a light was on, movement in the boat. A bald man, wide chest, in a tank top and boxer shorts, held a .357 pistol in his right hand. He peered through the window.

Russell said, "Craig … I've been stabbed. Need help."

Craig Moore looked beyond Russell, set the gun down and opened the door. "Good God almighty," he said, helping Russell inside the trawler. "We gotta get you to a hospital. I'm dialing nine-one-one." He helped Russell to the leather couch. Took a closer look at the wound, the pink of intestines visible through the ripped flesh and blood. Craig fumbled for his phone, put his wire-rimmed glasses on, tried to make the call, his hands shaking.

"Nine-one-one … what's your emergency?" asked the dispatcher.

"My friend's hurt bad! We need an ambulance!"

"What is the address, sir?"

"Umm … Marathon Marina off Route One. He's on my boat, a Helmsman-37. Name on the boat is *Lucky Strike*. We're at slip F-eleven."

"We're sending paramedics now. How was your friend injured?"

Craig looked over at Russell, sweat popping out on his forehead, his ripped shirt pooled in blood. Moore licked his lips and said into the phone, "He said he was stabbed. We need someone damn soon, okay?"

"I'm sending help to your location now."

Moore disconnected, set the phone on a coffee table and ran to the head. He came back with a large white towel, folded it and placed the towel against the open wound. "Hang in there, Russell. You hear me? Ambulance will be here in a minute."

Russell starred at a small oscillating fan on the top of a bookshelf, his bloodshot eyes following the movement of the fan. He was too weak to turn his head to look at his friend. He opened his mouth and tried to speak, his voice raspy.

"Save your strength." Moore said, holding the towel. "I think I hear the sirens down the road. Hold on, Russell. Don't you leave me! We still go a lot of fishin' to do."

Russell took a depth breath, his lungs on fire. He managed to turn his head a bit toward Moore, looked him in the eye and whispered, "Aphrodite." The life force in his eyes faded, and then Russell Moore exhaled his final breath on earth.

# SIXTY-FIVE

Katie Scott had never felt so alive in her life. She sat on one of the seat cushions near the helm, sipping black coffee, watching the sun peep over the Atlantic. The ocean was as smooth as a billiard table, a breaking dawn causing the low hanging clouds to blush with the color of sliced cherries. Last night, Katie and Andy had anchored *Dragonfly* in a quiet, remote cove at sunset, in an island chain near the Abacos. After a fabulous dinner of fresh-caught fish, salad and chilled chardonnay, they made love like they invented it and slept through the night, a cool sea breeze entering *Dragonfly's* open hatches.

At the break of dawn, there were no other boats in sight, only emerald green water fading into blue sapphire that went further than she could see. Katie sipped her coffee and looked at the lush island seventy yards behind *Dragonfly*. The rising sun now caressing the tops of tall canary palms bordering beaches with sugar white sand that seemed to stretch around the entire island.

She set her empty cup down, looked at her watch on her wrist, pursed her lips watching the sun open like a morning glory flower, gifting its rosy petals to a new dawn and those lucky enough to bask in its splendor. She unfastened her watch and took three steps to the transom, throwing the watch into the sea. Katie whispered, "We're in a land that time doesn't command." She stared at the splash, the ripple rings spreading into small circles until the last sphere flattened into nothingness. She turned and went below deck.

At the bottom of the steps, Katie peered into the master cabin, Andy lying on the sheets in his shorts, eyes closed, dark stubble on his face. She looked at him a moment, more in love with her husband than she could remember. He'd always been there for her, through death, cancer, job changes—life changes. And now it was time to reclaim their lives because time had poured through their fingers like water through a sieve, never able to grasp it rationally or tangibly to alter the flow.

*Until now.*

She walked into the cabin, leaned down and kissed Andy on his forehead. "Good morning, handsome. At the risk of sounding like the alarmist I once was, would you get your butt out of bed? We have an island to explore. You missed the best sunrise I've ever seen."

Andy pushed himself up on his elbows. "You said that about yesterday's sunrise, and the day before, and the day before that. And you'll probably say it about tomorrow's sunrise as well." He smiled.

"I probably will, because now I'm getting up before the sun so that I can appreciate its arrival and offer it a proper greeting. We share light and coffee together. Let's take the dinghy to shore and explore the island."

• • •

A half-hour later, Katie and Andy, both wearing swimsuits, were motoring their nine-foot dinghy to the smooth sand of the beaches. They got out and pulled the inflatable onto the beach, tying the line to a low-slung palm filled with green coconuts, the scent of wild yellow elder flowers in the breeze. Katie laughed and said, "Okay, Robinson Crusoe, let's go explore. Maybe Gilligan is still here."

"Let's hope not. He'd be an old man with a beard down to his feet. Robinson Crusoe was a castaway. Legend has it, the real guy the book was based on, spent most of his life as a castaway on the island of Trinidad before being rescued."

Katie motioned toward the dinghy. "We have an escape route." She looked at the beach, palms, clusters of sea grapes, and hummingbirds darting in and out of the flowers. "Maybe it wouldn't be so bad to be a castaway for a few months on a place like this." She grinned, dug her toes into the white sand and kicked some toward Andy's feet. "C'mon, hubby. Let's do the island."

She took off running through the gentle breakers. Andy grinned and followed, quickly catching Katie and pulling her into the clear water. They swam for a few minutes, laughing and playing like children before coming back to shore. They held hands walking down the beach, following the terrain as it meandered around coves filled with water clear as a glass of gin.

Within fifteen minutes, they had walked more than half a mile, marveling at the flowers and birdlife. Katie glanced back at *Dragonfly*, the sailboat lying stationary, sails down. She smiled and continued walking with Andy. They didn't see the boat coming over the horizon.

Coming straight for *Dragonfly*.

# SIXTY-SIX

O'Brien drove his Jeep toward the historic sponge docks in Tarpon Springs when Nick, sitting in the passenger side, huffed like a bull that was just released into a new pasture, following the pheromone scent from a cow. O'Brien drove slowly down Dodecanese Boulevard, bounded on the right by the Anclote River, marinas and the fleet of commercial fishing boats. On the left side of the street were gift shops, Greek restaurants and bakeries, the smell of baklava and sunblock in the air. Between it all were tourists—herds of tourists. Cut-off jeans shorts. T-shirts. Flip-flops. Moving color.

There were dozens of commercial fishing boats moored on both sides of the Anclote River. More of the sponge diving boats appeared to be closer to Dodecanese Boulevard, the shops and restaurants. Some of the shrimp boats and larger crabbing boats were across the narrow river. O'Brien slowed to a stop. No traffic behind his Jeep. He observed some of the captains and crews unloading fish, crabs and sponges just harvested from the bottom of the Gulf of Mexico.

Nick said, "Did I tell you, when I was a kid, I used to free-dive for sponges back on Mykonos. Sponges rotting on deck in the hot Greek sun, man, it's a smell you never forget."

"You have told me that, but not recently. I gather you don't miss it."

"Not at all. But I learned a lot about the ocean and its currents. Today, I can track things at sea. Most of the time I don't need a fish finder to read the bottom. I can look at the movement of the water, the wind, the breaking of small fish on the surface to know what's probably lurking below."

O'Brien said, "It's what's lurking above the surface that concerns me. Things like that Top Gun boat I spotted the first day I met Katie and Andy."

"I can't track people, Sean. Only fish. You're on your own in the bounty hunter's world."

O'Brien half smiled. "What do you think we're doing here now? We're tracking people."

"But it's not like we're kickin' some killer's door down and goin' in with guns locked and loaded. Not that I'd stay back if you needed me to help you. But right now, I'm more like a tour guide, showin' my close friend, you, around my favorite city in all of Florida." He stuck his head out the window for a second, shouting something in Greek. He turned back to O'Brien and said, "Smell the air, Sean. I can already tell the difference between the east coast of Florida and the west coast."

O'Brien slowed for a small procession of tourists coming closer to a tour boat barker shouting, "Sponge diver goin' out in fifteen minutes … catch a boat ride and watch the man dive. No place else in Florida, folks. Sponge boat goin' out. Get your tickets!" He had a sundried brown, leathery face, and wore a red T-shirt that yelled, too. It depicted a wide-eyed natural sea sponge, fist drawn back, taking a swing at Sponge Bob.

O'Brien slowed his Jeep to the speed of a walker, glanced over at Nick and asked, "What's the difference between Florida's east and west coasts?"

"First the air … it's less salty over here, but a little more of a fishery or fishy odor. My Greek nose is like a trained birddog. I can smell sponges drying on at least one of those boats tied along the docks." He looked out his open window, the breeze tossing Nick's wavy black hair, his dark eyes ignited.

"Is there a second reason?"

"Man, I got a dozen reasons. Second, that would have to be the Greek women. A lot descended from the genes of Aphrodite. Such beautiful creatures."

O'Brien said nothing.

Nick grinned and said, "Speakin' of women … Wynona, with her olive skin, could pass as Greek. Maybe from the southern Islands, places like Santorini. She doesn't look like a former FBI agent."

"What do former FBI agents look like?"

Nick pulled out a toothpick from his shirt pocket and stuck it in one corner of his mouth. He said, "I don't know. The picture I get of FBI types is white guys, probably attended some of the best colleges … frat boys turned federal agents."

"There are plenty of women in the bureau. She was one of the best."

"Yeah, I got no problem with her pumpin' rounds into a dude stabbing his teenage daughter."

O'Brien didn't comment, observing the docks and fishing boats.

Nick took the toothpick from his mouth and said, "I can tell she likes you a lot. Is it mutual … or you gonna say Nicky, it's none of your business?" He grinned. "She's a keeper, Sean. Smart. Freekin' gorgeous. And she seems damn fearless. Maybe my man, Sean O'Brien, finally found a woman who can go toe to toe with him. She's got the whole package."

O'Brien smiled. "I won't disagree with any of your musings. And that's all I'm saying because, right now, we have to concentrate on finding people who want to slit Dave's throat and stick a piece of paper with a verse from a nursery rhyme on his body."

Nick watched a fisherman, wet jeans, shirtless, yellow rubber boots, spraying water on a pile of sponges heaped in the cockpit of a boat tied to the docks. He said, "The Greeks came to Tarpon Springs in the late 1800s to dive for sponges and build businesses. So, there are a lot of bloodlines that go back to the islands and Athens. These are my people." He slipped on his sunglasses. "I got a couple of hole-in-the-wall bars over here I want to take you to."

"Let's save that for when this is finished, and we can bring Dave to celebrate with us."

"We need to dig for information, right? Well, two of the best places are the outta the way bars the locals go to … and the coffee shops. There's one coffee shop that Greek women don't go inside. It's an old custom. Mostly retired spongers and fishermen. I speak their language, and I'm not just talkin' Greek." He laughed.

"When was the last time you were in Tarpon Springs?"

"I'd say five months ago. Used to come more regularly when I was dating Mona Pappas. But those long-distance romances don't last, at least for me." He grinned watching a shapely woman walking near the sponge docks.

O'Brien smiled. "Tarpon Springs is about three hours from Daytona. That's not much of a long distance."

"No, but somehow the distance created distance. That causes excuses and hurt feelings. So, as a gentleman, I gave her a courteous out. I just hope I don't see Mona here today."

O'Brien slowed his Jeep to a stop, waiting for a family to cross the street from the docks to the shops. He looked at a bronze statue of a Greek sponge diver erected in the near center of the main dock area, and then he studied the fleet of commercial boats. "Any suggestions on where to start? If one of those boats in the harbor is smuggling assassins into this country, which one might it be … and how do we find out?"

Nick grinned. "I got an idea."

# SIXTY-SEVEN

They could still hear the breakers. Barely. Katie and Andy explored some of the island's interior, stopping to snap pictures of flowers. "Look at that!" Katie said, pointing to four parrots in a gumbo-limbo tree, the birds feeding on fruit. "They're so colorful. I had no idea that parrots even lived in the Bahamas." The birds had emerald green feathers, snowy faces and scarlet throats, giving the appearance of red scarfs on their necks.

Andy watched the birds for a few seconds. "I didn't know that either. I wonder if they were blown here from hurricanes in the past or if they're native to the islands?"

"We'll have to inquire with some of the native island folk at the next rustic bar close to a beach." She laughed, the birds eyeing them from the tree. "I'm going to take their picture." Before Katie could lift her small camera up, one parrot turned its head toward the north and squawked, its call traveling across much of the small island. "Wow, he or she is vocal. Maybe it's their way of saying hello."

All four of the birds cocked their heads in a northward angle, as if they were hearing something beyond the range of humans to detect. Within seconds, they jumped from the limbs, soaring though the gaps in trees—green, white, and red splashes rocketing through the foliage, screeching, each parrot trying to shout louder the other.

Katie laughed and said, "Maybe they were actually saying good-bye, or they just didn't want their picture taken."

Andy glanced back over his shoulder. "I don't think it was that. You see them posing on postcards everywhere." He grinned. "Before they flew the coop, they all appeared to be looking or listening to something toward the beach."

Katie stared up at the gumbo-limbo tree. "They could have had a bird's eye view from there." She laughed. "We should head back, check on our dinghy. Who knows if that boater's knot, that half-hitch you tied, is still holding. A receding tide might have worked it loose."

"Not a chance. Before I was a sailor, I was a boy scout. I've got lots of experience tying knots."

She smiled. "If that's so, why do the laces on your boat shoes seem to come undone a lot?"

"I like a loose fit."

"Sure. Let's go check on the dinghy. We don't want to wind up like Robinson Crusoe."

They left, walking back down the white sand path until they came to a fork in the path. Katie stopped and said, "We know the one to our right is the trail we walked down to get here. You can see our tracks. What we don't know is where the other path might lead us. It appears to go in the general direction as the other one. But, there is something about the road less traveled, in this case—the path … that best fits our mission of new discovery. It might take us back to the beach. If not, who cares?" She started walking.

Andy said, "I thought you were concerned that my half-hitch may have turned into a slip knot and the dinghy is floating away."

She looked back at him and smiled. "If that happened, we'll have to swim back to *Dragonfly*. Come on, lover. I have a feeling we're going to see something different on this path—the path less traveled."

# SIXTY-EIGHT

The divers were as close to human tourist's attractions as a small Florida town could hope. They were the few dozen men who still departed from Tarpon Springs each week, taking their boats out to dive for natural sponges on the ocean floor. O'Brien thought about that as he and Nick walked down the sidewalk adjacent to the sponge docks. A few deck hands were stocking two boats with ice, food and provisions as they prepped for departure at first light. Tourists kept a respectable distance, snapping pictures, the deep-water tanned divers and deck hands indifferent to it.

A half block away, a sightseeing "dive boat" was loading tourists aboard, some stopping near the gangplank to pose with a middle-aged diver wearing one of the rubber dive suits often used during the 1960s. He held a brass dive helmet that bolts to a metal collar on the neck area of the suit. When air from the single air hose attached to the boat is pumped to the diver, the suit can sometimes have a slight resemblance to the Michelin Man.

Nick grinned and said, "Yeah man. You gotta love it. The Greeks are good at figuring out how to capitalize on their heritage and the legend of the sponge diver. It's definitely in the top ten most dangerous jobs in the world. You gotta put up with changing currents, sharks, staying focused as you walk for miles on the bottom of the ocean. Very few men can do it, and even fewer can do it for very long."

O'Brien nodded, "There's a mystique about it. How long do they usually stay out?"

"Some captains and crew—for a week to ten days. For the bigger boats, they can stay out a month."

O'Brien stopped and looked at the fleet. "A few of these boats are large enough to smuggle people aboard. Others, probably not, risking getting caught." He looked across the narrow river to a dozen or more shrimp boats tied to the docks. "But the shrimpers, that's a different story. They have larger boats. More places to stow people."

Nick eyed the shrimp boats, sea gulls shrieking overhead. "Some of those boats are owned by Greek captains. But I guess it doesn't make any difference who the hell owns them. The color of money speaks many languages. Let's go see if we can find out stuff you'll never spot from standing here on the docks."

They walked across Dodecanese, sidestepping tourists who strolled in and out of the shops, the scent of coffee, grilled lamb and baklava in the air. Nick led O'Brien down Athens Street, past Café Anastasia, past Mama's Greek Cuisine, and then he stopped and motioned to a shop with no sign on the window or hanging from a post. It was a nondescript gray building tucked away between a bakery and a gift shop.

Nick said, "The place is called George's. They make Greek and Turkish coffee the old-fashioned way. Cook it on a gas stove in special metal coffee pots called brikis. They boil the coffee. In Greek it's called ellinikos kafes. Served in small, half cups with water on the side. It's rocket fuel." He watched two older men sitting in one of the three round tables outside on the sidewalk. "Sean, maybe you can hang here at Mama's cafe, maybe get a beer while I go speak real Greek to the real Greeks."

O'Brien looked at the two elderly men, one wearing an Aegean fiddler's cap. They had cards on the table, and in their hands, two small white coffee cups next to them. Nick said, "They're playing a card game called bastra. My father and his father played it after church. They taught me how. Give me a half-hour in there. Maybe I can get somebody to talk. They always have bottles of ouzo behind the counter. That's where I'll start."

O'Brien said, "Maybe you can find something in two shots or less. Otherwise …"

"C'mon, Sean. This round is for Dave. I'll do what I gotta do to help him. Hey, we're partners. Hang tight. Relax. Be right back." With that, Nick strolled down the sidewalk, head held high, whistling, nodding at the two older men and walking into the coffee shop like he owned the place.

# SIXTY-NINE

Katie and Andy followed the white sand path as it meandered closer to the shore, the rolling sound of the breakers not far away. They came upon a tall banyan tree, its girth larger around than two semi-truck tires, the roots from a strangler fig cascading down the tree in shoots as thick and large as a python's body. The tree and all of its prop roots gave the appearance of a long-ago volcanic eruption, the streams of lava hardened into a candle wax drip of wood art.

"Oh my God," Katie said, staring up at the tree. "It looks like it was planted five hundred years ago. Maybe it was growing on this spot when Spanish pirates sailed the islands."

"Check out at all of the nooks and crevasses in the trunk. Some look deep enough to stick your arm in all the way past your elbow. Maybe a few Spanish doublons are hidden in there."

Katie walked up to the tree. She reached out and ran her fingertips across the tree's gangly trunk, the bark cool to her touch—a coarse but soothing feel. She looked up at its canopy. "It's as if the tree is reaching to the heavens for some celestial hug. When I was a little girl, I used to sit under a big oak tree in a remote spot in our back yard. I somehow felt protected under its strong limbs. It was a special place where I could find some quiet times. And the old tree was always a great listener. Although once, when I was complaining about doing the dishes, the tree dropped an acorn on the top of my head." She laughed.

"Be glad it wasn't an apple tree. Although I believe that incident got Isaac Newton to start thinking about gravity and how our little planet stays in sync with the sun and moon."

"Let's follow the unbeaten path." She touched the tree one more time, as if she was caressing it, turned and left.

Andy walked next to Katie, ducking under some of the banyan's low-hanging branches, the prop roots like cave-dwelling stalagmites holding up the extended limbs. They went another fifty feet, no other human tracks on the path. But there were other tracks. Andy stopped walking and pointed. He said, "Take a look at those. I wonder if the tracks were made by a raccoon dragging its tail?"

Katie studied them and said, "I don't know if raccoons live in the Bahamas." She took three steps further, looked around a grove of sea grapes and stopped. "Wow! I feel like we're trekking back in time. Those tracks weren't made by a raccoon, they were made by that iguana strolling over the path less traveled like he or she doesn't have a care in the world."

They watched the iguana waddle down the trail, stop and eat a sea grape from a limb close to the ground. The reptile was about three feet in length, its skin a deep-sea green and gray. The iguana ate a second grape, crossed the path and disappeared in the undergrowth.

Andy said, "That iguana saw us, but he or she didn't look scared. I can't imagine that iguanas would see many people on the island."

"Then they'd have no reason to be frightened of humans because their species probably hasn't seen many people since the conquistadors trampled through here with gold dust in their dark and steely eyes. I'm ready for a swim."

They walked another fifty yards, following the sandy trail as it twisted through tall coconut palms and sea grape trees. The path led them to within one hundred feet of their dinghy. Andy grinned, pointed to the dinghy and said, "Not a hitch in my half-hitch knot. The dingy is exactly where we left it."

Katie looked at the dinghy, cutting her eyes to *Dragonfly*. She stared, trying to process what she was seeing. "Andy ... there's a boat anchored right next to *Dragonfly*."

Andy looked, lifting his right hand to his eyebrows, shielding the sun from his eyes. "What the hell are they doing? Why get so close to our boat?"

Katie touched two fingers to her throat, her pulse quickening. "That's the same boat I saw when we were docked in Bimini. And I think it's the same boat that I saw at a distance when we were making the crossing to the islands. What if it's the identical boat Sean O'Brien saw that day at Ponce Marina?"

"Then we have serious trouble. I can see two men in the boat. I don't know if any are on *Dragonfly*. The gun that Dave gave us is in the master cabin."

"What can we do? Maybe they haven't seen us. We can hide on the island."

# SEVENTY

Wynona stood inside *Jupiter's* salon and glanced at her phone again, hoping a text from Sean would arrive. Nothing. She walked over to a port window and looked down L dock. Dave was due to return to the marina, and she was anxious. She watched the houseboat tied to the next dock. No sign of the FBI agents. And that was a good sign. Surveillance works best when nobody knows you're there.

Her phone buzzed softly on the table next to her Beretta. She looked at Max resting on the couch and said, "Maybe it's Sean with some good news. Max seemed to nod as Wynona picked up the phone. She recognized the Miami area number—the FBI office. She answered.

"Wynona, it's Mario. Thought I'd give you the heads up on our questioning of Jason Thurston."

"Where'd you find him?"

Special Agent Mario Hernandez sat behind his desk in his corner office of the FBI's Miami bureau. His hair was dark as a crow's feather. Penetrating black eyes that didn't seem to blink as he spoke. "We picked him up at the Magic City Casino in West Flagler. He was losing a month's pay as we observed him. We brought the guy in and questioned him for about two hours. The deputy director and other honchos watched it via closed circuit in Quantico. Jason said that he and has father had an estranged relationship at best up until about eighteen months ago. He said his dad told him he's suffering from prostate cancer, and it's a slow death sentence. Said, before he died, he wanted to square things with Jason. We have our forensic psych people looking at the interview. He seems deceptive and robotic at the same time … as if he's resigned to the fact his old man is one of the nation's worst traitors and that's going to follow junior the rest of his life."

"How about the letters … anything there?"

"He denies going to the places listed in that one letter, the Middle East, Caribbean and so on. There's nothing on his passport, and Homeland has no data of him traveling there. If he was trying to deliver money to Aswad in any of these places, I'd suggest that he handed that task off to someone else to make the runs, or there was some sort of a wire transfer."

"And we have no idea who that someone else might be."

"We do have ideas … just nothing with tangible proof behind it. These people move in and an out of some countries by paying immigration officials to look the other way."

"Where is Jason Thurston now?"

"Back at his grandmother's condo. We asked him to stick around, otherwise he may appear as an accomplice and, if proven, he could sit in a cell right next to his daddy."

"You said Thurston was losing a month's pay at the casino as you closed in on him. His grandmother lives in a high rent district with no known or visible means of income. Where are they getting the money?"

"The condo is paid off. No mortgage. She owns it free and clear. All we could find is a trust fund set up in her name by Wevco LLC. There is only a P.O. box in Zurich, Switzerland. That's where it begins and ends."

"No … it doesn't end there. It ends with Richard Thurston in federal prison."

"And he's going to go to his grave with a smirk on his face and silent taunts."

"Maybe not."

"Well, his son is claiming ignorance, and Richard will be evasive or lie, even if he does answer questions."

"Maybe there's another approach. I'm sure you recorded video of you questioning Jason Thurston, right?"

"You know its standard procedure now."

"I have to ask you for another big favor."

"What is it?"

"Send me the link or make a copy of the video and send it to my email address. I want to study Jason Thurston. I have no idea if it'll help, but sometimes another set of eyes and ears can pick up on something." She heard him exhale through the phone.

"Wynona, you're the first to know that's strictly prohibited. I could lose my job if anyone found out."

"No one will find out. I'll delete it when I'm done. Any information I might come up with goes straight back to you. Please, Mario, I'd never ask you if lives weren't at risk. I'm in a marina looking across the dock at a boat owned by retired CIA officer, Dave Collins. And on the next dock are three special agents from headquarters rotating shifts, staking out Dave's boat and the perimeter area. Dave is one of two remaining CIA officers still alive after the assassinations in the last ten days. Anything Jason Thurston said that may lead us to the killer or killers, ostensibly Abdul Aswad and his band of merry psychopaths, will help."

"Okay. I'll send it through a secure protocol in a reduced file size. It'll make viewing easier. What's your most secure email address?"

Wynona told him and added, "Thanks, Mario. Please keep me updated if anything breaks."

"No problem. We miss you in the bureau. I mentioned this once to you, but I believe it bears repeating. Any of us would have done what you did. Okay, Wynona?"

"Thank you. That means a lot. We'll talk soon. Bye."

She disconnected and started to set her phone down when it made a slight buzz. She could see an anonymous file arrived. Wynona decided to make a cup of tea and watch the video. She set her phone down, standing and glancing out the port window. She spotted Dave Collins coming down the dock.

In the distance, a man was following him.

# SEVENTY-ONE

Nick Cronus sat at a corner table in the coffee shop and sipped a strong black coffee. There were no paintings or pictures on the walls. It was a simple shop with a dozen chipped Formica tables, foldout metal chairs, white sugar in glass containers on each table, and the smell of coffee and cigars. There was a makeshift worn bar in the rear with a four-burner gas stove, coffee in a metal pot boiling on one burner. The front door was propped open, an occasional fly entering, a half-dozen lying dead on a windowsill.

Nick casually watched the men—there were eleven customers, most over sixty, at least three eighty or older, all Greek-Americans. Some played bastra. They talked local and national politics. He could hear them speaking about the downturn in fishing and the effect of the red tide outbreak still lingering almost two months later.

Nick watched a man in his late forties wearing a traditional-style Greek fishing cap. He had broad shoulders, thick hands and forearms, dark complexion. He sipped ouzo from a small glass that looked like a shot glass in his big hand. The man sat alone, looked beyond the front door, as if he longed to be somewhere else.

Nick got up and approached the rear of the shop where a bald man, quarter-inch whiskers the color of dirty silver, mid-sixties, poured thick coffee into a small cup and set it on the roughhewn bar. In Greek, the man said, "Darius … coffee's ready."

A man with rounded shoulders, shaggy white eyebrows, bulldog jowls, stood from a chair next to one of the tables, shuffling back to get his coffee. After he returned to his table where two other men sat, Nick looked at the shop owner and, in Greek, said, "I like your coffee. Best I've had since my last visit to Patmos."

The old man cocked his head, listening, his mind locked on the images of a special place—Patmos. He nodded and said, "The sacred island. You got family there?"

Nick nodded. "Don't all Greeks have relatives on the island that was the home to Saint John?"

"Of course. I'd like to go back one day before I die."

"Maybe, if you're lucky, you can one day die there."

The old man smiled. Nick said, "How much for a bottle of ouzo?"

"Thirty."

Nick peeled off two twenty-dollars bills and set them on the counter. "Keep the change."

The shop owner grunted and reached under the counter, handing him an unopened bottle. He said, "You can't take the bottle out the door. You can drink in here. But when you leave, the bottle has to stay. Not my law."

Nick grinned, lifted the bottle, and said, "I'm thirsty, my friend. What's your name?"

"Gus."

"Good to meet you, Gus. I'm Nick." He lowered his voice a notch and said, "If a man was lookin' for work on the boats, don't matter if it's sponge fleet, charter fishing, or shrimp boats … who'd he see?"

The shop owner used a cloth towel to mop up a few drops of spilled coffee from the counter top. He lifted his eyes up to Nick and asked, "What kinda work you want? Deck hand? Diver? Looks like you got the shoulders to pull crab traps, too."

"I can do all that … but I was thinkin' if you might know somebody who's lookin' for a hired hand to run anything. If I'm not too picky, it might be easier to find a job quickly, and I need the money bad to pay off some bills I got hit with recently. I know my way around the Keys, the Ten Thousand Islands south of Everglades City, and even many of the Bahamas … like the back of my hand. Sort of been there and done that, know what I'm sayin'? And I can keep my mouth shut."

The man filled a coffee pot with water, set it on the stove and turned on the gas, the blue flames licking and hissing around the dark base of the pot. He looked up, his left eye slightly uneven, a small bleached scar across the bridge of his nose. "You might want to check with the fella in the hat, Kenny Drakos. He knows some of the newer captains. The rest of the guys in here have all been drawing Social Security for years."

"I need a second glass."

The shop owner nodded, setting another glass on the bar, turning to his boiling pot of water.

Nick walked to the table where the man in the fishing cap sat alone and, in Greek, said, "Gus sent me."

# SEVENTY-TWO

None of the people with boats tied to L dock would know that the man walking less than fifty feet behind Dave was an FBI agent. Wynona knew. She could tell by the way the agent watched the periphery, watched the people lounging and working on their boats. She saw the way the agent glanced at the man fishing from the pier, how he looked at the rooftops of the marina and buildings in the distance. The agent wore dark glasses and a flesh colored earpiece in his right ear that someone would think was a hearing aid.

Dave walked quickly, a small suitcase in one hand, the Wall Street Journal in the other. He stopped a second as he came up to Nick's boat, *St. Michael*. He seemed to know that Nick wasn't there. And then Dave glanced down the dock toward *Jupiter,* lifted his eyebrows, almost a signal—as if he somehow knew Wynona was there, too.

She watched him enter *Gibraltar's* cockpit, quickly inspecting various parts of the trawler before unlocking the doors leading to the salon. Within a minute of boarding, he was inside, the salon doors closing, the federal agent looking at the houseboat tied to the next dock, no doubt communicating with the agent or agents aboard.

Wynona turned to Max, picking her up and setting her on the couch. "Max, we haven't heard from Sean. So, what should we do? Since it's just us girls, we can put our heads together and come up with a solution."

Max sat up and sniffed. Wynona smiled. "That's exactly what I was thinking. He should know about the conversation I just received from my friend in the FBI. Let's call Sean and tell him, okay?"

Max moved closer, propping her chin on Wynona's thigh, looking up at her with soft brown eyes. Wynona couldn't help but laugh. "You're so darn cute. Okay, let's call Sean. I'm tempted to put him on speakerphone so you can hear his voice." She made the call, and O'Brien answered in two rings.

"How are things at the marina?" he asked.

"As good as can be expected considering we have a rotating shift of special agents from the FBI watching Dave, his boat, and the general area. Dave arrived a few minutes ago. Are you making any progress in Tarpon Springs?"

"Nick is at a coffee shop a few doors down that appears to have men only as customers. He thought he could get more mileage in there alone. It's Greek to him, and he understands it."

"What exactly is he trying to learn?"

O'Brien sat on a stool at a bar inside the restaurant. The lunch crowd was gone. It was too early for dinner or happy hour. He was the only customer. A middle-aged bartender, a woman, black hair worn in an attractive, natural hairstyle, used a soft white towel to dry wine glasses. O'Brien lowered his voice and said, "He's looking for a lead on boats down at the city docks. Nick's trying to find out which captain or captains might transport more than fish, crabs, sponges or shrimp."

"And where are you?"

"In a bar two doors down."

Wynona smiled. "Sean, I just heard from my friend Mario, bureau chief with the Miami office. He spent almost two hours interviewing Jason Thurston."

"Good. What'd he find?"

"Deception, of course." She filled O'Brien in on the conversation and added, "The son of one of the worst traitors in the history of the United States alleges he's been estranged from his father for years, only recently did Richard Thurston reach out to him because Richard supposedly is dealing with prostate cancer. Mario is sending me a link to the video interview with Jason Thurston."

"Please copy me on it. Maybe there is something I can use when I meet his father."

"Okay but delete it when you're done. It violates FBI security protocol, and Mario could get in hot water if this gets out. Can you imagine Jason Thurston, on video, becoming a viral phenomenon with no talent beyond a bad blood connection to the man who cost American lives and millions of dollars? Frightening possibility."

"No, I can't imagine that. How's Max?"

"I think she wants to speak with you. Can I put you on speaker for a second?"

"Sure."

Wynona hit the button and said, "Max is on the couch with me. She's all ears, hound dog ears."

O'Brien said, "How's my girl? Are you helping Wynona take care of *Jupiter*?"

Max's tail twitched. She let out a bark that sounded like a yodel. Wynona laughed and said, "You've got the magic touch with Max. You ought to see her eyes. They reflect pure doggy doxie love." She took the phone off speaker and held it to her ear. "I think you have a ten-pound, spoiled lady."

O'Brien smiled, "She's easy to spoil."

"We miss you. Come home soon and stay safe."

"I miss you both, too." O'Brien disconnected.

Wynona looked at the phone in her hand, petted Max and whispered, "He's a good man, Max. But you know that. Speaking of good men, Dave's back. Want to go visit him?"

Max let out a slight yap, jumped off the couch and scampered to the glass doors, pausing to look over her shoulder at Wynona.

"Just how good is your understanding of English?" Wynona asked, getting up from the couch. "I know that your vocabulary includes the key words, such as food, treat, outside, and go for a walk, but how did you know I just asked if you'd like to visit Dave? Is Dave a buzzword for you, too?"

Max cocked her head, sniffed, and then stared out the door in the direction of *Gibraltar*. Wynona looked at her phone and hit Dave's number. When he answered, she said, "Dave, it's Wynona, AKA Linda.

Max and I saw you board your boat. Sean and Nick are in Tarpon Springs. Can we join you for a cup of coffee?"

Dave sat at the bar on *Gibraltar*, a scotch in one hand. "Absolutely, you can join me for a drink, too. We have to restrict Max to light beer, though."

Wynona laughed. "Nothing worse than a wiener dog that looks like an inflated sausage. Can we come over now?"

"Of course. See you in minute." He disconnected.

Wynona looked at Max and said, "Okay, we're officially invited to come aboard."

She picked up her Beretta from the table, looked out the port window one more time before stepping off *Jupiter* to walk fifty feet to *Gibraltar*, a boat bearing the name of the fabled Rock of Gibraltar. Solid. Known through the ages as the Pillars of Hercules. Unyielding. She stared at the trawler tied to its slip like Gulliver not *Gibraltar*, she thought. *Dave's boat doesn't seem to reflect the strength symbolized in the legendary rock. It looks defenseless. And even in a marina filled with hundreds of boats, Gibraltar seems alone.*

# SEVENTY-THREE

Katie and Andy Scott stood next to their dinghy tied to a swayback coconut palm tree and watched trouble brew on the horizon. The two men in the red and white Top Gun boat sat behind the console, dark glasses on, looking back toward the dinghy on the beach. Andy reached for the line and untied the knot. He said, "We need to see what the hell they're doing so close to our boat … our home."

Katie stared at the men. She could see no one on *Dragonfly*. "This is related to my father … to his former job with the CIA, and they've gone to great lengths to follow us. Dave Collins said it's about a vendetta. We're being stalked for something we didn't do."

"We can try to hide out in the interior of this island, maybe they won't find us, or we can head for *Dragonfly*. If I can go below deck, I could get Dave's gun that I've hidden. That would help equalize the situation."

"What if somebody's already there? We're already out manned and probably out gunned. Our phones are on board. Even if we had them, we couldn't get a decent signal."

"Maybe they're hired guns—men who will change sides quickly for more money. We can try to negotiate with them."

"We don't have that much cash on board. I don't think it's about money. What if they're here to retaliate for something my father and Dave Collins did to them or the guy Dave mentioned, Abdul Aswad?"

Andy looked back at the dozens of tall coconut palms growing near the beach. "There's really no place we can go here. According to the charts I looked at, this island is close to twenty-five acres in size. It's not like we have mountains or caves to help us hide. Let's just take the dinghy back to our boat. Play dumb. Ask if we can help them. Find a few seconds when I can go below and get the gun."

Katie looked at her husband. She knew he was trying to appear brave, self-assured. But his eyes reflected deep fear. She said, "Andy, I don't think that's a good idea. At this point, I just wish we had the gun."

"That's far enough," said a man stepping from behind a cluster of royal palm trees. He held a semi-automatic rifle in his hands, the barrel pointed at Andy and Katie. He was large with powerfully built arms. Face dark, mouth small and turned down. He said, "I like his idea of taking the dinghy back to the boat—you both get in the front of the dinghy. We're going for a boat ride. If you refuse, I have orders to put a bullet in both your heads."

Andy raised his hands, looked at his wife, her eyes fearful. They did as ordered. The man used one hand to shove the dinghy into deeper water, climbed aboard and started the motor. Within seconds, they were heading toward *Dragonfly*.

The men in the cigarette boat remained seated as Andy and Katie approached with their armed escort. Both men wore wrap-around dark sunglasses. Short beards, frayed. Stoic expressions. Olive skin that had darkened in the Caribbean sun. They watched the dinghy approach.

The man piloting the dinghy pulled up next to *Dragonfly's* transom. "Get out!" he shouted. Katie and Andy stepped onto the sailboat's swim platform. The other two men stood, hands on the grips of their pistols. One used a line to secure the dinghy to *Dragonfly*, the other motioned with his pistol for Andy and Katie to stand in the cockpit.

In less than thirty seconds, a man came out from below deck. He held Dave Collins' pistol, pointing it at Andy and Katie. The man had a second handgun wedged under his belt. He was tall and gangly. The Smith and Wesson looked strange in his hand with his long, slender fingers and uncut nails. His face was weather-beaten, skin brown.

Dark, raccoon shadows under his coal black eyes. He was expression-less, as if he were a bricklayer arriving to the jobsite and surveying the day's work in front of him, calculating.

The man said, "Sit down." Andy looked at him and then at his wife. He was hesitant and then sat near the helm. The men in the boat were now standing. Both held pistols.

The tall man took a step closer to Katie, his eyes boring into her and then scanning her body as if he detested her swim suit. He said, "I am Abdul Aswad. So, you are the daughter of Sol Lefko?" His voice was emotionless. Nonthreatening.

Katie said, "What do you want?"

"You do not question me. Where are your phones?"

Katie motioned to an area near the wheel. "They're on the small shelf below the compass."

"You need to cover your body. Go below and put on clothes. You have one minute!" He looked at one of his men and said, "Go with her." Then, gesturing to Andy, Aswad said, "Hand me your phones."

Andy picked up both phones and gave them to Aswad, who stepped back and looked at his men. Trying to put distance between her and the man following her, Katie returned wearing a sundress she had pulled over her swim suit and quickly sat next to Andy. "If either one makes an abrupt move, shoot both of them." He scanned through Andy's phone first, set it down and did the same with Katie's phone. He paused and looked at some recent pictures she'd taken. One was the image of Dave, Nick, O'Brien and Wynona standing on the dock about to wave goodbye to Katie and Andy.

Aswad held the phone in his left hand, the gun in his right, pointing to the screen a few inches from Katie's face. "Who are these people?"

"Friends. They were on the dock when we left the states."

"Who are they? Names!"

Katie looked at the picture. 'The tall man is Sean O'Brien. The older man is Dave Collins, but I assume you're acquainted." Aswad remained expressionless. Katie lowered her eyes to the image. "The man with the moustache is Nick Cronus and the woman is … um … Linda. I don't remember her last name."

"Um …? Liar! Tell me her real name, or I will put a bullet between your husband's eyes." He aimed the gun at Andy.

Katie licked her lips and said, "Wynona. Her name is Wynona Osceola."

Aswad stared at her. Unblinking. The only sound was the *Dragonfly's* halyard clinking in the breeze against the top of the mast. Aswad's eyes bore into Katie. His lower jaw popped as he clenched his teeth. He said, "Where does this woman live?"

"I don't know, and that's the truth. We just met her before we left Ponce Inlet."

"So, we can assume she lives somewhere in that area. Who was she with … the man with the moustache or the tall man?"

"The tall man."

"The one you call Sean O'Brien. Where does he live?"

"He has a house somewhere in the forest, by some river. I don't know."

"Does he have a boat in the marina?"

"I think so, but I can't remember the boat's name."

Aswad looked at Andy and asked, "Can you recall the name?"

"No. We barely knew them. They're friends of Dave, and they were there to see us off. That's it."

"That's not it," Aswad said, smirking. "This is a new chapter in an old battle."

.

# SEVENTY-FOUR

A large man entered the coffee shop just as Nick was making an introduction. The new arrival—guarded eyes, prominent Greek nose, thick shoulders, walked by the table nodding at the man sitting and then went up to the bar. Nick grinned and said, "Looks like you're out of ouzo. Everyone else in here's drinking coffee. Thought I'd share a drink with you. My name is Nick Cronus. I'm originally from Mykonos. Seems like lots of people here in Tarpon Springs trace their roots back to the islands."

The man looked up at Nick, studying him for a few seconds. He glanced at the bottle of ouzo and said, "Mykonos. I won't hold that against you. My Greek's shitty. If we talk, let's talk in English. I was born in Tarpon Springs, not some distant island my grandfather called home. I'm Greek by blood but American by birth. I fought for this country in Iraq, two fuckin' tours of duty. Name's Kenny Drakos."

"Okay, got it. No sweat, Kenny. Let's pour a shot and drink to America … the best country this side of Greece." Nick sat down and half filled Kenny Drakos' glass. Then he poured a shot in his glass. "To Uncle Sam and America," he said, lifting his glass in a toast.

Kenny Drakos did the same, not touching glasses but rather knocking back a shot. His eyes watered a second, cheeks flushing. He looked at Nick, face filled with suspicion and said, "Cronus … Nick Cronus. Never heard of you. Where you from?"

"For the last seven years, in the Daytona Beach area. Before that, I lived all over Greece, Santorini, Mykonos, Hydra … and even Patmos, the island of the holy man, Saint John."

"I've heard of the place. Remember my grandfather sayin' God picked that island so some dude could hide out and not get his ass hung from a cross."

"That dude, Saint John, wrote the Book of Revelation, man. All the information was spoken to him from God."

"You really believe that?"

"Yeah, I do."

Drakos used two fingers to slide his glass a little closer toward Nick. "Hit me, Father Nick." He grinned and swatted at a large black fly.

Nick made the pour, refilled his glass, and knocked back the ouzo. He looked toward the open door, watching two men silently play bastra on one of the tables outside. He said, "The man pourin' the coffee said you might know of any work to be found on the docks."

"That right?"

"It's what he says."

"He doesn't know much. What sort of work are you lookin' for?"

"Usually work finds me. I don't have to look too far. Things between Daytona and Miami are a little slow. I heard there's some action over here. Thought I'd check around. See if anybody is lookin' for a deck hand that's used to … let's just call it, importing stuff. Stuff that doesn't need for some county, city, state of federal agency to slap a duty tax on it. We Greeks have been in the import-export business for centuries."

Drakos swatted at a fly. He shifted his eyes to the man in the back of the room at the bar and said, "I don't know you. So, I sure as hell can't refer you to anybody. No offense. You're on your own in Tarpon."

Nick finished his drink. He said, "No problem. Gotcha. Lemme put it this way … if I was goin' down to the docks, checkin' out the fleet, should I keep an eye out for a few captains that might be looking to take on a man or two? I don't need the names of the captains. If I got a name of a boat, I could just ask to see if anybody's hiring. I could use some time at sea. Been too long. Maybe it's the Greek in me, but I need the ocean. And, as I said, things have been slow—I really need the money, man. You know what I mean?"

Drakos pushed his empty shot glass closer to the bottle. Nick refilled it, slid it back toward him and leaned forward slightly. Drakos downed the ouzo, licked his wet lips and said, "I used to do some midnight runs. Last time was more than a year ago. If I were lookin' for that kind of work, I wouldn't mess with the spongers. The shrimpers … 'em boys go all over the place. Never can tell what they drag up."

"Sometimes it's even gonna be shrimp." Nick laughed. "Other times, who knows what the ocean will send your way. Looks like there are at least a dozen shrimp boats at the docks, probably that many more are at sea. I'd hate to knock on ever'body's door. What would you do?"

Drakos took a deep breath, glanced in the back of the coffee shop, the man at the bar speaking quietly with the shop owner. He lowered his voice and said, "I'd just get the hell outta Tarpon Springs. Nobody at the sponge docks, the municipal pier, will trust a stranger."

"I may be a stranger but I'm not strange. I'm Greek. That ought to mean somethin' over here. 'Nough said. Kenny, you told me your Greek is kinda shitty. You know what the word sigao means?"

"No, should I?"

"It means silence. The ancient Greek meaning is sacred silence as in secret silence. I have practiced it all my life." He refilled the two shot glasses.

Drakos looked at the milky white ouzo a second before downing it, his eyes misting. He said, "Sigao may mean sacred silence. But the one tough bad ass in Greek history was Jason. He led the Argonauts on a journey of no turnin' back. There's a boat down at the docks called *Argos*. The captain is Rastus Dimitrious. He runs a tight ship, if you know what I mean."

"Maybe he could use a hand."

"Dude's legendary around Tarpon Springs. A few years back, his boat got caught in Hurricane Charley. He personally tied his crew on, strapped 'em down when the waves turned into rolling mountains.

They say he navigated up and over fifty foot or better waves. One of his mates said it was like *Argos* came on the other side of mountain, wave after wave. Somehow Rastus kept her from splintering into a million pieces. I don't know if the captain's takin' anybody on or not. They could be way the hell out to sea for all I know. They could be lookin' to diversify their catch from time to time. I wouldn't know. It's on you now."

Nick slammed back his drink, slid the bottle toward Drakos, stood, and said, "Thanks."

Drakos pulled the bottle close and half filled the shot glass. He looked up at Nick and said, "Rastus didn't name his boat *Argos* because it's a cool name. He called it that because he'll sail into hell and back, like ol' Jason and the Argonauts. Rastus has faced monsters out there … and I hear he'll go anywhere and get anything if the price is right. I also hear that you'd better not even think of crossing him. Cheers, Nikolas."

Nick watched a large black fly orbit around the table. He used his right hand to snatch the fly in midflight. Then he rested his forearm on the table and slowly turned his hand around, opening his fingers. The fly stood in the middle of his palm, shaken but alive. Nick pursed his lips and blew on the fly. It lifted its wings and flew out the door. Nick cut his dark eyes over to Drakos and said, "Sometimes I catch 'n release. Sometimes I don't." He got up and walked out into the bright sunshine.

# SEVENTY-FIVE

A bdul Aswad held the Smith & Wesson, sitting in the shade under *Dragonfly's* canvas canopy and thinking about his dead brother. *A great warrior, a strong believer in the Koran, a brother who died when a woman infidel shot him like a rabid dog.* Aswad shifted his detached eyes from Katie to Andy and then down at his men who kept two Sig Sauer 9mm pistols aimed at the couple.

Aswad looked through more pictures on Katie's phone. Inspected the sent and received calls. Scanned people on her contact list. He lifted his eyes up at her and said, "Your father, and others, violated many prisoner-of-war conditions of humane treatment. The Geneva Convention, time and time again, established conditions of humane protocols when dealing with prisoners. The American government, its CIA, choose not to abide by those protections established under international humanitarian law. Me, and the two men you see in that boat, suffered horribly under the hands of your father and others at CIA torture camps, including Guantanamo Bay. Dabir lost the use of his left hand because it was so badly broken. The torture and sexual cruelties at Abu Ghraib were only a small part of it."

"Andy and I had nothing to do with that. You can't hold us responsible or complicit for something we had no knowledge of it happening."

Aswad half smiled, he glanced at his men. "When the wind blows the seeds of the weed—the dandelion, is the wind responsible for their growth or is the responsibility spawned by an evil father?"

"I assure you, whatever you think my father did to you, is much more humane than what you have done to people you consider your enemy. How humanely have you treated them? You stand here alive and able to condemn my father. You couldn't do that so well with your head cut off. Do you call beheading people you kidnapped humane treatment? I'm certain that's a blatant violation of every POW rule ever written in the Geneva Conventions. Those rules don't apply to you because you believe you are superior to people in the West who don't follow your personal interpretation of the Koran."

Aswad backhanded Katie, knocking her to the deck. Andy stood and drew a fist. Aswad leveled the pistol barrel near Andy's forehead and whispered, "You should learn how to keep your woman's mouth shut."

Andy said nothing, his fists clenched at his side. Aswad slowly withdrew the gun from Andy's head, still pointing it at him. Andy knelt down and helped Katie sit up, blood pouring from the left side of her mouth, bottom lip starting to swell. Her eyes watering, pink fluid dripping from one nostril.

Katie looked up at Aswad and said, "You're a tough guy when you and your thugs are holding guns on a woman. I don't think you're so tough when you are all alone."

"Silence!" shouted Aswad.

Katie wiped the blood from her mouth with the back of her right hand. She said, "You can just get in your boat and go away. Andy and I will continue on with our lives like nothing happened here today. But if you harm us, I promise you that the full force of the CIA and FBI will hunt you to the ends of the earth. The stuff that happened to you at Guantanamo will be a warm-up session to what will happen to you the second time."

Aswad smirked, his face pinched. "The ends of the earth. There are no ends of the earth. It is round, like a circle. Many places to stay secluded. Your CIA is searching for me in many parts of the Middle East. I have been in the Caribbean for years. And we have spent this time planning the vengeance that is ours. There is no place safe in America for the CIA devils to hide."

Katie looked at him, the breeze shifting, his body odor sour. "You said we. Is the we your friends in the boat or someone else?"

Aswad looked at Andy and said, "Your woman asks too many questions. I blame that on you. Stand up!"

Andy slowly stood. He said, "If you want our boat … take it. We can swim back to the island, or we can take the dinghy. Below the wheel, in the console, are the keys to *Dragonfly*. Take *Dragonfly*. Sell her! Whatever. Just let my wife and I go. We'll make do on the island."

Aswad shook his head. "No, not that island. I have chosen another one for you. You both get in our boat, and we will take you there. Do it or we will shoot you on the spot. And then we shall dump your bodies into the ocean. Between the crabs and sharks, there will be nothing left. Now, get in the boat."

# SEVENTY-SIX

Wynona hung her purse from her left shoulder to her right hip, the purse unzipped, the grip of her gun in easy access. As she and Max stepped off *Jupiter* and walked to Dave's boat, she looked down L dock toward the marina and saw the FBI agent watch her approach *Gibraltar*. She could barely see his lips move for three seconds at that distance.

Wynona lifted Max up and over onto the trawler's cockpit. As she approached the salon doors, Dave opened them and gave her a hug. He smiled and said, "Greetings ladies." Max seemed to nod as she blew past Dave and trotted toward the galley.

Dave chuckled. "Max has fantasies. She thinks I always have a pot of food on the back burner as Nick often does. She'll come to her senses and remember that I cook to live, but Nick lives to cook, and eat, of course." He smiled. "Did I ever tell you how much you remind me of my daughter? I know it sounds like a line of bull that an old man like me might use to flatter beautiful young women, however, in your case and that of my lovely daughter, Linda, the similarities are indeed true."

Wynona smiled. "You did tell me that I look like her but didn't mention other reasons." She gestured to the photograph of Linda on the end table near the sofa. "She's beautiful, and I hope she's safer now."

"I believe so. Your training and experience as a former federal agent make you uniquely qualified to work the alias. I want this over and not have anyone else put in jeopardy, including you. Come in, please. I was watching the news. I'm not sure if television news is real news anymore. Lots of opinion. Talking heads. Agendas. All I want are accurate facts about the story, both sides of the story, if possible, and a chance to come to my own decisions. Otherwise, I'm in the opinion brigade without any definitive information or objective facts. Please, have a seat. What can I get you to drink?"

"Red wine would be nice if you have some." She sat in one of two canvas deck chairs.

Dave poured a glass of wine for Wynona and gave it to her. He lifted a TV remote and muted the sound on the screen above the bar and sipped his scotch before sitting on the couch. "You have a preciseness about you that Linda has. And you're curious and candid, yet there's an easy-going comfortableness about you that's engaging. Linda's like that, too. She laughs easily."

Wynona said, "Well, if that's how you see me, too, that's quite a compliment. Thank you. On another note, I hate to ask anyone how a funeral went, especially someone very close to the deceased, but I hope the memorial went as well as could be expected."

"Indeed, it was touching. All the right things said at the right times. The eulogies were poignant and personal. However, the irony in the death of a former CIA officer is that ninety-nine percent of family and friends have no idea what his or her professional life was really like. They know the side of that person that could be revealed, and that's the loving side of a close relationship shown to family and friends. That's the persona they know, and for the most part, that's a very accurate assessment of a spy's personal life. The other side, the professional, covert life, is as obscure as the dark side of the moon."

Wynona nodded, sipped her wine and said, "It's not like a CIA officer can talk about his or her day at the office. Mergers and acquisitions, in the business sense of the words, supply chain economics, the market—all mean nothing. The spy's occupation is another real world that cannot be revealed. The façade, the occupation that family and friends think they know, is pure fiction from their stand-alone perspective. That's got to make for some interesting funerals when the mourners get in the same room."

Dave glanced up at the muted TV for a second, cut his eyes back to Wynona and said, "Often, it's too bad we never know how much we're loved, or not, until our own deaths. And we never see that scorecard. The true testament, I suppose, is the size of the crowd that shows up for your funeral. That, of course, isn't the case all the time. Although, it's a fair barometer to our worth—the love a person had and still harbors in the hearts of those who remain behind is personal—memories, some good, some bad, but collective … perhaps vulnerable. I'm sorry if I sound morose, like a miserable old man who wants others to bathe in the waters of his sorrow."

Wynona smiled, leaned forward in her chair and said, "Dave, you're human. You've lost some good friends in the last two weeks. You had an assassin fire down on you. You have every right to feel the way you feel. You have every right to feel sorrow … and also to feel anger for what's happened and how it hasn't been stopped until we can locate the perps and literally blow them out of their nest. And, you have every right to feel fearful for your family, who you've shielded all your life to keep them protected."

"Between the CIA and FBI, we have people fanned out everywhere. Thus far they've found nothing but false leads. It's like Abdul Aswad vanished from the face of the earth, left a hit list and enough money for a small army to carry it out. And if Sean is right about Richard Thurston's involvement, how did that happen? Was it the letters to his son, or something else?"

Wynona told Dave about the FBI questioning of Jason Thurston and added, "I have a video copy of the interrogation. You can watch it with me. I emailed one to Sean. He and Nick are in Tarpon Springs looking to find some connection, if it exists, between the two men on camera who bought the burner phones and a way they may have entered the country."

"That's assuming they actually came in through Tarpon Springs. There's a lot of shoreline from Brownsville, Texas, to upstate Maine. And there is the West Coast, too. I hope Sean's not looking for the needle in the entire hay field. The FBI already has scoured the place.

Tarpon Springs is a small town. I'm not sure that's the best use of Sean's time. However, it makes sense to include Nick. He'll fit in like he's attending a big fat Greek wedding. Sean stands out. He's tall. Handsome. And because he stands out—often people will remember him … he's the exact opposite of what the CIA looks for when recruiting new people."

Wynona smiled. "That might be looked at as an asset, depending on where someone like Sean was stationed and what he was asked to do."

Dave nodded, took a sip from his drink and said, "Let's take a look at that video interrogation of Jason Thurston. I met him a couple of times when he was a kid. He appeared reserved in those days. He was the type of teenager who seemed to hold his cards close to his chest in a cloistered and odd kind of way. And I didn't know why. Maybe now, all these years later, the seclusion I saw in the son was always there in the father, I just never recognized it. Mostly, I thought, it was because of what we did—deception. Let's take a look at the video. I'm anxious to see what kind of man young Jason Thurston has become."

# SEVENTY-SEVEN

O'Brien sipped a cup of black coffee at the end of the bar, waiting for the video to fully download. He glanced at the widescreen TV mounted on the wall above the mirror behind the bar. The room was full of ghosts—relics and remnants of Tarpon Spring's past. Its history lined the walls in vintage photographs depicting the town's symbiotic relationship with sponge diving. The old bar carried the smells of uncorked bottles of red wine, peanuts, and a lingering hint of perfume from the leather barstools.

There were framed photographs of Greek divers wearing their hardhat bronze helmets, sitting on the transoms of boats, grinning. These were young Greek adventurers ready to drop to the seafloor and walk miles on the bottom of the ocean in search of new sponge beds. One picture was a large black-and-white photograph of Greek-American teenage boys diving for the renowned white wooden cross that is tossed into the Spring Bayou by the priest during the celebration of Greek Orthodox Epiphany at Easter.

When the video file had loaded, O'Brien reached in his pocket for a small set of ear-buds. He put them on and watched Jason Thurston being questioned. The FBI's interrogation room at its Miami bureau was austere. Pale green walls. A steel table in the center of the room. Four metal folding chairs. Thurston sat opposite one FBI agent who introduced himself as Mario Hernandez. He had a closed file folder in front of him.

Hernandez used all the right body language. Open posture. Slow hand gestures. A smile when appropriate. His voiced modulated from normal speech to softer as he went through the warm-up routine with the man sitting across from him.

Jason Thurston hid his anxiety well. He had a narrow, hatchet face. His steely gray eyes seemed to follow Hernandez's questions as if he were watching a fly on the special agent's nose.

Hernandez asked, "How would you describe your relationship with your father?"

"We didn't have one up until a few months ago. In a weird way, I suppose you can credit his prostate cancer for inciting some new desire to connect." He looked down and picked at a callous on his left thumb, then raised his eyes to Hernandez. "Too bad he didn't make the effort years ago."

"I understand. My dad was raised old school. He told me he loved me a day before he slipped into a coma and died. I was twenty-seven."

Jason nodded. "Too late then."

"You're right. It's all about the living years, my friend. It looks like your dad's sentencing took a toll on your family."

"Yeah, it did. It took more than a toll. It took years off my mom's life. The stigma was horrible, like being married to Bernie Madoff or something. For her not to be the brunt of people spewing their hate, she took back her maiden name when she divorced him. Then she developed cancer, and none of that mattered anymore … she died without even putting up a fight."

"And now your grandmother is ill as well. She told us that she used to read to your father a lot when he was a boy. One of his favorite nursery rhymes was Ten Little Indians. Do you know it?"

"Of course. My dad used to tell it to me."

"Tell it? Didn't he read it to you?"

A slight smile tugged at the right side of Jason's mouth. "He didn't have to read it. He memorized the lines years ago."

"Did he memorize any other nursery rhymes?"

"I don't know. That was a long time ago." Jason pushed back from the table. "What's this about? I'm not in any way responsible for my father's decisions, but I'm still catchin' shit because of what he did."

O'Brien sipped his coffee and watched the interview, impressed with Special Agent Hernandez's skills.

Hernandez said, "It's not just what he did … it's what he's doing."

"What the hell are you talking about? He's locked away in a federal pen. He can't piss without being seen on surveillance cameras."

"But he can write letters to you. And he can receive letters, even visitors. So, he still has communications to the outside world. Your dad has become a fairly prolific letter writer. Looks like he's trying to make up for lost time. In one letter, he's encouraging you to see the world, offering suggestions about places to visit. He'd certainly know about those places, having worked in and around many of them. Did you visit any of the areas he suggested?"

"No, not yet. It's on my bucket list. So are a lot of other things, too."

"Did you share that particular letter with anyone?"

"Did I share it?" Jason looked away for a second. "You mean with my grandmother?"

"Sure, your grandmother or anyone else. I'm sure your dad had plenty of friends."

"No, I didn't share it with anybody."

"Where do you think Abdul Aswad is right now?"

"Who?" He tilted his head as if to better hear.

"Abdul Aswad."

"I got no idea who he is. Never heard of him."

O'Brien leaned a little closer to his phone screen, studying Jason's face.

Hernandez lowered his voice, leaning into the table. "Where'd your grandmother get the money to buy that pricey condo on South Beach?"

"Maybe you ought to ask her. Something you should understand is this … because my father was deep cover into the CIA, our whole life was one big sham. He was a professional at becoming something he wasn't. And he could maintain it through different scenarios, year after year. My old man was a chameleon. Ask him where he got the money. All I know is that my grandmother holds the deed on it. Free and clear."

"Speaking of your grandmother, and she is a delightful woman, we spotted some rum in a cardboard box. Two bottles of Brugal 1888 Grand Reserve. It's distilled in the Dominican Republic. It's rare and pricey. She said the bottles were yours. How'd you get them? Were you in the Dominican Republic?"

"It was a gift from a friend." He laced his fingers together, eyes flat.

Hernandez smiled. "I wonder if your friend bought it duty free?"

"I didn't ask him. It was a gift."

"May I see your cell phone?"

"Why?"

"I know it's in your front hip pocket. Please put it on the table."

Thurston complied, setting the phone in the near center of the table. Hernandez picked it up and gave it a cursory inspection. He said, "If you have this new iPhone, why do you feel the need to buy burner phones?"

"I don't use burner phones. And if I did, unless it's against the law to buy one, that's no one's business but mine."

"You didn't just buy one. You bought at least four." Hernandez opened the file folder and slid an eight-by-ten, black-and-white picture toward Jason. "That still was lifted from surveillance video in an electronics store on Bird Avenue. It's time stamped. We know when and where you bought them. But we don't know why. Tell us."

"This is over. Either charge me with something or get outta my face. I want to speak with my lawyer. I'm not saying anything more. Arrest me or let me go."

The image faded to black. O'Brien set his phone on the bar and removed his ear-buds."

"Would you like a warm-up?" asked the bartender as she approached O'Brien, coffee pot in her hand.

"Yes, thanks."

She flashed a wide smile. Pretty face. Black hair worn down and slightly angled over her bare right shoulder. Misty blue-gray eyes. Early forties. A string of pearls looped around her long neck almost to her exposed cleavage. She refilled his coffee and said, "I've worked here for almost two years, and I can't recall any man sitting at the bar and ordering coffee. It's kinda nice, you know?"

"It's what I prefer before five." He smiled and sipped from the cup.

"If you're thinking about staying for dinner, tonight would be a good night."

"Oh, why is tonight a good night?"

"Because it's Friday. A lot of the boats came back to port this morning. The fishmongers line the docks like a farmer's market. Our chef went down there earlier today to buy. It's hard to get seafood any fresher than what you'll find here tonight."

"That's good to know. Did you grow up in Tarpon Springs?"

"I was born in Crete. It's the largest of the Greek islands. We have more than six-thousand islands, and less than two-hundred-thirty are inhabited full time."

"What brought you to Tarpons Springs?"

"My parents. They decided to move here because my uncle came twenty-five years earlier and painted a picture of milk and honey. Of course, the sponge business was much larger than it is now. I married an American. At the time he was a tourist visiting Florida and his grandmother was in Clearwater for a month. After a long two years, he went back to Philly, and I stayed here. I thank the Lord above that we never had children. Can't imagine. As a matter of fact, today I'm celebrating my twentieth year as a U.S. citizen. I might buy myself a drink after work."

"When does your shift end?"

She looked at a digital clock next to the cash register. "In twenty-three minutes."

O'Brien smiled. "I'd be honored to buy you a celebratory drink."

Her eyes beamed. "And I'd be honored to accept it. What's your name?"

"Sean O'Brien. And your name is …"

"Sofia Alanis."

O'Brien shook her hand across the bar. "You mentioned today most of the commercial fleet is in selling fish."

"Straight from the Gulf. And the Greeks know how to prepare and serve them."

"No doubt. How about the shrimp boats … when do they arrive?"

"All kinds of different times and days. Some of those boats will go over to the Atlantic side, too. Many stay in the Gulf. Just depends on the catches and the season."

"I can tell you know your way around Tarpon Springs. Over that drink, I'd like to learn more."

"Happy to help the chamber of commerce." She smiled and moved down to the far end of the bar as a new customer took a seat.

O'Brien lifted his phone and punched out a quick text message to Nick: "I'm in Mama Penelope's. Give me an hour, and I'll come find you."

# SEVENTY-EIGHT

Wynona and Dave watched the interview with Jason Thurston in silence. When it faded to black, she said, "Well, what do you think?"

Dave took his bifocals off and cleaned them with a cloth. His eyes looked red and tired. "He may be grown, but I still see him as a teen. Evasive. And now, on camera, he's not very forthcoming. I think Jason knows more than he's willing to tell us.

"I agree. Was he lying about the rum from Dominica being a gift?"

"Good question. Even if it was a gift, it doesn't mean he didn't slip in and out of there, or anywhere else, under the radar. He appeared rather tight lipped through most of the second half of the interview."

"Does Richard Thurston have prostate cancer?"

"I'll find out."

Wynona set the wine glass on the coffee table. "No. It'll be interesting to get Sean's take on the interview."

"He may see something we didn't, but there wasn't a lot to see."

Wynona leaned forward in the deck chair. She watched Max lying on the couch near Dave. "I've seen Sean work," she said. "I'm not sure what it is … a gift is what I think it is. I never saw it with any of the agents in the Bureau, at least to the degree that Sean has it. It's as if he has some sort of perception allowing him to connect dots, incidents, people and places into a collective row. He sees things others often miss. And he usually sees them in people. It's uncanny."

"I'll concur with that. But it's a double-edge sword for him."

"What do you mean?"

"I suppose we're all a by-product of our past, at least to some degree. That doesn't mean we're chained to our past, whether it be an abusive childhood or anything we couldn't control that had a negative effect on us."

"Did Sean have a bad childhood?"

"He doesn't talk much about it. He discovered his biological mother recently. And he wasn't even looking for her. He found a brother he didn't know he had … and he unearthed depraved family baggage that no one should inherit."

"How so?"

"I don't know all the details, just what Sean allowed me to know. You'll have to ask him to get more. He may or may not share. The other parts of his world include tours of duty in Afghanistan. Sean, and a half-dozen of his men were held prisoners after a fierce firefight where they were pinned down in a valley. In the end, he was the only one of his squad that got out alive. He had to dig deep down into his DNA and survival instincts to escape. But he managed to do it, causing some serious destruction to the Taliban tribe that held him. You will probably never get him to discuss much of it, much less the specifics of his survival. But as a Delta Force team leader, I know he blames himself for what happened … even though it wasn't his fault. So, the Sean O'Brien you see is a man with a strong sense of right and wrong that was hammered out on the anvil of good and evil."

Wynona said nothing. She looked through the glass doors toward the houseboat with FBI agents behind the tinted windows. She watched a forty-foot Catalina sailboat motor between the moored boats as its crew headed out to the main channel. She turned to Dave and said, "I had no idea. Sean rarely talks about his childhood or his time in the military. I don't push him either."

Dave nodded, sipped his drink and glanced at the TV screen. He said, "So those powers of observation, his uncanny way of looking at the details, could have formed in the womb … but they were no doubt refined in childhood and during his tours of duty in the service. Also, his time working as a homicide detective gave him another insight into the criminal mind that he didn't already pick up through the earlier part of his life."

"I can relate."

"You like him a lot don't you?"

She smiled. "Is it that obvious?"

"Yes. He's a good man, but an extremely complicated man. He's fearless and yet somehow more complex than ever. It seems that after his wife, Sherri's, death from cancer, any illusions Sean may have had about life … and death, for that matter … evaporated."

"How do you mean, evaporated?"

"Most of us have a normal human tendency to let difficult things percolate. When extreme things happen to people—or to people they care about, often we need time to process it—to wrap their heads around it, so to speak. Sean's life has made him razor-focused. He makes lightning quick decisions, not with reckless abandonment, or in a cavalier kind of way. But there's a complete absence of fear or the usual *what ifs*, the repercussions that come with a split-second decision. It's not that he operates with some death wish bravado … on the contrary. He's one of the most docile men I've ever known. He's also one of the deepest thinkers I've ever had the privilege of knowing. To defeat evil, he goes deep into its source. And that is not a scenic place to be. He somehow manages to enter the criminal mind, with all of its cobwebs of wickedness, poke around those dark places, and find the horror of breadcrumbs that lead him to the perpetrator. But there seems to be a price to pay, a personal toll, every time Sean wades into the sludge of malice."

"How's that?"

"I think you know. You probably experienced it or still undergo dregs of it after you tried to defend that helpless girl in the murderous hands of her father."

Wynona was silent.

Dave said, "Sean, I think, has to reveal a small part of himself to sit at the table with pure evil. It's not some Faustian pact, or selling his soul at the crossroads, however, there is a trade-out—a compromise, a chink in his armor. He comes away with scars. Some are visible. Others internal. It's his toll when crossing the bridge over the River Styx. But he's willing to pay it because the good, in his mind, is greater than the bad."

Dave set his drink on a coaster with an image of a marlin on it. He looked at the TV screen and said, "I need to turn up the sound for a minute. A reporter is standing in front of a marina where I used to keep *Gibraltar* until I brought her up here to Ponce Inlet." He pressed a button on the TV remote.

A female reporter with dark shoulder-length hair stood near the entrance sign to Gangway Marina. She looked into the camera, pulling a lock of hair back in the breeze, and said, "The murder of seventy-year-old Russell Douglas, a retired fisherman, marks the third homicide in the Florida Keys in the last three weeks. The first was in Key West when police found the body of Lorenzo Alvarez in his car. He'd been shot once in the head. Last week, the body of a thirty-five-year-old Miami man, Blake Webber, was found behind a dumpster in the rear parking lot of the *Mile Maker 21 Bar*. No one has been arrested in these two killings. And now, with the stabbing death of Russell Douglas, police aren't sure if it's the work of one person. If so, they have a serial killer roaming the Florida Keys. However, in the other two killings, a gun was used. That's not the case with Douglas who was stabbed and left with a long and deep wound to his abdomen. Everyone here at the marina tells us he was a kind man, someone who'd go out of his way to help people. Perhaps that generosity, in some way, led to his attack and death late at night here at the Gangway Marina. Back to you in the studio."

The image cut to a split screen, the reporter on the left and a jowly anchorman on the right. He said, "Leslie, we understand the difference in this last murder is that the victim actually made it to a friend's boat before he died."

"That's right, Paul. Police say Douglas had been stabbed on one of the docks close to the channel. They found blood on the pier, but no blood trail. They said his clothes were drenched. That suggests that his attacker, or attackers, had pushed Douglas off the dock after stabbing him. Somehow, he made it to shore and managed to walk to a friend's boat." She glanced down at her notes. "He is forty-seven-year-old Derek Johnson. Mr. Johnson said the victim pounded on the door of his boat late last night, basically collapsing in his arms. He told police that Douglas only had the strength left to utter one word. He said … *Aphrodite.*"

The live shot cut to a video interview with Derek Johnson, standing on the docks, moored boats in the background. "Russell was kind and caring. I never heard him say a bad word about anybody. At first light, I walked down to the end of dock nine. There was a lotta blood on the docks. Police were taking pictures and whatnot. I saw a rope tied to a cleat. It looked brand new, and it appeared like it had been cut rather than untied. That rope wasn't there yesterday."

The image cut back to a live shot of the reporter. She said, "Police aren't speculating as to the importance of the rope, if any, or to the significance or the victim's last word, Aphrodite. But obviously it is believed to be someone, or something connected to the brutal murder of Russell Douglas. Reporting from Marathon Key, Leslie James, Channel Ten News."

Dave muted the sound, looked at Wynona and said, "I remember Russell Douglas. He wasn't retired when I docked *Gibraltar* there. He was a deck hand on fishing boats from Alaska to the Keys. He lived part-time on his boat, a boat that he always seemed to be restoring. He did most of the work by himself, so he could save money to retire and live on the boat. He said he might try to live in a house or an apartment, but he feared he'd miss the rise and fall of the tide and the laughter of the gulls as he tossed them bread after his morning coffee."

"What a senseless killing. Beyond its association to a mythical Greek goddess, I wonder what the significance is of the word Aphrodite. Maybe it's the name or the nickname of someone he knew."

"Or maybe it's the name of a boat."

# SEVENTY-NINE

*Dragonfly* seemed like an illusion to Katie, turning her head and staring at the sailboat anchored in the distance. She sat in the transom area of the long cigarette boat with Andy and tried not to look at the Sig Sauer aimed at her chest. Two of Abdul Aswad's men pointed guns at Katie and Andy as Aswad piloted the boat at a high rate of speed.

There were no other boats to be seen in this remote section of the Bahamas. She looked ahead and saw nothing but open sea, the sun hot on her shoulders, back, and arms. A fine spray from the boat slamming against the surface shot a spatter of water onto her left shoulder, cooling it. Her thoughts were jumbled. *Were they going to kill us? Shoot us and dump our bodies far out at sea? How can I possibly reach Dad? Dear, God … please help us.*

Andy reached out and took Katie's hand in his, gently squeezing, trying to bluff courage into a situation that drained hope down a dark whirlpool. There was simply no bluffing because it wasn't a card game, a dare, conditions, and there were no opportunities for negotiations. Aswad gripped the wheel as if he wanted to crush it, white knuckles. Jaws clenched. Andy knew deep inside that Aswad's mind was made up. The only chance for survival was to disarm one of the men, get the gun and use it. Use it quickly. There would be no second chances.

Katie could see land in the distance. A brown smudge on the horizon toward the port side of the boat. She used her left hand to shield the sun from her eyes, squinting. She squeezed Andy's hand and pointed. He looked in the direction and nodded. The guards with the guns were stoic. Indifferent tanned faces. They could have been androids, robots wearing dark glasses. Their only moves were to alternate the Sig Sauers from their right to left hands and then back again though the hour trip.

Within five minutes, the boat was coming closer to the island. Katie wanted to stand to get a better look at it. But she dared not to. From her perspective, the island didn't look foreboding. It looked different. The vast majority of the islands in the Bahamas seemed to have palm trees and dense green foliage. Not this one. It reminded her of a desert island. Very few trees. There was windswept scrub brush, none higher than three feet at the most. The island had an odd sepia tone color and look, as if the sand and scrub had been painted in the brown ink found in Old World drawings and calligraphy.

Aswad dropped the engines to near idle speed, the boat coming close to shore. He nodded to the man in the seat next to him and said something in Farsi. The man waited a few more seconds and eased off the side of the boat. He held a line attached to the front of the bow. The man, wide chest and thick arms, pulled the boat a little closer to shore.

Aswad stood and turned to Andy and Katie. He said, "This is where you get out."

Andy stood first, reaching back to help Katie up, the boat swaying in the gentle surf. The guard closest to them used his Sig to gesture toward the transom, indicating that's where he wanted them to exit the boat. Aswad folded his arms across his chest and said, "Leave my boat. This is your new home."

Katie glanced at the ominous island, made a dry swallow and said, "You don't have to do this."

Aswad shook his head. "Yes, I do have to do this. It is written that I do this. Considering what your father did, I have no choice."

She started to respond, and Andy interjected. "Katie, let's just do as they say. This is the better option."

She said nothing, glancing at the man in the knee-deep surf
holding the line to the boat. She walked to the transom and stepped
down a small aluminum ladder, then dropping to her waist in the
warm water. Andy followed. They both waded to shore and were
greeted with the smells of schooling baitfish, dried salt, and driftwood
rotting in the sun. When they stumbled onto the beach, clothes heavy
with water, Katie looked back over her shoulder and grimaced.

Aswad was following them.

He sloshed by the man holding the line and shouted an order in
Farsi. Then he turned and approached Katie and Andy. Aswad's eyes
were hard, black marbles wedged between the eyelids. He lifted the
Smith & Wesson revolver from his belt, and opened the cylinder,
pointing the gun at Katie. He spun the cylinder like a roulette wheel,
sunlight reflecting from the white breakers through the holes.

Andy could see that there were no bullets in the gun. He folded
his arms, the powdery sand soft under his feet. He said, "I'd like to
return that gun to its owner. It is not ours. Who is the owner?"

Andy paused a moment, exhaling. "Dave Collins owns it. He let
us borrow it."

Aswad grinned. "Perhaps I will return it for you." He paused and
made a motion toward the interior of the island. "That should be in
about one week. Probably less. That is the time I predict you have left
here. As you can see, this island has few trees. No shade. The daytime
temperature is at the one-hundred-degree mark or more. There is no
drinkable water. There is nothing to eat. No coconuts. No berries.
Very little, if any, wildlife here. Maybe a lizard or two. You have no
way to catch fish. You see, a massive hurricane made a direct hit on
this island five years ago. Most of the trees were blown away. The ones
that survived were under many feet of seawater as the giant waves
covered the land. It did not take long for the island to become what
you see here today—a desert island in the Caribbean."

Andy glanced back at the men with guns aimed at him and Katie.
He eyed Aswad and said, "Your plan is to leave us here to die a slow
death."

Aswad shook his head. "No, that will be your choice. Slow or
relatively quick." He lifted the pistol above his head, walked fifteen feet

inland and set the gun on the sand. He reached into his front pocket and lifted out something, closing his fist. Aswad walked back to Andy and Katie. He looked at Andy and said, "Put your hand out. Palm up."

Andy slowly reached out and turned his right-hand palm up.

"Good," Aswad said, opening his fist. Two bullets were in his palm, the bright sun winking off the shiny brass. Aswad dropped the two rounds into the center of Andy's hand and said, "As I suggested, that will be your choice. These two bullets go to that gun on the beach, the gun that was a gift to you from Dave Collins. Perhaps Collins did you a most humane favor. Here is your choice: after two to three days without water and food in this scorching heat, and with no shade, you will begin hallucinating. As your tongues start to swell, your heads will pound with the worst headache you have ever had. In Iran we call then death-march headaches. Most often happens to people lost in the desert. The body knows it is dying, and the brain is going through a kind of cerebral hyperventilation. It's gasping for nutrients to sustain itself while it's cooking inside your skulls."

Katie's fists clenched at her side. "You will never get away with this. My father and the entire CIA, Navy Seals, and Special Forces' troops will track you down. There will be no holding you at Guantanamo. They'll put a bullet through your head, you sick freak."

Aswad's nostrils expanded, like a dog catching scent in the breeze. He said, "I should cut your throat right here on the spot and leave you two for the crabs. As I said, you have two options … you can either both starve to death from lack of food and water, or you can use Dave Collins' gun to put one another out of your misery. For example, Andy, you can shoot your wife in the head after she begins having extreme hallucinations. And then, when she is dead, you can use the remaining bullet on yourself."

"Go to hell!" Andy shouted, his face crimson.

Aswad looked at him like a raptor bird surveys prey on the ground. He turned to one of his men and shouted, "Shoot the husband in the head!"

"No!" pleaded Katie. "Please … just go away."

"We have every intention of doing so." Aswad reached in his back pocket and pulled out a phone. "I am going to make a short video and you two will be my actors. However, there is no acting. It is very much reality TV, yes? The audience will be your father, Katie. You can say anything you want, with the exception of your location."

"We don't know our location," Katie blurted.

"It is sad," mocked Aswad. "Such a big ocean and such a small island. I will send the video to your father. Perhaps he will try to rescue you before it is too late. I do not think so. You get one chance to briefly speak. Make it the best speech of your life." He took a step back, pointed the camera phone lens at Katie and Andy. "You are both on camera."

Katie looked into the lens, licked her lips and said, "Dad … we've been taken hostage from *Dragonfly*. Abdul Aswad and his men took us to this desolate island somewhere in the Bahamas. We're at least an hour to ninety minutes southeast of Cat Cay in a fast boat. We have no food or water. He's leaving us here to die. If you get this in time, please have someone in a plane fly over the islands. We'll do what we can to signal them. This freak gave us a gun with two bullets. He wants the situation to get so drastic for us that one of us does a mercy killing and then commits suicide. He's sick, Dad. Whatever you did to him in Guantanamo wasn't nearly enough—"

"It was enough!" shouted Aswad, still holding the camera lens on Katie and Andy. "It was enough because you, Sol Lefko, reinforced to me and my people just how vile you are and what extremes you, Dave Collins, and your people will go to destroy Muslim brothers who are willing to fight your imperialism. Brothers are believers! I warned you I would remove your seed from earth. That will happen in such a tragic way … dust to dust." He ended the recording, backed away toward the boat and his men. He stood in the gentle breakers, grinned, and said, "I wish I could be here to see who takes the first shot. After that, will you have the courage to take the final shot?"

# EIGHTY

O'Brien sat at a small table in a dimly lit corner of the bar and watched Sofia Alanis approach. Her shift was over, and a man in his late twenties was behind the bar. He wore his blond hair in a ponytail, broad chest and sculpted arms of a weightlifter. Sofia smiled as she took a seat across from O'Brien. She set a half-filled glass of chardonnay on the table, the golden neon light from a Coors Beer sign trapped in the dark, iridescent pupils of her eyes.

"Welcome to my corner of the world," O'Brien said, lifting his glass of dark beer. "Cheers."

"Cheers," Sofia said, touching her glass to his. She sipped the wine.

O'Brien nursed the beer in a glass mug. He noticed that Sofia had brushed her hair and reapplied her lipstick. He could smell a floral perfume, the slight hint of jasmine. He said, "Tarpon Springs seems like a town that somehow manages to display its unique history all around the area and yet not be chained to the past. I see substantial growth since the last time I was here a few years ago. Lots of diverse businesses, a convention center, and it still manages to leverage its Greek sponge diving history to attract tourists year-round."

Sofia smiled and said, "It's definitely growing and changing as it grows. But it's the famous Tarpon Springs Sponge Docks that keep all these restaurants, bars, bakeries, and T-shirt shops hopping.

Hollywood has filmed movies around here. God only knows how many TV documentaries have been made. All that publicity, the books, and travel magazine stories, keep the mystique going. Also, the city is aggressive in its promotion of all things Greek." She sipped her wine, a trace of red lipstick on the edge of the glass. "What brings you over here? Where are you from?"

"Daytona area. I'm here with a good friend."

"Oh, really?" Sofia pursed her wet lips.

"He's having coffee down the street. He knows a few people in the area, likes to come and brush up on his Greek."

"So, you're saying your friend speaks the language?"

"Yes, in his own inimitable style. He's a fisherman by trade. Probably by birth, too. Born in the Greek islands. He loves to walk the docks over here and look at the catches, chat with the fishermen, swap stories. Work has been slow for him lately, so he might be trying to find out what's going on in Tarpon and possibly pick up some extra work. Anyway, he likes stopping in his favorite coffee shop."

"The Greek men, not so much the new generation or even the millennials, but the older men—the ones who carved a living at sea, they love to hang out at the old coffee shop. Just yesterday, I saw an elderly woman, no doubt one of the wives, stop at the door to that shop and send her teenage grandson in to get her husband. It's still an Old World tradition in there. Anyway, I'm sure it is a good place to see who's hiring." She sipped more wine.

O'Brien said, "That strong sense of community and friends … probably helps them live longer. Are any of your family members sponge divers or commercial fishermen?"

"My uncle, who's retired, was one of the best sponge men. He's probably at the coffee shop." Sofia laughed, her dark eyes misting for a moment. "He worked the docks for almost forty years. One of his three sons is a fisherman. Like his father, my cousin is one of the best. They're a very close-knit, Greek Orthodox family. I envy them sometimes." She drank more wine.

"What kind of fishing does your cousin do?"

"Deep sea. He goes out a couple of times a week. It's amazing how much they can catch. But when the red tide comes through the Gulf, forget it." She signaled the bartender, wide smile, pointing toward her empty wine glass. He nodded, reached under the bar and picked up a bottle of chardonnay, bringing it to the table.

"You're my hero, Michael," she said, watching him refill her glass, pouring beyond the halfway level. "Thanks."

"No problem," said the bartender. He looked at O'Brien and the glass of beer half full. "Can I bring you something?"

"No thanks. Not yet."

The bartender nodded and left. Sofia said, "His name really is Carl. Doesn't look like a Carl, though."

"What's a Carl look like?"

"Oh, I don't know. Someone who's good at numbers … an accountant maybe." She laughed and sipped her wine, glancing around the empty bar and then looking at O'Brien. "Your eyes are different. They're like sapphires with slate gray and even flecks of gold and emerald green. I've never seen anyone with eyes quite like yours. As a matter of fact, you have the most handsome and penetrating eyes I've ever seen. It's almost as if you can see through my clothes. Like Superman with those X-ray eyes." She laughed.

O'Brien smiled. "No, they have limitations. I can't see through lead."

She laughed, again, and sipped more wine, her pupils large, lips wet. She adjusted her body in the wooden chair, moving slightly closer. "How long will you be in town?"

"It depends on what we find."

"Okay … you told me what your friend was doing, but exactly what is it that you're looking for?" She sipped more wine.

"I'm not sure. Maybe I'll know when I find it."

"Can you give me a hint? Are you a cop?"

"No, I'm not a cop. I don't carry a badge."

"Do you carry baggage?" Sofia smiled. "Sorry, that just popped out. Seems that so many people our age do. I suppose it comes with living, the mileage. The key is to get over it and move on. I think a lot of people have a hard time doing that."

"No doubt. I guess that's part of being human." O'Brien studied her for a minute and trusting his intuition, said, "Sofia, you seem like a woman with a good heart. I want to share something with you.

Can you keep it confidential, something you and I can share together and discuss?"

"Yes, of course. What is it?"

"A close friend of mine, a retired man, is having his life threatened. It's coming from a radical Islamic group, men who will cut your head off just because they can and want to make a statement. Two of these men were recently in Tarpon Springs. There was surveillance video of them buying something at a local store. They were, no doubt, passing through the city. The question is, how did they enter Tarpon Springs? I think it was by boat … smuggled into the country. If you were looking for a boat and crew that might be importing more than sponges or fish, any idea where you'd look?"

She leaned slightly back in her chair. Her eyes were a little suspicious, less amorous, some of the arousal fading. "You said you're not a cop. Who are you? Or what are you, some kind of FBI agent?"

O'Brien smiled. "No, none of those things. I'm just a guy who cares deeply about an old friend. Some of his retired colleagues were recently killed. The trail is leading me to Tarpon Springs. But I've come to a dead-end." He reached out and touched the top of her left hand. "Maybe you can help. If one or more of the boats at the sponge docks were bringing people into the country, getting them by U.S. Customs, any suggestions as to who it might be? Your answer could save the life of my friend, a man who worked hard all his life like the elder Greek men who first came here."

She looked at his hand on hers, sipped the remaining wine from her glass. "You seem like the real deal, Sean. There are a lot of boats down at the sponge docks. I've heard a rumor that a couple of them will import or export more than fish, sponges, or Greek olives. But it's only a rumor."

"I understand. I don't operate on rumor. I only go with the facts. Which boats?"

She glanced back toward the bar. A middle-aged man and woman came in and sat down at a table in the center of the room. Sofia lowered her voice. "I've heard that a couple of captains and their boats are for hire to import and export stuff. Both are shrimp boats. One is called *She Devil*. The other is *Argos*." She paused her lips wet from wine, eyes pensive. And there may be a third boat. I say this only because the captain's wife rides around in a new Mercedes. They just enrolled two kids in private school. Boat's called *Aphrodite* … like the goddess. You know, the beautiful one who slept with gods and mere mortals?" She squeezed his hand. "But I guess we're just mere mortals, right?"

O'Brien smiled, "Well, I'm merely a guy trying to help an old friend."

"Ahhh … a mortal knight." Sophia laughed.

"That doesn't sound very Irish. I think my ancestors might object."

"Well … English … Irish … Greek … looks like you can carry your own weight. But I'd be very careful if I were you. You start poking around the sponge docks, asking questions like a cop, it could stir up some nasty stuff. Especially if your friend is asking for work."

"I understand."

She started to say something when two men entered the room, walked up to the bar, and sat on two of the stools. She watched them for a few seconds. O'Brien read her eyes. *Fear.* He looked across the room at the bar. One man had the shoulders of a buffalo, muscle rippling beneath the stretched white T-shirt, scruffy face, sea blown black hair. The other was tall and long-limbed, hard tissue and muscle on his wiry frame. They drank Miller Beer from cans.

Sofia lowered her voice and whispered, "The tall guy at the bar is the captain of one of those boats … *She Devil.* His name is Alex Trakas. The other guy, the one who looks like a wrestler, is Mike Rivera. I heard he served ten years in prison for something like manslaughter. Trakas is one of those guys always trying to make a fast buck. The irony is that I hear he's actually a good captain. But he lives beyond his means. On his third wife—they get younger each time. The guy pays lots of child support. If I were a betting woman, I'd bet his boat, *She Devil*, probably even more than *Argos* or *Aphrodite*, would be the one. But, I don't know that for sure."

O'Brien studied the men, their body language, the way the taller man postured his frame in a position of power, tossing some money on the bar, as if he were bluffing in a high-stakes poker game. O'Brien started to respond when Nick came through the front door, a crooked grin on his face. He walked around the tables, heading for O'Brien in the far corner of the bar.

# EIGHTY-ONE

Katie and Andy stood on the shore and watched the Top Gun boat disappear into the vista of sapphire, vanishing into an abyss at the threshold of the blue horizon. It was as if the boat sped off into another hemisphere, leaving them on the dark side of an uninhabitable planet. Katie turned toward her husband and said, "We will survive this situation. We have to believe that with all our hearts to convince our minds. Okay?"

Andy shoved his hands deep in his pockets, his anxious eyes surveying the barrenness. "Okay. Our first priority is food and water. I doubt we'll find water on this windswept island. But we will find food. I know you've never like sushi, but this is the time to gain an appreciation for it. I'll figure a way to catch or spear some fish and crabs. Drinkable water will be our big challenge."

"Maybe it'll rain."

"How will we catch rain? We have no buckets."

"We have our hands and our mouths. We'll catch what we can if it rains. We might be able to find some conch shells to trap raindrops. We'll do what we have to do to survive."

"Let's hope a low-flying plane will come over the island, or maybe a boat will come close enough for us to signal it." Andy glanced toward the sky, the sun hot and bright. No clouds. He could feel his skin beginning to burn.

Katie said, "Let's look around the island. Possibly we can find shade somewhere. We have to find shade or figure a way to create it with these twisted and splintered remnants of trees tailor made from the hurricane." She scouted about, gnarled and dead trees and vegetation everywhere. She managed a smile. "If I were a movie producer looking for some place that probably resembles Mars, this might do it. Everything is drenched a peculiar brown and grayish color, as if the whole island was seen through the lens of an Ansel Adams' camera."

"One good thing … there's a lot of dead trees. We could make a bonfire and hope a boat or even a ship might see it and investigate. It would have to look like a distress signal from an island that is devoid of trees and green vegetation."

"The only problem is we don't have matches, a lighter or a way to make a fire. But the idea was good. Let's call our temporary home driftwood island." Katie half smiled and looked at the gun in her husband's hand. She glanced to the spot in the sand where the brass bullets glinted in the sunlight. She walked over, picking up the rounds, and coming back to Andy. "The only reason I got these is because there may be some opportunity to shoot the gun to let a passing sailboat know we're here."

• • •

O'Brien could tell Nick had been drinking. He said, "Nick, have a seat. This is Sofia Alanis. Sofia, meet my friend, Nick Cronus."

Nick extended his hand to her and said, "Sofia, the pleasure is mine. I can tell you have Greek blood in you, probably descended from one of the gods of beauty."

Sofia smiled, glanced at O'Brien and said, "Are all your friends this charming?"

Nick grinned and said, "I can count his Greek friends with one finger, and since I'm his only Greek friend … I gotta be prince charming." He looked at her wine glass. "Your drink is almost gone. Lemme buy you a refill." Nick hiccupped, pulling out a wooden chair, sitting opposite O'Brien and Sofia, signaling for the bartender.

Sofia said, "I appreciate the offer, but I've reached my limit. Sean tells me you're a commercial fisherman. Where do you keep your boat?"

The bartender approached, and O'Brien, gesturing toward Nick, said, "My friend, here, will take a cup of coffee." The bartender nodded and left.

"Ponce Marina," Nick said. "I like the Atlantic side of the state. Not that there's anything wrong with fishin' in the Gulf, I just like the Atlantic better. Maybe it's 'cause, if I ever get the urge to sail back to Greece, the Atlantic is a closer course."

O'Brien glanced at the two men sitting at the bar. He cut his eyes to Nick and asked, "How was the coffee shop?"

"Good. Reminds me of a lil' coffee shop on Mykonos where my papa and uncles used to go. When they weren't fishin', they'd be down there just about every day at three in the afternoon."

Sofia smiled. "I haven't been back to Greece in seven years. I miss it. Something about the pace of life in the islands—it's unique."

Nick grinned. "Seven years. If you got the seven-year itch, you gotta scratch it. Come over to Ponce Marina, and maybe we'll sail all the way to Greece." He held up his thumb and forefinger, separated by a half inch. "I'm about this close to sailing back. I wanna come back like Jason and the Argonauts. Come back as a hero."

The bartender brought Nick's coffee and left, two more customers entering. Sofia smiled, her lips wet and said, "To come back as a Greek hero, you have to do heroic things. Have you?"

O'Brien smiled and said, "Nick's entire life is an adventure."

Nick's eyebrows arched high. "You got that right!" He took a sip from the cup. "I saved a mermaid in distress one time."

"Really?" asked Sofia. "How'd that happen?"

"It was on the Atlantic side, of course. She was sittin' on a rock near the Island of Abaco. I brought my boat, *St. Michael*, close, dropped anchor, dove into the sea and swam up to her. She told me she'd lost her way in a storm. She wanted to swim to Andros Island. But she was damn tired. So, I helped her to my boat, let her sit on the swim platform so she could keep her tail wet. I set a course for Andros, giving her time to rest. After miles at sea, toward sunset, the lovely mermaid said she had the strength to make it on her own. We bid adieu. She slipped off the platform and started her journey. Last thing I saw was when she dove, her tail fin splashing the surface of the ocean as the sun set like red wine in the sky. It was a beautiful moment." He grinned.

"Wow, I'm impressed," Sofia said. "The story of the Little Mermaid that I haven't heard. It's a good one." She smiled and glanced at her watch. "I need to give my sister a ride to the doctor's office. It's close by, but she isn't driving. She broke her right ankle in a fall about a month or so ago. Suppose to get the cast off today." Sofia pulled a pen from her purse and wrote across a white bar napkin. She folded the napkin and handed it to O'Brien. "Here's my number. Give me a call sometime when you're in the area."

O'Brien reached in his wallet and pulled out a card and gave it to her. "Will do. Here's my number, too. If you see anything that might help me help my friend, please let me know."

She looked at the card for a few seconds and cut her eyes back up to O'Brien. "It just has your name and number. Doesn't have your profession. You know, like a consultant or something. What is it you do?"

"Consultant will work."

She smiled, put the card in her purse and stood to leave. Nick stared at her, his eyes uncertain. O'Brien stood, kissed her on the cheek, and said, "Thanks for the information."

"Don't mention it." She glanced at Nick. "Those two men at the bar work on *She Devil*. The taller man is the captain. His name is Alex Trakas. The other one is Mike Rivera." Sofia shifted her eyes to O'Brien, then to Nick, and back to O'Brien. "I wish you two luck. If you start messing with those guys and their friends, you're going to need it." She smiled at Nick and said, "My hero ... it was good to meet you. Bye." She walked across the tile floor.

Nick looked up at O'Brien and said, "Remind me never to use the mermaid story again. Doesn't matter. She's got a thing for you, Sean."

Sitting back down, O'Brien said nothing, glancing at the two men Sofia had pointed out at the bar. They were watching her leave, the lean one staring at her butt. When Sofia walked out the door, the men spoke, heads nodding. Two seconds later, both turned and looked at the table where Nick and O'Brien sat. O'Brien locked eyes with the big, tall man. He gestured, said something to the bartender, who was making a drink for a customer. And then the captain stared into the mirror behind the bar.

He could see that O'Brien was still looking at him.

# EIGHTY-TWO

Sol Lefko was making a cup of coffee in his kitchen when he received a text—a message that was synonymous to a death sentence. A message that would change his life forever. But he was excited because the text was from his daughter Katie. "It's about time," he mumbled as he walked from the kitchen to the front window. He peered through a crack in the curtains and could see a parked car in the shaded and woody cul-de-sac. He knew that two federal agents were behind the dark, tinted glass.

Sol turned and walked through the house. He stopped at a banister, his wife Brenda slowly coming down the staircase.

"Shouldn't you be in bed?" Sol asked.

"His wife stopped, her right hand gripping the banister. "No, I've been in bed long enough. I feel much better. As a matter of fact, I'm going to make a cup of decaf coffee."

"We got a text from Katie. I was just about to read it."

"Oh, read it. Let's see how Katie and Andy are doing. Maybe they've found an Internet connection in the remote islands, and they're homesick." She smiled.

"I wouldn't go that far. I doubt if they're ever going to be home-sick, primarily because that boat's their home now, and they can bring it back here to the states if they miss what they wanted to get away from … the corporate grind."

They stood next to the kitchen table. Sol put his glasses on and read the text message aloud. "Lefko, we have your daughter and her husband. They will die soon." He paused and looked at his wife who grabbed the back of a high-back chair to steady herself.

"Sol … dear God … no."

His lips tightened, face ashen, taking a deep breath through his nostrils. He continued reading. "Not from us, but from dehydration, sun and starvation. It is such a horrible way to go. Muscle atrophy. Hallucinations. But the heart keeps pumping, trying to preserve the brain, skin and bones. A video is attached. See for yourself. You can intervene and save them. But you must do something for us. That request will come later … perhaps in a day or two into your daughter's suffering. You will still have time, but not much. Enjoy the video. It may be the last time you see them alive."

Sol sat down at the table. He looked up at his wife and said, "I know who's behind this. I should have killed him in Cuba." Lefko's heart raced. He took deep breaths to control the trembling that started in both hands. He held the phone and pressed the mark to play the video. The image was that of Katie and Andy standing on a beach somewhere, windswept brush in the background.

Brenda stood next to her husband, her hand gripping the back of his chair, watching the video.

Their daughter looked into the camera: "Dad … we've been taken hostage from *Dragonfly*. Abdul Aswad and his men took us to this desolate island somewhere in the Bahamas. We're at least an hour to ninety minutes southeast of Cat Cay in a fast boat. We have no food or water. He's leaving us here to die. If you get this in time, please have someone in a plane fly over the islands. We'll do what we can to signal them. This freak gave us a gun with two bullets. He wants the situation to get so drastic for us that one of us does a mercy killing and then commits suicide. He's sick, Dad. Whatever you did to him in Guantanamo wasn't nearly enough—"

"It was enough!" shouted Aswad, still holding the camera lens on Katie and Andy. "It was enough because you, Sol Lefko, reinforced to me and my people just how vile you are and what extremes you, Dave Collins, and your people will go to destroy Muslim brothers who are willing to fight your imperialism. I warned you I would remove your seed from earth. That will happen in such a tragic way … dust to dust."

Brenda touched her throat. She ran into a small bathroom off the kitchen, fell to her knees, and vomited in the toilet. Between vomiting, she cried, a deep and painful sobbing.

Sol stood from the table. He stared at the last still frame of the video locked on the screen, Katie's face frozen in a distraught plea for her life. Andy helpless. Heavily armed men just off the visible periphery of the camera lens. Sol's thoughts played back the one line of text that might lead to Katie and Andy's survival. *That request will come later … perhaps in a day or two into your daughter's suffering.*

# EIGHTY-THREE

O'Brien listened to Nick tell him about his conversations in the coffee shop, concluding with the information concerning the boat called *Argos*. Nick added, "Maybe, because I'd just heard about the boat, *Argos,* that's what I had on my mind when I was chatting with Sofia and talked about Jason and the Argonauts."

O'Brien half smiled and said, "That part was fine. I think you lost credibility with the story about the mermaid."

"Sometimes I get carried away. I can only blame it on the ouzo. It's deceptive because it looks like mother's milk but kicks like a mother mule."

"The guy you shared the bottle with … what exactly did he say about the boat, *Argos,* and its crew?"

"Nothing much more than what I already told you, Sean. Man, you're always lookin' for hidden meanings, but trust me, this fella was too buzzed to have much of any meaning in anything he said. He told me that the guy, Rastus Dimitrious, is a legendary captain. He said the dude runs a tight ship … if I knew what he meant, and basically will fish for more than what's swimmin' in the deep blue sea. Now, does that mean he's haulin' terrorists into the states through Tarpon Springs, I don't know. But it's worth checkin' out. Don't you think?"

"Yes. I also think you need more coffee and some food to cut the booze. If we start walking the sponge docks, and if you somehow wind up in the water, you need to be sober enough to swim."

"Sean, Greeks come outta our mama's womb knowin' how to swim. I got fish gills on the sides of my chest."

"Let's go find a sandwich and some black coffee."

O'Brien left money on the table to cover the drinks and tip. They walked across the room, Nick a bit unstable, but walking straight. As they got closer to the door, O'Brien heard someone say, "Dude, if you're smart, you'll keep your distance from Sofia. She's damaged goods."

O'Brien stopped just as he reached for the door handle. He turned and looked at the two men sitting at the bar. He said, "Excuse me. I didn't quite hear what you said."

Captain Alex Trakas grinned, his eyes dull. "I said Sofia is one of 'em chicks who bounce from husband to husband like she's gettin' a new model car. Lots of baggage. Just some friendly advice."

O'Brien turned around and approached the men, Nick walked next to him, his eyes red and bleary. O'Brien said, "I appreciate that. You never know what you're getting into sometimes until you're too far in to turn back."

"No shit. Where you boys from?" asked Trakas.

Nick said, "Greece. Where you from?"

"Right here in T Springs. Born and bred. Mike's from Georgia. Son of a hog farmer. Mike butchered his first pig when he was nine, right Mike?"

"That's right." Mike Rivera leaned back against the bar, eyes taunting.

Trakas asked, "How long y'all in town?"

O'Brien said, "Don't know yet. Since my friend's Greek, he comes over to get his refill. Mostly the food."

Trakas scratched his whiskered chin and said, "You boys here on some kinda gay holiday? We got no gay bars in Tarpon Springs. You can probably find plenty down the coast in Tampa."

Rivera snorted and laughed.

Nick's chest swelled. He started to respond as O'Brien said, "We'll ignore your little editorial comment. Because, to continue this line of conversation wouldn't work out well for either party … especially yours. As I said a moment ago, sometimes you never know what you're getting into until you're too far in to turn back." He paused and looked the captain square in the eye. "Sort of like when you stop hauling shrimp and cast your net for human cargo."

O'Brien didn't blink. He watched Trakas' pupils. Saw the instant dilation, watched his chest expand. Could see his carotid artery pulse on the side on his neck. And then O'Brien cut his eyes over to Rivera, the man's nostrils wider, his dim eyes blinking as if gnats were flying in his face.

Trakas chuckled and said, "Why don't you go on and take your friend outta here, and we'll call it a slight misunderstanding. All I was tryin' to do was give you a little advice about sweet Sofia, the taste of the town. And here you go makin' some weird damn claims about how we make a livin'."

O'Brien smiled. "Thanks for the advice. You've given me a lot to go on. You gents have a nice afternoon."

Rivera inadvertency pulled at his crotch, his thick jaws made a popping sound, as if someone were clipping fingernails. Trakas said, "Be damn careful what you say, smart ass. Mike here will put you and your ass wipe friend in wheelchairs if I say so. He bench presses five hundred pounds. You still got a couple of hours before sunset. It'd be a good idea not to be in Tarpon Springs after dark." Trakas turned his back to O'Brien and Nick, his eyes watching them in the mirror behind the bar.

O'Brien motioned to Nick with his head and started for the door, the only sound coming from the slight hum of a slow-turning paddle fan hanging from the ceiling. As O'Brien walked to the door, he looked at one of the old black-and-white photographs on the wall. It was a picture of young men, Greeks, all standing on the sponge docks with mounds of natural sponges in front of them. They had the look of pride. Hard working men who went to sea to bring back its bounty.

Smuggling human beings aboard was not part of it.

Outside the bar, Nick stopped and said, "Sean, man you tipped 'em off. If they're doin' the smugglin' thing, they're gonna hide it now."

"Someone here is doing it. Sometimes you have to set the trap. And this is one of those times. Dave's life is on the line. His daughter's life is at stake. So are others. We don't have the time to wait. But we can bait and see who shows up."

Nick made a hiccup. "But there goes the element of surprise that I know you use."

"Still plan to do so, only now it's in a little different way. Let's go."

"Where we gonna go?"

"To get something to eat, and then we'll visit the sponge docks. Maybe we'll see the captain and his first mate again … after dark."

# EIGHTY-FOUR

Dave Collins watched condensation roll down the side of his scotch glass and thought about a dead man. He sat on his couch in *Gibraltar's* salon and remembered the times he'd spent chatting with Russell Douglas at the Gangway Marina on Marathon Key. He recalled Russell lending him a moisture reader to locate a tiny water seal leak in one of *Gibraltar's* windows. *"You don't need to poke the wood with this device,"* he remembered Russell saying. *"Just move it slowly around the inside seam. It'll find where water's coming in."* Dave glanced at the water droplets on the sides of his glass.

He sat forward and looked at the notes he'd jotted down when he watched the news report with Wynona. Dave thought about what the TV reporter said and her interview with live-aboard resident, Derek Johnson. *"He told police that Russell Douglas only had the strength left to utter one word. He said ... Aphrodite."*

*"Saw a rope tied to a cleat. It looked brand new, and it appeared like it had been cut rather than untied. That rope wasn't there yesterday."*

Wynona came up from the galley with two plates of food, Max in step with her. On each plate, there was a triple-decker club sandwich, chips, black olives and potato salad. She handed a plate to Dave and said, "You need to eat. Man or woman does not live by scotch alone. In my case, wine."

He took the plate, smiled and said, "You didn't have to make this."

"No, I didn't, but I wanted to. A daughter can make her dad a plate of food. I don't go the culinary extremes that Nick uses, primarily because I don't have the talent or expertise. But I make a mean club sandwich. I was surprised you had the ingredients to pull this together."

"It looks wonderful. Thank you. Speaking of daughters and dads, tell me about your father." Dave sat the plate on the coffee table and picked up a chip, taking a bite.

She sat opposite him. "My dad was of Irish-American ancestry. My mom is full-blooded Seminole. They met when my mother was attending Florida State, fell in love and got married. A hit-and-run driver killed Dad when I was thirteen. He was coming to pick me up from gym practice. A witness said a man in a green pickup truck ran a red light and T-boned my father. From reports of erratic driving, most likely a drunk … making it murder by vehicle. Police never caught the guy. I think that's one reason I studied criminal justice, I always wanted to find the man who killed my dad."

"I'm sorry to hear that story. It's heartbreaking to lose a parent, someone who's in good health, especially to a hit-and-run driver. And you were at such a tender age … and age where a teenage girl really needs her father for a lot of reasons."

"Mom never remarried. She'd found the love of her life, and that was that."

Dave sipped the watered-down scotch in his glass and took a bite from the sandwich. "This is good, thanks."

"Better hold the thanks until after you've finished. If you get heartburn, blame it on the scotch and olives. A bad combo, not like vodka and olives." Wynona smiled and took a bite from her sandwich. After a moment she said, "Dave, my heart aches for you today. You just came back home from a funeral of a close friend, a former colleague, and then you see a news report about the murder of a man you knew at a marina in the Keys. The black cloud is descending too low. You need a break, a breather, just to collect your thoughts."

He cleared his throat. "I keep thinking about the senseless killing of Russell Douglas and his last dying word … *Aphrodite.* Maybe the guy on camera that was interviewed, Derek Johnson, heard or saw something else before Russell died."

"I can always ride down to Marathon Key to question him."

Dave smiled, "I don't want you to take any more risks than necessary. I feel guilty that you're even here."

"Hey, none of that talk. Your daughter's relatively safe. And you, Dave, keep forgetting that I spent a lot of time as an agent who was often in perilous situations. I'm a grown woman who can take care of herself. Trust me on that. Now, eat before Max has a conniption fit and steals your food."

Dave exhaled, a slight wheeze in his lungs. "I know. My apologies. In terms of the respite you mentioned … I don't need that. What I need is to hear that Aswad has been caught and the further threat of violence and death has been eliminated. I wonder how Sean and Nick are doing in Tarpon Springs?"

"Maybe their silence is a sign that they're plugging away, finding leads and following them."

Dave sat back on the couch, rubbed his eyes and said, "I hope Nick's presence is more help than hindrance. Sean moves extremely fast, doing subtle scratch and sniff tests throughout his investigations."

"I bet that Nick is getting Sean into places and conversations that he otherwise might not find alone."

Dave nodded. "You, dear Wynona, in spite of your training in law enforcement, are an eternal optimist." He took a bite from his sandwich, chewing thoughtfully, watching a sunset through *Gibraltar's* port window. "I've been around death much of my life. But never have I witnessed the type of death that I've seen in the last three weeks. And, it's beginning to look as if the shared evil is ostensibly tied to the sick, vengeful musing of a psychopath locked in a federal prison, and a sworn terrorist who'd love to be the next instigator of another 9/11."

"I hope Sean can question Richard Thurston. I have no doubt that senior is directing junior, Jason. To what extent and how … maybe Sean can find something."

"The agencies will want to question Richard Thurston. My guess is they'll learn nothing more than what we already know. For a guy like Thurston, he's usually a chess move ahead of most investigators. And, when you toss in the fact that he's in prison with absolutely nothing to lose, there's no incentive for cooperation or even for a meeting."

"The agencies might not have any luck—but if you can help get him in, I still think it's important for Sean to try," Wynona said.

Dave's phone buzzed on the counter. He rose from the couch, walked over, and looked at the ID. Glancing at Wynona, he said, "I need to take this. You can stay here." He answered and said, "Hey, Sol. I trust that you and Brenda are back home now."

"Dave … something horrible is happening." Sol stood in the center of his living room, looking at a portrait of Katie hanging on the wall. It was an oil painting, commissioned when Katie started college. She stood in a field, flowers in bloom around her, a small white flower in her hair, wide smile. Sol pinched the bridge of his nose and said, "It's Katie and Andy …" his voice cracking.

"What happened," Dave asked, setting his half sandwich on the plate.

"They were kidnapped from their sailboat and left to die on an island somewhere in the Bahamas or the Caribbean. No food or water. Scorching daytime temperatures. Aswad did it. I could hear his voice on the video, and Katie pleading for her life."

# EIGHTY-FIVE

It was getting close to 9:00 p.m. when O'Brien and Nick were finishing dinner at a rustic waterfront restaurant, one that offered outdoor dining and an opportunity for O'Brien to watch the sponge docks. He and Nick sat at a table under the stars and finished their meal of grilled sea bass, chargrilled octopus, Greek salad, and grape leaves stuffed with lamb and rice.

Less than a dozen other people sat at tables on the deck, soft, vintage white lights were strung around the perimeter of the dining area. They drank black coffee. When the server, a brunette in her late twenties, brought the check, Nick said, "Let's split it."

O'Brien took the check, glanced at it before handing the check back to the server with a one-hundred-dollar bill and said, "Keep the change."

"Thank you, sir," she said with a wide smile.

"You're welcome. How long have you worked here?"

"About a year. I like serving on the deck. I think it's the best place to eat."

"The only better place would be on the deck of those yachts." He motioned toward the docks.

"We get more of a boater's view in here than you might think— and it's year-round. Mostly with the change of seasons, heat in the south, cold up north and whatnot, we get visitors from everywhere. Some stay in hotel rooms … others stay on their boats."

Nick grinned and said, "Nothin' beats livin' aboard. Life gets simpler."

She smiled and nodded. O'Brien asked, "How about the commercial boats … you ever see people living on them?"

She thought for a moment, looking toward the docks and adjacent city marina. "It seems like you'll see that more often on the shrimp boats. Usually when they're getting ready for a run. I've seen their lights on a couple nights before they leave, and sometimes on when they get back. I guess they stay aboard because they're waiting for buyers to make them an offer. The price of seafood is up and down, you know. There's one boat, I believe it's called *Argos,* it seems like they're busy all the time. Hey, I need to get to a table. Y'all have a good night, thanks." She turned and walked back to the interior portion of the sprawling restaurant.

Nick sipped his coffee and said, "She's a looker. Hey, what'd I tell you about *Argos,* eh? Sounds like that could be where the action is 'round the docks."

O'Brien's phone vibrated on the table. He looked at the ID and said, "It's Wynona." He answered, "How's Max?"

"She's fine. I can't say the same for Dave, though."

"What happened? Is he with you?"

"Yes, I'm spending time with him on *Gibraltar.* He just went into the bathroom. Sean, Sol Lefko called Dave a little while ago and told him that Katie and Andy were kidnapped from *Dragonfly* and taken to some desolate island somewhere in the Bahamas or Caribbean and left there to die from exposure, lack of food and water."

"Tell me everything you know. Don't leave anything out."

Nick raised his shoulders, his eyes worried. Wynona gave O'Brien the details and added, "Dave immediately called some of his top contacts at the CIA and FBI. He sent them the video of Katie and Andy on camera. It's heartbreaking to watch. The FBI, in tandem with the Air Force, will fly over as many islands as possible tomorrow to see if they can find them. They'll work with the Royal Defense Force in the Bahamas, essentially that's their navy. They don't have an air force in the islands."

"Maybe they'll spot *Dragonfly*. If we're lucky, Katie and Andy may not be too far from there."

"For all we know, Abdul Aswad could have sunk *Dragonfly*, or had some of his men sail her to a more remote location just to throw us off the trail to Katie and Andy. We don't see Aswad on camera, but we hear his voice. He's speaking directly to Sol Lefko, taunting him."

"Beyond the obviously warped pleasure Aswad is getting from having the upper hand, the provoking … is there something specific that he's asking for?"

Wynona thought for a few seconds, playing back Aswad's words in her mind. "No, nothing specific. He just talks about the mistake that Lefko, Dave, and the others made in Guantanamo. How the Muslim brothers were deeply offended. And how the seed of people like Lefko, and apparently Dave, would be wiped from the earth in a dust-to-dust scenario."

O'Brien was quiet. He stared toward the docks, the blue flicker of a TV coming from the salon windows of 65-foot Sea Ray tied to the posts. He said, "Aswad has to want something more than ridiculing Lefko and Dave through a video. The question is … what is it?"

Nick sat straighter and asked, "Is Dave okay?"

O'Brien nodded. He listened as Wynona said, "Abdul Aswad used Katie's phone to email that video to Lefko. Either Aswad or one of his men shot the video. You only can see Katie and Andy on camera. The island looks bleak as hell, more like a desert than the tropics."

"Islands, like Aruba and Bonaire, have cactus and an arid feel to them. People live on those islands and thousands of others visit. But there are hundreds of islands that are only a few acres in size, uninhabited, and slow death traps to anyone stranded on them for too long. But something's not making sense?"

"Which part?"

"Aswad's part. The video, the bad it represents, is horrific … but it doesn't make sense to send it for shock value alone. He could have simply killed them on camera to achieve that result. Ask Dave if there was anything else Aswad sent Sol Lefko … some demand to do something to save the lives of his daughter and son-in-law."

"That crossed my mind as well. But Dave told me what Lefko shared with him. And I could hear at least one half of the conversation—Dave's comments and questions. There was nothing leading to anything else." She paused and stood from the couch, Max standing and yawning. "When it rains, it definitely pours. It's been a really bad day for Dave. Back from a funeral, he gets this information and video from Sol emailed to him courtesy of a cutthroat terrorist, and on top of that, one of Dave's friends at a marina in Marathon Key was murdered."

"Murdered? What friend? Was he or she former CIA?"

"I don't think so. At least Dave didn't mention anything like that. The victim was a man who Dave had known when he docked *Gibraltar* in the Keys at a place called the Gangway Marina."

"I'm familiar with it."

"The victim was a retired commercial fisherman who was stabbed late last night, probably somewhere around the marina. He managed to make it down the docks to bang on the door of a friend's boat for help. That's where he died, as his friend was calling 911. Dave's been nursing scotch most of the evening."

Dave approached the salon. "Hold a second," Wynona said. "I'll put him on the phone with you."

Ten seconds later Dave said, "Wynona told me she brought you up to speed. It's a hell of a mess, Sean. We'll have a lot of eyes in the sky at first light. But there are so damn many remote islands in the Bahamas, if that's where they were dumped to die."

"I'm sure the FBI and CIA are trying to track the email to locate where it originated. Aswad's people might have had it routed through dummy servers with near untraceable IP addresses prohibiting them from discovering the physical location of the phone."

"Maybe in his zest to bully Sol, Aswad didn't take those defenses."

"I'm trying to make sense out of Aswad's motivation, beyond the obvious abhorrent satisfaction a killer would get from hurting others … but is there something else that Aswad wants? Maybe there's something Richard Thurston wants and is orchestrating from prison."

"Sol didn't mention it. He was in such a state of shock I'm sure his mind was numb."

"Can you find out if he received a text from Aswad or an email with a demand, maybe a subtle threat … anything?"

"Sean, even considering the state of mind that Sol's in, he would have mentioned that to me."

O'Brien said nothing for a few seconds. "There may not have been an accompanying text since Aswad's voice can be heard on the video, but it wouldn't hurt to check with Sol. Can you send the video to me?"

"Of course."

"Another thing … can you ask your CIA contact to set up that face-to-face with Richard Thurston and me? It's time we met."

"I can make those arrangements. When do you want to fly out there?"

"Tomorrow."

There was a long pause. "I'm assuming you still think it's worthwhile considering the latest developments."

"We need whatever we can get to save Katie and Andy. I'm hoping I find that locked away in a prison cell."

"All right. I'll see what I can do."

"Thanks. Oh, Wynona told me a friend of yours was killed on Marathon Key. I'm sorry to hear that, especially in light of what's happening. Who was it?"

"His name was Russell Douglas. He was always a stand-up guy. He'd give you the shirt off his back if you needed it. There's apparently some physical evidence. Police found blood at the end of one of the docks. And there was a new boat line, a rope, which was cut and left on a piling. Looks as if the person or persons on a boat were in too much of a hurry to untie the line. So, they just cut it. Police believe Russell was stabbed there, on the dock, and pushed into the water. Somehow he managed to get out and sought help from a boater friend, a live-aboard. He told police that the last thing Russell said before he died was one word … Aphrodite."

O'Brien closed his eyes, Sofia Alanis' comments echoing through his mind, *"Boat's called Aphrodite … like the goddess. You know, the beautiful one who slept with gods and mere mortals."*

# EIGHTY-SIX

Katie looked at the night sky and said a silent prayer. The stars seemed closer than she'd ever seen them at any point in her life. She felt drenched in light from the heavens on a tiny speck of an island surrounded by thousands of miles of dark water. She only had one outfit, a sundress, which she had hurriedly pulled over her bathing suit to escape the prying eyes of Aswad's soldier, and flip-flops. Andy had nothing but his swim trunks and white T-shirt. A cool wind blew across the wide face of the Atlantic. Katie hugged her upper arms.

Andy said, "Let's build a lean-to or makeshift shelter. We'll pull in some branches and sticks to make a windbreak."

Katie glanced around and said, "We have plenty of material to make a stick house. I always wanted a brick house, but a stick house will do just fine at the moment." She began scouring the area, dragging some downed branches to the spot where Andy was repositioning a severed tree limb.

After fifteen minutes, they'd erected a structure similar to a teepee without the animal hide to break wind and repel rain. Andy said, "I hope in the morning light we can find some palm fronds to give it a covering, some outside walls."

"I'm cold and exhausted," Katie said. "I just need to sit down." She sat on the sand beneath the makeshift structure. Within five seconds she slapped her left ankle, staring at an insect that didn't appear to be visible.

She smacked at a second bite on her left leg. "What are these … bugs? They're biting like crazy, and I can't even see them."

Andy slapped an insect below is right calf muscle and said, "They're no-see-ums. So small they're hard to see, especially in this light. They're sometimes called sand fleas."

Katie looked at her husband as if he just started speaking a new language. She said, "No-see-ums. I can certainly feel them. What can we do? We can't lie on the ground with sticks and branches around us with sand fleas crawling over our skin and biting us." She smacked at her lower leg again. "Andy, they're getting bad. I almost want to run into the water to stop their biting. I feel them in my hair, my scalp." She stood. "If we even attempt to lie down, we'll be eaten alive."

"Maybe we should get closer to the breakers. The no-see-ums might not be close to the water. If the tide comes in, they'd go out."

Katie sprinted toward the gentle breakers, walking into the warm surf, the small waves rolling across her legs up to her knees. She splashed water over her forearms, felt more biting into her scalp. So, she pulled the sundress over her head, threw it back toward the beach, walked farther into the sea, and dove in, letting the salt water cover her entire body.

"Don't go too far out at night!" Andy shouted.

Katie swam for a few seconds on the surface and then dove under, the water like a bath. She wanted to swim all the way back to *Dragonfly*, climb up the dive ladder, lay across the swim platform and rest on her floating home. Her lungs began to burn. She swam for the surface, popped through, rolled onto her back and looked at the night sky. She stared into the infinity of space, the twinkling cosmos so vast and so far away. The Big Dipper looked as if all the water on earth would only fill a tiny portion of it. Never had the universe appeared so grand and immense.

She thought about what Dave Collins had said the last night she and Andy were in Ponce Marina. They were standing in *Dragonfly's* cockpit when Dave looked at the stars and said, *"Not long ago, a new galaxy was discovered with the aid of a super telescope. Astronomers are calling it Dragonfly 44. It's as large as our Milky Way … but they believe it's made from dark matter."*

Katie floated on her back, staring at the heavens, feeling so small in the universe, empty and abandoned.

# EIGHTY-SEVEN

O'Brien and Nick moved to a remote table on the expansive wooden deck, away from the few remaining diners eating baklava and sipping after dinner liquors. "Let's sit here," O'Brien said. "No one can see or hear the video from this corner. He scanned the docks, the moving shadows, boat lights flickering off the black river. They sat at a table, O'Brien finding the downloaded video on his phone.

Nick shook his head, rubbing the back of his wide hand against three days growth of dark whiskers on his chin and said, "From what Dave told you, I'm not sure I want to see it. I say this only 'cause I feel for Katie and Andy, and I gave them a loose sailing map to follow. Now, they've disappeared."

"Maybe we can make them reappear." O'Brien pressed the start button on his phone, the short video playing.

They watched the video closely, Nick cursing under his breath. When it ended, Nick ran his fingers through his thick, black hair and said, "What a freakin' son-of-a-bitch! Sean, we gotta find that dude. He's the devil on two legs. Katie and Andy won't make it too long in the heat with no food or water."

O'Brien nodded. "In that sun, dehydration comes quickly. One thing Aswad said … brothers are believers."

"What about it?"

"It's a motto for the Muslim Brotherhood. B-a-b are the letters the FBI found in the transfer of funds through one of Aswad's offshore accounts, the money going to someone or into something with the letters b-a-b. Nick, more importantly, right now, is the island that Katie and Andy are stranded on, it is different."

"What do you mean?"

"I'm backing the video up to the widest shot and let's freeze the frame." He used his index finger to move the video in reverse, it played for a second, and he stopped it, using two fingers to enlarge the frame, studying the image. "Nick, take a close look at the terrain behind them. It doesn't resemble Aruba or Bonaire. Have you seen an island like that? This is the result of what would happen a few months after a strong hurricane. What the wind didn't destroy, the storm-surge, with sea water, left its unique mark here."

"Lemme see closer." Nick took the phone and examined the picture, the rumble of diesels in the background as a boat came closer to the docks. "I've never seen that particular island … the way the trees and stuff look, before now. When a cat five hurricane whips up through the islands, lots of little ones can look like the surface of Mars after a while. If we can find *Dragonfly*, though, could be that island isn't too far away."

"Let's take a walk."

"Where we headin' to?"

"To where the boats are all tied up."

"Maybe *Argos* is one of 'em hauling weird stuff. My man, Sean … it's good to be hangin' with you."

"You might not say that in the next twenty minutes."

"We're brothers, bro. I always say that. I wouldn't be breathin' this sweet night air, drinkin' ouzo and flirtin' with women if it weren't for you savin' my life that night. C'mon, who knows, I might return the favor. Then we're even." He grinned.

They left the restaurant, walking down the sponge docks under dimly lit street lamps, moths looping through the soft glow, the smell of fish scales from an aging steel trawler with streaks of coffee-colored stains etched below a port window like rusty teardrops. They paused near a bronze statue of a sponge diver, midways down the docks, the diver holding his dive helmet in one hand.

O'Brien surveyed the boats, most dark, scarcely rocking in the current. Others were lit, soft light coming from salt-stained porthole windows, live-a-boards moving about open cockpits. Greek music came from a tavern across the street, the profiles of tourists strolling beneath the glow of neon.

O'Brien looked farther down the docks where most of the shrimp boats were moored, one boat just arriving, the Anclote River glossy as a black cat's fur under the moonlight. He counted eight shrimp boats, including the new arrival. Six were dark. Two had lights on, people in silhouette moving inside and on the exteriors, port side.

Nick followed O'Brien's eyes and said, "I see where you're lookin', and I think the best way to check 'em out is to take a midnight stroll in that direction."

O'Brien nodded, watching the boat, trying to read the name on the bow. As it approached a dock light, he saw it. "Nick, hang here a few minutes. I need to get something from my Jeep."

"What'd you forget?"

"Nothing. But I didn't know I might need it until I spoke with Dave on the phone."

"What do you need?"

"My gun."

"You think it's gonna be that kinda night?"

"You never know." O'Brien stared at the boat that was easing into its slip, the captain a half-lit figure in the wheelhouse, two crew members ready with lines on deck.

"Sean, why are you starin' at that particular boat? I can see from here it's not *Argos*. That's the one we should be checkin' out, or maybe *She Devil*."

"No, those aren't the boats. From here it looks like the name is *Aphrodite*. Dave said his friend, who was just murdered in Marathon Key, mentioned one word before dying. And that word was *Aphrodite*. In a few minutes, maybe we'll know where that boat was recently."

O'Brien turned and left, walking through the pockets of dim light, around tourists going in and out of the bars, and to the lot where his Jeep was one of a dozen remaining vehicles. He thought about what Sofia had said and he walked faster.

"And there may be a third boat ... called Aphrodite ... like the goddess."

# EIGHTY-EIGHT

O'Brien ignored the sign hanging from the locked gate: *Boat Owners and Guests Only.* He and Nick climbed over a waist-high gateway leading to the last dock—the dock where shrimp boats, trawlers, a houseboat and a crab boat were moored. The long pier was dimly lit, one security light bolted to the top of a twenty-foot, wooden beam, the square post weather-beaten and partially coated in sea gull droppings.

O'Brien lowered his voice and said, "Let's stay to the far-right side of the dock. It's the darkest."

"You packin' your gun?"

"Under my shirt."

"Let's do this." Nick used the palm of his right hand to wipe the perspiration from his forehead. He cracked his knuckles.

O'Brien said, "I assume every one of these guys speak fluent English, but if one pulls the Greek language card, talk the talk with him."

"I'm ready. What do you want me to ask him?"

"Nothing. You don't have to ask him anything, but you can tell him your pal, that would be me, is one crazy dude who once walked alone into a motorcycle gang's clubhouse and came out with a murder suspect. In the aftermath, seven of the gang members did serious rehab time in the county hospital."

"Sean, there's a lotta shit you never told me about. What—"

O'Brien placed one finger on his lips for silence. He whispered. "I hear voices coming from the end of the dock. Let's head that way … stay in the shadows."

They moved past the first shrimp boat, *Miss Jenny*. There were no lights anywhere on the boat and no sense of movement. O'Brien looked at the name on the hull near the bow of the second shrimp boat, *She Devil*. They continued walking, the muffled conversations becoming louder, the odor of rotting shrimp heads growing stronger. The next boat on the left side of the dock was *Argos*, and the interior lights glowed pale yellow through the portholes. The outriggers were dark like a butterfly's wings resting in the upright position.

O'Brien could see silhouettes moving in the wheelhouse, could hear the faint beat of a Bon Jovi song—*Wanted Dead or Alive*. "Looks like somebody's home," he whispered to Nick. "We'll let those sleeping dogs lie. Our destiny is at the end of the dock. We have a date with *Aphrodite*."

Nick shook his head and mumbled, "To the ancient Greek men, she was bad news. Aphrodite was born from the severed testicles of Uranus when they were tossed in the sea. I do know a little Greek history, the important stuff, at least."

They walked past a sixty-foot crabbing boat, dozens of wire mesh crab traps stacked on one side of the docks like small pyramids, the briny smell of decaying crab claws drifting up from the traps. O'Brien used the cages as a place to stand behind, unseen, and observe the deckhands tying down *Aphrodite*. He and Nick watched the men move around the boat, securing lines, coiling ropes.

Johnny Hastings placed an unlit cigarette behind his left ear, stepping from the stern onto the docks. He said, "Bear, throw me a line."

O'Brien watched the man called Bear, a man who'd earned his name from his girth. Beefy arms and the thick chest of an NFL lineman. Shoulder-length hair and dark beard reminiscent of Grizzly Adams. O'Brien observed how Bear used his hands and arms. *Left-handed*. That would be good to know if push came to shove and shove came to handguns. Bear tossed a line to Johnny, who stood on the docks. In seconds, Johnny whipped the lines around the dock cleats like a rodeo cowboy tying the three legs of a calf. Finished and done.

O'Brien watched the captain in the wheelhouse, a cigarette dangling from his lips, working the controls to the diesels and the bow thrusters, the whiff of diesel fumes in the night air. The captain lifted a phone to his ear, talking to someone. He waited for a stern line to be secured and then shut off the engines, the sound of prop wash splashing against the pilings. And then the dock was quiet. The men continued moving about the boat, coiling lines and locking down hatches.

The captain stuck his head out of an open window on the wheelhouse and said, "We got another run comin' up. Big money."

Bear looked up at the wheelhouse and said, "How big?"

"So big you won't have to make another run for a long damn time."

Johnny Hastings glanced up from coiling a line and said, "Man, I don't know. My ol' lady is already pissed. She says she's a single mom 'cause I gotta make a livin' at sea."

Kalivaris said, "Then make this the last one. You'll pocket enough to wine and dine Beth for a lotta Saturday nights.

• • •

O'Brien turned to Nick and whispered, "It's show time. Let's roll out the welcome mat."

Captain Santos Kalivaris noticed them first. He glanced out the open wheelhouse window and did a double take as O'Brien and Nick approached. Kalivaris picked up his 9mm Sig, lifting his shirttail, and wedging the pistol under his belt. The two deckhands stopped what they were doing, both men looking surprised and edgy as O'Brien and Nick stood dockside.

"We help y'all?" asked Bear.

O'Brien nodded. "We hear you might have some shrimp for sale."

"Where'd you hear that?"

"Around the docks."

"That right?"

"That's right."

Bear folded his big arms. "Not tonight, pal."

Captain Santos Kalivaris came out of the wheelhouse, wiping his hands on a stained, red-checkered cloth, his dark eyes shadowed under the bill of his cap. He looked down from the boat to O'Brien and Nick. "Like he said … we got no shrimp. Happens from time to time. You hit a dry run. You fellas might want to check with the Rusty Pelican. If anybody's got 'em, that's the place."

O'Brien glanced at a bowline that hung over the gunwale. He could see that the line appeared to have been slashed, the end of the rope frayed in an unraveled cut. He thought about what Dave had said on the phone, *'There was a new boat line, a rope, which was cut and left on a piling. Looks as if the person or persons on a boat were in too much of a hurry to untie the line. So, they just cut it.'*

O'Brien looked up at the men and said, "The Rusty Pelican … we appreciate the referral. I'll tell them you sent me."

Kalivaris used one hand to slide his ball cap back a little on his head, his dark hair feathering out from the sides of the hat. "Y'all don't know my name."

O'Brien smiled, able to see the captain's eyes now. "But we know the name of your boat, *Aphrodite*. That should be enough. Sorry you guys had a dry run. Where do you trawl for shrimp?"

Johnny Hastings pursed his lips and stroked his unkempt goatee with a nicotine-stained finger. "Hey, dudes. No disrespect, but we got work to do. So y'all need to take a hike. Cap's more diplomatic. But I'm dog shit tired and want to go get some sleep."

Nick grinned and in Greek said, "Know how you feel, man. I fish, too. Wears on you."

Kalivaris tilted his head at a right angle, staring at Nick and, in English, said, "Your Greek is all right, guy. So, I'll just say it in plain English. Leave us the fuck alone right now. We got stuff to do." He hooked his thumbs under his belt, rocking slightly in his orange rubber boots.

Nick started to say something when O'Brien interjected, took two steps closer and said, "Sure, but before we go … are you needing any more crew members?"

Kalivaris looked doubtful. "We just told you it was a dry run. Don't need help."

"You gents have a good night. We'll head on back down the docks, see if we can buy some shrimp from the locals on the water. If not, I guess we'll have to seek out the imported shrimp. You know, the catch that comes from other parts of the world." He didn't blink, looking straight at the captain, watching the two other men in his peripheral vision.

Kalivaris moved his right hand near his jean's pocket. He made a dry swallow, mocking smile. Bear folded his arms across his chest. Johnny removed the cigarette from behind his ear, used a silver Zippo lighter to light it, taking a deep drag, blowing smoke through his nostrils. Kalivaris said, "We don't bring in anything but Gulf pinks. Take a hike."

O'Brien smiled. "No sweat. Hope you guys can get some rest and better luck next run." O'Brien watched Bear's eyes. Then looked at Johnny, taking a drag, his eyes following something.

And then there was a creaking sound in the boards behind them.

# EIGHTY-NINE

Katie and Andy stood on the desolate beach and watched hope appear at the rim of the world. They stared at a ship, a freighter in the black of night. The lights on the ship, from bow to stern, gave an indication of the length, more than a thousand feet. But in the distance, it appeared a few inches long. Katie hugged her bare arms in the breeze and said, "Maybe you can fire a shot. Somebody might see the flash out of the end of the barrel and think it's a distress signal."

Andy considered the ship for a few seconds. "I bet that freighter is three or four miles away. Let's see if it comes closer. Right now, the chances of someone on board seeing a muzzle flash are next to none. And even if they did see something, it'd look like a firefly in the distance. It would be a waste of a bullet."

Katie looked at her husband, unblinking, and lowered her eyes to the pistol in his right hand. She said, "At this point, we need to do whatever we can to get somebody's attention. If we don't, we'll die out here."

"No, we won't die. In the morning, I'm going to catch something in the ocean for us to eat."

"Right now, I'd just like to be able to lie down without being eaten alive by some bugs we can't even see." She stared at the ship, the only visible lights in the Atlantic. "Does it look to you like it's coming closer?"

Andy watched the freighter for a few seconds and said, "Maybe, but it's hard to tell. The ship came from the northeast. Could be heading to someplace like Nassau or Freeport, maybe Miami."

"I'm going to be an optimist. I think it'll come close to our little no name island, close enough for you to signal with one or two bullets. They can send a rowboat for us or maybe call for help."

Andy moved closer to his wife. He carefully tossed the gun farther up the beach, out of the way of the rolling surf. He said, "Let's just sit on the beach and rest. The sand fleas aren't near the breakers. Tide's going out. The beach is damp. We'll sit here. You can put your head in my lap. I'll do what I can to keep you warm."

He took her hand, and they slowly sat on the hard sand. Andy put his arm around his wife's bare shoulders, and they stared out to sea, watching the freighter. After a few minutes, the ship's lights grew dimmer as did their chance for rescue. They said nothing, sitting on a remote beach, rolling breakers the only sound. They sat there, together and yet so alone on a sliver of land in a sea of islands, the freighter vanishing over the horizon and taking their hopes with it.

• • •

Sean O'Brien didn't have to turn around to know someone was behind him and Nick. He could tell it in the eyes of the three men on the moored shrimp boat. The captain, Bear and the man called Johnny all three pretended not to look at whomever was approaching. O'Brien knew by the trajectory of their eyes, and the creak in the boards on the dock, that the person or persons were at least twenty feet behind him. He assumed that the captain was armed, the long shirt covering his belt area. He had no idea if the new arrival behind him was carrying a gun.

There was another sound. Now ten feet away.

O'Brien turned around to face the same two men he and Nick met in the bar. Nick looked over his shoulder just as O'Brien said, "The fellas on *Aphrodite* tell us the best shrimp can be bought at the Rusty Pelican. Do you gentlemen concur?"

The taller of the two, Alex Trakas, shook his head, grinning. Mike Rivera folded his arms across his chest. Trakas moved a toothpick from the left side of his mailbox mouth to the right side. He glanced up at Captain Kalivaris and said, "Santos … last I recall, the dock's private property and reserved for boat owners and their guests. Are these two dudes your guests?"

"No … make that a hell no."

Nick glanced over at O'Brien, looked at the three men on the boat and said in Greek, "Come on brother, we're Greek. We're all brothers. Greek blood is thick. The same."

Kalivaris shook his head. "Don't think so," he said in English. "You boys got a smell to you. Like somethin' ain't quite right. Sorta like three-day-old fish."

Trakas chuckled and said, "That's what I thought. Kenny Drakos told us that the guy with the mop hair was askin' some serious questions in the coffee shop. The sort of questions that got nothin' to do with shrimp."

"No shit," said Bear. "What kinda questions?"

"Stuff about the import—export business here at the docks. Nasty and serious stuff."

O'Brien sized up the two men closest to him and Nick. The breeze changed, and he smelled weed mixed with whiskey on their clothes. He thought, if he could take down the taller man first and then compromise the second man, it might give Nick time to prepare for an assault, assuming the guys on the boat make a fast charge. O'Brien said, "Let's chalk this one up as a miscommunication. My friend and I will head down the dock and call it a night. No harm done. We'll be on our way."

Trakas took two steps closer. Rivera did the same. Trakas said, "I'll agree with you on that. We definitely got a failure to communicate. But the fly in the ointment is your pal. He was communicating real good to Kenny Drakos in the coffee shop." He reached under his belt and pulled out a knife. "Maybe the failure to communicate is 'cause you got that big damn mustache … messes up your speech. I'll shave it off. You boys are trespassin', and Cap'n Santos tells us he saw you tryin' to steal a downrigger off *Argos*. That's theft of a man's property … his livelihood."

O'Brien saw Trakas look up at the three men on the boat and nod. It was the half-second he needed. O'Brien lunged forward, grabbing the man's wrist, twisting it behind his back, pulling up hard. The arm snapped at the shoulder socket with a noise that sounded like an egg dropped on a tile floor. Trakas screamed, dropping his knife.

Rivera swung at O'Brien's head, missing by a half-inch. O'Brien countered, driving his fist into the man's left jaw, dropping him to the dock.

Nick picked up the knife as the three men from the shrimp boat descended. They stopped momentarily, Bear grinning. He said, "You think you're gonna stop the three of us with that blade?"

O'Brien had his gun out before Nick could answer and said, "Maybe my friend's knife won't stop the three of you, but this Glock will. Hands up! All three!"

"Screw you!" Johnny said. "Who do you shit heads think you are?"

"The last two people you'll see alive," O'Brien said, slight smile. "Hand's up or I'll put one right between your eyes." O'Brien aimed his pistol. The man's hands shot up, as did the other two. "Nick, walk over there and relieve the captain of the gun he's carrying on his left side under that shirt."

Nick grinned, held the knife in his right hand, walked around the three men and came up behind Kalivaris, reaching under his shirt and lifting out the gun. Nick walked back to O'Brien.

Trakas, crumpled with a fractured arm and dislocated shoulder, lay on his side and groaned. "I need an ambulance!"

O'Brien said, "Maybe one of your pals here will call 911 for you." He looked over to Kalivaris and said, "We're going to be generous. Rather than toss your gun into the bay, we'll leave it on top of the last piling at the end of the dock. But I wouldn't advise you to pick it up until we're off the dock."

Kalivaris pointed his finger at O'Brien and said, "You better get you asses outta Tarpon Springs. We catch you here … we'll take you out to sea. Nobody will find you."

O'Brien smiled, "Seems like we've heard that before in this town, right Nick?"

"Yeah … same ol', same ol' stuff."

O'Brien said, "Maybe your next run won't be a dry run. I hear shrimping is pretty good down in the Keys." He backed away, Nick following, three men cursing, one moaning and one knocked out cold.

# NINETY

O'Brien looked in his rearview mirror as he and Nick left Tarpon Springs, the lights of the town reflecting in his eyes. He glanced over at Nick and said, "I think that all those guys on the shrimp boats are in the import—export business to some extent. But I'd put money on team *Aphrodite* when it comes to smuggling in terrorists."

"All of 'em look like they'd pry the silver dollars from the eyes of a dead man."

"But only one of those boats was probably in Marathon Key recently, that boat is *Aphrodite*—the last word Dave's friend uttered before dying." O'Brien stopped at a traffic light, watching a police cruiser pull up behind him. The light turned green and O'Brien slowly pulled through the intersection, the police cruiser not far behind him.

Nick looked in a side-view mirror. "I wonder if he's a good guy or a bad guy?"

"I hope we don't have to find out. Since we left the docks, no sound of a siren from an ambulance. The shrimpers probably didn't want to make the call. They'll pick up their wounded warriors and get to a hospital emergency room somewhere." He watched the police cruiser turn down a street. "And that will give us a window to go back to *Aphrodite*."

"Go back? Tonight? That could be risky."

"It could, yes. But we don't have a choice. Katie and Andy are in serious trouble. We have to find them … alive. My gut is telling me a lead might be right here in Tarpon Springs."

"I got that, but why the hell would we wanna go to those docks tonight?"

"Because I'd like to know where *Aphrodite* goes on her next run. We overheard them planning, what Kalivaris called, a big run." He reached in the glove box and pulled out a round disk, black and smaller than a doughnut.

"What's that?" Nick asked.

"State-of-the-art GPS tracker. I'm going to board *Aphrodite* and hide it someplace. I also want to get a pic of that sliced rope while it's still hanging off the boat."

"What if one or more of the dudes is still there?"

"I doubt it. They looked like they needed showers and beers. But if one or two of them are still there, I'll deal with it."

Nick said nothing for a few seconds. "I liked your comment about how shrimpin' is pretty good down in the Keys."

"I liked the look on their faces. They're not good actors. Let's check in with Dave and Wynona." O'Brien picked up his phone and made a call. Dave Collins answered and asked, "How's Florida's original Greek town, Tarpon Springs?" Dave sat in a leather chair on *Gibraltar*, Wynona sitting on the couch with Max sleeping by her side.

O'Brien looked in his rearview mirror and said, "Can't complain. We have five shrimpers with a bad attitude. The good out of that bad is Nick and I found a shrimp boat called *Aphrodite*."

"Hold a second, Sean. I'm putting you on speakerphone so Wynona can hear this." He pressed the button and said, "Okay. Wynona, Sean and Nick located a shrimp boat called *Aphrodite*. Sean, do you think there's a connection to the murder of Russell Douglas?"

"Probably. The boat and crew were just arriving from somewhere. We approached them at the end of a dock and asked if they had any shrimp for sale. You'd have thought I asked them to explain the theory of quantum physics." O'Brien explained what happened and added, "You mentioned something about a new boat line, a rope that was cut and left on a dock piling."

"Yes, what about it?"

"On the shrimp boat, *Aphrodite*, there's a half-inch bowline that's cut. Partially frayed. It looks new."

"Interesting."

"Maybe you or Wynona can speak with the detective investigating the murder in the Keys. A forensics exam under a microscope could tell us if it's the same rope."

Wynona said, "Sean, I can make the call to the investigators in Monroe County. If there's a match, we definitely know that boat was there. Nothing beats physical evidence."

"It could be a long shot, but I doubt it, considering what the victim said before he died. Dave, maybe one of the three men on board had some reason to kill your friend at that dock."

Dave nodded. "The question is why? Trust me on this one … Russell Douglas was not a criminal. Maybe he was in the wrong place at the wrong time. He was always the kind of guy who kept an eye out for others."

"Could have been he heard a noise at that dock late at night. Maybe it was the sound of that shrimp boat dropping off or picking up illegal passengers. And if that's the case, could be that one of them killed him … especially if they're trained assassins."

Wynona said, "So this could boil down to Abdul Aswad's killers entering the country on a shrimp boat that calls Tarpon Springs its port of call."

"At this point, it's a good probability."

Dave set his empty glass down on the coffee table and said, "Katie and Andy Scott are in dire straits, courtesy of Aswad. Sol Lefko and his wife are coming unglued. If we don't find Katie and Andy soon, I'd hate to be part of the recovery team that finds their bodies later."

O'Brien drove down Highway 19 and said, "We have to keep that from happening."

Wynona said, "Sean, we have three FBI agents on rotation watching Dave and his boat twenty-four-seven. Is there anything that you think I should be doing to expedite some of this?"

"Your presence with Dave, as his daughter, is crucial. Your training and experience will add an upper hand should someone get beyond the surveillance team."

"In other words, you think I should stay put, right?" She smiled.

"Right. And, on second thought, maybe it wouldn't be a good idea to have detectives from Marathon Key investigating *Aphrodite* in Tarpon Springs."

"Why?" she asked. "The chain of evidence, if the pieces of rope match, would be irrefutable."

Dave stood and said, "I agree. If it's the same rope, a good detective can squeeze these three suspects. Mostly likely, one will crack. Spill his guts in a plea deal."

"Yes, but I've seen it have the alternate result … at least initially. And we don't have time. I have a plan B that I think might get us closer to the island where Aswad dumped Katie and Andy. If the shrimpers are hauled down to Marathon Key for questioning, it may be to the detriment of Katie, Andy and even you, Dave. We can't take that risk right now."

Nick looked over at O'Brien and arched his thick, black eyebrows, a slight smile working at the corner of his mouth. He cut his eyes down to the GPS tracker on the Jeep's console.

Wynona said, "We understand."

O'Brien shifted the phone to his left ear. "We overheard the captain tell the deckhands they have another run soon. I want to go back to the city docks and hide a GPS tracker on *Aphrodite*."

Wynona said, "Sean, you told us two of the men from another boat were hurt in your confrontation with them. There may be police and others around there."

"Don't think so. For guys like them, it's just another bar fight. But, tonight, they lost. They're probably in an ER ward somewhere."

"You and Nick be careful. Please call us when you're done. Okay?"

"Okay."

O'Brien pulled into a convenience store parking lot, turned the Jeep around and back on the highway, heading toward Tarpon Springs.

# NINETY-ONE

Sol Lefko sat alone on the couch in his darkened living room and sipped bourbon on the rocks. He picked up a framed picture of Katie from an end table, used the light on his phone to shine upon her face. The photo was taken right before her marriage to Andy, and she never looked happier, never looked more joyful than in that period of her life.

Lefko blinked back a tear, trying not to think about the possible looming death of Katie and Andy unless they were found ... and found very soon. In his mind, he played back her voice on the video— the look of absolute horror on her face. Andy tried so hard to put up a brave front but struggling to appear fearless in an ominous situation.

Lefko remembered the time he'd interrogated Abdul Aswad in Guantanamo. After an hour of hard questioning, Aswad spit blood, looked him straight in the eye and said, *"I will come back and remove your seed from earth ... remember that."* And now the same voice, the same strain of intense hate, *"I warned you I would remove your seed from earth. That will happen in such a tragic way ... dust to dust."* And, finally, Lefko thought about the text Aswad sent on Katie's phone: *That request will come later ... perhaps in a day or two into your daughter's suffering.*

Lefko walked through his dark home, his wife upstairs crying herself into some form of listless sleep. He peered through a fold in the curtains of a front window near the formal dining room. The two FBI agents were in a dark car at the end of his driveway. He slowly removed his hand from the curtain, walked into his home office, slid open a drawer at his desk and removed a 9mm Beretta. He loaded the gun, looking through a window into his moonlit backyard. He watched leaves on a large oak waft in the breeze. He whispered, "We'll find you, Aswad. This time, no interrogation. This time I will kill you. And I will do it before the FBI or CIA can whisk you away."

• • •

A crescent moon hung over the Tarpon Springs sponge docks like a crooked smiley face perched in a milieu of black as O'Brien lifted binoculars to his eyes and looked for threats. He and Nick sat in the Jeep, parked on a side street off Dodecanese. O'Brien searched for any signs of life on the dock. Most of the shrimp boats were dark. Two had diffused lights coming from wheelhouse windows. No indication of movement. He lowered the binoculars and said, "Nick, maybe you ought to stay here. I can move quicker alone. No need in putting you in any more danger that we have to."

Nick shook his head. "You can't expect me to sit here while you risk your life with a bunch of badass Bubba Gump types."

"All right. Let's hustle down to the crab traps piled on the dock. Listen for a few seconds. If all seems quiet, I'll board *Aphrodite*, hide the tracker, and be done in less than a minute."

"What do you want me to do?"

"Keep watch."

"Do you have a spare gun in the Jeep somewhere?"

"No."

Nick looked down at his hands, stretched his fingers and said, "I got ten friends here. They all come together for me in two fists."

"Use a couple of your friends to text me if you hear or see anyone while I'm moving around *Aphrodite*." O'Brien got out of the Jeep. Nick followed him through the parking lot and down to the docks, tide rising, boat lines creaking—the faint odor of sponges coming from the stern of a weary and worn boat named *Salty Dawg*. They stepped over the rusted gate and walked down the dock, staying in the smattering of shadows across parts of the dock.

They paused again at the crab traps and listened. The only sound was from an adjacent dock, a sailboat halyard tinkling on a mast. O'Brien whispered, "Okay … I don't hear any music or talking. *Aphrodite* looks dark." He glanced down at the GPS tracker in his left hand.

"Where you gonna hide that?" Nick asked.

"I don't know. Keep an eye peeled." O'Brien walked to *Aphrodite*, his boat shoes silent across the dock. He slipped the tracker in his pocket, stepped up on a wooden ladder and was aboard the boat within seconds. He stared at the fresh cut bowline, almost wanting to take it, or to take a picture of it. The picture wouldn't be good enough for a forensics match, but it would prove it was once on the boat if they disposed of it. To take the line, though, would break a possible chain of evidence. Get the tracker in place first, then snap the picture on the way out, he thought.

O'Brien tried the main door leading to the wheelhouse. Locked. He removed the two paperclips from his shirt pocket, bent them, inserting one in the lock as a tension wrench. And then using the second to rake back and forth, applying slight pressure until the lock turned. He entered the wheelhouse, looking beyond the big wooden wheel to the console, an ashtray filled with cigarette butts, screens that monitored weather and GPS locations, a dozen gauges, marine radio, microphone and cord attached to the ceiling near the wheel. O'Brien couldn't find a place to hide the tracker. He went back on deck and decided to climb on the roof of the wheelhouse.

Nick licked his dry lips and looked around, eyes scanning the boats, ears primed for the slightest sounds. He heard three car doors shut in the marina parking lot. After a second, he peered around the mound of crab traps. Three men were walking toward the gated entrance. Nick watched them for a few seconds. The men paused at the entrance gate, one man unlocking it.

Seconds later, all three were walking down the dock.

O'Brien jumped up, grabbing the eave on one side of the wheelhouse, pulling himself to the top, slinging his legs to the roof area.

He crouched down, looking for a spot to secure the GPS tracker. He took it from his pocket, squatted next to a Furuno radar antenna and pressed the suction cup onto the roof, securing the tracker in place. He slid the switch to the on position.

His phone buzzed.

O'Brien looked at his phone screen and read the message from Nick: *Get out! Three guys coming.*

# NINETY-TWO

N ick watched O'Brien on top of the wheelhouse as the three men came closer, less than one hundred feet away. Nick ducked behind the crab traps, peered around the wire mesh. Even at that distance, he recognized two of the men. One was the captain of *Aphrodite* and one was the man the others called Bear. The third man was someone he didn't recognized, at least at first.

And then he came into view.

Nick knew the man was Kenny Drakos, the guy he'd drank ouzo with in the coffee shop. "Oh, shit," he mumbled. He looked at the shrimp boat, watching O'Brien drop from the top of the wheelhouse, catlike, to the deck. But there was no time for him to go over the gunnel ladder and climb down to the dock. O'Brien dipped around the winches and outriggers, crouching behind the large nets as the men approached *Aphrodite*. He could overhear them talking.

Captain Kalivaris said, "The doctor said Trakas will be outta work for at least two months. It's gonna take that long for three broken bones to heal. He's out."

Bear spat off the dock and said, "Those two dudes got a death wish. I guarantee you that, when Trakas is healed, he will hunt the tall dude down, and he'll kill him. Weight the body down and drop the guy in that deep trough west of Cedar Key. Won't be his first time either."

Kalivaris shook his head. "It's gonna take more than Alex Trakas to take that guy down. I've seen a lotta fights in my life, been in a lot, but I never saw a guy move that fast. He knocked out Mike, snapped Trakas' arm, and pulled a gun like he'd rehearsed it a hundred times."

"Maybe he's actually done it a hundred times," Kenny Drakos said, lighting a cigarette. "From what you and Bear said, the guy's like some kind of ninja warrior. But his Greek pal has diarrhea of the mouth. What a freakin' team."

Nick could hear the mocking jabs, his temper building. He looked for O'Brien, couldn't see him in the layers of nets, outriggers and dark places on the boat. The three men boarded *Aphrodite*, Kalivaris reaching in his pocket for a key. "Damn," he said, "I wonder if I left my boat keys in the truck."

Bear reached for the lock and turned the handle. "He said, "Don't need 'em. You forgot to lock up."

"I never forget to lock her. Not in ten damn years." He stepped in the wheelhouse and looked around, eyes filled with suspicion. He turned toward the men. "Check out the boat. Make sure nobody's on her." Kalivaris reached for his 9mm Sig in a drawer, chambered a round, and walked back on deck.

Nick folded his arms, straining to see what was happening, as the men appeared to be searching the boat. And then he heard something to his right—something in the water. He looked between two moored boats. One was a shrimp boat; the other was a crab boat.

O'Brien held his Glock and phone in his left hand above the surface, quietly treading water. "Shit!" Nick muttered. He glanced back at *Aphrodite*, heard muffled conversations and cursing. And then looked at O'Brien as he reached for a rubber tire hanging on the side of the crab boat, the tire used as a bumper. O'Brien quietly pulled himself out of the water, his clothes soaked. He crouched down in the boat and stepped off onto the dock, near the mound of traps.

Nick's face was filled with surprise and awe. He whispered, "How'd you get off *Aphrodite* without 'em dudes seein' or hearin' you hit the water?"

"Hung onto one of the stern lines and lowered myself into the water. Then it was just a quiet swim to the crab boat. Let's get out of here.

Unless they start looking on top of the wheelhouse, the tracker should be okay." He watched the men checking the boat, Kalivaris lighting a cigarette and staring up at the crescent moon as if he were gazing at a celestial emoji in the heavens while silently condemning O'Brien to hell.

• • •

O'Brien and Nick drove south from Tarpon Springs to Tampa International Airport. He glanced at Nick and said, "I'll leave on the first flight out tomorrow to Denver and then drive a rental car to Florence. It's about a ninety-minute drive to the federal supermax prison."

"Sean, in case you haven't noticed, your clothes are soaked. Where you gonna get clothes this time of night?"

"I have a shirt and jeans packed in the back of the Jeep. I'll get a hotel for the rest of the night. Can you take the Jeep back to Ponce Marina? Check on Dave? I'm sure he's in good hands with Wynona and a rotation of FBI agents."

"Sure. Not that she needs my help. Wynona is the kinda woman every man desires, but few can acquire."

O'Brien said nothing.

Nick continued, "She's smart. Drop dead gorgeous. She's kind. Funny. But there is somethin' mysterious about her … like she's never gonna put all her cards on the table for any man." He paused and looked at lights reflecting off Tampa Bay as they crossed the long Gulf-to-Bay Boulevard Bridge. "That's you, Sean. You're my brother. I'd take a bullet for you … but there's a lot I don't know about you. I respect that, your private world. But me, man … I wear my emotions on both shoulders. You and Dave know my whole life since I was a tadpole learning to dive off Mykonos."

"And we still like you." O'Brien smiled. "I've been thinking about the video of Katie and Andy."

"Yeah, it's hard not to think about it."

O'Brien exited the bridge and pulled into the parking lot of a Hyatt Hotel near the airport. He parked and reached under his seat, lifting out a laptop computer. He opened it and went to his email, quickly pulling the video up on screen. He used the toggle bar to move the video a few seconds past the starting point, freezing the image. He studied it for a few seconds, the light from the computer screen appeared trapped in his blue eyes.

"Nick, take a look at this." O'Brien angled the screen so Nick could see it.

"What am I lookin' at, beyond a couple scared to death?"

"Look at the way the trees and dead vegetation are all slanted toward the left behind Katie and Andy."

"What about it?"

"When a cat five hurricane whips through the islands, and I've seen the aftermath in the Caribbean, the winds are moving counter-clockwise. In this video frame, all the trees behind Katie and Andy are blown down and bent towards the left."

Nick studied the images and said, "That would indicate that the hurricane approached the left side of the island as it was moving, the gale force winds battering it like a clock's hands moving backwards."

"If the hurricane had passed by on the right side of the island, chances are the winds generated would have the opposite effect, pushing the trees the opposite way."

Nick grinned and said, "The winds moving on the right side of a storm are the bad side. Like people, a good and bad side."

O'Brien smiled. "There's no good or bad side of a hurricane, but there is a dirtier side. And that's what we're looking at behind Katie and Andy."

"This means when the cat five hurricane roared through the islands, it came over the sea on the left side of this particular island. So, what we have to do is track … or backtrack the path of the last cat five hurricanes in the Bahamas," Nick said.

O'Brien looked at the video and said, "All of the islands to the left of its path can be excluded as the island where Katie and Andy are stranded. But any islands to the right of the storm's path can be included."

Nick sat back in his seat. "I know you've tracked a lot of bad guys when you were a detective … but I bet you never tracked a cat five hurricane."

"I will now."

# NINETY-THREE

I t's been called the "Alcatraz of the Rockies." It is the federal supermax prison near Florence, Colorado. Layers of concrete, twelve-foot high razor wire fences, a dozen guard towers—a bone white concrete and red brick fortress baking on the dry terrain in the shadow of the Rocky Mountains. For inmates arriving at the prison, the approaching view of the Rockies in the distance will be the last time they ever see the mountains. Or the sky. Or a tree.

For the rest of their lives.

Supermax houses many of the nation's most heinous prisoners— the worst of the worst. Many have or had the word *'the'* in front of their names, the Unabomber, the Shoe Bomber, the 9/11 Mastermind, the Oklahoma City bomber. The list is a who's-who of criminal minds. The roster includes men who are considered too violent to be housed in any other prison in America.

Entering supermax, O'Brien went through the mandatory screening, metal detectors, pat-downs, removing of personal items—watch, belt, keys, pens or pencils—to gain access to the gray and austere meeting room. He sat at a metal table in a metal chair. Both chair and table were bolted to the concrete floor. He counted five closed-circuit cameras. Two armed guards were positioned in corners of the room. Forced air-conditioning through a vent on two sides of the room with a slight metallic smell, as if the air also was a prisoner, trapped and recycled for years.

There was the loud buzzing and the sound of an electronic lock unlocking. The door to a corridor, leading to a wing of the prison, opened and two more guards escorted a lean man in shackles—leg irons and handcuffs. They led him to the center of the room, the ankle chain scraping across the concrete. At the table, they motioned for him to sit. He robotically extended his forearms to the tabletop.

The guard with the nametag, *J. Tilton*, locked the handcuffs to a secure pin bolted to the table. No one uttered a single word. And then the guards backed off, moving to the corners of the room, one plump guard looking in a single camera and nodding to someone watching.

Richard Thurston said nothing. He sat opposite O'Brien and simply stared at him. Thurston looked older than his CIA peer group. His had ashen white hair combed straight back. Dark raccoon rings under darker eyes—eyes that could hide deep secrets. Facial skin pale and flaccid—a ghostly parchment look. His thin lips were moist, mouth turned down. Fingers long and thin.

O'Brien sat straight, almost unblinking. He said, "Thank you for agreeing to meet with me."

Thurston didn't move. Silent.

O'Brien leaned back a little, opening up his posture. "Your son, Jason, sends his regards."

No reaction. Not a bat of the eye. Thurston seemed to study O'Brien's face as if he had a spot of pasta sauce on the tip of his nose.

O'Brien smiled. "Your mother seems to be doing well, too. Nice place she has in Miami Beach. You've taken good care of her."

No reaction.

O'Brien continued. "Dave Collins sends his regards."

Thurston folded his hands across the table, the sound of the shackles against the metal surface. "Mr. O'Brien, you can skip through the pleasantries, the chitchat, the synthetic words … all designed to illicit a reaction from me. I assure you that will not happen. What do you want? Why are you here?"

"Why are you killing your former CIA colleagues?"

Thurston squared his head a bit and made a half smile. "You flatter me. I spend twenty-three hours a day in solitary confinement. Even if I wanted to cause harm to someone, I could not from inside here. No one could."

"You didn't ask me about the killings of your former team members. Aren't you curious? Or do you know what happened?"

"No, I'm not curious. Why should I be? They conspired to put me in here."

"And you've had a lot of time to think about that. Time to plan. Time to recruit people." Out of the corner of his eye, O'Brien noticed one guard shift his weight, folding his arms across his chest.

"You've wasted a lot of time coming here. However, for me, it's a diversion. I get out of a cell to do something different. You see, Mr. O'Brien, difference isn't designed into this prison. What is designed is a sameness that seems to go on into infinity. It is designed to break the human spirit by numbing the mind. There are no windows. I haven't seen the sky in years. I get fifty minutes a day to walk in a circle in what's known as the exercise area. It's really a large room in which inmates walk in chains for an hour before escorted back to our cages. So, your little trip is a mild diversion from the insanity of monotony. It is rather amusing to sit here and watch you try to figure out how to get some tiny morsel from my soul. But you fail to recognize I no longer have a soul. It's the first thing you trade off in the CIA, because to keep one is a liability, an invitation for death."

"You lost your soul long before the CIA."

"Oh, is that so? Tell me, how did that happen, sort of analogous to losing one's virginity … a coming of age tribulation perhaps?"

"It's when Tucker died." O'Brien said nothing else, closely watching Thurston's eyes, nostrils, his jawline. His pupils grew a little smaller. The carotid artery on the left side of his neck slightly enlarged. O'Brien said, "That's where and when your mother believes you changed. When your father blamed you for your dog's death. He made you dig a grave and bury Tucker in the rain. The good thing about the rain is that you could cry, and your father wouldn't see your tears. But you couldn't cry that night. There were no more tears. What was left of your innocence was buried that night with Tucker. In the coming of age for you, Richard, you crossed the bridge to becoming a psychopath that night."

Thurston smiled, unblinking. "You bore me, O'Brien. I'm used to destroying men like you and then having a gourmet meal and not thinking twice about my conquest. I became what the CIA strives for but fears as well. A killing machine that you never see coming or going."

"You know the interesting thing about childhood, Richard … it manipulates adulthood. Not completely, but enough that we often define good or bad, by those experiences we go through at a tender age. For example, take something as innocent as a nursery rhyme. Sweet stories that have been handed down for generations. The classic, *Ten Little Indians*, your mom said it was your favorite. It's been used as a teaching tool for counting—backwards. But when you read between the lines, as told in Agatha Christie's book—*And Then There Were None*, it's about murder—genocide. Innocent people die, and it's implied that someone else is to blame, someone other than the real killer. In Christie's novel, it was Justice Wargrave. In real life, it's you. And then there were none. It has been your calling card since you killed your dog … Tucker."

Thurston's eyes burned. He reached for O'Brien, the locked chain stopping movement. Two of the guards started across the room, then stopped, taking a few steps back to their positions. Thurston leveled his intense eyes at O'Brien and said, "Don't you try to psychoanalyze me. You don't have the talent or the insight. I'm done—"

"Is that why you commissioned Abdul Aswad to send his assassins in when all along you are the real killer?" O'Brien leaned forward. "I would think, considering your life in prison status, that you'd enjoy your final psychotic mission. Like Wargrave, you have a sociopathic ego that needs feeding. That's why you will take credit. You can't help yourself. Sort of how Joker in a Batman movie enjoys a short-lived win. Because in the end, Richard, you will lose again … like you always have. Your father got it right. You are a sick loser."

Thurston's voice dropped, almost guttural. "In the end, I win because they all lose. I'd suspect that Sol Lefko's daughter and her helpless husband will be dead in a couple of days. Next on my list is your friend, Dave Collins—the arrogant son-of-a-bitch. After that it will end with … and then there were none. Guards! I'm finished with this man."

Ignoring him, O'Brien said, "The offshore accounts you tried to launder Russian money through, using the name Burgh LLC … Burgh Island is the real island off the Coast of Devon, England. Agatha Christie used it as a source of inspiration in *And Then There Were None*. She changed the name to Soldier Island in the novel." O'Brien stood and added, "By the way, nice fatherly reach out after all these years … your fake love for your son, Jason, will land him in prison, too. Nice gift."

"He lowered his voice to a whisper, glaring at O'Brien and said, "I am like Justice Wargrave … right down to the last murder … yours, O'Brien."

"I will agree with you, Thurston, you are like Justice Wargrave … just not as clever. You see … I got your game, and there's two of us playing now—you and me."

# NINETY-FOUR

The morning sunrise brought the hope of rescue to the exhausted minds and hearts of Katie and Andy. They stayed awake all night, keeping away from the vicious and hungry bites of the sand fleas. The couple had walked the shore, talking, not sleeping, and now they sought refuge—a place to rest. Katie moved slowly, her body exhausted, mind lethargic. Lips sandpaper dry. Andy was no better, but he tried hard to bolster optimism.

"The no-see-ums don't bite during the day," Andy said with a smile. "So, we can go back to our small lean-too shelter and get some rest. The palm fronds over the structure should keep the direct sun out of our faces."

Katie nodded. "Maybe we can find something to use to dig a hole."

"Why do we want to dig a hole?"

"To find fresh water somewhere underground. We can use conch shells and start digging."

"I don't know if there's an aquifer under this island or any others in the Bahamas. A lot of the islands use desalination plants. To dig a well, we'd probably have to go down a hundred feet. We could never hand-dig that far."

"We need water. We have no choice. Maybe it's not a hundred feet."

"I'll see if I can catch fish."

"We can't drink fish."

"At least we won't starve to death."

"Okay." She managed a smile. "We'll hang on until we're rescued. Somebody will find us. I know it in my heart."

• • •

O'Brien awoke early in the hotel room, set up his laptop computer on the small table, sipped a cup of black coffee and looked at the GPS coordinates of the tracker he left on the shrimp boat. He could tell it hadn't moved. His phone buzzed. Nick calling.

"Sean, I've been online lookin' at data from hurricanes in the Bahamas. I looked at the computer renderings of a path left behind from Hurricane Irma, followed the course of Hurricane Maria. Then I examined the islands west of Nassau, looking at satellite images— seeing dozens of no-name islands, sand spits surrounded by the dark blue waters of the Atlantic Ocean. Irma came over Dominica, went north of Cuba, stayed near the Turks and Caicos, and east of Nassau. Her wind action would produce the buzz-cut we're talking about."

"No doubt. Nice work, Nick. Thanks. That'll help narrow the search. Talk to you later." O'Brien disconnected, looked at his computer screen, examining the proximity of the Dominican Republic to the Bahamas. He thought about the letters he'd read, letters written to Jason Thurston from his father, Richard … remembering the reference to Hispaniola. He hit keys on his keyboard, pulled the image of the letter up on his computer screen, scanned partway down, and read in a near whisper, *If you make it there, visit the caves of El Pomier, the Tito Indians—the first indigenous people to greet Christopher Columbus, left behind hundreds of cave paintings in the NW part of the island, dating back 2077 years ago. After that, have a toast of Clement Rum at Captain Cooks. They may still have a few bottles from 1952. It's superb, and it was distilled in the year of my birth. Follow your journey. Write to me when you can, I want to hear more about your adventures.*

He leaned back in his chair, picked up his phone and called Dave. When he answered, O'Brien asked, "Have you seen Nick this morning?"

"Briefly. Wynona, Max and I are having breakfast with Nick in a little while. He did share what happened when you returned to the docks in Tarpon Springs. So, the GPS tracker is secure."

"It was when I left." O'Brien looked at the screen on his laptop. "And it hasn't moved from the docks. I'd bet *Aphrodite* is still there … but not for long."

"How'd your meeting go with Richard Thurston?"

"He sends his regards. And he also sends his assassins."

"You're sure he's part of Aswad's group."

"Aswad is part of Thurston's group. Is Wynona there?"

"Yes—good timing, she came aboard a few minutes ago. I caught her coming back from walking Max."

"Put me on speaker so she can hear, too."

Wynona stood from one of the canvas chairs in *Gibraltar's* salon and came closer to Dave's phone, which he set on the coffee table. He said, "Okay, Sean, we both can hear you."

"Good." Max lifted her ears, a slight whine, tail wagging. "Thurston knows about Katie and Andy. He's aware they have little time left. Just like Justice Wargrave in Agatha Christie's book, Thurston wants us to know he's the mastermind … someone who can plan and execute the sequential murders of his former CIA colleagues one by one, leaving those notes on or near the bodies." O'Brien gave the details of the conversation and added, "Dave, he made a point of saying you're next on his list. Until we find and stop Aswad, you need to stay totally out of sight."

"All right. But, why would Thurston choose to talk to you?"

"I called him out on his game and told him I was playing, too."

"That's not good, Sean. Now you'll be on his hit list," Dave said with concern.

O'Brien said nothing.

Wynona asked, "Sean, how do you think Thurston is getting information in and out of that prison? It seems apparent that he's using his son, Jason, as the go between—the carrier pigeon. But Jason's not visiting the prison. So, how's it getting out?"

"Ask the FBI to pull every bank account and phone transaction that can be connected to a prison guard with the last name of Talbot. His nametag had a first initial of J."

"Why do you think he's the breach?" Dave asked.

"Because of the subtle ways he reacted when he overheard my questioning of Thurston."

"We'll make the calls to the bureau immediately," Dave said.

"While you're at it, maybe you can have them check out a couple of places in the Dominican Republic. It's second in size to Cuba and a large place to hide. Abdul Aswad may be there."

"Where do we look?" Wynona asked.

"Richard Thurston doesn't mention the island in his letters, but, as you know, he does mention Hispaniola, the name it went by for years, since Columbus. Thurston's letter references two places: El Pomier Caves, and a bar or restaurant called Captain Cooks. Somehow, I believe, Jason Thurston got there and gave messages from his father to Aswad, along with money. Enough money to move assassins in and out of the country on a shrimp boat docked in the peaceful little town of Tarpon Springs. It's a place far from the ebb and flow of immigration law violators. Draws little suspicion as a tourist's town on Florida's Gulf coast away from places more often used by smugglers, such as the Keys or Ten Thousand Islands near the Everglades."

Dave said, "Sean, there are dozens of aircraft and boats combing the Bahamas. They've been at it since daybreak. We'll find Katie and Andy. I'd love to be the one to call Sol and Brenda Lefko when we have good news."

"You should be the bearer of good news. To save the search parties time, you might want to let their operations people know to comb the islands east of Nassau."

"Why east?" Wynona asked.

"Because the last cat five hurricane left the island Katie and Andy are on with trees and debris pushed in a northward direction, indicating the island took the brunt of counter-clockwise winds on the hurricane's right side. It's the bad side, if you will, as Nick calls it."

Dave shook his head, a slim smile on his face. He glanced at Wynona. "So, Sean, can we assume that you picked that up from the video?"

"When the video was shot, the sun is more in their faces. Based on the timestamp of the email, I think they were facing west. The debris behind them is slanted in a northward angle. Nick did some hurricane tracking this morning and agrees on the direction—said it helps, but there's a lot of islands out there."

Wynona said, "Yeah, but that narrows it down to a few hundred. I'll pass the information on to the rescue ops people, suggesting they concentrate on the islands east of Nassau. When are you leaving Colorado?"

"I made an appointment to speak with the warden. I have some hunches and unanswered questions. It's a two-hour drive to Denver. I'm taking a red-eye flight into Orlando, renting a car and driving to Ponce Marina. It'll be a long night. How's Max?"

Wynona smiled. "She's fine. When she heard your voice on speakerphone, her tail started wagging. She misses you ... we all miss you."

• • •

Katie's mind seemed immersed in quicksand—a bog that trapped her subconscious mind, holding her between reoccurring nightmares and reality. She could hear the noise of a motor—a drone-like sound far away, as if it were a background sound in her dream.

And then the noise was right over them. She and Andy, exhausted, lay hidden under the dry palm limbs and dried palm fronds as a U.S. Coast Guard Jayhawk helicopter approached. Katie's eyes fluttered open, rays of sunlight pouring through the small slats in the thatched roof. She blinked twice, looked over at her sleeping husband and stared through the cracks in the roof as the orange and white helicopter flew over them.

"Andy! Wake up!"

Andy shot up, wiping the sleep from of his red eyes.

Katie crawled out of the makeshift entrance, Andy following her. They stood on weak legs and watched the helicopter pass over the island.

Katie ran toward the beach as the chopper flew beyond the vast chain of similar islands in the distance, the orange and white now a speck in the deep blue sky.

Katie fell to her knees, hands clenched in her lap. Too drained to scream. Too weary to cry. The breaking of the surf was the only sound for miles.

# NINETY-FIVE

Deckhand Johnny Hastings was climbing one of the outriggers on *Aphrodite* to fix a joint when he spotted something strange. He stopped and stared at the roof of the wheelhouse. Something about the size of a doughnut was near the radar antennae. He descended from the outrigger and climbed the ladder-like steps to reach the roof of the wheelhouse. "We'll … I'll be damned. Looks like somebody wants to keep tabs on us."

He reached over, used the blade of his knife to gently pry under the section cup, lifting the GPS device. He climbed down the ladder and entered the wheelhouse where Captain Kalivaris was watching porno on his laptop.

"Look at this!" Johnny said, holding up the device.

Kalivaris eased down from the captain's chair, closed his laptop and stared at the GPS tracker. "Where'd you find that?"

"Right above your head. Top of the roof. Near the radar. That tall dude must have left it. He really wants to keep an eye on us."

"Who the hell is he workin' for?" Kalivaris shook a cigarette loose from the pack on the console, lit it and deeply inhaled. "Let's fuck with him and whoever he works for."

"What do you mean?"

"Hide it on *Lucky Strike*." He looked at his watch. "Nobody's on her right now. That gambling boat goes out tomorrow. Let's see if that tall boy wants to mess with the Boloros family. They're old school, the old school of real hard knocks."

● ● ●

The phone call was first—a call that opened a hole in Sol Lefko's heart. It was followed shortly after by a life-changing text message. He watched the progress of the search-and-rescue operations, in contact with team leaders from the Coast Guard, Air Force and the FBI. A dozen planes and as many helicopters and boats had crisscrossed the seven hundred islands of the Bahamas and northern Caribbean in search of Katie and Andy. The call arrived late in the day from the Deputy Director of the FBI, Marshall Wilson.

"Sol," he said, his voice soft and compassionate. "We found their sailboat, *Dragonfly.*"

"Where?"

"In a remote cove near Eleuthera. It was anchored about a hundred yards off shore. No sign of foul play aboard. The dinghy is there. The Coast Guard is impounding it at the docks at Governor's Harbour for a more thorough inspection. We've concentrated the search more than a hundred miles in every direction from where the boat was found. It's just a matter of time before we find them."

"That's the problem, Marshall. They don't have a lot of time."

"It's still a rescue mission … not a recovery mission. We'll find them, and we'll find them alive. I'll keep you posted."

"Thank you." Lefko disconnected, started to set the phone down on his kitchen table when the text arrived. He lifted his glasses out of his shirt pocket and read the message. He used his right hand to brace himself on a high-back chair, his heart pounding, breathing shallow.

He paced the kitchen area for a moment, his mind racing, thoughts jumping to different scenarios and possible outcomes. "Focus," he whispered. "Do what you've always done in these situations. But there's never been a situation like this." He stopped at the kitchen table, slowly slumped into the chair, looked at the tiny scars and age spots on the back of his hands.

And, at that moment, his thoughts crystalized into a plan. A plan he must carry out to save the life of his daughter and her husband.

Andy waded in waist-deep water and felt the ocean bottom with his toes. He walked through eelgrass, the emerald grass caressing his knees. He could see the white sand, the shadows of the eelgrass wafting in the bright sun. And then he felt something hard, like a rock. He stopped walking, lowered himself under the water and used his hands to lift a large conch shell from the sea grass.

He carried it to shore, Katie walking toward the breakers with a rock the size of a coconut in her hands. Andy looked up and said, "Great. Where'd you find that?"

"Under the brush. Everything is under something on this island."

"That's the truth." Andy set the conch shell on a hard area of impacted sand. He gripped the rock in both hands and slammed into the mollusk shell. There was a small chip. He raised the rock and struck with all his strength. Another chip, this a half inch long. "Katie, see if you can find a bendable short limb or a stick. Maybe I can pry it out of there." He hit the shell again as she found a stick and returned with it.

"See if this will work," she said.

Andy broke the tip of the stick off, giving it more of a point. It had a bamboo like litheness. He shoved the stick into the opening of the shell, the pink and white colors gleaming in the hot sun. He stabbed again and again, reaching into the shell with his fingers and pulling out the queen conch, flesh the gray hue of a slug, the flesh wriggling. Andy set it on the rock and used the edge of the shell to chop it in pieces.

"Oh, God," Katie mumbled. "It looks like a giant snail."

"It's all we have to eat." He handed his wife a small piece of conch. She took it, staring at the flesh a moment, then slipping it across her cracked and bleeding lips, chewing the tough meat, the taste of saltwater, guts and gristle in her mouth.

Andy ate a piece, his hands trembling from dehydration and lack of food. A seagull circled overhead, watching the humans below struggle to survive. Katie looked at the bird, her face sunburned, dried blood in one corner of her mouth. She lowered her swollen eyes to the beach where a crab scurried across the wet sand.

# NINETY-SIX

It was getting close to 11:00 p.m. when O'Brien walked to his gate at Denver International Airport. He checked his flight schedule: delayed one hour. He looked at his watch and took a seat in a remote corner near the gate. There were not many passengers at that time of night. A few business people, men and women, rumpled clothes, weary faces, anxious to get back home. A man in a brown jumpsuit used a rotating polisher to wax the floor in one area.

O'Brien thought about his conversation with the warden, a balding man who resembled the late Senator John McCain. The warden said life in supermax is much worse than death. "It's designed as punishment, not rehabilitation," he said, sitting behind his large desk, a framed photo of him, the FBI director, and the president of the United States. "These men are far beyond rehabilitation. Most, if not all, are psychopaths. This is the most secure prison in the world. No one escapes or gets out alive."

"How would you describe Richard Thurston?" O'Brien asked.

"He came in here conditioned to withstand deprivation, with all the CIA training and whatnot, but after a while, even Thurston can go a little stir crazy. We have 440 men in here. Every one of them could kill you without so much as a bat of an eye. If anybody doubts the existence of pure and absolute evil in this world, let them come work here for a couple of weeks. Not only will you see it, you'll feel the evil. It makes the hair on the back of your neck stand up."

"Do the same guards watch the same prisoners?"

"There's not a whole lot of watching. There's no prison yard. No exercise area. These men are in eighty square feet for twenty-three hours a day. For the most part, guards rotate. With seniority, some can ask for certain assignments. We run three shifts, twenty-four-seven for life." He grinned.

"Are there any areas where the guards or prisoners aren't on camera?"

"No sir."

"How much seniority does James Talbot have?"

The warden paused before answering. "He's been here a good while, probably more than ten years. Why?"

"Because I think he's on the take. I believe Thurston is having someone pay Talbot to smuggle information in and out of here. Maybe no one escapes, but even this place can't trap information or cage greed."

• • •

Dave Collins didn't like to dream. Unlike most people, Dave remembered his dreams. He remembered because, for the most part, he'd lived them. Some were good. Most were not. The bad ones seemed to hang around more often, like a shadow that follows you because it's attached to your psychic profile. It was part of the inner baggage he still carried from three decades of covert intelligence service.

He thought about that as he had a final nightcap of single malt scotch before going to bed. He stood in *Gibraltar's* master cabin and peered through the blinds at the houseboat on the next dock. He could see an occasional soft light pop on near the steering console. The light from mobile phones as the FBI agents took or received calls.

He raised his glass and toasted them from the dark shadows of his trawler, reflecting on the events leading up to this very night. He thought about Richard Thurston, the good, bad, and ugly.

He remembered Abdul Aswad. The good was always conditional, the bad his philosophy, the ugly—the result of his actions.

He finished his drink and lay down on the bed in a T-shirt and boxer shorts. He thought about his daughter Linda, her husband and children. He reflected on his contentious divorce with his ex-wife, Deloris. In the thick of the proceedings, he remembered her saying, "I never really loved you. You know why, Dave? No one can love a ghost. Even when you're home, you're not really here."

He closed his eyes, hoped his demons would be held at bay, and drifted off into a languid sleep.

• • •

O'Brien's phone buzzed. He looked at the ID. It was Wynona. He answered, and she said, "Max and I were just checking to see if you made it to the airport."

"Yes, but my flight is delayed. I'm not sure if it's weather-related or mechanical."

"We'll hold the fort down until you get back. Max is ready for bed. But we thought we'd stay up. Do our nails, watch a romantic comedy and sip wine."

O'Brien smiled. "Sounds like a plan. Have you heard anything more about the search and rescue for Katie and Andy?"

"Dave's been on and off the phone just about every hour. They found *Dragonfly* near Eleuthera. No sign of Katie and Andy, of course. There were no obvious indications of foul play on the sailboat. Coast Guard and FBI are securing it. And speaking of FBI, we have four agents in the Dominican Republic staking out Captain Cook's Bar and the Pomier Caves. So far, nothing."

"If Aswad's not there, it may be because he's relocated. But there are a lot of places to hide on an island that size, even if he had to enter Haiti. I'll see you tomorrow."

"Maybe I'll read Max a bedtime story. I'd try nursery rhymes, but most are too dark with strange endings you never see coming. Good night, Sean. Stay safe. We miss you." She disconnected.

O'Brien leaned back in the hard chair, looked out the window and watched a jet taxi onto the runway. He thought about what Wynona had said in reference to nursery rhymes, and he remembered the ending to *Ten Little Indians*. He recalled the ending of Agatha Christie's novel, *And Then There Were None*. Suddenly, something Richard Thurston said resurrected like a cold chill under a door: *"Next on my list is your friend, Dave Collins—the arrogant son-of-a-bitch. After that it will end with … and then there were none."*

O'Brien picked up his phone and called Dave.

And he hoped it wasn't too late.

# NINETY-SEVEN

O 'Brien counted the number of rings before the phone went to voice-mail. Five rings, and he could only leave a recorded warning—a warning that might, if heeded, save his old friend's life. He said, "Dave, listen closely. When I was questioning Richard Thurston, he said next on his list is your friend, Dave. He said after that it will end with … *and then there were none*. In Agatha Christie's novel, Justice Wargrave did not kill the last two people. He tricked them into fighting each other. There is no one you can trust. Call me!"

• • •

After decades in the CIA, many of those years sleeping in hotel rooms, tracking or dodging foreign agents, Dave Collins never slept soundly. He'd developed the ability to catnap, to catch sleep when possible—to run on reserve, and to detect sounds in his sleep that were unrelated to the environment.

A noise. Was it on *Gibraltar* or the dock?

Dave lay in his bed. He cut his eyes over to the digital clock on the nightstand. 4:02 a.m. Thought the trawler made a slight move, but there was no sound of a passing boat to create a wake.

The noise was foreign. Something unfamiliar from the night sounds of the marina, the slap of the sailboat halyards in the breeze, the groan of boat bumpers against the dock in a rising tide. His eyes burned.

The barrel of a pistol pressed hard against the side of Dave's head.

"Don't move." The man's command was just above a whisper, calm and self-assured. "Get out of bed."

Dave recognized the man's voice.

• • •

Max lifted her head, listening. Her dachshund ears rose as high as they could go, cocked, searching for the source of the noise that had awakened her. She slept next to Wynona in the master berth on *Jupiter,* less than seventy feet from *Gibraltar.*

A low growl came from the back of Max's throat.

Wynona opened her eyes. She didn't turn her head. Just listening. One of the bowlines creaked, stretching against the tide.

Max growled again.

Wynona whispered. "What do you hear, Max? Is it just the bowlines, or maybe it's Ol' Joe the cat looking in a trash can."

Soft moonlight poured into the master berth through three port windows, two of them wedged open, allowing the night breeze to enter the cabin. Max stood, trotting to the edge of the bed facing the windows. Another low growl.

Wynona got out of bed, Max following. She walked from the master berth into *Jupiter's* salon, the cockpit facing the dock and some of the boats on the far side of the dock. A slight mist rose from the marina water. Most of the boats were gently bobbing silhouettes in the moonlight.

All but one.

Wynona stood at the sliding glass doors. She looked at *Gibraltar,* studying it for a moment. A light was on inside the salon. "Max, it looks as though Dave didn't shut his lights off. That's not like him. He's usually asleep sometime between the news and the sportscast."

Wynona slipped on jeans, T-shirt, and her boat shoes. She picked up her Beretta and quietly opened the sliding glass doors and stepped onto *Jupiter's* cockpit. She glanced down the long dock, the fog building, the light from the lighthouse diffused in the fog.

"Max, stay here." Wynona left *Jupiter* and, in less than thirty seconds, walked down the short auxiliary pier leading to the rear of Dave's trawler. She intuitively felt something was wrong before she got there.

*Maybe Dave is sick*, she thought. *Maybe not.*

She stepped along the dock wet with heavy dew. Then she stopped. In front of her were tracks left in the dew by someone else. By their positioning, she could tell they were not tracks made by Dave Collins.

Wynona quietly lowered herself over the boat's transom side railing. She looked at the houseboat, used her hands to signal for help. She waited a moment and signaled again. There was no visible response. No flash of light. Nothing from an FBI agent. She could see that the cockpit door was slightly ajar, soft jazz playing inside the salon. *Maybe Dave came out a moment for some fresh air. Maybe he's in his cabin.* Her pulse raced. She lifted her Beretta, entered the salon, and listened for a few seconds.

"Dave, are you here?" she asked.

Nothing but the sound of the piano jazz.

Wynona quietly moved through the trawler, her gun extended. All was clear. The last area to search was the master berth. The door was closed. She stood outside, her hand on the doorknob. She turned the handle quietly and opened the door. In the diffused light through the window from the lighthouse, she could see Dave sitting on the edge of his bed. But she couldn't see the look of concern on his face.

"Dave ..." She took one step inside and felt the gun barrel on the side of her neck.

Sol Lefko said, "Drop the pistol."

# NINETY-EIGHT

S ol Lefko turned the overhead light on inside the master berth. He pointed his gun at Wynona and said, "Stand next to Dave."

She followed his orders and walked around the bed and stood next to Dave in the corner of the cabin. Dave looked at Lefko and said, "Sol, you don't have to do this."

"I have no choice. Katie and Andy have gone without food and water for days. I can't let them die, trapped on an island that no one in the Coast Guard or FBI can seem to find."

"Do you really think Aswad is going to give you or anyone directions to where he left them?"

"He dealt this hand. I have to play it. It's a gamble, but I'm willing to do it if it'll spare the lives of two people who never asked for this. Two people never in the business. Victims only because they're related to me. For you and me, Dave, we're lucky we lived this long. I never thought we'd retire in the traditional sense of the word." He glanced at Wynona and said, "I'm sorry you got involved. Somehow Aswad knows who you are, and he knows what you did to his brother. How you wound up here helping our old employers and the FBI with surveillance, I don't know. But I know that sometimes fate can be cruel."

Wynona shook her head. "If Aswad promised you he'd spare Katie and Andy's life in exchange for our lives, it won't happen. Fairness is not in his genetic DNA. Everything else is an illusion, something that should have been the first thing you lost working for the CIA."

"The CIA also taught me how to negotiate in extreme circumstances." He punched numbers on his phone, waited for an answer.

After five rings, "Abdul Aswad said, "Let me see your captives."

Lefko held the phone up, the image of Wynona and Dave on the screen. In a small box in the corner was Aswad's live image. He stood next to a docked boat. No one else was visible. Aswad looked at them and smiled. "It is good to see you, Dave Collins. Even with all the time that has passed, I find you even more repulsive than I did in the place you called Strawberry Field. I would surmise that you never thought I would be released in any kind of prisoner exchange."

Dave shook his head, looking over his bifocals. "We caught you once. We'll do it again."

"Not this time. The CIA doesn't employ anyone who can find and capture me."

Dave said nothing.

Aswad taunted. "Your leaders are so prudent. They do not understand the mind of a devoted Muslim man. We never forget. I have not forgotten the bombs dropped on me and my brother and sisters by your planes. It was 1983. Our father and sisters were killed that day. Our mother never walked again. Luckily, our youngest brother, Mohammad, was away or he would have been killed, too." He paused and looked at Wynona. "You … Wynona Osceola. It was your hand that put bullets into the body of the brother that was there that day, all those years later. You must now reap what you sowed. Allah, in his wisdom and in his time, decreed justice."

Wynona said, "Where's the justice for the daughter your brother was butchering?"

"Enough!" Aswad paused. "Sol Lefko, let me see you." Lefko moved the phone to where he was now partially in the picture. Aswad said, "Richard Thurston wanted it to end with you killing your friend Dave Collins. Followed by you committing suicide. But now that the woman is here, I have a better idea. There is a large boat at your disposal. I want all three of you on it."

Lefko shook his head. "Not until you tell me where you dropped Katie and Andy."

Aswad smiled. "You will be very near them. As a condition of our agreement, I will instruct the captain to drop you off on the same island. And then you can either help them or die with them. I really do not care which. I will deal with Collins and the woman. Leave now. I will text the departure information to you." He disconnected.

Lefko looked at Dave and said, "Get dressed."

Dave slipped on a shirt, reached for a pair of jeans near his bed. He watched Lefko's eyes. As Dave placed one leg in the jeans, Lefko shifted his eyes to Wynona. It gave Dave time to lift his phone off the nightstand, slipping the phone into his underwear before zipping up his pants.

# NINETY-NINE

As soon as O'Brien's plane landed at Orlando International Airport, he tried Wynona's phone. After three rings, it too went to voicemail. O'Brien got into his rental car, drove well above the speed limit and called Nick.

"Hey, Sean," Nick said, his voice throaty and sluggish. "Where are you?"

"Driving from Orlando to the marina. When's the last time you saw Dave?"

"Last night. He had a scotch. I drank—"

"How about Wynona? Was she there?"

"Yeah, she was. Max, too. Hey … what the hell happened inside that prison? You sound like a big sink hole just opened up in the road ahead of you."

"Nick, check on Dave and Wynona immediately. Call me back." O'Brien disconnected.

Nick slowly removed the phone from his right ear, glanced at it and mumbled, "No problem." He slipped his phone in one of the pockets on his shorts and bolted from *St. Michael*, jogging over to *Gibraltar*. He boarded the trawler, finding it unlocked. Nick quickly checked all the cabins, galley and topside. "Shit!" he said under his breath, climbing off *Gibraltar* and sprinting down the dock to *Jupiter*. He jumped into the cockpit, opened the door to Max sitting on the

406

couch. She barked once. Nick looked at her, his eyes taking in the emptiness—the silence. "Max, where's Wynona?"

Nick flew through the boat, checking the cabins. He climbed the ladder to the fly-bridge. Nothing. On the bridge, he placed a call to O'Brien. "Sean, Dave's gone. Nowhere on his boat. And Wynona's not on *Jupiter* either. No sign of them. Max is here. I wish she could talk."

O'Brien drove faster, pushing the speedometer near 100-miles-per-hour. He said, "Go to the houseboat. Check with the FBI agents. See if they saw anything and call me back." He disconnected.

Nick jogged down L dock, holding his phone, the sun breaking over the palm trees behind the Tiki Bar. He sprinted over to M dock and ran up to the houseboat. Standing on the dock, he could not see anyone in or around the long boat. He stood near the fly-bridge, the glass around it tinted dark. "Anybody home!" Nick shouted. No response.

A woman walking her black lab down the dock stopped and looked at him briefly before continuing. Nick walked across a short gangplank and boarded the boat. He entered the wheelhouse, immediately bracing himself on the doorjamb. Nick made the sign of the cross, whispering, "Holy Mary … mother of Jesus."

He stared at the body of an FBI agent dressed in tan shorts and a white polo shirt. He was slumped in the captain's chair, a single bullet hole in is right temple. Dried blood turned the collar of the shirt dark red, a single blowfly buzzing in the wheelhouse. Nick shut the door, his hands shaking, backing down to the gunnel area and called O'Brien. "Sean, there's a dead body in the wheelhouse of the houseboat. Looks like it was one shot to the head. Should I call the cops?"

"No, I'll call the FBI. They need to take it from here."

"One of those assassins somehow got the jump on Wynona and Dave. Let's hope the FBI can find them before the same thing happens. I wonder why they were taken and not shot like the poor dude on this boat?"

"Because I think the assassin this time was one of Dave's old CIA colleagues, Katie's father is desperately following orders to save the life of his daughter and her husband. It may be him."

"Whose orders?"

"They started with Richard Thurston, and the facilitator is Abdul Aswad. Nick, check the parking lot. See if Dave and Wynona's cars are there."

"Okay." Nick looked around the marina to the adjacent boats, wondering if anyone had seen or heard something, the smell of bacon coming from a sixty-foot Hatteras motor yacht docked near the houseboat, a news anchor on the television screen.

In the parking lot, Nick quickly found Dave's SUV. It was parked next to Wynona's car. He called O'Brien and told him. "Sean, I got no idea how long they've been gone. I was wiped out and fell asleep kinda early for me last night."

"Did you put my Glock back on *Jupiter*."

"No, I still have it."

"Do me a favor. Put it back on *Jupiter's* bar. See if you can find Dave's phone anywhere on *Gibraltar*. And please walk Max because I won't have time to do it when I arrive, and then keep her with you. I may need to leave immediately."

"Where you gonna go? You don't know where they took Dave and Wynona, unless the dude in the prison told you something more."

"He told me enough to know who's got Dave and Wynona. And I have a feeling the reason the abductor didn't kill them is because Aswad wants them alive—so he can do it. See you soon." He disconnected, and his phone made a *ping* sound. He slowed some and looked at the GPS tracking app. He could see movement from the docks at Tarpon Springs. "*Aphrodite* is leaving," he whispered.

O'Brien watched the tracking and called the FBI, getting quickly put through to the deputy director's office. O'Brien told him about the killing on the houseboat, the kidnapping of Dave and Wynona and added, "I think it's Dave's former CIA officer Sol Lefko."

FBI Deputy Director Marshall Wilson stood by a window in his corner office, looking down at the traffic on 10th Street. He said, "I was just at Robert Lewis' funeral with Collins and Lefko. They seem to be solid friends—working together. What makes you think Lefko's behind this?"

"He's not, ultimately. Richard Thurston is or was calling the shots."

"We interviewed his son and got nothing useable. We know money has moved to offshore accounts and dummy shell addresses. But we can't prove it was through Jason Thurston's efforts, and we have no record of Abdul Aswad receiving it. We have four agents in the Dominican Republic looking for Aswad. So far there's been no sign of him. We did pull bank records for prison guard James Talbot. He's banking three times his salary. Maybe the source is Thurston through his son, Jason. But, so far, we have nothing tangible. And it's hard for me to think that Sol would fall into their trap, because that's what it would be."

"I have no doubt that Jason is the connection. And, as you know, Sol Lefko received the video of his daughter and son-in-law from Aswad after they were left behind on an island somewhere. So far no one has found them. Assuming they have no food or water, considering the tropical heat, time's about to run out for them. Do you have a daughter?"

"Yes."

"If you faced the same circumstances, what would you do?"

"I tell you what I would not do … I wouldn't kill a federal agent, kidnap a former agent and CIA officer, and I wouldn't yield to Aswad's demands. If it is Lefko, I hope we find him before Aswad does."

"You might want to start near Tarpon Springs."

"Why there?"

"Because there's a GPS tracker on a shrimp boat that's leaving Tarpon Springs right now. Dave and Wynona may be on that boat. It's called *Aphrodite*. A few days ago, it dropped off or picked up illegals—most likely from Aswad's group, on Marathon Key. A witness to the arrival or departure of the boat was murdered down there. *Aphrodite* should be in the open Gulf of Mexico in a half hour."

# ONE HUNDRED

Katie squatted, hunched over in the blistering sun using a conch shell to dig a hole to nowhere. Her hands bled. Her shoulders and face severely sunburned. Lips cracked and bleeding with open sores. Andy's condition was no better. From the shade of the lean-to, he watched his delusional wife attempting to dig a well like a dying person stranded in a vast desert hallucinates the image of a cool oasis with a bubbling spring under palms and lush ferns.

Andy stood on weak legs, walked to her, stumbled once, got back up, placing a hand on her hot shoulder. "Katie … save what strength you have left. Let's lie back down, okay?"

"No!" she shouted, her voice raspy and hoarse, looking up at him through bloodshot eyes and an emaciated face. "I just have a little farther to go. There's water here … somewhere. I know it."

Andy slowly straightened up and looked around. No sign anymore of planes or boats. Nothing but the vast ocean. Undrinkable blue water that seemed to bend at the curvature of the earth.

• • •

O'Brien jogged down L dock to *Jupiter* and entered the salon. Max jumped off the couch, her bark almost a yodel. O'Brien picked her up and held her to his wide chest. He kissed the top of her head.

Max licked O'Brien's cheek, her eyes bright. "What happened to Wynona? Did someone come on the boat and take her, or did she try to help Dave, and someone took her from there?" Max uttered a noise somewhere between a bark and growl.

Nick entered the salon as O'Brien set Max down. O'Brien grabbed his black leather duffle bag and placed his Glock inside with two boxes of ammo and a change of clothes.

Nick said, "No sign of Dave's phone anywhere on *Gibraltar.*"

O'Brien pointed to the coffee table. "Wynona left her phone on the table. I'd bet she didn't take it with her because she was awakened in the middle of the night and investigated Dave's boat. If that's the case, that means she didn't come back here … and she was taken right along with Dave."

"Taken where? Maybe to someplace where Aswad's killers can finish them. What if it's an old or abandoned warehouse someplace in the Daytona area?"

O'Brien said nothing, his thoughts racing. He checked his phone, finding a GPS app he sometimes shared with Dave. He keyed it in and watched the screen.

"What are you staring at?" Nick asked.

"Somehow, Dave managed to take his phone with him and hide it. If Sol Lefko is the kidnapper, maybe he didn't notice Dave picking up his phone in the midst of whatever scuffle he caused by holding Dave and Wynona at gunpoint." O'Brien studied the screen. "Maybe Lefko found it later, destroyed it … or Dave's phone ran out of battery power."

"Why? What do you see?"

"They aren't in a warehouse somewhere in Daytona or Ponce Inlet. Four hours ago, the GPS left a trail of them headed west on Highway 44 toward DeLand."

"Why would he be taking them to DeLand?"

"I don't think DeLand is the destination. I think it's Tarpon Springs. The shrimp boat, *Aphrodite*, just left the docks. I wonder if Wynona and Dave are aboard?"

"So where are you heading," Nick asked.

"You may be right, Nick—nowhere just yet. But, I will find them."

# ONE HUNDRED ONE

*L*ucky Strike was three miles off shore in the Gulf of Mexico when all hell broke loose. Passengers were just starting to gamble, booze flowing, wait staff and dealers all smiles as eighty-seven passengers on the 175-foot, double-decker floating casino placed bets. "Let the good times roll!" said a large man in a Star Wars T-shirt and baggy shorts, a Budweiser in one hand, a long cigar in the other hand.

On the bridge, the sleepy-eyed captain, salt and pepper stubble on his heavy face, sat back in his chair, his short-sleeve, white shirt wrinkled, the gold and black stripes on his shoulders were frayed. He started to sip his coffee and almost spit it back in the cup when he looked over the horizon.

• • •

In the casino on the first deck, dozens of people stood at slot machines, blackjack tables, roulette, craps and poker tables. "What's that noise?" said one white-haired retired man to his wife of forty-nine years.

"This whole place is noisy," she said, rolling her pale green eyes, looking at him before feeding a dollar into the slot machine, a cigarette dangling between freshly manicured, bright red fingernails.

412

"Sounds like choppers I heard years ago in Vietnam," he said. "You never forget that noise."

"C'mon, Harry, we're here to have fun. After all those years, you still can't handle fireworks and strange sounds. Let's get a cocktail."

He stepped away from the row of slots, walked though second-hand cigarette smoke and peered out of the boat's salt-spray, discolored windows. "Oh shit," he mumbled, watching three-armed United States Coast Guard helicopters overhead, one slowly circling, the other two flying stationary in opposite areas of the blue sky.

"Margie!" he said, "Come take a look at all this."

His wife pulled the slot handle once more before slowly prying herself off the seat, slipping her flip-flops back on, and walking over to the window. "What the heck?" she uttered, smoke drifting from her cigarette up and into her left eye. "What's going on, Harry?"

Four Coast Guard cutter ships, each more than one hundred feet in length, bright white with a large orange stripe near the bow, circled the gambling boat. Each cutter was armed with machine guns, ensigns and officers carrying rifles and pistols. A fifty-foot, high-speed, search and rescue boat filled with FBI agents wearing bulletproof vests and heavily armed U.S. Marshalls approached *Lucky Strike*.

One of the federal agents stood near the port gunnel on the smaller boat and lifted a bullhorn to his mouth. "Halt any forward progress! Drop your anchor and prepare for boarding."

The gambling ship captain cut the engines. He turned to a young crewmember, soft blond stubble on his chin. The captain shouted, "Drop anchor! Looks like we just sailed into a sea of shit."

• • •

Five hours later, O'Brien received his first call from FBI Deputy Director Marshall Wilson. He said, "Your tip sent close to a hundred men on a wild goose chase."

O'Brien stood in *Jupiter's* salon, his laptop on the couch next to Max. He asked, "I assume you didn't find them."

"No, but we found dozens of gamblers, mostly retirees sipping beer and Bloody Marys. None too happy that we interfered with their excursion on the high seas. After interviewing passengers, crew, the captain, and a search of *Lucky Strike*, there was no sign of Dave Collins, Wynona Osceola, or Sol Lefko." Wilson stood in one of the FBI's command centers at its Washington D.C. headquarters. The massive room was filled with analysts in front of computer screens. There were digital, real-time world maps and large screen monitors receiving live video and satellite feeds from around the world.

"Did you find the GPS tracker?" O'Brien asked.

"That, we did locate. It was on the roof of the bridge. After that boondoggle, we had a team of agents hit the docks in Tarpon Springs. Once again, they questioned shrimp boat owners, commercial fishermen and even a few sponge divers. No one's seen anything or admits to seeing anything. The boat you mentioned, *Aphrodite*, was tied up and deserted. We found nothing on it. No one seems to have seen the owner or any members of the crew. Thanks for the tip. Too bad it cost a lot of time, money and manpower."

O'Brien said nothing, his mind working, replaying conversations from Richard Thurston, his son Jason, to the video tape Abdul Aswad sent of Katie and Andy on the island.

"O'Brien, are you there?"

"Yes, something's off … wrong. Sol Lefko is a desperate man. I believe he's cut a deal with Abdul Aswad to deliver Dave and Wynona. Dave is the former CIA officer that Aswad wanted the most. The same goes for Richard Thurston. He wanted Dave to feel the heat the most because Dave was the principle witness for the prosecution in Thurston's trial. The icing on the cake for Aswad would be Wynona, one of your best former agents. When Aswad would have discovered who the woman with Dave really was, the woman who killed his brother, and that she was helping to protect Dave, well Aswad would know he'd entered into a scenario he could only have dreamed of when his sick mind was plotting revenge."

The deputy director walked to one corner of the large command center. "We have eyes everywhere with some of the most high-level satellite surveillance in the world. But if you want to hide someone, dead or alive, it's easy to do it. Why would Aswad try to smuggle them out of the country when he's been able to assassinate victims almost at will right here?"

"Because this one's even more personal, and he wants to be the one to do it."

• • •

The sun was setting over the Gulf of Mexico when Captain Santos Kalivaris piloted *Aphrodite* out of the mouth of the Anclote River and into the Gulf, its emerald waters now reflecting pink and gold in the sunset. He held binoculars to his bloodshot eyes and watched ships in the distance. He shook a Camel loose from the pack, lit it, turned to Bear and said, "I bet ol' Capt Ted Laskaris pissed in his pants. When Sammy Boloros hears about it, he might try to sink one of 'em Coast Guard cutters."

"I just want this to be over with. This is my last run with you."

"You'll make so much off this run, you won't have to work for a year, that is if you don't suck the money up your nose. It's all about moderation, Bear."

Kalivaris made a sharp left turn in the Gulf, heading due south, pushing the twin diesels and bringing *Aphrodite* up on plane, the big shrimp boat humming. A mile later, he poured two fingers worth of Crown Royal into a red Solo cup and took a sip, the alcohol burning the back of this throat.

Locked inside the crew cabins were Dave and Wynona.

And the role Sol Lefko played was about to change.

# ONE HUNDRED TWO

Katie Scott could no longer dig. The hole was more than three feet wide and almost four feet deep. She sat at the edge of the pit and stared at the hard sand. She'd used two conch shells as primitive shovels, breaking the edge of each shell. She looked up at the windswept tree-scape. Watched sea oats bobbing in the sea breeze. She and Andy had very little sleep. No water in almost five days. Both were so severely dehydrated they had debilitating headaches, cramps, fever and even chills in the daytime heat nearing one hundred degrees.

Andy sat under the palm frond lean-to, his energy so depleted that he could hardly stand. His left eye was swollen shut from an allergic reaction to the scorching sun. Water blisters peppered his forehead and cheeks. He watched his wife, the deepest sorrow he'd ever felt moving through his body like a fever. *Katie's not digging a well,* he thought. *She's digging our graves. But there is no one here to cover us up.*

Andy's hands trembled. He reached under a palm frond on the ground and removed the pistol loaded with two rounds. "It'll ease the suffering ..." he mumbled, dried blood caked in both corners of his mouth. He slowly stood and started a sluggish walk across the hot sand to his wife.

Katie tried to remember the last time she peed. When she did, her urine was deep yellow. She could no longer make salvia or even tears— her glands were shutting down, her organs starving for hydration, her mind rambling. She stared at the sea oats, and they suddenly turned into stalks of green corn—crops she'd seen as a little girl when her family visited Grandpa's farm in Indiana. She remembered the old-fashioned scarecrow Grandpa had erected near the front row of crops in the field. The way Grandma had dressed and stuffed the scarecrow with fresh smelling hay, its gangly arms and legs, the worn brogan shoes Grandpa had tied to the feet.

And now the scarecrow was walking toward her. *How did it get down off the post?* Her thoughts were disjointed, vision slightly blurring. She remembered the scarecrow in the Wizard of Oz. *He had a caring face. Did the one coming closer have a caring face?* She couldn't tell. Too far away. She heard seagulls overhead, reminding her of the chatty crows on the farm. Katie sat on her knees, leaned back to see the scarecrow better as it approached.

"Katie …"

"Yes," she said, using one hand to shield the sun from her eyes, the scarecrow in silhouette.

"Katie … it's me, Andy."

She smiled. "Hi."

"Let's go back in the shade and lie down."

She felt a hand under her arm, helping her stand. "I'm so thirsty," she said, managing to stand up.

"Me too, baby."

"Andy." She was too weak to smile. She felt him leading her to their little house in the sand. He helped her to lie down, then laid next to her, the seagulls louder, screeching now. *What did they want?*

Andy, lying next to his wife, took her hand in his left hand, the pounding of the surf now louder. He turned to look at her, using two fingers to gently comb the hair from her eyes. A single tear spilled from his eyes. He said, "Katie … I love you so much …"

"Love you, too," she barely whispered.

"I can end this now for both of us. We're in such pain and misery." He coughed. "We have two bullets … I can end it for you first … and then turn the gun on me. We'll be together, baby. Just not here dying slowly. But I won't do it unless I have your permission."

Katie said nothing, her mind wandering. She felt someone squeeze her hand.

"Katie … do you understand me? I can end the suffering for both of us. We'll be together with no pain, okay, baby? We can't last much longer." Andy spotted a land crab—a large soldier crab the size of his hand. It stood defiant at the entrance to their lean-to. The crab's eyes black and the size of peas. "Katie, can you hear me?"

She gently squeezed his hand. "Yes … I'm here. I'll always be here for you, Andy."

He gripped the pistol, lowering his head back to the sand and holding his wife's hand, another tear spilling from his wet eyes, the sound of hungry gulls screaming in the sky above their tiny hidden world.

# ONE HUNDRED THREE

O 'Brien replayed conversations and events in his mind, trying to put the puzzle pieces together—trying to follow a path that wasn't there—wasn't visible. At least not yet. He stood in *Jupiter's* cockpit, Max at his feet. She could sense his fear—fear for the lives of at least five people: Dave, Wynona, Sol Lefko, Katie and Andy. Max uttered a soft whine.

"Hey, kiddo," O'Brien said, opening the doors to the salon, Max following at his heels. "We have to find Dave and Wynona very quickly because they don't have much time. Where are they, Max? Are they still in the country or on a boat headed for a horrible fate that Aswad will, no doubt, video record for his deranged followers?"

Max tipped her head and hopped up on the couch. O'Brien opened his laptop and keyed in his notes on Richard and Jason Thurston and on Abdul Aswad. He reread an excerpt from one of the letters Richard had sent Jason, reading above a whisper. "*If you make it there, visit the caves of El Pomier, the Tito Indians—the first indigenous people to greet Christopher Columbus, left behind hundreds of cave paintings in the NW part of the island, dating back 2077 years ago. After that, have a toast of Clement Rum at Captain Cooks. They may still have a few bottles from 1952. It's superb, and it was distilled in the year of my birth. Follow your journey. Write to me when you can. I want to hear more about your adventures.*"

O'Brien leaned back in his chair, staring at the words. He whispered, "The NW or northwest part of the island … dating back 2077 years ago …" He paused. "Why so specific? Why not simply round off the years? Maybe because they're not years … possibly they're latitude and longitude and the NW stands for latitude 20 north and longitude 77 west."

He tapped his keyboard and looked at the screen. The GPS location was a large swath of Cat Island. O'Brien keyed in real-time satellite maps and zoomed down into the area. He went to street view. Scanning the cross streets. He quickly spotted Cooks International Bank. The address was 1952 Columbus Street. O'Brien whispered, "To greet Christopher Columbus … few bottles from 1952 … the year of my birth."

O'Brien looked up from his computer screen, his thoughts racing. He reached for his phone and made a direct call to FBI Deputy Director Marshall Wilson. When Wilson answered, O'Brien said, "Marshall, I believe that Richard Thurston used some covert coding when he sent letters to his son, Jason."

"Do you really find that surprising, considering Richard Thurston's background and training?"

"No." Rather than take a dig at the FBI, he said, "I had to read one of the letters a dozen times to see it. He gave Jason GPS longitude and latitude coordinates to meet, or have someone meet, Aswad on Cat Island. He mentions Captain Cooks in the letter, but he's really referring to Cooks International Bank. They have locations in the Caymans, Bahamas, and Switzerland. The one in the Bahamas, at those coordinates, is located at 1952 Columbus Drive." O'Brien quickly explained how he decrypted the information and said, "I believe that your agents will find images of Aswad on bank cameras, maybe there with Jason. The shell banking account is most likely Clement LTD, the account that Aswad received money from Thurston and his son to fund the logistics and manpower to assassinate four retired CIA officers, one FBI agent, and to kidnap at least two other people and leave two more on an isolated island to die."

Wilson sat at his desk and took notes. "We'll have the bank records and surveillance video in a few hours. Even if Aswad is on camera, it doesn't mean we'll find him on that island."

"When I was in the military, I learned a lot from an old sergeant who was raised on a simple farm in the Tennessee hill county. He could track most any animal. And he used to say that once he found the trail, he didn't always follow the hoof or paw prints because sometimes they weren't visible. He had to rely on other signs along the path. The path to Abdul Aswad, and saving these lives, may begin with GPS coordinates disguised as the precise age of etchings on the walls of caves on Hispaniola. From there let's see where it leads us."

# ONE HUNDRED FOUR

Captain Santos Kalivaris didn't need depth gauges, charts, radar or GPS as he piloted *Aphrodite* into water he'd fished since his grandfather first took him to sea at age four. Kalivaris knew the marine routes south along Florida's west coast like the back of his scarred left hand. He could run just off shore from Tarpon Springs past Clearwater, St. Pete, Longboat Key, on down to Boca Grande, Fort Myers, Naples, and the Ten Thousand Islands. His second route was to take *Aphrodite* through the Gulf Intracoastal Waterway. He chose that option.

He knew the marinas—the good and the bad, waterfront bars, places to dock overnight using cash only. Places to score drugs and women. And he knew what to avoid. Kalivaris liked running *Aphrodite* after dark. He knew that once he entered the Ten Thousand Islands after a refueling stop in Everglades City, the maze of islands would create additional camouflage. The risks of running aground in a slack tide were always there. But he checked the tidal charts, knew his way through the labyrinth of islands, and wanted *Aphrodite* to keep a low profile en route to the Atlantic Ocean.

Bear was in the wheelhouse with him, Johnny Hastings on lookout near the transom. Kalivaris tapped his pack of Camels against the wooden wheel. He lifted a cigarette out, lit it, and blew smoke through both nostrils. His nervous eyes watched the port and starboard sides of his boat, his human cargo held in the cabins.

Bear folded his arms across his chest and said, "We need a plan?"

"We got a plan. We drop these towel heads and their hostages off at the rendezvous boat, collect the remaining quarter mil, turn back around and get the hell outta Dodge."

"Santos, it ain't Dodge City we're headin' toward. It's the fuckin' Atlantic, and this boat's not the fastest. We don't know where we're goin' and we got no idea who we're meeting out there. All we can go on is what that guy, Shahid, tells us."

"I may not agree with the way they interpret their religion, but I do know they've honored every financial agreement we've had with them. Far as I can tell, none of these goat herders are flyin' planes into American buildings. So, whatever they do when they come and go, it's not for me to question. Blame it on our immigration policy." He grinned and took a long drag off his cigarette.

"Who the hell is that woman and those two guys? They look American. Who'd they piss off to be taken outta the country?"

"The less we know about their passengers, the better. In a few hours, we say good riddance to these dudes, get the rest of the dough and spilt. This is the last damn run. I'm gonna sell my boat and get the hell outta anything to do with the sea. I plan never to eat seafood again." He crushed the remains of his cigarette into a Folgers' coffee can cut to the size of an ashtray, the can littered with a dozen cigarette butts smoked down to the last half-inch.

• • •

Sol Lefko sat to the right side of Dave and Wynona in the captain's cabin. Shahid Abboud, ratty black beard and languid dark eyes, sat on a metal folding chair in one corner. He held a small assault rifle in his lap, the tip of the barrel pointed toward the three. Lefko looked up and said, "I have an agreement with Aswad. I am not supposed to be held under guard. Did he inform you of that?"

Abboud didn't move for a few seconds, his face like granite. He exhaled and said, "Abdul always honors his commitments, the first being to Allah."

"I am supposed to be taken to where he left my daughter."

"Abdul is a man of honor and great vision." He looked at his watch for a moment and then used the butt of the rifle to pound on the wall behind him. In ten seconds, the door opened and two more of Aswad's men were standing there. In Farsi, Abboud said, "I need to piss. Watch these infidels."

"I will do it," said the taller of the two men.

Abboud handed his rifle to him and continued in Farsi, "If they move beyond a sneeze, shoot them. Try to keep the woman alive. Abdul says that he has special plans for her."

Dave listened closely, his understanding of the language was still very good in spite of the fact he hadn't used it in years. He made sure his eyes didn't register that he understood them. He knew Sol Lefko wasn't nearly as proficient with the language, but Lefko's grasp of Russian was flawless, and he could, at one time, hold basic conversations in the different Arabic dialects.

Wynona sat next to Dave, looked at the gun in the man's hands, looked at the contrast between his dead eyes and his long eyelashes. For a brief moment, she wondered what he was like as a young boy, when childhood innocence and curiosity were a compass he shared with the world. *What was he like playing with his sisters or brothers long before the time capsule of his forefather's suspicion and hostility imprisoned him into its intricacies of hate composing for generations?* Wynona closed her eyes for a brief moment, thinking about Sean. *Do you have any idea what happened? How can we get a message to you … to anyone?* She thought about the day she was shot and left for dead in the parking lot of an abandoned warehouse in Miami. Sean holding her hand and cradling her head as she lay on her back between broken wooden fruit pallets and telling her, *"You're going to rise up out of this dark rabbit hole and live, you hear me?"*

Abboud opened the door to the crew cabin and entered. He glanced at Wynona, Dave and Sol before turning to the guard and speaking in rapid fire Farsi.

Dave looked at a cigarette burn on a small table near one wall. He listened carefully and heard him say, "I spoke with Abdul. He will await our arrival and meet us between Rum Cay and Crooked Island in one of the fast racing boats and take us back to an island with an old abandoned castle. Allah is most great."

# One Hundred Five

O'Brien hadn't slept more than one consecutive hour all night. He'd drifted in and out of a restless sleep in *Jupiter's* master berth. He climbed to the fly-bridge before sunrise and sat on the bench in the dark with Max. Soon, there was a blush of pink, the rosy hue of dawn like a roseate spoonbill's feather, sprouting in the eastern sky over the Atlantic.

As O'Brien rubbed Max's head, she made slight cooing sounds. They watched the clouds above the horizon turn cotton candy pink, the sky itself becoming neon blue. Two large pelicans were the only movement in the still vista.

He thought about how little time Katie and Andy had remaining. He checked his phone every half hour, hoping that somehow Dave or Wynona might get a message to him. Nothing. O'Brien didn't know their location at that moment, but he had an idea where they'd be—delivered to a secret place, a place where Abdul Aswad waited to greet them with terror.

• • •

Two hours after sunrise, Captain Kalivaris stared at the Seven Mile Bridge as he piloted *Aphrodite* closer to the Florida Keys. In his mind, as soon as he crossed under the bridge, he was into the homestretch—in the Atlantic Ocean and heading toward the Bahamas. He just didn't know where in the islands.

He slowed the shrimp boat down, used his driver's license to cut and bead a line of cocaine on his navigation table. Bear and Johnny Hastings watched him and the surroundings, Bear using binoculars to canvas the bridge area. Kalivaris bent over the table and used a rolled dollar bill to inhale the cocaine, sucking the white powder through his right nostril, pressing a dirty finger against the left side of his nose. He stood, blinked three times and offered the remaining two lines to his crew, Bear and Johnny Hastings. Each man quickly snorting the drugs.

Johnny popped his knuckles, eyes wide, and said, "Who the hell needs coffee when you got the cream—the powdered cream."

Bear nodded. "We're gonna need all the stimulants we can get between now and dropping off our cargo."

Kalivaris got back behind the wheel, working the throttles to return the boat to a speed of about seven knots as they came closer to two bridges—the original bridge finished in 1912, and the latest one which opened in 1982. He guided the big boat in perfect alignment between the first set of bridge pilings. Less than a minute later, he piloted *Aphrodite* under the final bridge connected to the mainland United States. Ahead were thousands of miles of Atlantic Ocean and hundreds of islands in the stream.

Kalivaris turned to Bear and said, "Go back there and tell Abboud to get his ass up here to the wheelhouse. Tell him I'm not gonna go a mile farther 'til I know where we're goin,' and I mean exactly where we're headin' to. We won't have the fuel to zigzag around the islands like some damn cruise ship.

• • •

O'Brien stood in *Jupiter's* fly-bridge and looked down at *Gibraltar*, the trawler seemed different, as if its spirit had departed, leaving the hull behind—the vigor that Dave exuded had somehow drifted away with the receding morning tide. O'Brien thought about Wynona, how she'd volunteered to stay at the marina, doing what she could to boost the FBI's surveillance of Dave and the old trawler he called home.

Something caught Max's attention. She stood on the long bench seat, watching the water below *Jupiter*. She lifted her head as a large dragonfly skimmed above the surface, the insect ascended quickly up to the fly-bridge. It flew around the perimeter and then alighted on one of the aluminum railings next to O'Brien. He watched it, the dragonfly, its four wings motionless—the wings were light blue but translucent. The dragonfly's head was the color of a blue flame, its four-inch body tricolor—electric green, lemon yellow and the brown of new leather.

O'Brien and Max observed the insect. She didn't bark or growl. O'Brien remained stationary. He could hear Wynona's words the first time she told the story of what the elder medicine man, Sam Otter, said about dragonflies. *"He said, if a dragonfly comes into your life, maybe lands very near you, looks at you with those large eyes, just watch it for a moment, and be very still. Never harm or kill it. Sam told us the visit of a dragonfly often brings or signifies a change is coming into your life. He said, the key is not to fight change, but to embrace it."*

O'Brien watched the dragonfly, and it appeared to watch him. The insect moved its head in O'Brien's direction, its large, dark eyes filled with mystery. Three seconds later, the dragonfly flew from the railing, darting over the water, its colors becoming one with the ripple of blue and gold off the surface.

O'Brien's phone buzzed. He looked at the caller ID, quickly recognizing the area code and then the number. The call was coming from Sofia Alanis, the woman he'd had a drink with in Tarpon Springs. He answered, and after a quick greeting she said, "I was thinking about you this morning."

"Oh, how's that?"

Sofia stood near the Tarpon Springs sponge docks, tourists walking behind her, a breeze blowing her hair. She said, "I came to my favorite bakery for baklava and Greek coffee and happened to notice the boat, *Aphrodite*, is gone. It might not mean a thing, but the crew hadn't been back in town very long before they left again. That usually doesn't happen. Just thought you'd want to know, especially after all that federal hullabaloo in the Gulf with the casino boat, *Lucky Strike.*"

"Thanks, Sofia. I appreciate the call."

She smiled, pulling a strand of hair behind her left ear. "No problem. If you're ever in Tarpon Springs again, give me a call or text. I can show you around, maybe show you some of the town's history. There's a lot here."

"I'd like that. Thanks, bye." He disconnected and looked from the fly-bridge to the Halifax River and the marine channel leading to Ponce Inlet and the ocean. Wynona's words echoing in his mind, "*He said the visit of a dragonfly often brings or signifies a change is coming into your life.*"

O'Brien looked at Dave's boat, *Gibraltar.* He turned to Max, picked her up, and stood facing the Atlantic in the distance. "I have to go, Max. I'm not sure exactly where, but I believe Dave and Wynona are somewhere out there. I just have to figure out where, and I have to do it very quickly. You hang with Nick for a little while. If I have some luck, I'll bring two close friends back, and maybe save two more from horrible deaths."

O'Brien climbed down the bridge ladder with Max tucked under one arm. He entered the salon, set her on the couch and pulled a cigar box from behind the bar. He opened it and picked up a wad of business cards bound by a rubber band. He flipped through the cards, pulling one from the stack. He looked at the number and made a call. When a man answered, O'Brien said, "Dustin, it's Sean O'Brien."

Dustin Sharpe, mid-forties, salt and pepper hair, tanned face, stood on an airfield with a stationary helicopter and palm trees in the background. He held the phone to his ear and grinned, "Sean O'Brien. It's about time I heard from you. Ready to do some fishing in the islands?"

"Yeah, but not for fish. Are you still operating aerial sightseeing over the Bahamas?"

"Hell, yeah. Hey, I recognize that tone in your voice. Used to hear it sometimes in Afghanistan. Whatcha need?"

"A huge favor."

# ONE HUNDRED SIX

Dave looked at the man holding the gun on them. Wynona closed her burning eyes. From his wallet, Sol Lefko removed a picture of Katie when she was a teenager, staring at the image in his lap. Dave nodded at the stoic guard and said, "I need to pee. My plumbing isn't as good as yours." He started to stand.

"Sit down!" the guard shouted.

Dave smiled. "My friend. I either go piss, or I'll do it in my pants, and we all can sit in this small cabin and breathe the smell of an old man's urine until we get to wherever in the hell it is that you're taking us."

The guard used one fist to pound on the wall behind him. In seconds, the door opened, and another man stood there, armed with an Uzi. The two guards spoke in Farsi and the one at the door looked at Dave and said in English, "Get up!"

Dave stood, his legs and back sore, following the man to the small head located behind the master cabin. He looked at Dave and said, "You have thirty seconds. If you're not done, too bad."

Dave half smiled and said, "It may take me that long to get started. Come on, friend, I'm sixty-six. Things get a little slower. The upholstery has some wear and tear."

The guard stood stone-faced. Dave turned and shut the door. He reached in his pants, quickly finding his phone. No signal. He used his thumbs to type: *Island - castle. Bahamas.* He hit *send* and held the phone in one hand as he urinated.

"Ten seconds," said the guard standing at the door.

"Almost done." Dave placed the phone back in his underwear, zipping up his pants.

• • •

O'Brien was met by Dustin Sharpe at the small airport at Arthur's Town on Cat Island in the Bahamas. O'Brien carried a black leather overnight bag. He and Sharpe embraced, slapping backs, and O'Brien said, "Thanks for meeting me."

"After you explained what's at stake, man, I only wish I had a small air force with a fleet of planes and choppers to help you, Sean."

"We've been doing that with fleets of planes and boats. So far no luck."

"Yeah, I've been following it in the news, best I can. Getting most of my updates from stateside news sources. Not much journalism in the islands. Matter of fact, when conducting my sightseeing tours, I've kept looking for anything out of the ordinary on the islands. Problem is there are more than seven hundred scattered over thousands of square miles. You think the couple is still alive?"

"Something in my gut tells me yes. Having spent some time with them, you sort of get the feeling they won't give up as long as they can breathe. FBI still is calling it a search and rescue mission, but I believe in their hearts it's moved into a recovery mission. Do you run your business out of this airport?"

Sharpe pointed to a metal Quonset hut to the far right of the cinderblock building that served as the main terminal, a half-dozen tourists getting off a Beechcraft Bonanza that had just landed. The Quonset hut was made of gunmetal gray, corrugated steel. The roof formed a half circle and looked like it had been built during the World War II period. The sign out front read: *Island Charters, LTD.*

Sharpe smiled and said, "I do most of the runs. But I have two other guys, all former military, turned bush pilots, turned permanent holiday seekers, who help out when I need them. I have a chopper. It's a Bell Jet Ranger. The bird's got at max range of about 450 miles, depending upon the wind and conditions. I have one seaplane, a Seamax. It's tied up at the docks about two hundred yards on the other side of the terminal."

"Which one would give us the best eyes in the sky. We're looking for a seventy-foot shrimp boat with a blue hull. And we're looking for Katie and Andy on an island."

"Both have about the same range. I'd use the plane, because if we find them, it'll be easier to get them on board and headed to a hospital. Nassau would be a good destination."

O'Brien nodded. He lifted his bag. "I'm packing a Glock in here. It's not hard to do when you don't fly commercial. But we might need more firepower. Do you have anything here or at your house?"

"You know me, Sean. After carrying for three tours of duty, you sort of don't want to leave home without it. In my office, I have two rifles, an M24 and a McMillan TAC-50. Both with scopes."

"Let's carry everything you have. We don't know what we're going to run into out there."

• • •

Katie held Andy's hand, her breathing shallower, dreams mixing with hallucinations, not able to distinguish between them. Her eyes fluttered open. She looked at her husband, his stomach now concave, dried blood around his nostrils. She said, "Let's pray, Andy."

"Save your strength. We can do silent prayers."

"No … we need each other's strength by praying together." She managed to make a dry swallow and whispered, "The Lord is my shepherd … I shall not want. He maketh me to lie down in green pastures … he leadeth me beside the still waters … he restoreth my soul …"

Andy opened his eyes and softly prayed with his wife. Together they whispered, "He leadeth me in the paths of righteousness for his name's sake … though I walk through the valley of the shadow of death … I will fear no evil … for thou art with me …"

• • •

O'Brien and Dustin Sharpe boarded the seaplane and left the dock on Cat Island, flying west into the afternoon sun. Sharpe sat at the controls, gaining altitude and airspeed. He leveled off at twelve hundred feet. He turned to O'Brien and said, "I know the search teams have been concentrating on places from Spanish Town all the way down to Long Island, Crooked Island, over to Duncan Town and a hell of a lot of smaller, no-name islands scattered over a few thousand square miles. Where do you have in mind?"

O'Brien thought a moment, holding and studying an aerial map of the Bahamas. He said, "Their sailboat, *Dragonfly,* was found on the west coast off Eleuthera, opposite Rock Sound. If someone were using a high-speed cigarette boat and wanted to put distance from where they abducted Katie and Andy … where would they go?" He scrutinized the maps, looking toward Crooked Island and the areas Sharpe mentioned. "Let's stay east of Nassau." O'Brien looked at the map again and said, "The long chain of islands, an archipelago, northwest of Rocker's Point and past Great Guana Cay … there are a lot of small islands dotting a huge swath of ocean."

Sharpe slipped on sunglasses and said, "I know for a fact they searched those. A buddy of mine spent a few days fishing areas of that chain. He said planes and choppers buzzed over at least twice at different parts of the day."

O'Brien smiled. "But my pal, Dustin Sharpe, wasn't behind the wheel. I saw how you could find our guys in the mountains of Afghanistan. I'm betting you might do the same in a place that has no mountains. We're looking for a shrimp boat on the water and two people on an island no one can spot. No pressure, okay?"

Sharpe shook his head, "Yeah, right." He banked the plane to the south, heading to Rocker's Point before flying northwest over a strand of islands that, even from the air, looked like a four-hundred-mile necklace surrounded by the deep waters of the Atlantic.

# ONE HUNDRED SEVEN

Captain Kalivaris was about to enter seas he'd never sailed before today—the southwest side of Andros Island. He needed to refuel *Aphrodite* and still make the rendezvous with Aswad that evening. Kalivaris was glad their meeting was to be in the remote southwest side of Andros Island, south of Ratman Cay, but he was nervous because of what he'd heard about the area through the years.

There was a reason it was uninhabited.

He examined the charts and looked at satellite images. Looked at the depth in the areas, seeking the best route in and out of what amounted to shallow, dangerous shoals and hundreds of coral reefs and small islands. The west side was a remote, very large slice of Andros Island, abandoned long ago and designated as a national marine park.

Bear entered the wheelhouse, his mouth turned down, eyes bloodshot. He said, "I'm sick and tired of the attitude these fuckers are sportin' as we get further from the states. They're actin' like *Aphrodite* is theirs. One of 'em slapped the guy sittin' to the left of the woman, I think the dude is named Sol something or the other. He's got a busted lip. Bled like a stuck mackerel on the front of his shirt. And, tall ass, the guy wearin' the sweatband around his head and carrying the Uzi, he looks like he's thinkin' about how he's gonna rape the woman when they get to wherever it is they're goin' to."

"You and Johnny remind those SOB's that nobody gets slapped around on this boat. What they do after they're gone, that's their business. Last thing we need is to deal with a dead body or bodies. Quicker we can get 'em all off the boat, the better. We'll gas up at Driggs Harbor and head south to the remote part of Andros past Ratman Cay. I don't like the shallows and reefs, but, at this point, we don't have much choice."

• • •

As *Aphrodite* came close to the east side of Andros Island and chugged south down its one-hundred-mile coastline, the boat was within range of cell tower signals. Dave Collins sat still, sipped from a water bottle, when he felt a two second vibration against his lower stomach area. At that point, he knew his text had been sent to O'Brien. He leaned closer to Wynona's ear and whispered, "It's going to work out … I promise."

She looked at him, pleased for his optimism, but not sure how to respond or even whether to respond. She licked her bottom lip and nodded. The guard stared at Dave and said, "No whispering. If you talk, then you speak up so everyone can hear, otherwise Khalid may choose to cut out your tongue. He has done it before, and now he is more efficient.

• • •

Dustin Sharpe flew as slow as aeronautically possible, flying the seaplane between five hundred to eight hundred feet above the islands. He turned his head toward O'Brien and said, "If you see something, shout it out. I can go low as a telephone pole if I have to. And we can land anywhere there's water, and that's everywhere."

"Okay." O'Brien used a pair of binoculars when he thought he saw an anomaly on any of the islands. For the most part, they looked the same. Some verdant green rimmed in snow-white sand beaches. Others were windswept. Trees scattered from massive hurricanes that plummeted the islands in recent years. These were the islands that he concentrated on observing from the air. He also looked at boats—the ones that had the distinctive outriggers of shrimp boats. There were none, at least none shrimping in the area below their flight path. If *Aphrodite* were in the area, it would be an easy vessel to spot.

From Rocker's Point, Sharpe guided the seaplane in a north to northwest direction. He glanced at the setting sun in the west and said, "We won't have as much time as I'd hoped. Sunset happens real fast over the sea. It's like the ocean just swallows the sun during the last twenty minutes or so."

"I've noticed that through the years. Sometimes, when I've spotted the flash of green at the moment of sunset, it's as if fire and water had a quick fusion." O'Brien continued watching. He spotted two people walking the beach on one of the windswept islands. He got Sharpe's attention and pointed toward the island. "Looks like a man and a woman down there."

"We'll go in for a closer look." Sharpe banked the plane to the left and dropped altitude to five hundred feet. "They have a small powerboat anchored right off shore."

The couple looked up and waved at the plane. Smiles. Healthy. The woman in a white bikini, the man shirtless and wearing trunks. "Obviously, not Katie and Andy," O'Brien said.

"I hope your hunch is right about this big area, Sean, because there has been a lot of eyes on these islands."

"And there are a lot of islands. One can slip by many people, just like an inconsistency in a photo that not everyone sees. We just have to force ourselves to see if it's somewhere down there."

Sharpe banked the plane back in a north to northwest direction, the sun now getting lower in the western sky. O'Brien looked at the sunset and cut his eyes back to the islands. A long freighter plowed through the deep blue water, churning a snowy wake from its bow to beyond the stern as the ship headed towards the north Atlantic.

Something caught O'Brien's eye.

He stared at it for a few seconds. It appeared to be a hole in the sand about one hundred feet inland from the beach. In the twilight, it was getting harder to see. The binoculars weren't much help. He said, "Looks like there's some sort of hole dug there." He pointed.

Sharpe glanced down for a few seconds. "Hard to tell in the fading light. Probably a sea turtle hole. It is egg-laying season. The big loggerheads can dig a helluva hole."

"Yes, but after they dig, the turtles cover them up with sand and crawl back out to the sea."

"It's getting too dark to safely land on water with so many reefs, rocks and sand spit of islands down there. Let's call it a night. We can start back out right here tomorrow."

O'Brien said nothing for a few seconds. Then he said, "Okay. I appreciate what you've done so far. But somewhere out here, I believe, is a shrimp boat carrying two people I care a lot for, and two others close to death on one of these desolate islands. We just have to find both before it's too late."

"Sean, you did some impossible stuff in Afghanistan. I'm betting you can do it here, too. Let's go back to the airport. I have some old single malt with our names on it." Sharpe turned the plane around, flying lower over the island.

O'Brien looked out the window trying to see what could be seen in the twilight.

• • •

From under the palm frond lean-to, Katie Scott opened her eyes. She listened for a second, trying to squeeze Andy's hand. "A plane …" she whispered. "It's so close … please come back."

The last thing she heard was the seaplane's engine fading as it flew toward the east, the drone of the motors replaced by the constant crashing of the surf as high tide rolled up on the sand for another long night.

# ONE HUNDRED EIGHT

C aptain Kalivaris was getting more nervous. He and the crew had anchored *Aphrodite* in twelve feet of water four miles south east of Ratman Cay. He stepped out of the wheelhouse and walked along the gunnel. Two of Aswad's men watched him. Neither man said a word. They looked to the southeast, anticipated the arrival of Abdul Aswad any minute. Kalivaris knew the other passengers were confined to the crew's cabin with a guard that rotated out every couple of hours.

The captain lit a cigarette and looked at the sky, stars so close he felt as if he could touch them. Except for the single red and green lights on *Aphrodite*, the stars were the only light for miles. No manmade light pollution because they were not near any port of town.

Johnny Hastings and Bear walked up to the captain. "Got an extra smoke, Cap?" Johnny asked. "I smoked my last one after we refueled at Driggs Harbor."

Kalivaris shook a cigarette loose from his Camel pack and handed it to Johnny. He took it, used his own Zippo to light it, and blew smoke up into the night air. He said, "This guy's a half-hour late. What the hell we gonna do if he never shows. We sure as hell can't go back to the states with all these people."

Kalivaris said, "He'll show. For some reason, I believe, he really wants those two dudes and the woman."

Bear looked back over his shoulder and said, "After they get off here, and we get our money, we got to swing the boat on a wide half circle to get beyond what appears to be the most dangerous reefs and shoals in the Bahamas."

Kalivaris nodded. "The crazy thing is we're just off the edge of what they call the Tongue of the Ocean. It's that big damn trench, three miles east, and it's at least four thousand feet deep. You go a hundred miles northeast of Andros, and it's more than five miles deep. But, of all the places in the Bahamas and Caribbean, Aswad picked these shallow and dangerous shoals."

Johnny blew smoke out of his mouth and said, "It's probably on account nobody's around for God knows how far. And I bet he's got his hideout not too far from here."

Bear started to respond when Kalivaris held up his right hand, pointing to the southeast. "I'd wager the towel head's got his hidey-hole in that direction. I see the runnin' lights from two boats. Looks like they're movin' it." He glanced around and lowered his voice. "I expect things will go fine, just like they always have, but y'all make sure you got a full clip in your guns. If one of 'em old boys so much as scratches his crotch, take a fast bead on him. Don't let 'em pull first. Let's try to keep Aswad's dudes and their hostages between us and the new guys arriving."

Bear sucked air in through his nostrils, his massive chest expanding. He exhaled and said, "It's show time." He looked back over his shoulder as one of Aswad's men held up a flashlight, pointing it at the approaching boats and turning it on and off three times."

• • •

Dustin Sharpe sat in his aviation office with O'Brien and reached in a desk drawer. He lifted out a new bottle of Macallan scotch. He picked up two glasses from a shelf behind his desk and poured the drinks. He slid one across his desk to O'Brien. Sharpe said, "To our latest mission turning out successful." He raised his glass in a toast.

O'Brien did the same, and they both sipped. Three seconds later, O'Brien's phone pinged. He lifted it from his right pocket and read the text. He looked up at Sharpe and asked, "Is there a Castle Island in the Bahamas?"

"Yeah, why?"

"Because Dave Collins, I mentioned his name and situation to you, he sent me a text. No doubt made when he hit cell services somewhere and did it, somehow, without his captor's knowing."

"What'd it say?"

"*Island - castle. Bahamas.* There's a dash between island and castle."

"Castle Island is damn remote. It's south of Acklins, which is way south on Crooked Island. Castle Island is fairly large. Totally uninhabited. There's a lighthouse on the southern tip. It has a long history as a stopping off island for pirates."

"Interesting how often history tends to repeat itself."

"Castle Island is at least two hundred miles from here, Arthur's Town."

O'Brien looked at the text. "I wonder why Dave just didn't key in Castle Island rather than Island - dash - castle?"

"Maybe he didn't have the time if he's being held hostage."

"The FBI has a presence in attaché offices with our embassies in the Dominican Republic, San Salvador, and Barbados." O'Brien glanced at his watch and punched numbers on his phone.

"Who are you calling?" Sharpe asked.

"The FBI. Let's see if they can pull together a team to hit Castle Island."

# ONE HUNDRED NINE

For years they were called cigarette boats. Then rumrunners. And some simply referred to them as go-fast boats. Two of the sleek boats, each nearly fifty feet in length, and an opalescent, silver color, approached *Aphrodite*. Both boats popped on powerful spotlights, blinding Kalivaris and the crew. Together the two boats had more than twelve hundred horsepower, their big engines reverberating as their crews came within fifty feet of *Aphrodite*.

Captain Kalivaris held up one hand and shouted, "You mind turnin' off the spots. We can't see a damn thing?"

Abdul Aswad stood in the boat that inched closest. He nodded to his crew, and they lowered the lights to the surface of the clear water, fish and crabs easily visible. Aswad gave a sign, and his men cut the engines, sounds of water slapping against the hulls. He said, "Captain Kalivaris, I do apologize for being late. The seas were a little rougher than anticipated."

Bear and Johnny stood near the crew cabin, both men watching two of Aswad's men on board *Aphrodite*, the third was still in the cabin. Kalivaris smiled. "No harm done. Stuff happens at sea." He turned to one of the sentinels and said, "Why don't you bring your people on out here? We'll do the exchange, and ever'body can go their separate ways."

The man looked over at Aswad who nodded. He dipped slightly in return and opened the crew cabin door. Sol Lefko, his shirt red from a smashed lower lip, came out first. Wynona and Dave followed him. The guard inside came behind them, an Uzi in his hands. Bear and Johnny watched him carefully, both ready to quickly shoot if need be.

Aswad stepped out from the open overhang above the seating and cockpit area. He looked at Dave, Lefko, and Wynona and said, "So good to see you three. I doubt if the feeling is mutual. However, Dave Collins and Sol Lefko, I warned you years ago what would happen after Guantanamo. And now is that time." He paused and cut his dark eyes over to Wynona. "You, failed FBI agent Osceola … did you think you could shoot my brother like a rabid dog and stay forever safe? You reap what you sow."

She looked at him a moment and said, "Your brother was a cold-blooded murderer. My only regret is that I just had eight rounds to use on him."

Aswad clenched his fists at his side, his face twisted, eyes hot with rage. Kalivaris looked at him and then at Wynona and said, "Y'all can work out your differences somewhere else. Right now, my crew needs to be paid. So, you fellas, hand over the cash, you get your people off my boat, and we'll all call it a night."

Aswad motioned to one of his crewmembers in the adjacent boat. The man nodded, picked up a pewter suitcase and walked down the bow. He handed the suitcase to one of the guards on the boat. The man carried it over to Kalivaris. He looked up at Aswad and said, "Much obliged. We don't really need to count it, but we need to take a look at it." He unlatched the suitcase, lifted the top, and his eyes widened. "What the fuck you doin' Aswad? You put sand in here!" He reached under his shirt just as Aswad fired a bullet into Kalivaris' forehead, his men opening fire on Bear and Johnny Hasting before they could pull their pistols. Both men dropped dead where they stood.

When the smoke cleared, Aswad smiled, looked over to Lefko and said, "You're number four," shooting him in the center of his chest. Lefko's body fell backward against one of the tall outriggers. Aswad eyed Dave, grinned and said, "I have a message for you. He tossed an envelope onto *Aphrodite,* falling at Dave's feet. "Open it Collins! If you don't, Abboud, who is standing behind the woman, will cut her throat."

Dave stared at Aswad for a second before bending down to pick up the envelope, taking his bifocals out of his pocket and reading silently. He cut his eyes up at Aswad who shouted, "Read it to all of us!"

Dave said, "And now there is one ... best wishes ... Richard Thurston."

Aswad smiled. "One of your very own. I believe he converted to Islam at Guantanamo. And, all these years later, he had even more reason to destroy those who conspired to send him to prison." He looked at his three men on *Aphrodite* and said, "Load them on board. Cut the anchor rope on the shrimp boat and let her drift with the dead men aboard."

• • •

Two hours later, the fast boats were approaching a dark island with an even darker history. It was a haven for pirates before it became a sanctuary for a former Nazi sympathizer suspected of war crimes. Before the war, he'd built a fortress in the center of the island. A home he called his castle. It was to be his sanctuary—a place he was thought to have gone to during the war and planned to live in for his remaining years.

• • •

*Aphrodite* drifted northeast of Andros, the shrimp boat screaking and rocking in the moving current, illuminated by a full moon and stars. It moved in the moonlit night, a silhouette pushed by an unseen hand and drifting to an unknown destination, a ghost ship trapped in the stream of forfeiture.

# ONE HUNDRED TEN

T he call came at midnight. O'Brien and Dustin Sharpe had been waiting for it. They were still in Sharpe's airport office, half eaten sandwiches and chips on paper plates. Two half consumed bottles of water. O'Brien answered, and the FBI Deputy Director, Marshall Wilson said, "Hate to tell you this, O'Brien, but you're two for two. First the casino boat and now Castle Island."

"What did you find?"

"It's what we didn't find … people. We flew a chopper and a plane with infrared imaging over the island. We've been monitoring live satellite feeds. The only movement we could spot were sea turtles laying their eggs in the moonlight. We're calling it a night, O'Brien. I suggest you do the same. Let's regroup in the morning." He disconnected.

O'Brien turned to Sharpe and said, "FBI flew over Castle Island. They used all the electronic surveillance toys. Couldn't find anything but sea turtles." He walked over to a large map of the Bahamas on one wall. He found Castle Island, touching the spot with his index finger. "Dustin … I keep thinking about the way Dave jotted that text message. Are there any islands in the Bahamas that have castles on them?"

"Man, there's so much wealth on some of the islands, their homes look like castles. They're huge mansions. Some billionaires, like Richard Branson, own whole islands."

"I'm talking about some place that has a building or home that resembles a castle … maybe an abandoned chateau."

"Let me think a sec … I do remember flying over an island, not too far from here, that has a huge white structure right smack dab in the center. It's southwest of Musha Cay. The island I'm thinking about is called Darby Cay." Sharpe tapped his laptop keyboard and brought up images. "Here it is, Sean."

O'Brien walked to the desk and looked at the screen. "See if you can get closer." Sharpe zoomed into the picture, and O'Brien said, "Take a look at that … it resembles an old English castle, right down to the turrets." The pictures were of a massive old home, bone white, with enormous arches and two spires.

Sharpe said, "Now I'm remembering more about this place. The property is large, and it's for sale." He read the description online. "It's three hundred acres. Four beaches. Even has a fresh water pond in the center. It comes with an abandoned airstrip. It says it took the Brit five years to finish the place. He was thought to be a traitor, helping the Germans navigate through that area. After the war, he and his mistress disappeared from the island—a mystery to this day. Take a look at this. The island has steep banks on the west side with the entrance to two caves. These caves are large enough to hide a U-boat in them."

"Or maybe a cigarette boat. Let's study the pictures and the terrain and plan our approach. It looks like the northeast might give us more camouflage from the trees and vegetation. If Aswad's there, he'll no doubt have men posted … maybe even booby traps rigged." He studied the images on the screen and pointed to one section of the island. "Here's our best approach. We have to go. No time to call the FBI, not that they'd come again. It's just us."

"When?"

"Tonight. We can't waste a minute. If Dave and Wynona are in there … we have to try. You said it was close. How close?"

"Exactly sixty-one miles. In the seaplane, it's fifteen minutes. One cool component of that plane is this … once I land on water, I can use the silent underwater props to get closer to where I'm going. It's two small props powered by electric motors. Very quiet."

"That's what we'll need to get close. Let's take the rifles and plenty of rounds."

Sharpe said, "I also have a twelve gauge, sawed off. Plenty of buckshot."

"Let's take it."

• • •

Dave and Wynona stood in the great room of the old castle, the room lit by candles and a dozen battery-powered lanterns. One of Aswad's guards watched them. The room had twenty-foot ceilings, a mural of England's Sherwood Forest painted across one wall. The floor was marble, quarried and imported from Italy. The thick walls were constructed from cut granite. In the center of the room was a long concrete table, strewn with broken plates and metal cups. A fireplace in one corner was large enough for an average size man to walk in without hitting his head. The home had the smell of wet timbers and old stone, windows gone, the salty breeze coming up from the sea.

Aswad entered from an arched doorway with one of his armed men. He approached Dave and Wynona and said, "How does it feel to know that this is your last night on earth?" He motioned toward the full moon shimmering across the Atlantic. "To know that this is the last time you will ever see the moon or smell the scent of the ocean. We are setting up a room with video cameras and chairs. Not only will your deaths be recorded, but your confessions to your sins will be as well." He smirked, the moonlight through two mammoth arched windows caught in his dark eyes.

Dave looked at Aswad, "You won't leave this island alive."

Aswad smiled. "Really? I will be on a private jet bound for Iran before the sun rises." He stared at Dave. "You look amused, Collins. Even for you, the tough ex-CIA officer, I find that rather interesting."

"You won't make that flight because you won't see the sunrise."

"Not only will I see it, I will see it as my men put your dead body on a raft and set it in the current. Some people place notes in bottles and toss them in the ocean. How romantic. However, for you, we will dog collar a note on your corpse that reads … *and then there were none*." He turned to his men and said, "Take them. Prepare them for what I've waited so many years to see and do."

# ONE HUNDRED ELEVEN

A mile away from the island, Sharpe turned to O'Brien and said, "I'm going to do something I haven't done since my last tour of duty."

"What's that?"

"Fly like a freakin' bat with the lights out. The full moon is enough for me. Besides, there's no FAA rules in the islands. You more or less make your rules to fit the situation. And we sure as hell don't want them seeing the lights from my plane."

O'Brien looked around the horizon. "The sky is clear. Let's do it."

Sharpe hit a switch and the exterior lights on the plane went dark. "I'm flying the perimeter around the outer edge of the island. See if you can spot any lights down there."

O'Brien said, "Already have. I saw someone with a flashlight near where I think the caves are located." He used binoculars to look out the plane's window and said, "It appears to be a slight illumination coming from one of the windows in the castle, the north side."

Sharpe smiled. "Looks like somebody's home."

"Let's go introduce ourselves."

Sharpe turned the plane, flying to the north side of the island, skimming across the water and landing quietly about a quarter mile off shore. He flipped a switch and engaged the electronic props. He said, "Hopefully no one saw or heard us. I'm gonna take us to the northwest side … where I believe we'll find the caves." The seaplane moved slowly like an amphibious creature over the dark water, a transplanted silhouette reminiscent of Lock Ness, as it came closer to the island.

"There's an outcropping of rock and some palms sloping over the water," O'Brien said, pointing toward a steeped bank area lush with small palms. "We can tie up there or anchor near there."

Sharpe looked at his depth gauge. "It's about forty feet deep right here. Let's drop anchor. I have a small, one-man inflatable and an air pump."

"We can use it to off-load the guns and ammo."

"How do we get it to shore?"

"I'll swim and tow it," O'Brien said.

"All right. I just hope sharks aren't feeding during the full moon."

O'Brien smiled. "Me, too. You have a rope?" He looked in the direction of the castle. It stood in silhouette, a medieval stance—white exterior pale in the moonlight, a soft glow coming from two large arched windows.

"Of course," Sharpe said. "One for the anchor and one to tie up. Sort of like hitching your seahorse to a rail."

The inflatable, not much larger than a car inner tube, inflated in less than a minute. They loaded the rifles, two pistols and one shotgun onto it. O'Brien said, "When I get there, toss a rope to me. I can tie the plane to that long palm that sticks out over the water." With that, O'Brien quietly entered the sea, swimming with one hand, pulling the raft and guns to shore.

• • •

Before it became a death chamber, the room in the old castle was the master bedroom. More than twelve hundred square feet with a domed ceiling that looked more like the interior of a church than a bedroom. A dark and deep fireplace in one corner. An immense wrought iron chandelier, its decorative crystals long since gone.

Below the chandelier sat Dave and Wynona, their hands tied to heavy chairs, a bright light pointed at their faces, one video camera near the light. Abdul Aswad stood next to the camera. Three of his men were in the room, one holding a long knife with a serrated blade, the knife large as a machete.

Aswad looked at Dave and Wynona and spoke in a low voice that was devoid of any emotion. It sounded as if it came from a machine, artificial intelligence speaking in innocuous sentences about philosophy and impending death. "You both know why you are here. And, you both know that you would not be here had you decided not to initiate the actions you chose to do. When you inflict hurt or damage to the cause of our people, more than two billion of us, you must expect fierce resistance."

Wynona squinted through the glaring light and said, "You don't speak for two billion people. You speak for your little band of renegades who interpret what they want to satisfy what they lack."

"Quiet!" Aswad shouted. His men looked at each other, anxiety arising in their faces. "It is time." He pressed the record button on the video camera.

• • •

Within one minute, O'Brien was on the rocky beach, water dripping from his face and clothes. He walked to the outcropping of rock, caught the end of the rope that Sharpe threw and tied the plane to the palm tree. Sharpe lowered the anchor into the water and swam less than twenty feet to shore. They quickly armed themselves and then used hand signals, moving around the cove to an area with a steep cliff. O'Brien pointed toward two cave openings, both partially filled with seawater. He whispered, "Look at that. Even in the moonlight, I can see the sterns of two boats. Two very fast boats."

Sharpe nodded and said, "That's why no one could spot them from the air. Hidden in their own watery and private cave boat slips."

They climbed a rocky path, following a moonlit trail. The scent of night blooming jasmine in the breeze, the castle on the hill a forgotten fortress withstanding time, hurricanes and curious interlopers.

There was a light only for a brief second. It appeared from a mobile phone, the light catching O'Brien's eye. *Maybe the guard checking the time.* O'Brien pointed, and Sharpe nodded. The man was more than two hundred feet away and near the castle, walking close to what seemed like a short retainer wall or trellis covered in bougainvillea vines.

O'Brien and Sharpe came closer. They could see the man was armed with a rife slung over his right shoulder, a pistol wedged under his belt. O'Brien squatted, picking up a small rock. He hurled it into the foliage some fifty feet in front of the guard, the opposite direction from where they approached.

The man gripped his rifle, walking away from the trellis toward the sound. O'Brien whispered to Sharpe, "This has to be silent." Sharpe nodded as O'Brien ran in a stealth-like crouch, approaching the man from his back. The guard turned when O'Brien was less than five feet from him, making a futile effort to raise his rifle. O'Brien used the stock of his rifle to smash the man in his mouth, pulverizing lips and teeth. The man fell. O'Brien used the stock against the man's head.

Sharpe kept his eyes moving around the perimeter of the old castle, looking for more sentries. He didn't have to look far. A second man came out of the shadows, his 9mm pistol drawn and cocked. He yelled something in Arabic. Sharpe was faster, firing a single round from his rifle into the man's chest, the sound of the shot traveling across the entire island.

O'Brien ran up to Sharpe and said, "Two down. Don't know how many are left. But I do know they probably heard that and are about to come out of the hive like angry hornets."

"Let's storm the castle before they can get their shit together."

# ONE HUNDRED TWELVE

From inside the castle walls, the gunshot sounded like the pop of a firecracker. But it was more than enough to get the attention of Aswad and his men. Dave and Wynona heard it, too. Neither acknowledging the sound to Aswad or his guards. Dave glanced over to Wynona, his eyes reflecting courage. She nodded and then turned her head toward Aswad and his men.

Aswad looked at her with absolute disgust. He turned to three of the five men and, in Farsi, said, "Go! See if that sound came from Nazeeh or Saleh. If not, find the source and eliminate it. Do you understand?"

"Indeed, Abdul. Consider it done," said the tallest man, a dark red taqiyah on his head, his sooty black eyes wide. He ordered two other men to follow him, all armed with semi-automatic Bushmaster rifles, pistol and knives. They left the room, weapons drawn.

• • •

O'Brien and Sharpe waited at opposite ends of the castle. Sharpe took a position behind a gumbo-limbo tree less than one hundred feet from the back portion of the castle. In the moonlight, he could see the two rear doors, the wood rotted away. Two men emerged, each crouching around the native palms running in the opposite direction.

450

Sharpe drew a bead on the man with the red cap, which looked dark burgundy in the subdued light of the moon. He aimed for the cap and squeezed off a round, the man's head exploding. Sharpe reloaded and followed the second man across the property.

• • •

One man exited the front of the castle just as the sound of the rifle shot echoed across the island. O'Brien had the man in the cross-hairs of his rifle, the man bolting when he heard the gunshot, waving his rifle barrel, and darting into the night.

O'Brien followed him, chasing the guard through the sand and sea oats. The man zigzagged, rolling and coming up behind a thick strand of sable palms. He aimed at O'Brien and fired five consecutive shots, the white muzzle flare glowing in the night, one round whizzing by O'Brien's left ear. He stooped behind a concrete cistern that, years ago, was used to capture and store rainwater. He aimed one foot above the muzzle flare, firing a single shot from his Glock. The man was hit just above his right eye. And then silence.

The silence lasted for less than five seconds.

The other soldier came from the shadows and took aim at O'Brien's head, firing once. The shot hit the concrete cistern and ricocheted into the bush. O'Brien turned and shot the man in the center of his chest.

Dustin Sharpe came from around the side of the castle. He nodded at O'Brien, looked at the dead man and said, "That guy was one of two that came out from the back. I plugged the tallest dude. Looks like you got his little buddy."

O'Brien wiped the sweat off his forehead, waving away mosquitoes, and said, "We don't know what's inside. Aswad, no doubt, has Dave and Wynona held in there as hostages. It'll be hard to storm the castle when he has a gun to their heads or a knife to their throats." O'Brien looked at the castle. In the moonlight, he could see a side entrance, a broken door. He cut his eyes up to the sky and then to Sharpe. "A cloud is covering the moon. Let's use the cover of darkness to approach the east side—the gapping door. Maybe, at one time, it was the servant's entrance. Let's see where it'll lead us."

Sharpe nodded and, as the cloud crept in front of the moon, they darted across the overgrown grounds. They paused at the open door, nodded and entered, moving back-to-back through the hallway and looking into rooms. O'Brien held the shotgun. Sharpe with his rifle gripped at his hips, muzzle pointed in front of his every step.

A shadow moved.

"To your left!" O'Brien shouted.

The shadow fired three quick bursts. One round hit Sharpe in his upper left arm, almost knocking the rifle from his grip. O'Brien squeezed off a single round of buckshot, the full force hitting the man square in his chest. The impact blew him hard against one of the concrete walls, where he collapsed to the marble floor.

O'Brien looked at Sharpe. He saw the blood pouring out of his friend's' arm. He said, "Go back outside and sit. Keep your heart rate down. We can't have you bleeding out."

Sharpe shook his head. "It's okay. I'm not leaving you alone to fight the rest of the good fight."

O'Brien took his knife to create a slit in the fabric at the base of his shirt, tore a strip, and quickly tied it around Sharpe's arm to slow the bleeding. Then he nodded. "Let's roll."

They entered the great room. Wide and large. Flickering candles on the mantle and table. Dark shadows in corners. O'Brien looked up just as the cloud cleared the moon, light streaming through the arched windows and a hole in the roof. His eyes followed a winding marble banister, steps leading to the second floor.

Something moved at the top of the stairway.

A burst of white muzzle flash. A .30 caliber round hit the wall three inches to the right of O'Brien's head. The bullet ricocheted off two other walls, whizzing down a dark hallway.

Aswad and his last man stood at the top of the stairway, firing a half-dozen more rounds at O'Brien and Sharpe. Both men dove around and under a thick marble table, the rounds shattering pieces of marble like broken glass flying. Sharpe used his 9mm pistol to return fire. The distraction gave O'Brien a second to run behind a large concrete beam, firing a blast from his shotgun. One piece of buckshot hit Aswad's soldier in the throat. He collapsed and fell down the flight of steps like a ragdoll. Aswad turned and ran through an upstairs hallway to the master bedroom.

The great room was partially filled with smoke from the gunfire, the smoke drifting across the area and curling out of the arched windows. O'Brien waited a moment for it to clear, loading more shells into the shotgun. He motioned to Sharpe and darted across the floor, stepping over the dead man at the foot of the banister and climbing the steps to the second floor. Sharpe was right behind him. The tourniquet on his left arm seeped in blood.

O'Brien gestured with his head and started down the hallway, moonlight pouring through the open windows. Sharpe kept up with him, his 9mm in his good right hand. The corridor led to one area—the master bedroom. O'Brien shouldered the shotgun, one hand on the forestock grip, the other on the trigger. He signaled to Sharpe, and they burst into the room.

Aswad stood behind Dave and Wynona, the barrel of his Sig Sauer pushed against her temple. She looked at O'Brien and then at Dustin Sharpe. There was no expression of fear on her face. Dave nodded toward O'Brien and then looked at Aswad holding the gun against Wynona's head. Aswad grinned. "One of you may get me. But not until after I kill the woman. It was a very difficult decision, whom to kill first, the woman or Collins. She has more time left, with the possibility of producing more infidel offspring. She dies first."

"Neither one of them will die today," O'Brien said. "But you … that's a different story. You're next in line for a one-way ticket to paradise, pal."

"I recognize you." Aswad said, smirking. "The tall man in the photograph at the docks. Katie said your name is Sean O'Brien."

Dave glanced at Aswad and said, "Where'd you leave Katie and Andy?"

Aswad ignored him, holding Wynona by her hair with his left hand, the pistol hard against her skull. He said, "O'Brien … you and your injured friend can leave now and she lives. If not, it will be your hand that puts the bullet through her brain."

O'Brien took a step closer and said, "Answer Dave's question. Where are Katie and Andy Scott? Where'd you dump them? What island? Tell me!"

"Why, Sean O'Brien … they are dead. Sol Lefko sowed the seeds. In the end, we removed his seeds from earth. By now, I suspect the scavenging birds and land crabs have enjoyed their rotten flesh."

"Dustin, keep a bead on our host," O'Brien said, shifting the shotgun to his left hand, using his right hand to reach in his belt and pull out the Glock, dropping the shotgun to the floor.

Aswad smiled. "You will not fire from across the room and risk killing the woman."

O'Brien concentrated on one spot—Aswad's forehead. He could see the beads of sweat on the man's brow. "You're right. I won't risk killing her," he said, lifting the gun in a blur and firing one shot. The round hit Aswad in the center of his forehead. His body falling between Wynona and Dave.

O'Brien sprinted across the room, holstered his gun and used his knife to cut the ropes on Wynona's arms. Sharpe did the same for Dave who looked at him and said, "We need to stop your bleeding."

Sharpe smiled. "Later."

Wynona stood and embraced O'Brien. "How did you find us?"

He started to answer when something caught her eye. A man, face streaked with dried blood, stood in the doorway, his rifle aimed directly at O'Brien's back. "Down!" she yelled, pushing O'Brien as a round from the rifle flew over his left shoulder.

Wynona snatched Aswad's pistol off the floor and fired a shot directly into the chest of the shooter as he was trying to get off another round. She shot twice more, each round hitting him in the chest and gut while he struggled to aim his gun. He crumpled, his body falling into a shaft of moonlight coming from one of the glassless windows.

Silence. The only sound now coming from the surf pounding the beach.

Dave stood slowly, massaged the rope marks on his arms, glanced at O'Brien and said, "For a while you had me worried. What took you so damn long?"

O'Brien smiled. "We had some diversions along the way. We'll get you and Wynona back to Arthur's Town. You guys can get rooms, showers and food. You can call the FBI. They're tired of hearing from me." He looked at Sharpe. "Let's get you patched up. If you feel up to it, we have a flight at daybreak."

"Where to?" Sharpe asked.

"To where I think we'll find Katie and Andy. I just hope we're not too late."

# One Hundred Thirteen

The ocean was flat, reflecting a sunrise of crimson and slivers of yellow gold to the east over Cat Island when the seaplane with O'Brien and Dustin Sharpe aboard took off from the surface. Sharpe's left arm had a large white bandage under his black T-shirt that read: *Island Charters.* He looked over at O'Brien and said, "We have bottled water, fresh sandwiches and fruit. Let's hope the couple is, by some miracle, still alive."

"I'm hoping that they managed to catch something in the sea for food … maybe captured rain somehow and saved their energy."

"What makes you think they're stranded on that no name island?"

"Turtles."

"Turtles?"

"The female will dig half the night, lay her eggs and cover up the hole. They will not return to the sea leaving their eggs exposed. It's imprinted in their DNA. I didn't see a pile of white eggs in the bottom of that hole, and it looked freshly dug. I think Katie and Andy dug it. I don't know why … seems like a waste of energy. But, if it saves their lives because it caught our attention, it was worth the effort."

Sharpe slowly banked the plane left, heading southwest. He said, "Seems more effective if they'd just made a big S-O-S in the sand or used fallen palm fronds to make some kind of distress sign."

"They've never been in a life and death situation like this. After being deprived of food and water, then toss in the extreme heat … all of that can play hell on the mind."

"Sean, I've always admired your optimism. How you still maintain it after some of the stuff we experienced over there, and how you sustain it after your time working homicide in Miami, couple that with Sherri's death, well, it's a wonder you've never just said screw it, I'm outta here."

"Where would I go, Dustin? What would I do?"

"I don't know. But since we've stayed in touch through the years, some of the crap that lands in your lap …" He paused and looked to the east, the rising sun reflecting off his dark green glasses like two egg yolks. "It seems like a lot of bad stuff happens to you. And, as your friend, it just feels damn unfair."

O'Brien smiled. "I've sort of shelved the fairness doctrine a long time ago. What's not fair is for people like Katie and Andy, an innocent couple trying to turn the page in their lives, getting swept up into a black storm they didn't create. Bad stuff doesn't necessarily happen to me. It happens to people like them, and I'm often on the sidelines watching a near slaughter. I just choose to insert myself in the game to see if I can help take one across the goal line for the underdog."

Sharpe shook his head. "Let's see if there's a little overtime left in this game. God knows they deserve it."

• • •

In less than a half hour, Sharpe was within a quarter mile of the island. He slowed the plane and came closer. "Here we are," he said circling the island at an altitude of five hundred feet. "I can see the hole, but that's all I see. No signs of people. Nothing but a lot of blown down trees and brush."

O'Brien studied the terrain closely. He said, "When was that last time you saw mother nature build something in right angles and straight lines?"

"What are you talking about?"

O'Brien pointed to a spot less than one hundred feet from the hole. "Right down there, not far from the hole, you can see what looks like somebody put together a crude roof. The palm fronds are all lying in the same direction. No storm leaves that. Let's get closer."

Sharpe descended to about three hundred feet above the island and did a slow 180-degree turn. O'Brien said, "Not only is it a roof, but it looks to have branches and limbs stacked on at least three sides for walls. Let's get down there. Maybe Katie and Andy are right below us."

• • •

Katie heard the strange sound in her dreams. Loud. Intrusive. *Just go away*, she thought, her mind alternating between subconscious and conscious. The noise sounded like someone with a leaf blower somewhere. She was too weak to open her eyes. She only wanted to sleep ... *to sleep forever.* She could no longer feel Andy's hand in hers. *Are we still holding hands? Can't tell. Can't hear him breathing, the deep obstruction in his lungs when he awoke coughing. When was the last time he did that? Think. The noise ... go away ... so tired.*

• • •

Sharpe landed the seaplane and taxied it to within seventy feet of the shore, the plane slightly bobbing in the gentle swells that rolled toward the island. He glanced at O'Brien and said, "We're in about four feet of water. I'll drop anchor."

O'Brien looked at the plane's shadow on the white sand bottom. He said, "I can walk in from here. I'll carry a couple of bottles of water ... just in case ..."

Sharpe nodded. "Just in case." He reached in the back seat, pulled out two bottles of water and handed them to O'Brien. "Want me along with you. You don't know what you might find there."

"Yeah, I know. You can hang back. I'll signal you."

"All right."

O'Brien dropped into chest-deep water, holding the bottles up as he moved toward shore. Within thirty seconds, the water depth was at his knees, and then he walked onto the beach. He approached the hole, studying the excavation. He lifted up one of two discarded conch shells, knowing someone had used them as shovels. He set the shell down and looked at the tracks—human footprints in and around the hole.

He followed the tracks to the west and quickly came upon the lean-to he'd spotted at a very low altitude. He stared at if for a second, looked at the numerous tracks that led in and out. One set of prints was larger than the other—a man and a woman. O'Brien sprinted the last thirty feet to the structure, pulling a few palm fronds that appeared to be a makeshift door.

He stopped at the entrance.

They looked dead.

Two sunburned, emaciated bodies lying next to each other, hands clasped together, dappled sunlight coming through the cracks and spaces in the thatched roof. O'Brien moved next to Katie and Andy, kneeling down and feeling for a pulse on her right hand. Faint, but it was there. He looked at Andy' chest. *Was it moving? Was he breathing?* O'Brien reached over and felt for Andy's pulse. A heartbeat ... and another.

He unscrewed the first bottle of water and said, "Katie ... Andy ... can you hear me? I have water." No response. He poured some water into the palm of his right hand, letting it trickle onto Katie's face, the water dripping over the dried blood around her mouth. Her eyes fluttered open. Her mind not registering what was happening.

"Katie, it's Sean O'Brien. I'm going to pour a little bit of water into your mouth. It won't be much. I want you to drink. Do you understand?"

"Drink ..." Her voice was softer than a whisper.

O'Brien carefully lifted her head and poured a small amount of water through her cracked and blistered lips. She managed to swallow. Her eyes closing. "Let's take another small sip," O'Brien said. He gave her the water, and she drank. Slowly her eyes opened.

"Sean ... you're real. Tell me you're real ... no dream ..."

"It's me. Save your strength. I need to help Andy." He moved over to Andy, gently dripping water against Andy's face, his lips scorched, eyes swollen. "Andy … it's Sean O'Brien. Katie is alive and lying right next to you. I'm going to drip some water into your mouth. Try to swallow." He rubbed more water on Andy's face. "Okay … here's a little sip."

Andy managed to partially open his left eye, strawberry red. He barely nodded his head.

O'Brien gently held the back of Andy's head and poured a swallow of water into his mouth. He drank, his eyes closed. "Let's take another sip." He did, some of the water dripping down his hot cheeks. "You guys are going to be okay. We have a seaplane here. We'll get you to a hospital quickly. I want to get more water into both of you." O'Brien reached down and took both of their clasped hands in his and said, "You're going to make it now. You hear me?"

Andy nodded. Katie looked over at O'Brien, a single tear spilling from her eye. She whispered, "I didn't think I could cry … thank you."

# ONE HUNDRED FOURTEEN

### Two months later - Ponce Marina

Andy and Katie walked down L dock at Ponce Marina, smiling, skin glowing, their normal body weight restored. She wore a tropical green summer dress, a scattering of freckles across her shoulders. Andy in shorts and a polo shirt. They approached Nick's boat, *St. Michael*, Nick loading bags of ice in the hold. He looked up and grinned. "You two are definitely a sight for my sore 'ol sea eyes. You both look great."

"Thanks," Katie said, wide smile. "It's amazing what a few weeks eating anything you want can do for your body and soul."

Andy grinned and said, "But none of the food we ate could hold a candle to your cooking, Nick."

"You haven't tried my specialty yet."

"Oh," said Katie. "What's your specialty?"

"The meal begins with clams Kronus, sautéed in wine and garlic, followed by my Mediterranean-style, grilled swordfish with a feta and spinach stuffing between the filets, virgin olive oil from Greece dripped in all the right places, and cooked to perfection on my wood grill."

"You really need to publish a cook book. I think it'd be a huge hit."

Dave Collins walked from *Gibraltar* across the dock to Nick's boat. He embraced Katie and said, "You look lovely."

"I feel great. Things are better. We're better."

"Andy," said Dave, "I can recognize you again." He hugged Andy, slapping him on the back.

"Good to see you, Dave."

"I think I may have aged a lot in the last couple of months." He looked at Katie. "I'm so sorry about your dad. He was truly a decent man who always did his job well, and he loved you very much. I'm sorry I didn't make it to Sol's funeral."

"I understand. There were way too many funerals of your old friends happening too close together and by heinous circumstances."

Dave nodded. "We, your dad included, never had any misconceptions about what we did in the CIA. However, after our time … after what we all went through, we did have illusions about retirement. Thought we could enjoy it like any other American, but the fact is, we're not like any other American, except those who trade a lot of themselves to do covert work where everything and everybody is suspect."

She looked at a sailboat putter from the marina to the channel. "Maybe that'll change for you, Dave. We hope so."

Dave pursed his lips and put his bifocals in his shirt pocket. He said, "An old Irish pal of mind used to say something like this: 'A dog owns nothing but is rarely dissatisfied.' For us poor humans it translates to something like this: 'May you live as long as you want … and never want as long as you live.' You and Andy are so fortunate to have somehow survived your ordeal. We had searchers all over the islands looking for you."

Katie smiled. "And one guy found us." She looked toward *Jupiter* at the end of the dock. "Is Sean here? We flew back to surprise him, and to properly thank him."

Dave glanced at *Jupiter* and said, "Sean's sort of like the tide. He comes and goes. We never know until we hear little Max barking hello as she trots down the dock."

"Where do you think we might find him?" Andy asked.

Nick folded his thick arms across his chest and said, "Sean's got this old cabin way the hell back in the sticks, on the banks of the

St. Johns River. Out there, it's just him, Hot Dog, and a few hundred gators. I call 'em land sharks."

Dave said, "I can call him. See if he's in the area and coming to the marina. If I tell him you're here, he'll drop everything to see you. But your presence will no longer be a surprise." Dave glanced over their shoulders, his eyes scanning the marina. "Where's *Dragonfly*?"

Katie said, "That's what we want to talk to Sean about."

# ONE HUNDRED FIFTEEN

Only Max heard the phone buzz. She stood by a screen door on the river cabin's roughhewn back porch. She looked up at the wooden table where O'Brien had left his phone, and then she peered through one of the porch screen panels, watching and waiting. A mile away, O'Brien ran alone along a backwoods trail adjacent to the St. Johns River near the Ocala National Forest.

It was the same primitive Florida that greeted the Conquistadors. Sprawling Southern live oaks, their thick lower limbs draped in Spanish moss, the pewter beards motionless in the humid morning. Crimson bromeliad air plants rode the backs of the old oaks. A water moccasin slithered across the path, disappearing in the bush.

He jogged by clusters of sabal palms, bald cypress trees growing tall by the riverbank, white egrets step dancing on the limbs, eyeing O'Brien as he ran under them. He breathed though his nose. Shirtless. Old, faded jean shorts, sweat dripping down his face, the musty smell of rotting leaves near the river. He watched a six-foot alligator slip down from the riverbank, making a splash to disappear under the water. O'Brien ran harder on his way back to his cabin.

The trail meandered toward his large yard that sloped down from the cabin to the river and his dock that extended fifty feet over the slow-moving dark water. O'Brien walked the last fifty yards on his property, letting his heart rate slow, wiping the sweat off his muscular arms. The cabin was built seven decades ago with cedar and hard white pine, a tin roof and screened back porch. He opened the door to the porch and stepped inside, Max turned a circle and let out two quick barks.

"Good to see you, too, kiddo. I was gone less than a half hour, and you act like you haven't seen me in days." He picked up his phone and said, "One missed call. Maybe they left a message. Maybe we'll check it." He looked down at Max. "Let's go to the dock."

Max barked once, snorting and trotting down the yard. O'Brien followed her. She scurried onto the dock, watching a bald eagle pull a bass from just under the surface near the center of the wide river.

O'Brien set his phone on the arm of an Adirondack chair, paused at the end of his dock, his eyes scanning the riverbank for gators. He dove head first into the river, swam twenty-five feet out, turned around and swam back, climbing the wooden ladder bolted to the dock and partially submerged under the surface. He shook the water from his body, picked up his phone and listened to a message. "Hey, Sean … it's Wynona. I've been thinking a lot about what we went through with Aswad and Thurston. What happened to Katie and Andy … and what almost happened to Dave and me. I'm having a serious career crisis. I'm not sure this is what I want to do anymore. I know you reached a crossroads at one point, too, and made a decision. At least on a professional level you did. Anyway, I just wanted to talk if you had some time. Maybe I just need a real dose of the islands to clear my head—a real vacation void of being strapped to a chair with a gun held to my head. Call me when you get a moment. Bye."

• • •

Andy and Katie met O'Brien in the Tiki Bar. After hugs and catching up, they sat at a round table in one corner and Katie said, "There's no way we can ever repay you, Sean, for what you did."

O'Brien smiled and said, "Repayment never comes into the equation. Just the fact that I'm sitting here having a drink with you two, is payment enough. And, please remember it wasn't just me. Many very good people spent a lot of time searching for the two of you. Dustin Sharpe and I were lucky enough to find you."

Andy said, "You guys saw what no one else did. The hole my wife dug, for one, and somehow you managed to see our tiny lean-to among a few miles of similar material. Katie and I want to offer you a small token of our appreciation."

O'Brien said, "That's not necessary because—"

"Hold on," Katie said, leaning forward. She opened her purse and pulled out two keys on a key ring. "These keys are for *Dragonfly*. One's for the engine, the other unlocks the hatch. We want you to take them. We want you to take *Dragonfly*."

"I can't do that. *Dragonfly* is your blood, sweat, and tears. It's your hopes and dreams for a different life, a better life."

"Yes," Katie said. "It helped us head in that direction. Prepping the boat, planning, and even the sailing, up until the moment we were hijacked, was a great bonding and learning experience for us. But, after what we survived, we just lost the taste or the desire to own a boat. *Dragonfly* was, and still is, symbolic of our journey in life."

Andy said, "But we're not going to be the ones behind the helm. We actually booked an extended cruise that will take us half way around the world. And we'll have a crew of fifty and a couple of hundred passengers to join us."

Katie said. "Andy and I want you to have *Dragonfly*. You gave us so many pointers about sailing. It's obviously a great love of yours. You said, when your wife was alive, you both did a lot of sailing together. Perhaps, you can again." She grabbed O'Brien's hand and placed the keys in his palm. "We won't take no for an answer. We had the paperwork and bill-of-sale drawn up. It'll cost you one dollar to take possession. She's in slip B-17, Harbor Island Marina at Governor's Harbour in Eleuthera. Please take her, Sean. *Dragonfly*, we believe, will be in better hands with you than with us. And, hopefully, it'll mean just as much to you as she has for us."

Andy leaned forward and said, "Maybe you can sail her back to Ponce Marina. Maybe you can have an exotic get-away port for relaxation and discovery."

Katie smiled and said, "Who knows what you could discover about yourself."

• • •

O'Brien took Max for a walk along the beach before making the call. He strolled from the gentle roll of the surf up to higher dunes with sea oats dotting the sand. He called Wynona, and when she answered he said, "On your phone message, you said you could use a real dose of the islands. I think I have a viable option for you."

Wynona was standing at her mailbox, roses blooming near it. She said, "You do? Tell me more."

"Can you take a month off?"

"If I do that, I won't come back. And that, I'm convinced, would be a good thing."

"You've earned it and a lot more. Come and let your hair down."

# Epilogue

Two weeks later, *Dragonfly* was almost prepped for sail. O'Brien and Wynona were stocking the boat with food, water, essential wines and liquors, and two salt water fishing rods. *Dragonfly* was tied to an older dock in the port of Harbour Island Marina, the water beneath her was gin clear. Dozens of powerboats, sailboats and yachts were moored to the five docks. *Dragonfly* was in the most remote section, red bougainvillea wrapped around a long trellis near the docks, the hum of bees whizzing in and out of the flowers, gulls chortling in the hard-blue sky above the waterfront.

O'Brien and Wynona walked along the docks, Max darting ahead of them, her head high, nostrils filled with the scent of tropical flowers, salty breezes and the smell of red snapper grilled over hot charcoal. An older black man sat on an upside down, plastic bucket and fished in the waters to the far right of *Dragonfly*, his hair mostly snow white, a beard like steel wool streaked in shades of gray and silver. His skin was creosote black, wide smile.

"Hi," Wynona said. "How's fishing?"

The old man smiled, a gold tooth reflecting in the sunlight. He tilted a second bucket next to his knees, showing two fish and said, "Pompano. You don't haf' to go far to get 'em. Dey good to eat, too." His accent was thick, smile wide, brown eyes gentle." Something caught his eye. A dragonfly skimmed just above the surface of the clear water, coming up quickly and alighting on the end of his fishing pole. The old man held the pole still and grinned. The dragonfly was as wide as O'Brien's hand, its body neon blue, its head the color green that the ocean turns when sunlight shines through a curling wave.

O'Brien asked, "What kind of dragonfly is that?"

The old man looked up, his eyes playful. "That'd be a blue dasher. I hadn't seen one in a few months. They's special."

"How so?" Wynona asked.

"'Cause they means good things is gonna be hap'n soon." He grinned. The dragonfly darted off the tip of the rod and flew over the water, vanishing in a sea of bougainvillea and palms.

• • •

A breeze from the northeast pushed *Dragonfly* off shore, the island in the background, blue water in the distance, crystal clear water under the sailboat. Max darted from the cockpit to starboard to port side to the bow, wind flapping her ears like bird wings. A few miles at sea, two porpoises came from nowhere and swam less than thirty feet to the port side of the boat, leaping out of the water, whimsical porpoise smiles etched on their faces. Max barked as if she was challenging them to a race.

Wynona stood in the cockpit with O'Brien at the helm. They laughed watching Max and her two new friends. Wynona turned to O'Brien, looking at him behind the wheel, the wind in his hair, the sky somehow making his eyes even bluer. He sailed *Dragonfly* with one hand, a natural ease—some kind of camaraderie with the wind and sea that seemed an extension of his calm demeanor. Something, she felt, that could be taught at some level, perhaps. The rest was an innate talent that wasn't teachable, something built into his DNA. She wondered about his parents—family, why he never spoke of them. *Doesn't matter*, she thought. *What matters is here and now.*

"I think you've found your calling," Wynona said. "You handle this sailboat like you were born on the water."

He looked from the horizon to her face. "Conceived maybe, but not born on the water. I'll leave that claim to Nick." He smiled.

"I like your friends, and I can tell how much they appreciate you." She looked at Cat Island in the distance to the east. "I could live here. The pace, the food, the people—I think the word stress doesn't have meaning in the vocabulary of the Bahamians."

"It's illegal to practice stress in the islands," O'Brien said, smiling.

"Oh, really?"

"Absolutely. They passed a law prohibiting it years ago. You can import it, but you certainly can't export it because it doesn't happen in the islands."

"None of the islands?"

"None. If you're caught doing it, you could be fined and not allowed a rum drink for a month—or you might be forced to drink way too many."

She laughed. "I think that might qualify as cruel and unusual punishment, either way."

"You think?"

"Yes, most definitely."

"Where are we heading, Captain O'Brien?"

"Oh, no particular island. We'll just see what's over the horizon." He took his hand off the wheel and reached for her hair clip. He removed it, her dark hair falling in a twisted drop below her shoulders. "I invited you to come and let your hair down. That's the first step to throwing stress overboard."

Wynona smiled, used the fingers on both of her hands to comb out her hair, which was now cascading over her brown shoulders and down her back. "If this is the first step, what's the second and third."

O'Brien leaned over and softly kissed her. "That's number two," he said with a smile.

The breeze shifted, Wynona's hair flowing like the water off the bow, her face relaxed in the morning sun. "If a kiss is number two, what's number three?"

"That happens later. After we put Max to bed."

"That sounds like captain's orders."

"Let's call it a special request."

"Okay, I have one, too."

"What?"

"Teach me to sail." She placed her hand on O'Brien's hand as he held the wheel. He motioned for her to take the helm. She did, the wind popping the sails, the sound of water spray breaking across the hull. "I love it!" she said. O'Brien stood behind her, his hands on hers for a moment, guiding.

"You're a natural born sailor," he said, taking a step back, Wynona steering the sailboat. She looked toward the bow, and burst out laughing. Max's ears were pushed back in the wind, the porpoises racing in front of *Dragonfly*, leaping from the water, their tails seemed to wave goodbye in unison. Max cocked her head, a quick bark protesting their departure.

"Hey, Max ... they'll come back," O'Brien said. Moments later, they reappeared, two porpoises leading *Dragonfly* to unplanned destinations. Under a blue sky that stretched from the depths of the universe to the ends of the sea, the sailboat skimmed over the water, following the wind, following the spontaneous flight of the dragonfly.

# The End